THE CUCKOO'S CALL

LILY MORTON

Warning

This book contains material that is intended for a mature, adult audience. It contains graphic language, explicit sexual content and adult situations.

For my darling Dan
My sunshine boy
I love you

Can a summer romance last forever?

Wren Roberts thought he'd found his fairy tale when he met Mateo Rossi on holiday in Majorca. The wealthy and successful older man swept him off his feet, and before he knew it, he'd thrown caution to the wind and was living in Mateo's waterside apartment in Venice. It's a far cry from his harsh upbringing and crummy flat in London.

But as the summer turns to autumn, cracks begin to show. Mateo's family aren't welcoming, and there doesn't seem to be a place for Wren in Mateo's world. He could have coped with all of that, but Mateo himself seems like a different person away from the sunshine island.

Should Wren have been more cautious in riding off into the sunset when he wasn't sure what lay over the horizon?

From bestselling author Lily Morton comes a romance about two men who find that sometimes happily ever after doesn't end there.

"A man travels the world over in search of what he needs and returns home to find it."
George Augustus Moore

PROLOGUE

Wren

I stare at the woman behind the airport checking-in desk. "I'm sorry. Can you repeat that?"

She eyes me, as if assessing for sarcasm, and then relents. "As I have said twice before, sir. Your flight is delayed due to the fog."

"But it's only a little mist. Don't the planes fly above it?"

She glances out the nearby window where the fog continues to move thickly against the glass. "Yes, sir," she says slowly. "But they have to get up in the air first."

"But how long will it last?" I ask, desperation eating into my voice. "I need to leave here as soon as possible."

"You and everyone else in the airport." She waves a careless hand. "It will last as long as the fog is there. And they've forecast this weather to last until the evening." I bite my lip, and as I run a shaky hand through my hair, her expression softens a little. She leans forward. "Hopefully, it will lift sooner than that, and if your flight is cancelled, your airline will provide you with a meal and a hotel room.

Do not worry. Just stay close to the desk and keep checking the flight information board."

I want to tell her that having a meal is the very least of my concerns at the moment, but it isn't her problem, so instead, I smile and take my ticket and passport back from her and step aside so she can deal with the next customer.

Shouldering my rucksack, I wander over to the huge plate-glass window. The fog moves sluggishly, offering a teasing glimpse of the outside world one minute and then moving lazily back to cover it in the next. I rest my head on the glass, feeling the coldness against my sweaty forehead, and take a few deep breaths.

It's only a slight delay, I tell myself. *Mateo won't come after me. He's away until tomorrow, so he won't see my note until he comes back and by then I'll be in London.*

I imagine what he'll think when he reads it, and sadness curdles my stomach and takes my breath away. Then I remind myself of why I'm leaving. He won't miss me. I bite my lip, the small pain bringing me back to the here and now. I straighten up from the window determinedly.

My reflection resembles a ghost against the foggy background, my brown hair tumbling around a face that's pale and still too thin. My full lips are drawn tight, and my eyes are shadowed. Shaking my head, I move away from the sad image and head to the coffee shop to get into the queue.

The board displays a multitude of hot drink choices, and for a second, I can hear Mateo's laughing voice in my ear asking which froufrou drink I want next, but I dismiss him and draw out my wallet. A quick glance at the contents makes me order the cheapest coffee they have and forget the idea of getting something to eat. I need to conserve my money and buying expensive food will see it dwindle very quickly. Not to mention the thought of food makes me feel sick.

Taking my drink, I find a seat that gives me a view of the information board. My wild hope that they've decided to fly through the fog is dashed. All flights are still delayed. The coffee is bitter and sour, and after a few mouthfuls, I grimace and opt to hold the cup between my palms, letting the warm cardboard heat my cold fingers.

"No good, eh?"

The cheerful voice breaks into my thoughts, and I find an older lady looking at me.

"Sorry?" I ask.

She has grey hair and the greenest eyes I've ever seen. She gestures at my cup. "Your drink. You don't seem very enthusiastic."

I jerk. "Oh no, it's fine. Just a little bitter."

She smiles at me. "I'm Margery and this is my husband, Len." She points to the man sitting next to her. He has grey-brown hair and a resigned expression. "We were just saying that we can't wait to get home and have a nice cup of tea."

"You're English, then?" I say wryly. "It's the number one thing I hear in Venice from English people."

"They heat the milk," she says with a shudder. "It's like stewed dishwater." Her companion shakes his head, and she nudges him affectionately. "You hush," she says even though Len hasn't said anything and doesn't look as if he intends to. She turns back to me. "Have you been on holiday?"

I shrug. "I suppose you could call it that." She raises her eyebrows in question. "A holiday from life, I suppose," I say slowly. "Chasing a dream."

She cocks her head to one side like a bird. "Well, I suppose you couldn't pick a better setting than Venice for that. It's a beautiful city."

"It is," I say, emotion clogging my voice. "I'll miss it."

Her eyes sharpen, and her smile turns kind. "I'm sure you're taking away good memories."

Am I? I wonder, as she turns to say something to Len. I trace my fingers over the bracelet on my wrist. The dark brown leather is woven of three butter-soft strands. It's one of the two things he gave me that I'm taking with me. The other is wrapped in tissue paper in my bag.

I pull my fingers back and curl my hand into a fist as the memories flood my brain.

PART ONE

CHAPTER ONE

Wren

"I'm sorry. Could you repeat that, Owen?"

My best friend of seven years has the grace to look awkward. "I said that we're thinking of flying to Madrid to finish the week out. Josh's friend is having a big party, and they're bored of Majorca."

I sit down heavily on the chair in our room. "Yes, that's what I thought you said."

He paces over to the window and then turns to face me, his expression one of truculent surprise. It's because I'm questioning him when he's got his mind set on something. I can understand his astonishment, because I usually let him have his own way.

"You can still come with us," he says.

I give him a wry glance. "No, I can't, and you know it. I maxed out my credit card to come here. The flight to Madrid alone would bankrupt me."

He gives an exasperated sigh. "You're being so dramatic, Wren."

I shake my head. "I'm really not. I can't pay for whatever expensive place you're going to stay in. I don't think I could even afford half the plane journey. They'd have to open the hatch and dump me out over Valencia."

"Well, I'll pay"

"No, you *won't*." My voice is sharper than I'd like, and he flinches. I moderate my tone. "I won't let you pay for anything for me. Your mother is convinced that I'm constantly in the process of fleecing you. She always looks surprised that I'm not twirling a handlebar moustache and giving an evil laugh. I'd hate to prove her right."

"She doesn't think that," he predictably protests. "She *loves* you."

I roll my eyes. Only if love means she wants to remove my intestines with a teaspoon. I let it go. After all these years, I'm still unsure whether he was born with a happy filter over his eyes or whether he got it through his upbringing, but I've always found it very endearing regardless.

"I can't come," I settle for saying again.

"But what will you do on your own?"

I'd been expecting the question, but I still flinch. We've been friends since our schooldays and when he went to university, I held out hope that we'd stay friends even though I couldn't afford to go. This holiday has taught me how naïve that was. When he first mentioned us going to Majorca, I'd been thrilled. I thought it would be just the two of us and I'd have a chance to reconnect with Owen. The hotel had been very expensive, but he'd pushed for it and finally, I'd maxed out my credit card, feeling guilty that he was reining himself in and thinking it would be a memory I could hoard. My first time abroad.

However, when we got here, it was to find his friends from university waiting for us. The first night he'd enquired breathlessly whether I minded them going out with us. Of course, I'd agreed, and I've hardly seen him alone since. Wherever they went, he had to follow, and he dragged me along with him on outings to private beaches, expensive bars, and yachts belonging to their parents. I'd tried to break off on my own, telling him honestly that I was happy to explore and do other things while he was with his friends, but he wouldn't hear of it. Maybe it was guilt on his part, but it's a sure fact that my wallet would have been fuller and I'd have had a better holiday if he'd left me alone.

It's sad to realise finally that we won't ever reconnect now. He's moved away from me and the gap is too wide to breach. It hurts but he isn't the first to let go of me and I'm sure he won't be the last.

Owen runs his hand through his hair agitatedly, and I realise I've been quiet for too long. "I'll be fine," I say coolly.

"Oh, don't be like that," he bursts out. "I wouldn't go, but Josh wants me with him, and he's split up with his boyfriend. He won't be single for long."

"Well then, you have to go." I stand up. "You need to beat the race of all the stupid people who think he's wonderful. You'd better get your stuff together. Take a camping chair for the queue."

"Will you be alright on your own?"

"I'll be fine," I say lightly. "You're leaving me in a very expensive five-star hotel. Not the toilets in King's Cross."

His face clears. "So, you're okay with this?"

I shrug. "Of course." I wonder whether he'll be bothered when it finally dawns on him that our long friendship is just about over.

I potter about while he packs and then make my way downstairs with him. The others in the group are waiting for him in the lobby lounging on the sofas, looking tanned and very relaxed.

Josh stands up when Owen nears him, reaching for his bag. "You're coming, then? I told you Wren would be fine." He gives Owen a warm smile, completely ignoring my presence.

Owen steps back and gives me a nervous smile. "Are you sure you'll be okay?"

I'd like to know what he'd do if I gave him an honest answer.

Not really, Owen. I have very little money left in my budget after having to pay for food in the expensive restaurants your friends like, and the fact that you made me go to the nightclub with you last night so I could stand to one side sipping water that cost nearly ten frigging euros while you snogged Josh. So, I'm a little unsure what I'm going to do for an entire week on my own with no money.

But I've learnt not to tell people my problems. It bores them or makes them uncomfortable. "I'll be fine," I say for probably the hundredth time today. Maybe I should tattoo the words on my forehead.

Josh wraps an arm around Owen's shoulders. "Told you," he says.

"He'll probably be glad to get rid of us. I think we're a bit too much for Wren and his purse strings."

I glare at him. I've spent the whole week ignoring his jibes and silly jokes at my expense. All so I wouldn't upset Owen. However, I don't have to bother about my former friend anymore, and Josh has finally pushed my patience to its end.

"Not at all," I say sharply. "I adore a spoilt, ignorant man-child, so you've been an absolute *joy*. I'm unsure what I'll do with myself when you leave. And the staff will miss you just as much. What will they do without you here to explain things to them slowly and very loudly? How will they get on without you clicking your fingers at them so much that someone thought you were part of the hotel cabaret act yesterday? And surely they'll lose valuable income without you here drinking more than a professional footballer on tour."

Josh recoils, and Owen gasps in horror.

Then I hear a soft snort of laughter from behind me. I turn around and find a dark-haired man in a light grey suit leaning against the reception desk and watching us, his face alight with laughter. We look at each other for a long moment, his eyes running over me, but then the receptionist says something to him, and he turns back to her, his interest gone.

I let out a shaky breath and turn back to my ex-best friend and his band of merry men. "Well, enjoy Madrid," I say. "I hope it manages to recover from your visit."

"We'll be back before the end of the week," Owen says, taking my arm.

I shrug off his hand as an idea comes to me. "I might not be here then. I'm going to see if I can get an early flight home."

"Oh no." He pauses, obviously unsure what to say now.

I give him a bright smile. "Have a good time, then. You'll miss your flight if you don't get a move on."

"Oh, Josh has asked his dad for his plane, so we've got a bit of time," he says casually. "We're okay, aren't we?" he whispers.

"Of course." I don't think we'll ever be the same again, but my hurt and anger are making that seem like a good thing at the moment.

"Have a good time," I say politely to the group who really don't give a shit about me.

I wander back up the stairs to my room. When I get inside, I throw myself on the bed and scrub my eyes with my hands. "Shit," I say out loud and then curl into a ball, dragging the sheets over me, so they form a cocoon. It's something I've done since I was little when I honestly believed that a cotton cave could keep out the world. Nevertheless, it works its usual magic, and I drift off to sleep, inhaling the scents of sun lotion and fabric softener that cling to the cotton.

I come awake a while later. The room is warm with late afternoon sunshine, but the balcony doors are open, and they're letting in a cool breeze that ruffles my hair. I tilt my face into it, and my stomach rumbles loudly. I'm so hungry that I feel sick.

I sit up, stretching, and consider my options. I've eaten a lot at breakfast for the last week as it was part of the hotel package. I've looked longingly at the cheap restaurants we've passed every night but never suggested eating at one, so as not to embarrass Owen.

Well, now I don't have to bother, and if I can get a flight out tomorrow, I can maybe splurge on a paella tonight. The others had sneered at the dish, calling it cliched tourist food, but for someone who's never been abroad, it sounds lovely.

Mind made up, I pad into the bathroom and start the shower. Standing under the spray, I twist and turn, appreciating the water pressure. I have a room in a boarding house at home and a bathroom that I share with two other tenants. The water pressure there is comparable to sticking your finger under a tap and spraying someone with the water, and you need a Hazmat suit to get in the bathtub.

I rub some of the hotel shower gel in my hands and begin to scrub. It smells expensive if that's a thing—fresh and herby. But as I run my hands over my body, I can't help but notice how much weight I've lost on this holiday. Most people put it on, apparently, but a diet of bread and water is better than a visit to the spa. I consider marketing it and snort before washing off the suds and stepping out.

I wander naked over to the balcony and revel in the heat of the tiles under my feet. The sea is a constant presence here, and this week it's been a wonder to just stare at it and listen to the soothing sound of the waves. The only time I'd visited the sea before was a trip I'd taken with a foster carer's family to see the lights in Blackpool. We'd sat on the beach and eaten burgers and doughnuts hot from the fryer and sprinkled with sugar, and I thought I'd never had anything that tasted so good.

A five-star hotel in Majorca is infinitely nicer than Blackpool. The sun is going down, and I bask in the rays for a while before my stomach rumbles get too loud. I go to the wardrobe and view my options. I push aside the memory of Owen's friends' barely concealed sneers at my cheap clothes.

If it had been up to me, we'd have spent the holiday in swimsuits and eaten in places that welcomed jeans. I pull on the only things that are clean—my skinny jeans and a pink T-shirt that proclaims, *I may be wrong, but I doubt it.* Then I slide my feet into the cheap flip-flops I'd been forced to buy at the beginning of the week when I realised I couldn't stand on the sand at midday.

I grab my room key and stuff my wallet and phone into my back pocket.

Reception is full when I get downstairs, and I edge through the crowds of people checking in, dodging expensive-looking luggage and choking on perfume. I finally make it outside and pull out my phone to call the airport. It takes ages, and I pace up and down outside, inhaling the scent of flowers from the big tubs by the entrance and feeling the delicate mist from the sprinklers that are watering the plush green grounds.

I'm halfway through talking to the seventh person in twenty minutes when I realise that I could have done all this on the airline's website without wasting my minutes. At this point, as if synchronised, my phone beeps. "Crap," I say, breaking into the lady's spiel. "I'm so sorry," I apologise. "I'm going to have to ring off. I've used all my minutes. Could you ring me back or text me the flight and price?"

She starts to say something, but the phone dies, and I bite my lip to avoid shouting in frustration. *Great.* I now haven't got any minutes left and I'm stranded alone in a foreign country with hardly any money. For a second, panic bangs at my mind, but I take a few deep breaths in and out. I remind myself that I've been on my own plenty of times, and just because it's a foreign country, it doesn't mean I can't look after myself.

Feeling the panic subside a bit, I stroll around the outside of the hotel, intending to take the path leading down into the small village. However, I'm waylaid by the spectacular sky. The sun is giving its last flare of brilliance, and the sky is a pale lavender edged with pink and filled with the pinprick lights of the first stars. Against the dark waves, it's stunning, and I edge onto the hotel patio to lean against the stone balustrade and look my fill. The view seems perfect now that I'm on my own and able to appreciate it, and I relax into the moment for the first time this holiday.

From the nearby tables comes the sound of clinking plates and cutlery and the happy hum of conversation. Candlelight burnishes the guests' faces and arms in a golden glow. I take a breath and my stomach clenches at the smell of food.

"Excuse me, sir. Unfortunately, you are in the wrong place."

I spin around to find the head waiter glaring at me. He's dressed in his usual outfit of black trousers, a white shirt, and a black bowtie. His supercilious expression tells me that he recognizes me. During my first meal here, I'd scandalized him by assuming the finger bowls were for drinking. Ever since, he'd behaved as though I'd blow my nose on a tablecloth at any second. After Owen's friends joined us, he treated me like the poor relation, serving me last or passing me over. One less bill to pay for me, but his attitude rubs me raw.

"What do you mean?" I ask tersely.

He edges closer. "Your place is out there," he says in a low voice, pointing towards the lights of the village. "You'll find bars and cafes more to your taste down there."

Some people at nearby tables glance our way and my ears get hot. "I've been eating breakfast here all week," I say. I hadn't intended on eating here, but now I sort of want to. "So, why am I suddenly being directed a few miles down the road?"

He offers me a disdainful smile. "You were with the others then, sir. You're alone now, and this is *not* the place for you."

I open my mouth to argue, but a low, accented voice interrupts our standoff. "Excuse me, I think you're blocking my guest's way to the table, Felipe."

The waiter and I turn, and it's a toss-up who looks more surprised —him or me.

I recognize the man I'd seen earlier in the day in the lobby—he'd laughed after witnessing my conversation with Owen and his mates.

He rises from a table next to the balcony. It's the best seat on the patio, offering an unimpeded view of the sea. He's exchanged his suit for a pair of cream-coloured shorts and a pale beige loose shirt, and he's beckoning to me.

"Here you are," he says smoothly, his voice husky and deep with a Spanish lilt to it that makes my cock twitch.

I look around, wondering who he's talking to and then realise with a shock that it's me. "Excuse me?" I say.

He gives me a crooked grin, humour and enjoyment of the situation visible on his face. "You're late, but I'll excuse you. It's a beautiful night." He beckons. "Come sit down. I'm hungry for my dinner."

"Oh," the waiter says, obviously flustered. "I didn't know that the young man was with you, senor."

The smile falls from the man's face, the shadows turning his expression almost saturnine. "Obviously, Felipe," he says coolly. "Perhaps you would prefer me to go with my guest into the village too. Maybe we could eat at a burger bar, as we don't seem welcome in this restaurant tonight."

"Oh no, *no*," Felipe protests immediately. "My suggestion was just for *him*." The man's eyes flare, and the waiter adds quickly, "Obviously, this has been a huge misunderstanding."

My rescuer watches him intently. "That is *certainly* the truth."

Felipe's face is sweaty, his eyes panicked.

What on earth is going on?

I decide not to question the beauty of my nemesis getting told off. "Well, I'm here now," I say sweetly.

I step past Felipe and slide into the seat that the stranger pulls out for me.

Immediately, two waiters approach, and I jolt in surprise as they unfurl a napkin over my lap. Then they bustle about, pouring water into my glass, and when the stranger indicates, they fill my wine glass. We're handed two menus with a flourish, and then they step away, leaving us in silence.

"Well," I finally say.

His eyes twinkle as he observes me. "Well?"

"This is a fascinating twist to the night." I lean forward and whisper, "You are aware that we've never met, aren't you?"

I catch a lemony scent which must be his aftershave, and he grins. "My name is Mateo. You?"

"Wren Roberts."

He blinks. "Unusual name."

"I'm named after the architect."

"The one who designed St Paul's Cathedral?"

I nod.

"Didn't he die en route to visiting it?"

"Apparently so. It's why travel raises so many red flags for me."

He throws his head back and laughs. It's a big booming laugh that makes me smile. I eye him appraisingly. He looks in his late thirties or early forties, and he's not conventionally good-looking. He has a battered face with a big nose that juts out like a downhill ski slope. His eyes are hooded, and there are deep grooves down the side of his nose to his mouth. However, that mouth is full and soft, and his eyes are a strange golden colour. There's something magnetic about him, as if he's used to commanding attention.

When he's recovered chuckling, he smiles at me. "Now we have been introduced. It's nice to meet you, Wren Roberts."

I return his smile. "Thank you very much for jumping in."

His dark, slashing eyebrows lower. "I don't like bullying of any kind and snobbish bullying least of all."

"I've had worse." I set my menu down. "I'll clear off in a second and leave you to your meal."

He looks startled. "Why?"

I gape at him. "Well, the table is laid for two, and I don't think your guest will want to sit in my lap. This place is far too posh for those sorts of shenanigans."

He shrugs. "My lawyer was going to join me for dinner, but he's been detained. So, you'll be doing me a favour eating with me. I grow so bored of my own company."

"How sad for you."

He chuckles, and the sound is warm and rich and makes my belly clench. Something about the way he looks at me tells me he's gay. However, it makes no difference. I'm leaving tomorrow and won't see him again, and he's way out of my league anyway.

I consider his offer and then decide, *fuck it, I'll just be honest.* "I don't have the money to eat here," I say baldly. "I'm off into the village to eat paella."

His eyes narrow. "Is the paella so bad here?" He pauses. "And why don't you have the money?"

I blink. "Well, that's a bit blunt." He continues to watch me intently, and I smile at him. "I don't mind bluntness. It's better than fannying about being polite all the time." The corner of his mouth ticks up, and I admit, "I used up all my money getting a room here and then hanging around with the rich bunch of wankers you saw in the lobby this afternoon."

"Yes, you didn't exactly look like a welcome member of their party."

I laugh. "Ouch!"

He raises an eyebrow which gives him a very devilish air. "I was under the impression that was a compliment. So, why were you with them?"

I contemplate his interested face. It's not very often a gorgeous older man looks at me like this. I tell him all about arriving here and the events of the week. When I finish, I take a sip of my water. He's a wonderful listener, and I haven't talked so much in ages, so my voice is a little hoarse.

"What are you going to do?" he asks.

"I'm going to get a flight back tomorrow." It must be my imagination or the candlelight because, for a second, he looks disappointed.

He sits back in his chair as a waiter moves in. "I'll have the sea bass," he instructs him and turns to me. "What will you have?"

"Oh, I'm not staying," I say, and he smiles charmingly at me.

"You must allow me to treat you to dinner. Unfortunately, you've not had the best holiday experience, and as a native Majorcan, I must remedy that."

"What utter bullshit," I say idly.

He laughs while the waiter just looks horrified. Mateo turns to him. "He'll have paella."

The waiter darts a worried glance at him. "Senor, there isn't any paella on the menu at night," he says in a low voice.

"Well, I'm quite sure the chef won't mind making a batch," my companion says. His voice is silky, but there's a steely element of command the waiter immediately responds to. He practically bows before gathering the menus and hotfooting it away.

"I'd have struggled to get something that was actually *on* the menu. You get so much better service than I ever have," I observe. "Why is that?"

For some reason, his eyes twinkle. "You haven't had good service here?"

"Good grief, no. I've had better service in my local Tesco."

"Why? Tell me everything," he orders, sitting back as another waiter appears, bearing fresh bread and little bowls of olive oil.

The oil is golden, warm, and speckled with garlic. I dip my bread into it and make a low sound of happiness at the heavenly taste. I practically inhale the first piece, and when I come up for air, he's watching me intently, his eyes dark in the candlelight.

I swallow. "Sorry. I'm starving."

"I can see." His voice has a rough edge to it, a stark contrast to his previously mellow tone. He pushes the plate towards me. "Eat it all," he instructs. "You're skin and bone."

I roll my eyes. "I'm just thin. It's my body type. But I'm plenty scrappy, though."

His expression clears, and he laughs. "I can see that."

I dip another piece into the warm oil and inhale the yeasty scent of it. "Why isn't paella on the menu?" I ask idly. "Is it too clichéd?"

He looks startled. "Of course not. I presume it's on the lunch menu. We don't usually eat such a heavy meal at night. That's for the tourists."

"Well, this tourist is very grateful. The chef, however, won't be. I can't believe he's cooking that just for you."

"Well, it's not for me."

I shake my head. "Oh, it's definitely for you. You must have some pull here."

He looks confused. "Pull?"

I cram the last of the bread in my mouth. "Pull, sway with the staff. Clout," I say thickly.

Something that looks like amusement crosses his face. "You could say that." He pushes my wine glass towards me. "Drink some wine. It'll put colour in your cheeks."

"I don't really like wine," I admit, but take a sip obediently. My eyes widen as the taste explodes over my tongue. "God, that's *lovely*."

He takes a sip from his glass. "Spanish wine," he says. "Nothing better, although I'd get shot at home for saying that."

"You don't live here?"

He shakes his head. "No. I was born here, but I live in Venice."

"Oh, wow," I say, resting my head on my hand and staring at him. "I've always wanted to go there. It's on my bucket lust."

"Isn't it a bucket list?"

"No. I don't have much cash, so a place has definitely got to be something I lust after before it makes my list. I feel the same about Rome, Prague, and Budapest."

"Rome is beautiful. Don't race to cram everything in when you go. Take it slowly and then you can really appreciate the city."

I finish my glass of wine and watch him pour me another. His hands are heavily veined, his fingers long and elegant, the nails perfectly manicured. On his wrist is a heavy silver watch that's very battered. It looks very old and not what I'd expect a rich man to wear.

"I'll get there one day," I say. "I'll just choose nicer travelling companions next time. Or even better, I'll go on my own."

He sits back in his chair. "You prefer to be on your own?"

"I don't *prefer* it," I say, considering the question. "It's just a natural state for me. And put it this way, I'd rather be alone than travel with Josh, who thinks people walk in front of him unfurling a red carpet."

His loud laughter seems to take him by surprise. We're interrupted by waiters arriving at the table. They set his meal in front of him and then put mine down with a flourish. I look at the wide china bowl. The rice is plump and golden, full of peppers and slices of chorizo and prawns glistening pinkly.

"Wow," I say to the waiter. "That looks amazing. Thank you so much."

He inclines his head to me, and after checking the settings in front of us, he leaves us with a nervous bow.

Mateo watches as I take a mouthful. "Good?" he asks with a smile as I groan in happiness.

"It's amazing," I say and fall on my meal hungrily.

He eats sparingly but with evident enjoyment, and for a few minutes, there's a contented silence at the table as we eat.

Then he leans forward. "So, tell me just how bad it has been staying here?"

There's a relish in his voice that makes me smile. I lean closer to him. "Well, meeting your receptionist feels a bit like I imagine it would be to meet Queen Elizabeth. Although, maybe our queen would be more polite, and she'd definitely handle the check-in process better."

This time his laughter doesn't seem to take him by surprise, and I regale him with my observations as we eat. His attention is a heady thing. He really listens, unlike many people who while away the time while you talk, working out what they're going to say next. Mateo, however, just eggs me on, filling my wine glass and watching me intently.

Finally, I sit back, putting the spoon down on my empty plate. I've just hoovered up a piece of homemade chocolate and honeycomb cheesecake which is the best thing that I've ever put in my mouth. I pat my stomach. "That was beautiful."

"So, you approve of the chef at least?"

"He needs a raise." I look around at the beautiful terrace and the restless movement of the sea beyond it. "It's a beautiful place, but the staff here are so *rude*. They're only polite to the rich people, which isn't fair. Everyone is entitled to civility. Especially at these prices. Anyway, I think they need to be careful with how they treat people who aren't obviously rich." He looks at me in query, so I elaborate. "Rich people are tricky buggers. They don't always *look* wealthy."

The waiter brings us coffee, and once we've doctored them to suit our tastes—him with it the colour of kreosote and me with enough sugar to stand the spoon up in the cup—he looks at me enquiringly.

"You were saying about rich people being tricky?" Something about that seems to amuse him.

"Once, when I was sixteen, I had a part-time job at a car showroom cleaning the cars. One day, this old bloke came in. He was dressed like a tramp and had dirty hands and clothes, but he wanted to look at the cars, and the salesmen were so *rude* to him. They practically ran him out of the showroom. I opened the door for him and said goodbye, so he gave me a tip." I shake my head. "Five hundred *quid*. I couldn't believe it. I'd never had that much money in my hands ever." I grin. "Or since, now I come to think about it."

He looks troubled, and I move the conversation on quickly. I don't need pity. He seems to have a way of bringing out honesty in me, which is probably why it's a good thing that I won't see him again.

"Anyway, they got a right telling off when the boss found out. They had no idea who the bloke was."

"Who was he?"

I grin at him. "He was a local man. A multi-millionaire who made his money from property development. He liked to get his hands dirty and work with his men. It turned out he'd been on site and remembered he wanted to buy a car for his wife. The showroom down the road sold him an Aston Martin twenty minutes later. A cash purchase."

He throws his head back, laughing, and I look around the patio. To my surprise, we're the only people left out here. It's fully dark now, with a thin moon and the coastline lights twinkling in the distance. The sound of the sea is loud in the empty space.

"I think it's time I was going," I say regretfully. It's been a fantastic night. One I'll pull out of my memory banks a lot.

"So soon?"

"Not really. We're the only ones left."

He looks startled, and it's a sweet feeling to think he's enjoyed himself as much as me.

I stand up, setting my napkin on the table. "Thank you for the meal," I say. "It really has been lovely, and you've given me a much nicer memory of Majorca to take home with me."

I offer him my hand, and he stands up to shake mine. I swallow as our palms slide together. His hand is so much bigger than mine. I quickly draw back. "Goodbye, Mateo," I say.

He inclines his head. "Goodbye, Wren Roberts named after an architect. I hope you have a safe journey back."

I bite my lip and then make a hasty departure. I look back as I get to the doors leading into the restaurant. Our table is empty now with no sign of my charming Sir Galahad. On an impulse, I turn to a tired-looking waiter who is folding napkins at a table.

"Excuse me," I say. "Could you do me a favour?"

"Of course, sir. What is it?"

"Could I buy a bottle of the wine we had at dinner and have you give it to the gentleman I ate with tonight?"

He looks startled. "You want to buy Senor Rossi a bottle of wine?"

"Yes, please."

He nods and names a price that makes the blood pound in my temples. It would pay my usual food budget for a month. Nevertheless, I swallow and hand him my card, hoping fervently that it doesn't bounce back faster than a kid on a trampoline. As he puts the payment through, I look around idly. There's something about Mateo's surname that rings a bell. I frown and then gasp as it comes back to me in the form of the name of the hotel.

"Did you say Mr *Rossi?*" I ask.

The waiter smiles. "Yes, sir. The Rossi family own the hotel."

"Oh my god," I say faintly.

CHAPTER TWO

Wren

The following day, I'm zipping my suitcase closed when there's a knock on the door.

I don't know anyone here, so who could want to speak to me? The tapping comes again, and I lope over to the door.

I throw it open and stop dead. "*You!*"

Mateo is leaning casually against the door jamb. He gives me a lazy grin. "Me. And you, Wren Roberts."

"What are you doing here?" A thought occurs to me. "Did you drink your wine?"

He blinks. "At ten in the morning?"

I rub my hand over the nape of my neck. "Well, needs must," I say awkwardly, which sounds rather like I think he's an alcoholic. "I sent you a bottle of the wine we drank last night to say thank you for dinner."

He looks stunned for a second, but to his eternal credit, he doesn't mention the price the way anyone else who knew about my impoverished state would. Instead, he smiles.

"That was a very nice thing to do, Wren Roberts, but I enjoyed your company. That was enough of a gift."

I think I'd rather have had booze than my company. "*Really?*"

He frowns. "Yes. Why not?"

"Well, you're you, and I'm me." I gesture between the two of us to illustrate my point.

"I do not understand you this morning," he says sadly.

I chuckle. He eases me for some strange reason. Usually, I'm polite and guarded with everyone, but I'm open in a bizarre way with him.

"Well, I'm pretty sure your outfit cost a lot of money." I gesture to his beige shorts, chambray short-sleeve shirt, and brown deck shoes. They're simple clothes that scream money.

"Is that a problem?"

"Well, my entire holiday wardrobe cost less than that bottle of wine. My flip-flops were three euros."

He looks down, and I wriggle my toes in the bright pink flip-flops. He makes a sound of disgust. "You were robbed," he advises me. "Are they... pleather?"

I nod. "Not very environmentally friendly, I'm afraid, but the plight of the oceans didn't seem so important when I was walking on sand doubling as burning lava. I spent so much time hopping from foot to foot on the first morning that an old lady thought I'd started a Zumba class."

He bites his lip, his eyes shining with amusement. "I wish I had been there."

I laugh. "So, why are you here, Mateo?"

He straightens from his absorption with my footwear and smiles at me. It makes his golden eyes glow, and his whole face soften.

"I need your help."

I wrinkle my nose. "How can I possibly help you?"

He indicates my room. "Do you mind if I come in?"

For a split second, it occurs to me that this might be part of his seduction technique, but I dismiss that straightaway. I'm not nearly good-looking enough for someone like him. Or worldly. So, I step back and gesture him in.

He steps through, giving me a waft of his lemony scent. He looks around curiously. "This is one of the superior rooms, yes?"

"Yes, and my wallet certainly knows that."

"And what do you think of it?"

"I know who you are," I blurt out. "You own this hotel." He looks startled and not very pleased. "Was I not supposed to know?" I ask.

He shakes his head. "It's of no real consequence, but it would have been nice to get to know you without you knowing everything about me."

"It's not like I know your inside leg measurement." I wave a careless hand. "Who you are doesn't matter to me apart from the fact that with your prices, my hotel bill probably paid for your monthly wine budget. I hope you enjoy drinking something that's been salted with my tears." He chuckles, and I smile. "I'm glad you're successful, but I'm only going to know you for a few more minutes anyway."

He catches sight of my luggage, and for a second, disappointment crosses his face. "You're leaving, then?"

I sit down on the end of the bed. "Well, hopefully. They're going to text me if a seat becomes available."

He studies me intently, and I wriggle. I'm not used to anyone looking at me so thoroughly. Usually, they spare me a second and then their gaze moves on to someone more interesting. It's almost thrilling to be the object of such attention.

"So, how can I help you, Mateo?"

He watches me for another second and then nods as if answering a question only he can hear. "What is right and what is wrong with this room?" he asks abruptly.

"*Pardon?*"

He waves a hand at our surroundings. "Tell me what is good and bad with this room."

"Why?"

"Humour me, Wren Roberts."

I bite my lip and then decide to categorise this as eccentric rich man behaviour.

"Well, the view is good." Beyond the window, the sea glints

turquoise in the morning sunshine. "You can't go wrong with that sight."

"Anything else good about the room?"

"The shower gel is bloody *lovely*," I burst out and then flush. "Sorry I made you jump, but last week I had to use Fairy Liquid to shower with when I ran out of money. The toiletries here are absolutely lush."

"Fairy Liquid?"

"Oh, erm, the stuff you wash dirty pots in." I shake my head. "I'm betting you don't know one single thing about washing crockery."

"You bathed in washing-up *detergent*?" He sounds horrified.

I laugh. "I've done far worse. I suppose I was just a big saucepan in that scenario."

His odd golden eyes are very focused on me for a second and then he smiles. "So, the view and the toiletries are a plus, yes?"

"Well, I wouldn't go that far. The soap stuff is lovely, but it's like you're supplying toiletries for pixies who have hygiene problems."

"Pardon?"

I stand up, grab his arm, and tow him into the bathroom, trying to ignore the firm muscle under my fingers. His skin is silky and warm, the hair on his arm tickling my fingers. I dismiss the silly thrill and gesture at the toiletries.

"There. Look at the size of that shower gel, Mateo. One squeeze, and it's gone. Do rich people need less soap to wash with?"

He chuckles. "Not noticeably." He takes the small bottle from me. His hand looks big and brown with long fingers and neat nails. "Hmm," he says. "You are right."

"Says no one ever." I bounce on my toes. "So, do you want the bad stuff now?"

His lip twitches. "That was it for the good stuff—the sea and the shower gel?"

I pat his arm. "You can't exactly take credit for the sea, Mateo. Poseidon might be a bit pissed off."

He chuckles and walks out of the bathroom. He sits down on the easy chair in the bedroom and gestures rather bossily at me. "Okay. Give me the bad things," he commands.

I pace the length of the room, marshalling my thoughts. Something about that must tickle him because his mouth quirks.

"Okay," I say, coming to a stop. "The hairdryers. They're travel hairdryers. They're so small it'd take an hour to dry a Barbie doll's hair, and you'd probably set fire to her because you have to hold the dryer a centimetre from your head. I thought the hotel was on fire the first few times until I realised it was just my hair follicles." I gaze around the room. "There aren't enough plug sockets. Most people have lots of things that need charging, and three plug sockets make you an electrical Scrooge. *And* one of them is under the bed. It means your guests are going to be commando crawling under the furniture at midnight. That does not lead to good things on *Tripadvisor*.

"The TV is nice and big, but it's not much use for people who aren't multi-lingual, as all the stations are in Spanish. I've had an interesting week making up what I think they're talking about, but it's wasted on your guests who are challenged in the imagination department."

He bursts into laughter, and I'm suddenly aware that all the stuff I'm slating is in his hotel. "Sorry," I say.

He smiles, looking much more cheerful than he should. He springs to his feet. "Excellent."

"*Really?*"

He nods. "Yes. You have a keen eye."

"Probably because this is the first time I've been abroad. It's all new."

"*Really?* This is your first time abroad?"

"Well, anywhere really apart from a weekend in Blackpool with one of my foster mothers."

"Your parents are...?" He hesitates, and I take pity on him.

"Who knows?" I say cheerfully. He blinks. "I was left on the steps of Guy's Hospital in Southwark when I was a baby. They were never able to find my parents. The lady who found me had the honour of naming me, and she was a trainee architect. Hence, my lovely name. I stayed at the hospital for a few weeks, and then I was taken into the foster care system."

"You were never adopted?"

It should be awkward to have this conversation with a stranger, but somehow it isn't. "With this nose, no way."

He chuckles, but his eyes are sad. "And what is wrong with that nose?"

"One of my foster mothers always swore I looked like a young Barry Manilow. I had to look him up, and it wasn't flattering." He grins and it chases the sadness in his eyes away. "So, have I helped you?" I say awkwardly.

He looks surprised. "Oh, that wasn't why I needed your assistance."

"What, then?"

"I am on the island to buy two more hotels. I need your help."

I bite my lip. "Well, money's a bit tight this week, Mateo."

He roars with laughter and then sobers. "I thought, as you have never been to Majorca before, you could come and view the hotels with me."

"Why?" I narrow my eyes. "It's not a pity trip, is it?"

"Not at all. You have a very keen eye, and I need that this week." He spreads his hands, attempting to look helpless and failing miserably. "I find myself suffering a little ennui. Everything looks the same to me at the moment. I need a fresh pair of eyes. I could drive us over the island and show you some of my homeland."

"But I'm going home today."

He purses his lips. "You are waiting for a call, yes?" I nod. "Then let us put your case in my car, and I can take you to the airport if you get a text. What do you think?"

I stare at him, excitement filling me. "And I can really help you?"

His gaze is steady. "I'd be very grateful, Wren Roberts."

I should probably turn him down, but I can't bear the thought of doing that. The holiday has been so shit so far, and this is completely out of the blue. I want to go with this man and have something exciting happen in my little life. Something I can remember when I'm back in gloomy London working my grey little job in my tiny office cubicle.

"Okay," I say. He grins widely which makes me feel quite awkward. I'm not used to people wanting me along. "And maybe you'd better call me Wren. Wren Roberts is a bit of a mouthful."

My words ring between us, and I flush, realising what I just said.

He bites his lip, his eyes lit with wicked amusement. "I'm sure he is."

I shake my head, and he bursts into laughter. It's loud and robust and rich and makes me smile.

He sobers. "Then we are agreed," he says, sounding relieved. "I have a small bit of business to do downstairs, so join me when you are ready. I'll be in the lobby."

CHAPTER THREE

Wren

When he's gone, panic descends. "I'm going out with him, and I haven't got anything to wear," I say out loud.

The absurdity of what I've just said shakes me back to reality. He probably wouldn't notice if I wore a thong, a snorkel, and flippers to lunch. I'm pretty sure that I'm well outside his usual type.

Rather than saddening me, the thought steadies me. He's taking me out because he's bored, and I've caught his interest in a small way. I entertain him.

"Like a jester," I say to the empty room and then shake my head. "No way I'm wearing bells on my clothes."

I look down at my outfit of yellow shorts and a striped T-shirt. Neither of the items were made to go together, but they'll have to do. I run a brush through my hair which immediately goes its own way, how it's been doing since I was born. I wriggle my toes in the flip-flops and roll my eyes. "He'll have to take me as I am," I say out loud.

I see Mateo as soon as I exit the lift. He's holding several files and surrounded by a group of four people, all hanging on every word he utters. I hesitate and then take a seat on one of the pastel-coloured sofas dotted about the foyer. I pick up a magazine and flick through it but abandon it in favour of looking out of the enormous front windows. Gardeners are bustling about under a sky that's as blue as a cornflower. The sun beats down, and there's the ever-present fizzing sound of the sprinklers.

Turning back to the foyer, I watch as Ava, the receptionist, sails past me to take a drink order from a couple who are sitting on a nearby sofa. Ah, Ava. Another joy of my Majorcan holiday. If I had ever harboured the wish to have invisibility as my superpower, it would have come true on this holiday. She seems incapable of seeing me no matter how hard I've tried to get her attention. I'd be prepared to bet that if I stripped naked and danced the tango in front of her, she'd still look over my head as if searching for something more interesting on the horizon.

It's been that way from the beginning of the holiday. I'm pretty sure that check-in isn't supposed to take an hour. If Owen hadn't come in with our luggage, I'd probably still be standing in the foyer.

Feeling brave because Mateo is here, I raise one hand and wave at her. "Excuse me," I say, hating the hesitancy in my voice. "Could I order a drink, please?"

There's no response. Honestly, at this point of the holiday I'd have fainted if she'd even acknowledged me, let alone got me a drink. I try another wave but it's no good.

At this point, Mateo glances around. When he sees me, he smiles, and the power of it makes me blink. But I don't have long to appreciate it. His gaze takes in Ava walking past me with her nose in the air while I hover with my hand up like I'm summoning a bus, and his expression clouds. He says something to the man in front of him, hands him the files, and stalks over to us.

Ava must sense a disturbance in the force, because she turns and blanches when she finds Mateo standing there.

"Oh, good morning, sir," she says, raising one hand to smooth her already immaculate hairstyle. I eye her hair enviously.

"Good morning," Mateo says, his expression still clouded. "What is going on here? This young man was trying to get your attention."

"Oh." She finally looks over at me. "I'm so sorry. I didn't see the gentleman."

"I fail to understand why. He was waving his hands around like a human windmill."

It's not the most flattering description I've ever had, but as he's telling her off, I roll with it.

He looks at me. "Would you like to order something? You can have whatever you like."

Ava's eye twitches at the corner. I'm very tempted to order something outlandish, but I bite my lip. Every time I do something even vaguely naughty, I hear the sisters from my Catholic primary school in my head. It's probably why I've led such a saintly life.

"No, I'm fine," I say.

Ava essays a smile at Mateo. "I'm so sorry, sir. I didn't see the young man. I've been very busy taking care of our other residents."

Mateo frowns again. When his expression suddenly smooths, I eye him suspiciously. He nods at Ava. "Wren is a personal friend of mine, so I'm always delighted to see someone taking care of him."

Her gaze flashes toward me, her eyes widening. Mateo drags her attention back when he says, "But we mustn't suppress your caring impulses, Ava."

"We mustn't, sir?" She falters.

His smile has a lot of teeth. "Why, yes. As you're so concerned about the guests, why don't you do a round of the sunroom and serve drinks to the people there? And when you've finished that, you can go out to the pool and help Armand out there. Lana can cover the desk."

"The *pool?* But I'm not dressed for that, sir."

"Oh, I think you are." His tone is pleasant, but there's a steely thread running through it. "And then we really must see about getting you and Felipe some extra training, as you're so obviously suited to looking after people."

She starts to say something, but he dismisses her smoothly. "I won't keep you, Ava," he says.

She stalks away, and I can't help my chuckle when she disappears.

He looks at me enquiringly.

"Remind me to take you everywhere with me, Mateo," I say.

"Why?"

"I wouldn't want to cross you. You're the Terminator of politeness. That was annihilation by good manners."

He chuckles. "And now your stay will be good, yes?"

"Or they'll just spit in my food." He blanches, and I shake my head and stand up. "Are you ready, or do you need to do something else?"

"I am sorry I kept you waiting."

I wrinkle my nose. "You were working. I was only sitting on a comfortable sofa being ignored by Olga the Oblivious." When his expression eases, I smile and bounce on my toes. "So, shall we go? I'm looking forward to seeing the island."

He turns, and we leave the foyer, the subject of a lot of covert observation from the staff. Even as the door opens for us, I'm aware of several conversations beginning behind us.

"Have you seen much of the island?" he asks as we get outside. I squint in the bright sunlight and feel sweat prickling under my arms already.

"I've seen a lot of the posh places. It's left me with the impression that Majorca is full of expensive carpets and chandeliers."

He steers me towards a Jeep parked to the side. "Is this yours?" I ask.

He grins, suddenly young and devilish. "It is. You seem surprised."

"That's because I am. I thought you'd drive a Porsche or something else really expensive." The Jeep is old. It's also dented, and the black paint is faded and chipped off in various places.

He pats the bonnet affectionately. "I've had this since I learned to drive. My mother bought it for me, and I keep it at her house while I am in Venice."

Before I can open the door, he leaps forward and does it for me. I'm surprised into silence.

One of his dark eyebrows rises.

I flush. "Oh, thank you," I say rather awkwardly. "It's like being Cinderella."

"If you lost one of those flip-flops, it wouldn't be a tragedy," he says dryly, closing the door and skirting the bonnet. He slides into the driver's seat and turns the key. The engine roars to life, and he looks over at me and grins, his teeth white in his tanned face and his funny golden eyes sparkling. "Ready to see Majorca?"

I grin with excitement. "Let's go."

He pulls out of the forecourt and onto the road. The traffic is heavy at first, but I quickly relax as he handles the Jeep with the same confident ease he seems to have with everything else. Soon we leave the town, and he takes a road that runs alongside the sea. We pass small coves surrounded by pine trees whose tall spikes shade our faces. Then we drive out into the open, where the sun shines down, bleaching everything into white. The roof is down, and the wind blows my hair about my face. Happiness bubbles up inside me like I've drunk a can of Coke too fast, and I can't stop my smile or the way I raise my hands over my head to catch the wind in my fingers.

He grins. "The sun is bright. There are some sunglasses in the glove box. Put them on."

I fumble in the glove box and draw out a soft leather pouch with the word *Persol* embossed on it. "These are expensive," I say.

"Yes, and they do their job. Put them on before you get a headache."

I slide them on. They're too big and immediately slide down my nose, but the light dims to something more comfortable than nuclear hot, and he nods in satisfaction. "Pick some music," he says. "You can sync your phone with the stereo."

"The age of this Jeep, I thought it would have a tape deck."

"Ah, the good old days," he says mockingly. "Perhaps I should have a CB system too."

"You know about those? A schoolfriend's dad had one. He never seemed to know what to do with it, which is understandable as he was an accountant in Bermondsey rather than a trucker on the M1."

He laughs, and I fumble my phone out of my pocket, and within a minute, the Jeep is filled with the sound of Madonna's "La Isla Bonita."

He shakes his head, and I grin at him. "*What?* It's perfect for today."

"The beautiful island," he translates and shrugs. "Why not."

We drive for a while as I choose songs, and he grumbles about them. Eventually, we come onto a winding road leading down to a cove. The road is so narrow that I could reach out and touch the bushes on either side. A fresh, herby scent fills the Jeep, and Mateo slows, cautiously steering through the steep curves. I look idly out of the window, and the foliage parts, revealing an eye-wateringly steep drop.

"Jesus," I say.

He smiles. "You are fine, Wren. I've driven this road many times. It's easy enough as long as you are not a reckless driver."

"I'm not worried." He shoots me an incredulous look, and I shrug. "I'm not. You're a good driver. I trust you."

"You're very quick to trust a stranger," he murmurs, his eyes back on the road, but his brow wrinkled in concern. "Maybe too much so."

His concern warms my chest. It's a rare occurrence for me and I push the feeling away. "I'm not. I just trust *you* for some reason." He shoots me a startled look and then turns his attention back to the road. "Unless you really are a murderer who's going to slit my throat and throw me down the gap." I pause. "Oh god, please say you're not and that I haven't just given you the idea of how to murder me."

He laughs. "Give me some credit. If I were a serial killer, I'd be an organised one, and I'm positive that I'd want to come up with my own killing ideas rather than just copying yours."

I relax back against the seat. "Thank goodness for fragile male pride."

His eyes are bright with humour, and he says in a low, hoarse whisper. "I'd let Felipe and Ava deal with you. They have a great deal of repressed antagonism."

"Goodness," I say faintly, and he chuckles again.

The road levels out, and then the trees clear, and I see a hotel in front of us. It's painted white and sits on the edge of a beach, the sand glowing white in the fierce sunlight. It looks elegant and very, *very* posh.

"Wow," I say. "I thought I'd seen all the rich places on the island." I look at him. "And you're thinking of buying this. How much is it up for sale?" He names a sum of money that makes my eyes water. "Fucking hell," I breathe. "You're joking."

He pulls up to a parking spot in front of the hotel and turns off the engine. "I rarely joke about money."

"Well, maybe you should start. That's *incredible*."

He shrugs. "We have a lot of properties," he says almost apologetically. "My family has been in the hotel business for a great many years."

"Do all your family work in the business?"

"No. My grandfather was ill and retired last year, and my father took over as CEO. When he retires, it will all be mine."

"What do you do now?"

"I used to be responsible for hotel acquisition, but I've been mostly based in the Venice offices since my grandfather retired. The individual directors report to me, and I oversee the properties in our portfolio and analyse current market trends."

"So, what does your dad do?"

He gives a humourless bark of laughter. "If you find out, maybe you can tell me."

"Ouch."

He grimaces. "He mostly tries to keep up with my stepmother's spending and her rather tumultuous moods."

"I think I'd rather troubleshoot sewage myself."

The shadow fades from his face, and he gives an easier laugh. "You must have met her." A concierge walks towards the Jeep. Mateo turns back to me. "We're incognito. I don't want people to know who I am. I don't need them to know that I'm interested in buying the place. It will send the price sky-high."

I nod as we get out of the car. The concierge gives an ingratiating smile and a bow, nearly kissing the pavement. "Senor Rossi," he says reverently. "May I say what a wonderful pleasure it is to have you here?"

Mateo looks over at me, and I bite my lip to stop my laughter.

Two hours later, we walk out of the hotel and slide our sunglasses on.

"Well," he says meditatively. "So that's how an anonymous hotel inspection works, Wren."

I start to laugh. "Yeah, that incognito wotsit went *really* well." He groans and I laugh harder. When I've finished, I look at him and snort. "So is the service usually that fawning for you, because that was like travelling with Brad Pitt. Minus all those children." I nudge him. "It's your own fault anyway, Mateo."

"How?" he says indignantly.

"You're very noticeable. You remind me of the queen."

"Can we get on to the portion of the day where you compliment me?"

I tap my finger against my teeth. "No," I say and grin when he slumps. I elaborate. "I once read that the queen thinks everywhere smells of fresh paint and new carpets, and that's because everyone wants her to see the best of wherever she's visiting. You're like that. I'm pretty sure there aren't that many Majorcan-born multi-millionaire hotel empire heirs floating around here. Of course, they knew you straightaway."

He sighs. "I have people who do this for me now. I have a wonderful acquisition officer. It appears that I've forgotten how to play the game."

"So why are you doing it now?"

He wanders over to stand by the beach. It's a long strip of golden sand dotted with comfortable-looking loungers shaded by umbrellas. Waiters in uniform dart about serving people, while a children's club plays far enough away not to disturb the parents. When I inhale, I can smell the salt of the sea and coconut sun lotion.

"I don't know," he says musingly. "Lawrence is fantastic at his job and picks perfect properties, and I always let my staff feel free to do their jobs. But I just woke up one morning a few days ago and felt..." He hesitates, looking out over the sea. "I felt restless," he finally says.

"Oh my god, you're *bored*," I say in a tone of revelation.

"I think it's a bit more than that," he says huffily.

I elbow him. "No, it isn't. You're bored."

He sighs. "Maybe," he finally acknowledges. I eye him beadily until he slumps. "Okay, I was bored. I wanted to get out of the office and see the island again. I love it here."

"It's home to you," I say softly. He looks at me, and I shrug. "I might not ever have had a proper one, Mateo, but I can recognise homesickness when I see it."

He returns his gaze to the sea. The breeze lifts his dark, wavy hair over his forehead. The strands look silky, and I know they'd be sun warm if I reached out and touched them. I shove my hands into my pockets, and he looks at me curiously.

I say quickly, eager to push away the odd, yearning awareness, "Well, if you want to look at new properties and inspect your own, you're going to have to *really* do it incognito." I stretch the word out to see him smile, and he immediately obliges.

"And how can I do that, Wren?"

"Get rid of those expensive clothes and designer sunglasses for a start." He eyes me, and I elaborate. "We've been here for two hours, and you've had the very best service, the chef cooked his heart out for you, and people bowed so low I'm pretty sure their noses polished the floor tiles." He laughs and I nudge him. "In short, you've only seen the beautiful surface. You need to be me." He raises his eyebrows. "I don't mean thin, big-nosed, and slightly lippy. You need to dress down and be a real tourist, and then you'll see the real side of the hotel. And I can tell you from experience that you'll have a very different view."

He contemplates me, a light in his eyes. "You're right."

"I usually am, but there's very rarely anyone around to witness it."

He laughs and steers me to the Jeep. "So that should be my new plan?"

"Yes. Operation Dress Down." This time I don't even flinch when he opens the door for me. I wonder how long it would take me to get used to a man being considerate. I shake my head. It'd be easier to meet a dodo. I become aware that he's still holding the door and flush before sliding in.

Then I pause. "What was that noise?"

He cocks his head. "Where?"

I listen again. "It's coming from the bushes over there." I climb out of the Jeep.

"Wren, I can't hear—"

I shush him. He obeys, his eyes sparkling and his lips twitching.

I move closer to the bushes and hear it again—a faint mew. I part the bush gently. "Oh, it's a cat," I say, looking down at the creature. It's a tiny grey and white thing with a startlingly loud miaow. "Are you lost, little one?" I crouch, holding out my fingers.

"Careful," Mateo says. "It's probably got fleas, and its claws are dirty. A scratch will make you ill."

"He's not going to scratch me, are you, sweetie?" I coo as the cat sidles up next to me. I run my fingers gently over his fur, feeling his ribs. "He's very thin," I say. "Would he be someone's pet?"

Mateo looks down at the both of us. "Unlikely. The hotel is the only building around here, and the staff do not keep pets. The nearest town is miles away." He straightens. "We must get on, Wren." He looks at me and groans. "No. Absolutely not."

"Oh, please," I say entreatingly. "We can't leave him alone. He's *starving.*"

He looks at me for a long second, and I put my best smile on. It doesn't usually work that well, but to my astonishment, he gives a wry chuckle and shakes his head. "I give in," he says, flinging his hands in the air. "I'll see if I can find him a home."

"Really?" I say, staring at him

His eyebrow quirks. "I rarely say things I don't mean."

"That's *amazing*. Thank you."

He looks somewhat bemused. "Why are you thanking me? I am not adopting him."

"You're doing something much better. You're finding him a home. Every person needs one of those."

His eyes are warm and golden in the sun, and he watches me for a long second before nodding. "Let me get my sweater."

"Why? It's not cold."

He chuckles. "Because that placid little creature will be enraged when we pick him up, and I have no desire to look as if I am dating Wolverine."

"That's an awfully nice image, though," I tell him earnestly.

He laughs and retrieves his jumper, and after a few attempts, he manages to get the cat bundled up in it and in the back of his Jeep. For such a small animal, the cat is rather forceful.

"Ouch," I say, looking at the long scratch on Mateo's tanned arm. "That looks like it hurts." I reach out, and before I know I'm doing it, I run a finger down the skin beside the cut. His arm is warm and silky beneath my fingertip, and he shudders. For a second, we stand very still and then, as if by mutual consent, we step back.

"So, what now?" I ask in a high, nervous voice.

He watches me for a second with a blank face and then smiles. "I will ring and see if I can find this creature a home."

"Thank you," I say fervently, and he shrugs.

"*De nada*, Wren."

We've been driving for a few minutes when my phone beeps. I pull my fingers away from the cat, who is batting them lightly with his tiny paws. He emerged from Mateo's jumper a minute ago, a little ruffled and on his dignity. But he quickly realised we meant him no harm and relaxed.

I pull my phone from my pocket and read the text. "Oh. They've got a seat for me on a flight at eight tonight." Disappointment is clear in my voice.

"What?"

I show him my phone even though he can't read the screen while driving.

"They've got a seat for me. Oh well, that's good," I say, trying for cheerful. "I can get back to real life and my job. I bet my boss will be glad enough to see me back early and—"

"Wren." He interrupts my blizzard of words. "Why don't you stay?" he says coaxingly.

"*What?* Why?"

"Because I need your help."

"I helped you today."

He shakes his head. "I have so much more to do. I need to look over another couple of properties, and I must perform Operation Dress Down, yes?" I nod, and he continues somewhat grimly. "I also need to do a spot of investigating in my own hotels. It appears that my managers may have become a little negligent and are letting the staff do what they want. You can help me with both of those tasks. You have a good eye and make astute judgements."

"I hope they're not in any trouble," I say, alarmed. "It's just little things."

"You have a soft heart," he says in a tone of revelation.

I'm immediately discomforted. "Not so you'd notice."

"I need your help," he says again. "Stay the week. You have the room until Sunday, yes?" I nod. "Excellent. Let me take you back to the hotel, and if you don't mind, you could spend the week helping me. You would be my assistant, and I would pay you, of course."

"Really?"

"You would be working for me. But, of course, I will pay you." He names a sum that makes my eyes go round.

"That's enough to pay my rent at home for three months. It's far too much money."

"No, it isn't," he says firmly. "You deserve it." He smiles at me, the sunlight showing flecks of copper in his golden eyes. "What do you say?"

"And I'd really be helping you?" He nods, and I bite my lip. "Well, that would be good, then," I say awkwardly, wishing passionately that I was as smooth as Josh and his friends.

Mateo looks pleased. "Excellent. I am very grateful, Wren. Now, let me take you back to the hotel and then tomorrow we will begin."

Excitement makes my stomach roil, and I fall quiet on the way back. He doesn't seem to notice and chats easily about all sorts of things, pointing out places of interest and telling me a little of the island's history. After we arrive at the hotel, he stays me with his hand before I can get out.

I meet his eyes, trying not to notice how much I like his hand on my skin.

"You can eat in the hotel tonight," he says.

"Oh no," I immediately protest. "It's not a place for me."

He frowns. "It most certainly is, Wren. I have found in life that if you act as if you belong somewhere, then people will believe you and invariably, at some point, you will believe it too." He lets go of my arm and says, a grim note to his voice, "I have issued instructions. You will be taken care of, and there will *not* be a repeat of last night."

"I hope Felipe didn't get into trouble." I think about that and amend it to, "Not too much trouble, anyway."

"Even after the scene last night, you still feel that?"

I frown at him. "Maybe he has something bad happening in his private life, Mateo. You should find out before you do anything drastic like sack him. Maybe he has family troubles. People don't always share their problems. They hide them," I say knowledgeably. "It could be the same for Ava."

He stares at me, his eyes dark, and then he relents. "You are right. I will discuss things with both of them, but I want you to eat at the restaurant. Everything has been paid for." I open my mouth to object very strenuously, but he puts his hand up. "You work for me this week, and it would make me very happy," he says smoothly, and I find myself giving in. I nod, and he smiles. "Excellent. Bon Appetit. I will see you tomorrow."

"Look after my pussy," I instruct him, tongue in cheek.

He grimaces. "Most people would have steered away from the pussy jokes," he says, his accent catching on the words.

"I'm a rare and unusual person," I inform him.

"Is that what they're calling it now?"

I laugh as I climb out of the Jeep. He waves and swings the car around, pulling out of the entrance and back onto the main road. I watch him go until he's a speck in the distance and then turn and make my way up to my room. I let myself in and then lean back against the door.

"What the hell are you doing, Wren Roberts?" I ask.

I don't care. For a week, I will go with the flow and spend time with the most fascinating man I've ever met.

Something on the neatly made bed catches my attention, and I walk over to it. There's a basket packed with the costly products from the bathroom, but the bottles are huge. Even the glass looks expensive. I run my finger down one cut-glass bottle, and a card comes loose.

Written in an elegant scrawl is:

. . .

For Wren,

    World travellers need the best accompaniments. No pixie products for you.
    Mateo

My laughter rings loudly, and I raise the card to my nose. It might be my imagination, but I swear I can catch a trace of Mateo's earthy, lemony scent.

CHAPTER FOUR

Mateo

I see him as I turn into the hotel forecourt. He's waiting by the door, an eye-catching figure in a pair of khaki shorts and a bright red T-shirt, the ever-present pink flip-flops on his feet. His thick brown hair is tumbling over his beaky nose, and there's an air of evident excitement about him.

I'm smiling before I even realise it. There's just something about Wren that makes me smile. He's a funny mix of spark and gawky awkwardness, and underneath there's a golden vein of kindness that I don't think he's aware of. He looks at the world a lot differently from me, and it's fascinating. I remember him crouched by the kitten, hand outstretched. Even the cat had sensed the gentleness in him.

I pull up beside him, and he looks up and grins, showing white teeth in a tanned, thin face. A dimple tugs at his right cheek like a little comma. It had been there the first time I saw him in the foyer speaking sharply to the spoilt rich boys—a sense of mischief.

It had been impulse that had made me invite him to dinner. I'd meant to reprimand Felipe and get them to give the boy a free meal, but then I'd looked into his warm brown eyes and found myself inviting him over. Then I'd increased my foolishness yesterday and asked him to stay for the week.

I don't regret that impulse, and I'm not sure why. I don't live my life by whims. I've seen the disastrous effects of that in my father's life. Mine is always calm and ordered. Just the way I like it.

Becoming aware that he's waiting for me, I reach over and throw the door open, and he grins.

"Morning," he says, climbing into the Jeep and bringing with him the scent of coconut sun lotion and the fresh smell of the hotel body wash. I think about the basket I'd had sent to his room. It had made me happier to do that for him than when I buy expensive presents for the men who pass through my life.

"Morning," I echo. When he thrusts a bag at me, I ask, "What is this?"

"A present." He buckles his seat belt. I scowl down at the bag in confusion, and he laughs. "It's my contribution towards Operation Dress Down. A new outfit for you." He pauses and says in a Spock voice, "It's life, Jim, but not as you know it."

I peer into the bag and see a bundle of clothes. "Wren, you shouldn't have bought me anything." Foremost in my brain is the fact that he's very obviously short of money.

He shakes his head. "I'd save your thanks until you've seen what I've bought you. You're going to look rather different from your usual suave self."

"Suave? You make me sound like James Bond."

"Then you can smack my arse and call me Miss Moneypenny."

He instantly flushes bright red, and I can't stop my laughter. "I think your private daydreams should maybe be kept to yourself."

"Shut up," he mutters. Even the tips of his ears are red.

I smile at him and then return to the topic of utmost concern. "You shouldn't have spent money on me," I protest.

His head comes up, and he narrows his eyes at me. "I can spend my money where I want," he says, a warning note in his voice.

I nod, respecting his pride. "Of course," I accede. "You know best." I add meekly, "Miss Moneypenny." His glare makes me laugh, and I reach to switch off the engine. "I'll park the Jeep and go in and change into the clothes, and then we will be ready for our work today."

He immediately shakes his head. "God, no. Can you do it somewhere else?"

I narrow my eyes. "Why?" I feel my anger rise. "Has someone else been rude to you?"

"No, no," he says, putting his hands up. "Quite the opposite."

"What do you mean?"

He thrusts a hand through his hair, and I smell the sweet scent of his shampoo. "It's just that everyone is being so *nice.*"

"And is that not good?" I ask cautiously.

He shoots me a wry grin. "It sounds silly, but it's a bit overwhelming to be the focus of that much attention. They're always offering to do things for me. It's like being a king or something."

And you've never felt that, I think, watching him. I wonder if anyone has ever looked after this sparky boy. Did those foster carers take care of him, or was everything done with a sense of obligation? It makes my chest hurt.

When he'd first told me about his childhood, the information had been offered so guilelessly that my suspicions had immediately been raised. Was he making the revelations because he knew that I had money? He wouldn't be the first man to spin a poor-me tale for me. He wouldn't even be the twentieth.

However, only a few minutes in his company had dispensed with such a silly notion. He's startlingly honest and forthright, with a deep compassion that someone who grew up like him should surely not possess. It made me ashamed to have thought ill of him.

I realise he's watching me worriedly as if I'm going to be offended. "Well, let's get on with our day, then," I say.

He instantly relaxes. "That's good." He hesitates. "I think we might be the subject of some gossip too," he says tentatively. "They keep eyeing me as if I'm the cheese in a Mateo sandwich. I'm sorry."

I turn to face him. "There's no need to be sorry. It's understandable. They've seen me with a lot of men over the years. They must think you're the latest. I suppose I should apologise to you."

My cheeks heat, and god only knows why. I'm not ashamed of my life.

However, he just laughs. "That explains everything, then. They keep staring at me with this air of disbelief as if there's a unicorn eating a croissant for breakfast. I'm guessing I'm not like your usual conquests."

He's actually correct. With his air of gentle naivety, he is nothing like the men who usually hang from my arm. They're toned, gym fit and tanned, and dressed in the best labels. They're the same age as me and mostly successful in their own rights. They wouldn't pet a stray cat or care about a waiter who'd been appallingly rude to them. We keep company with no commitments and no promises, and when it's finished, there are no scenes or emotion. And I like it that way. My relationships are honest and as far from my parents' choices as the moon.

"You're nothing like them," I say gruffly and only realise that it sounded like a criticism when he flushes. I put a hand on his arm quickly. "And I'm very glad of that," I say emphatically. "*Very* glad. I don't need other men this week."

He relaxes. "You won't be saying that when you see the outfit I've chosen for you."

"Oh god," I groan, and he laughs.

Ten minutes later, I stand by the side of the road. I've pulled the Jeep under a plane tree, and the road is quiet, the cloud of dust from the Jeep slowly dissipating. Cicadas whirr as I open the bag again and pull out the clothes Wren bought me.

My eyes widen. "I'm to wear this? *This?*"

He snorts. "It's very you, Mateo."

I look down at the bright pink T-shirt with the word "cocky" emblazoned across it in rhinestones. "Only if I was a stripper in Vegas." He laughs, and I lift the shorts. "Aren't these a little tight?" I ask, swinging them around my finger as if I am that stripper.

He contains his laughter and sits back. "I know you're used to wearing Ralph Lauren or whatever label the staff in your hotels seem to expect your customers to wear. But, if you need to assess the service at your hotels, then you have to dress like someone who'd experience bad attitudes and poor service. It's a little like being undercover."

"Well, that's appropriate. I don't think I'll even be able to fit underwear under these."

He bites his lips, his eyes sparkling. "Stop messing about and drop trousers, Mateo."

I shake my head and pull off my shirt and shorts, leaving me in just my boxers. I shake out the shorts and suddenly realise that Wren has gone quiet. When I look up, I find him watching me. His warm brown eyes have gone dark, and his cheeks are cherry red.

I swallow hard as a surge of lust surges through me. It's so sudden and powerful that I almost stagger. For a wild second, I imagine striding to him, taking his mouth with mine, and then having him against the Jeep on this lonely road. Then I make myself remember that he's only in his twenties. I'm forty and far too old for him. He's so new and fresh he should have dew on him, and I have no business with that. My men are experienced and know the score. This lovely boy doesn't.

I take a hopefully unobtrusive breath and turn to put on the shorts and hopefully hide my erection. Then I pull on the shirt, grimacing at how tight it is, and turn back to him, pulling a catwalk pose.

"Well, what do you think?"

"I'd make it rain for you, baby."

"The only rain I require is the sort that will shrink this clothing enough that I am unable to wear it anymore."

He laughs loudly, but there's a hint of relief in his expression that he can't entirely hide. The knowledge that he doesn't want this attraction to go anywhere should be a relief, but I can't help a small stab of disappointment. *Get over yourself, Mateo.*

"So, am I guaranteed bad service in this outfit then, Wren?"

He looks me up and down. "Depends where you are, I think. If you were on the pole at Sparkles in London, you'd have the best service ever invented."

"I'm fairly sure you are not talking about white wine being served in the correct glass and a top-notch turn-down at night." He snorts, and I pull the shirt away from my torso. "It's a bit tight."

"Mmm," he says dreamily and then bursts into more of his raucous laughter, scaring away a bird on a nearby bush. "I'm sorry," he says when he's recovered from his hilarity. "You just look so indignant and out of place. Like Nigel Farage at the Labour Party annual conference."

"I have no idea what you're talking about," I say loftily, not hiding the upturn of my lips.

I climb back into the Jeep, and he smiles at me. It's wide and sunshiny and sits on his soft pillowy lips as if made to do so, and I find myself helplessly returning it.

"So, what's the plan?" he asks.

I bring my mind back to the task at hand. It's harder than it should be. "We're going to my hotel near Canyamel. I got my assistant to make the booking. She's booked a double room in your name and paid for it with her card."

"What about luggage? We can't turn up at the hotel without it. They'll think I'm on the game."

"On the what?"

"Oh, hooking. Rent boy."

I blink. "I brought a small case of clothes," I inform him.

He chuckles. "That means I'll have to pack away my leather shorts and scarlet letter. What a huge disappointment this day is turning out to be."

I shake my head. "Idiot," I say, but he just laughs.

When we set off again, he turns to face me, drawing one long leg under him. His brown hair is blowing wildly in the wind and there's a visible air of excitement about him. "What happened to Mick Jagger?"

I hesitate. "The singer?" I finally say. "I believe he is still alive."

"No, the cat we rescued yesterday."

"We didn't so much rescue him as he inflicted his presence on us."

"You say potato. I say potahto. How is little Mick?"

"I know deep inside me that I'm going to regret asking this, but why Mick Jagger?"

"Because he's always out on the prowl."

I can't help my chuckle. "That's perfect. Well, Mick Jagger is fine. He's infinitely better than us at the moment, as he is curled up in the kitchen of my mother's home rather than dressing ridiculously and anticipating being treated appallingly by the very people whose wages I pay."

He laughs and then asks, "You gave Mick to your mother?"

"Of course. I can't keep him. I'm not on the island that much, but my mother loves animals."

"Thank you." His voice is soft and his eyes admiring. Warmth floods my chest. Like the best kind of praise. "You didn't have to do that."

I shrug and think of my mother's wry smile when I had shown up at her home last night and told her the story. She'd followed it with so many questions that my head had spun. I'd finally escaped, but I'm under no illusions that it's for good. My mother is relentless and very concerned with my private life. She's also interested in Wren for some odd reason.

I shelve that as a problem for a lot later and concentrate on driving. A silence falls between us that is strangely easy. Wren looks out of the window, his hair blowing over his face. I tap his knee and point at the glovebox. "Put some glasses on."

He reaches into the glove box and pulls out the leather pouch. "These aren't the same as the ones I had on yesterday. Where are they?"

"I left them at home. Try those on. They might fit you better."

He slides the Ray Bans over his eyes and turns to look at me. "These look new," he says suspiciously.

That's because they are. I'd gone shopping for them after leaving my mother's house, remembering how often he'd had to push up the glasses on his nose yesterday. I'd noted the patience with which he'd done it and the utter lack of expectation that something should fit him properly. It had angered me for some odd reason, and I'd spent a long time in the shop choosing something that he'd like.

I'm gratified to find how much the orange-framed Wayfarers suit him, showing off his tanned thin face. I become aware that he's staring at me.

"Oh, do they?" I say vaguely. "Oh, look over there at the cove. Beautiful place for swimming. The current is very mild."

He obediently looks away, and I let myself smile. I have every intention of putting those in his luggage at some point this week. Everyone deserves a good pair of sunglasses, but he deserves them more. He looks at himself in the Jeep's side mirror and touches them reverently. I repress another grin just in time as he turns to me.

"I do hope you didn't buy these for me."

I make myself look innocent. "Why would I do that?" Before he can ask more questions, I say, "Maybe I should tell you a little bit about the hotel we're going to."

He's immediately diverted. "Good idea."

"It's high on the cliffs looking out over the Bay of Canyamel and a very peaceful spot. We added it to the portfolio in the nineties and it used to be our big money maker on the island. But, in the last couple of years, the figures have dropped. At first, no one noticed." Mainly because it was my father's job to track earnings. "But then it caught my attention the other week." Probably because I'd been driven mad by boredom sitting in that office, staring at the same view every day and looking down to see the endless tides of paperwork on my desk. "I want to know what's happened to make bookings drop. After hearing what you had to say about the service in your hotel, I want to take an incognito look at the place. See what the guests are experiencing firsthand."

He wrinkles his nose in thought. It's extraordinarily charming. "So, what's our cover story?"

"Our what?"

"Our cover story. Who are we are? Are we brothers or boss and employee?"

"We're newly married," I say. The words come bursting out of me, taking me by surprise and making him jump. "Sorry," I say quickly. "If it's okay with you, we can be newly married." I think back to how Felipe treated him the other evening and the answering look of resignation on Wren's face. "I felt that some of your interactions with the staff had a whiff of homophobia. I will not allow that. Ever. So, if we're newlyweds, I can get a sense of the situation at this hotel."

"We're not only newlyweds. We shall be *poor* newlyweds," he says with relish. "We've saved up for a couple of years to afford this trip."

His tone indicates that he's familiar with the concept of saving for a trip, but there's no self-pity there. Some of the men I've been with would pout if they had to wait a few hours for something they desired, but Wren seems to view challenges with bright eyes and a relish of the absurd.

"I'll be Monty," he continues. "And you will be Bernard, but I always call you Bernie Boo."

I bite my lip. "What a delightful nickname. *That* is the only name you can think of for me, then?"

"It's the logical choice." The lilt in his voice betrays his amusement.

I turn onto the long avenue lined by gracious olive trees, and Wren looks around with big eyes. The hotel looms ahead of us. "Is that yours?" he gasps.

I look up at the huge stone building. "My family's," I correct him. "I don't feel any real connection to it."

"No, I don't suppose you do," he says, his tone oddly knowing. I glance at him, and he smiles. "You seem like the sort of man who wants to do his own thing. You're not the type of person to sit back and accept things being given to you. You probably don't feel ownership unless you've actually been responsible for it."

I draw the Jeep to a stop, parking it neatly in the car park. The sun is hot on our heads, and the wind in the trees is the only sound to be heard. He flushes when I turn toward him and meet his eyes.

"Sorry," he says quickly. "I've only known you for twenty-four hours. That was very rude."

"It was correct," I say. "You're a very clever young man."

A flush dapples his sharp cheekbones, and I get the sense he's not used to accepting compliments.

I don't like to see him uncomfortable, so I switch the engine off and tap the steering wheel. "So, are we doing this?"

"You bet," he says, sitting up straight. "We just need to do something with your face, though."

"I'm slightly worried by that statement. My face has been this way for forty years."

He chuckles, the sound warm and inviting. "No, you're too tidy, and you look expensive even with those clothes." He reaches into his bag and produces a baseball cap. "We'll just put this on," he says, placing it on my head backwards and pulling a few strands of hair loose.

I repress a shiver at the feel of those long cool fingers on my sun-warmed skin and eye him. "Why?" I ask.

"Because you're very noticeable." His gaze traces my features but then he looks away quickly. "This way, you look like a tired tourist. It's perfect." He glances out the window. "Why did you park so far from the hotel?"

"Because my Jeep is well known in the area. The news would have spread in a second that the boss's son was here."

"Good thinking. Are you ready?"

"I am prepared. That is as far as I can go."

"This is going to be fun," he says with more of that irrepressible optimism. He climbs out of the Jeep and grabs the case I indicate. "Let's go, Bernie Boo."

I wince. "Please, can you not call me that ever again?"

"I make no promises," he calls. "Honesty makes me tell you that I'm going to use the name at every opportunity."

I roll my eyes and follow him as he laughs.

When we get to the hotel steps, he stops. "Have you had any official complaints from guests?"

"Nothing direct that we could point the finger at and say what member of staff needed to go. It's more a general dissatisfaction with the hotel and the staff as a whole. It's an alarming theme."

"They're probably doing what the hotel I'm staying at does. They're killing with coldness. They make people feel unwelcome."

I shake my head. "Felipe has been dealt with."

He looks alarmed. "Not with the sack?" He pauses. "Or being thrown into the sea in a bag of bricks. Whatever being *dealt with* means in your family."

"We're not the Sopranos, Wren. Anyway, I promised you I wouldn't dismiss him." When he raises his eyebrows, I say indignantly, "Did you think I was lying?"

The concierge opens the door before Wren can answer. I guide Wren into the lobby, my hand at the small of his back. I look around, assessing. It's cool in here, with marble floors and walls stripped back to the stone. The reception desk is a slab of driftwood and currently empty, while the sofas dotted about are bold colours echoing the modern art on the walls. The whole effect is one of classy calm and coolness. I relax a little. At least the decor is on point.

Wren purses his lips and brings me back to the conversation. "I didn't think you were lying so much as just agreeing with me for a quiet life and then doing what you want."

I can't help my smile. "It wouldn't exactly be the first time I've been guilty of that, but this time I was telling the truth." I wink. "You didn't, however, prevent me from sending him on a customer relations course. A long one."

"He can pal up with Ava. They have so much in common." I laugh, and he shakes his head. "The way we're going, your hotels will be empty because all the staff will be on courses."

"The way we're going, I'm considering asking for a bulk discount." I look around. "Where the hell is the receptionist?" I grumble, and he shushes me as a woman comes around the corner.

She wears the uniform of a grey suit well, and her blonde hair is neatly held back in a bun. She spots us and her steps falter as she takes in our outfits and the old, battered suitcase that my mother had dug out for me last night with a great deal of hilarity about my plan. It's cracked brown leather with a tear on the side and a rainbow ribbon tied jauntily around the handle.

"Good afternoon," she finally says into the awkward silence. Her voice is frigidly cold. "Do you have a reservation, gentlemen?"

I open my mouth, but Wren steps forward. "We certainly do, don't we, Bernie Boo?" he says enthusiastically.

I narrow my eyes at him, and he pulls me forward, pinching me in the ribs.

"Ouf!" I grunt, but he talks loudly over me.

"My hubby will have made that. He's the organised one out of the two of us. Do you know I once went to the wrong place to take my woodwork GSCE? I'd forgotten where the building was. If only I'd had my boo with me, I'd have definitely gone to the right place. Maybe I'd have become a master carpenter rather than a pole dancer." He sighs.

"The paths that life takes us on." He winks at her. "Still, the good news is that the pole pays."

I promptly swallow my own spit but the receptionist, whose name badge says *Cecilia*, is made of sterner stuff. She says nothing, and her smile remains frigidly polite as she stares at Wren. She takes the printed sheet I offer and scrutinises it as if she'll be taking an exam on it at any moment. Or hoping to find a mistake.

Finally, she looks up. "Everything seems to be in order." There's a distinct tinge of disappointment in her voice.

I open my mouth to say something sharp, but Wren claps. *Loudly.* "Wonderful," he enthuses. "This is such a very special occasion for Bernie and me. We're actually on our honeymoon."

Now, I know that the hotel policy is to offer all newlyweds a room upgrade, a meal in the restaurant, and a bottle of champagne, because I wrote the rule, and I wait for Cecilia to do as she should.

Instead, she gives a chilly smile and rings the bell. "Wonderful," she says with no enthusiasm in her voice at all. "Rodrigo will show you to your room."

I narrow my eyes, but she looks behind us at the next set of guests. "Someone is waiting," she says coldly to me.

Wren pulls me to one side. Cecilia's expression becomes warm and sociable as she greets the middle-aged guests behind us. They have sweaters wrapped around their shoulders as if they're off to umpire the cricket, but Cecilia greets them as if they're the royal family. "Welcome," she says gaily. "How may I help you?"

"Bloody outrageous," I growl, but Wren shushes me.

I subside but not without a hint of amusement cutting through my displeasure. No one ever shuts me down like that.

"*Perfect*," he corrects me. "So, we know they're not exactly rolling out the welcome rug. Especially if you're gay or someone who doesn't own a Ralph Lauren shop."

I snort and turn as a throat is cleared behind us. An older man is standing there dressed in uniform. Unlike Attila the Hun behind the desk, his smile is warm and welcoming.

"May I show you to your room?" he asks, his huge moustache twitching.

Wren gazes at it in fascination, and it's my turn to elbow him.

"Ow," he says and then grins at the man. "How lovely. My Bernie and I haven't had a man carry our bags since we got mugged on Oxford Street."

I try to repress my laughter, but it comes out as a disgusting snort, and Rodrigo looks at me as if I'm going to drop dead in the foyer. I offer him a nod, and Wren tugs on my elbow as we follow him to the bank of lifts.

"This is the best fun *ever,*" he whispers. "It's like we're hotel private detectives." He pauses. "We're *the* mystery customers. Ooh, I always wanted to do that."

"Not exactly what I thought I'd be doing considering that I own the bloody place."

"Oh, *now* you own it," he says. "Interesting."

I shake my head. "What have I done?" I bewail.

His lip twitches. "You've set me loose. Feel bad, Mateo. Feel very bad."

CHAPTER FIVE

Wren

I walk into the room and whistle. "Wow."

Mateo sniffs disapprovingly. "*This* is the superior room?"

"Hmm. It's quite poky, isn't it? A bit like a prison cell with a nice view." He glares at me, and I spread my hands. "What? You wanted me to point out the problems."

He takes off his baseball cap and throws it on one of the beds. *Will we be sleeping in here tonight?* The beds are very close together. Somehow, I don't think Mateo figured on that when he thought up this plan.

He puts his hands on his hips and looks intently around the room. He somehow manages to be dignified even with that atrocity of a T-shirt. I shake my head. Even in those cheap clothes, he's *hot*. The tight T-shirt clings to his muscled torso and highlights the bulge of his biceps while the colour, which would be terrible on me, makes his olive skin glow. Even the shorts accentuate the tight fleshy curve of his buttocks.

He breaks the spell by moving over to the bed and lifting the mattress.

"Whoa," I say. "What are you doing?"

He grins wickedly. "An old tip given to me by a hotel inspector. Lift the mattress and check for dust and dirt on the frame and springs. It shows whether it has been turned recently."

"Aren't hotel inspectors supposed to be secretive?"

He winks. "Not when they're naked."

I shake my head and move to his side. "Ugh. Look at that dust."

He lets the mattress fall, wiping his hands on his shorts. "The mattresses are supposed to be turned every month."

"I bet Julio Iglesias was in the charts the last time that happened here."

He crouches and peers under the bed. "There is a condom wrapper under here," he says in disgust.

"Open or sealed?" He raises an eyebrow and I shrug. "Well, it changes things. Open is bad housekeeping. Sealed is helpful."

"It changes nothing." He stands up and runs his finger over the top of a picture. He turns his finger toward me, showing that it's covered in dust. "Housekeeping isn't doing their job."

"You remind me of an old foster carer I stayed with," I say idly, opening the drawer of the bedside table. I remove a copy of *Fifty Shades of Grey* and offer it to him. "Don't hotels usually provide the Gideon Bible? I'm not sure whether this is an improvement or not."

"Why?"

"Well, it's not the best read out there." I grin. "I remember reading this. It took bloody ages to get a copy from the library. I wanted to know whether I was suited for BDSM. I decided in the end that I could cope with the odd smacked bum, but I wasn't that keen on being told what to do. I mean, I might have been able to obey a handsome billionaire, but it didn't quite work with Trevor from Wapping, who was telling me to go to Tesco for him to buy his beer."

There's a long pause, and his lip twitches. "No, I mean, why do I remind you of a foster carer?"

I look at him and burst into laughter. "Sorry," I say when I've recovered. "This couple I lived with for a few months used to get us all out of bed at five in the morning and make us clean the house."

I'm startled to see a look of rage on his face.

"How old were you?" he asks.

"About ten, I think."

"That's fucking terrible."

I shrug. "I've had worse, and at least I know how to use a hoover attachment. I'm sure it'll come in useful sometime." I look around the room. "I could be in for a position with your housekeeping team with my superior cleaning knowledge. I'd probably be management material straightaway."

He watches me for a long second, his face turbulent, and I shift, wishing I'd never made that flippant remark. I'm never this honest with anyone. *So why is it different with him?* I give him an imploring look to drop the subject, and finally, he does.

Instead, he enters the bathroom and puts his foot on the bin to open it. "Fuck me," he mutters. "A night in this room costs a great deal of money, and they haven't even emptied the waste bin."

I move to the double doors and step out onto the balcony that looks out over the bay. There's a huge hammock in one corner and a squashy-looking sofa and chairs in another. "Now, *this* is five stars. I think you could fit my bedsit on this balcony." The sun is hot on my face and body, but there's a light breeze that blows my hair back. I lift my face to bask in the warmth and turn when I hear a footstep. Mateo is watching me, a smile on those full lips.

"Happy?" he says. "You look like a cat."

"Not Mick Jagger. He's even scrawnier than me."

"Not now that my mother is feeding him. I confidently expect that he will be the size of an elephant by the end of the summer."

"I'm glad he's in a good place." I look back over the view. "I love the sun. I didn't know whether I would. Living in Britain, we don't exactly get enough sunshine in the summer to make up our minds on it. It's more like a couple of hours. Just long enough for us all to moan about how hot it is, and then we get torrential rains for the rest of the summer and moan about how we never get any good weather."

"After looking at Tripadvisor, I can guess a lot of our customers must be British. There is always something to complain about."

"We *are* world-class whingers. It's a shame it's not an Olympic sport." He laughs, and I look at the blue sky. It's so much better with the sunglasses he lent me. "I wondered whether it would be too hot here for me, but I love everything about this place."

"You like the island," he says, a pleased tone in his voice. He leans against the balcony's railing and looks out on the view. The breeze blows his thick brown hair around his face, and the sunlight picks out the faint lines at the corners of his eyes. His stubble is that perfect length that only models and actors seem to attain. When I tried growing my own, it ended up looking like I'd got mange.

"I love it. It's so pretty, Mateo."

"There are many wonderful places on the island that I'm sure you haven't seen. We'll have to remedy that this week."

"Only for work, though?" I say, worry seizing me. "You're paying me to work for you. We can't skive off. It would make me feel awful about taking your money."

He shakes his head. "You are like no one I've ever met."

"I've heard that said a few times," I say wryly. "But not usually admiringly." I step back into the room and look at the curtains. "These curtains are frayed at the bottom."

He says something vicious in Spanish and leans down to inspect them. "I would very much like to see what the decorating budget is actually being spent on."

"Not curtains," I offer sympathetically. I gesture towards the room. "Or soft furnishings and bedlinen. The throw on the bed is bobbling badly." His cursing makes me chuckle. "This is good fun," I say happily.

Half an hour later, we've examined every inch of the room. We're sweaty and hot, and Mateo's face still wears the grim expression it got after he started moving furniture. Finally, he subsides onto the sofa on the balcony. "Shit," he mutters.

I pat his shoulder and settle into one of the chairs. "It's no longer surprising that people aren't happy with their stay here, but unless they've all shagged hotel inspectors, a lot of them might not even have noticed all the tiny things you looked for. From my observations this week, most people just want to get straight to the pool and start their holiday drinking."

"If I'm looking for dirt, I expect my staff to do the same." He shakes his head and seems to throw off his moroseness. "And you're right. So that's what we're going to do next."

"Drink our weight in beer and get sunburnt?"

He smiles. "No. We need to inspect the pool area facilities and see if the staff are any friendlier than our charming receptionist."

"That's not exactly difficult. Jack the Ripper was probably more sociable."

He stands and I follow him into the bedroom. He opens the battered case resting on the bed.

"Where did you get that?" I ask. "It doesn't look like something you'd own. Mind you, I thought that about your watch and your Jeep."

He pats his watch with one long finger. "This was given to me by my grandfather when I was eighteen. It was his when he was a young man. I know it doesn't exactly fit the image, but why would I throw it away for something shinier? Everything loses the shiny patina after a while, and an Omega Seamaster always keeps its value."

I smile at him. "I like the way you think." I feel myself flush because I sounded a little too enthusiastic, but luckily, he's staring into his case and hasn't noticed.

Inside the case is a stash of clothes neatly packed.

"Did someone pack for you?" I ask, coming closer and losing my self-consciousness as I reach out and touch a pair of blue and white patterned board shorts. I saw some like this in a shop in the resort, and I'd been consumed by want. I'd bought an old pair of shorts from a charity shop at home, and I'd thought no one would guess, but Josh's friends had taken one look at me and immediately broken into smirks.

Odd that the same pair of expensive shorts I'd admired are here in Mateo's suitcase. I shake my head. It's a small world.

There's a funny expression on Mateo's face. It isn't pity. I don't know what it is, but it makes me feel warm.

He gestures at the shorts that I'm touching. "Those are yours."

I snatch my hand back. "*What?*"

He eyes me steadily. "They're for you. I bought them yesterday."

"*Why?*"

"Because I saw them and thought of you."

"Really?"

He smiles kindly. "I felt like treating you. You're doing a huge favour for me this week, and I wanted to show my appreciation."

His explanation was nicely done. He acknowledged my pride and neatly circumvented it by being kind and not patronizing.

"You're paying me for this big favour, though, Mateo."

"Then look on it as a bonus." He rifles through the clothes, tossing them aside when he can't find what he's looking for.

I struggle with what to say before mumbling, "Thank you."

"*De nada.*"

"What are you looking for?" I ask, forgetting my self-consciousness.

"I asked my mother to grab me a pair of board shorts, and I can't see any." He stills and then lifts a piece of fabric, cursing long and low.

"Wow!" I say lightly. "Someone's cross."

He brandishes the material. "Bloody woman. Look what she's done."

I take the scrap of fabric from him and immediately snort. It's a tiny pair of bright red Speedos. "Oh my God, are these *yours?*"

He snatches them back, his cheekbones ruddy. "They are not," he says huffily.

"Did the person who owned them wear a gold medallion that nestled in his abundant chest hair?" I ask.

His crossness fades as he starts to laugh.

It suits him. His face is usually warm and his manner welcoming, but I've come to realise that he's also a guarded person. The laughter opens him up. It's a warm, intimate sound.

"That sounded alarmingly detailed," he observes.

I shrug. "A few months spent reading a foster mother's stock of Mills and Boon will do that to you. I like to read, and they were all she had. They were actually very informative. Someone wearing that swimming costume would have been a rich Spanish noble and the heroine would have been his young British bride who he'd had to marry because of a *scandal*."

He laughs, and I watch him. He's actually the epitome of a Mills and Boon cover from the sixties. Tall, dark, and craggy. It'd be titled something like *The Spanish Lover,* and he'd be appallingly badly behaved, but the woman would love him anyway.

He breaks me from my thoughts when he holds up the tiny costume. "One of my exes liked Speedos," he says. "I can't stand them myself."

I bite my lip. "They're quite... snug."

He shakes his head. "They make a leotard look like a kaftan."

"Would you like mine?" I've never owned anything as posh as those shorts, and it would crush me a little to give them up, but I like him, and I don't like the idea of him being uncomfortable.

He gives me a kind smile. I like to think it's bigger than the ones he gives other people—more special. I push that stupid thought away immediately. He wouldn't be attracted to me. I'm not his type, judging by the few comments he's made about his men.

"They're yours, Wren. I got them for you." He glares down at the scrap of fabric. "Piss-taking woman," he mutters. "I'm pretty sure these belonged to her last boyfriend." I bite my lips to stop smiling, and he rolls his eyes. "You can laugh."

"Okay, then." I burst into a fit of giggles while he watches me with amused eyes.

"He was built like a bull and would wander around the pool, and he always bought them a size too small so his balls would peek out. It used to quite put me off my lunch." That sets me off again, and I bend double. When I sober and stand up, he's watching with a huge grin on his face. "Finished?" he asks.

"Maybe. Put them on, and let's test it."

He shakes his head and wanders into the bathroom, shutting the door behind him. "Get ready," he calls. "We need to test the pool area."

"Aye-aye, Captain," I mutter. Then, with a quick glance at the door, I strip naked and slide the shorts on. They fit perfectly, but that doesn't surprise me. He has an eye for detail. I look in the full-length mirror and smooth my hand down the fabric, feeling it soft and new under my fingers. They smell fresh and clean without the frowsty smell that charity shop clothes always have.

I don't look half bad, I think, twisting to one side and the other. The shorts hang from my hips and cling to my bum, and the blue and white pattern suits the tan I've got this week. My hair is windswept from the Jeep and my eyes... My eyes are wide and sparkling. I look full of life. I frown. *Because of Mateo, or this adventure?*

The door clicks, and Mateo appears.

I bite my lip. "Will you be wearing the towel for the rest of the afternoon? It might raise a few eyebrows if you get in the pool."

He groans. "I'm going to kill my mother," he vows, and with a sigh, he loosens the towel and removes it, and my mouth instantly goes dry.

"Wow!" I say before I can censor myself.

He raises one eyebrow in a devilishly debonair way. "There is no need to be kind."

"I'm not," I say, staring at him until he shifts uncomfortably.

"I feel like a piece of steak."

"A fillet steak wearing Speedos. *Tight* Speedos," I finish in a reverent voice.

The red fabric clings to his hips, the colour accentuating the rich honey gold of his skin. He has the broad shoulders and stocky build of a rugby player, and a patch of hair on his chest that arrows down to his belly button. His hips are narrow and his legs thick and strong, and he seems to glow in the afternoon sunshine.

He clears his throat, and I flush. "Sorry," I say quickly. "It's just that I've not seen many—" I stop abruptly, unable to believe what I was just about to say.

"Not seen many what?" he asks curiously.

My mind whirs fast. "Oh, I don't think I've ever seen a tighter swimming costume."

I'm sure he mutters, "And getting tighter by the moment", but I dismiss the notion when he grabs one of the robes from the back of the bathroom door. "I'm wearing this downstairs," he says as if daring me to argue.

I nod meekly, and he looks me up and down. It's a quick look, but his eyes seem to darken as they play over the shorts and my body. Then he clears his throat and tightens the belt on his gown. "You look nice," he says, and it's awkward and almost unpractised, and for some reason, it makes me feel better and easier.

"Thank you. You look just like Hugh Hefner."

"I'm quite positive he never had to go undercover to see how idiots were ruining his hotels."

"No, but he did have that waterfall and all those women. I bet they took some upkeep."

He sighs and slides his glasses on. "Ready, Wren?"

"That's Detective Wren to you, but you can call me Mr Loverman."

His laughter is loud and almost joyous.

The pool area is beautiful. It's set against the backdrop of the bay with wooden loungers dotted about that look like something from the set of Titanic—pre-iceberg. Towels embroidered with the hotel monogram are folded ready on the loungers and bright red umbrellas offer welcome shade. A central bar with a thatched roof is doing brisk business and waiters dart about carrying trays of food and drink. The atmosphere is calm and inviting.

I come up next to Mateo. Bitter experience from this week makes me ask cautiously, "Do we just grab a sun bed, or do they allocate them to you after frowning disapprovingly and muttering under their breath for five minutes?"

His sharp eyes are taking in all the details of the bar area. "They'll come over and greet us and let us pick our own. I don't allow people to reserve their beds. It leads to towel wars and the sort of bad feelings that fuelled World War Two."

"You're what Genghis Khan would have been if he'd gone into the hospitality industry."

"I bet he had better luck with staff. Someone should have greeted us by now."

"Welcome to Wren's world," I say in a sing-song voice, craning around him to peer at the pool. It's huge, the green water sparkling in the sunshine.

"What are you looking at?" he asks, humour entering his voice and easing out the irritation.

"The love floats."

"The *what?*"

"I noticed them this week. You don't allow children at your hotels, so it's mostly couples, and it's *so* weird. None of them swim properly.

They just sort of get in slowly, so they don't disarrange their hair and then float around the pool hanging off each other."

He looks past me at the pool and does a double take. "You're right."

"I know. Love floats. You should market that."

"I definitely won't be marketing the service here." He walks to the side of the pool. "Come on. We'll find our own beds."

"But won't that upset the system? Pretty soon, everyone will be picking their beds. It'll be outright anarchy."

"I'm thinking of pushing you in the pool," he says in a conversational voice, and I can't stop my laugh.

He comes up next to a couple of beds set under an umbrella with a little table between them. "These ones," he says in an autocratic tone that shouldn't be as hot as it is.

I eye the reserved sign on the table. "It looks like they're taken." My mouth drops open as he takes the plastic sign and throws it into the pool, where it promptly sinks.

"No reservations," he says in a stern voice that has an immediate effect on my penis. I cough and slide onto one of the beds.

"Are you alright?" he asks, and I screw my face up as he removes his robe, tossing it over a chair nearby. The sight of his body tanned and fit in the sunshine is not helping my condition.

Movement nearby thankfully takes my mind off my erection, and I watch as a waiter stalks towards us. He's fit and very good-looking, with coal-black hair and dark eyes, but the whole effect is spoiled as he looks us up and down, his eyes registering my flip-flops and Mateo's Speedos.

"Not here," he says sharply. "These beds are taken."

"I wasn't aware that was company pol—" Mateo starts to say in a snotty voice.

I put my hand on his leg. My fingers register the wiriness of the hair there and the heat of his skin, but I push the awareness away.

"Really? But me and my boo want to lie here."

"*Boo?*" Mateo mouths in a disgusted fashion. The waiter misses it, because he's eyeing my hand on Mateo as if we're something he's found under a rock.

"Not here," he says again. "Your beds are over there." He points to somewhere vaguely in the distance.

"Ah," Mateo says. "And let me guess. They're over in the nosebleed area where we'll need hiking boots to reach the pool."

"Ooh, my baby is *hangry*," I say loudly. "Could we get some food, please?"

"The restaurant is closed," the waiter says and then adds "sir" as an afterthought. "Maybe you should walk to the village. It would be better for you."

Mateo is still fuming half an hour later.

"Disgusting," he says for the fiftieth time.

We're lying on beds set back from the pool and under the shade of a big tree. They're nice but not as nice as the other loungers, and waiter service doesn't appear to stretch this far, so Mateo has had to trek over to the bar a couple of times. That didn't improve his mood, and neither did the avaricious gazes of two women who are eyeing him in his Speedos like he's lunch.

I roll over onto my front and look at him. "So you've said. Quite a few times. Surely you should be thinking up some new words for your report?"

"Who would I report to?" he huffs. "Myself. *I* am the unfortunate person in charge."

"Well, never mind. If you lose your job, you can always pursue the option of gigolo," I say, eyeing the two women who've moved closer under the pretext of getting some shade. Mateo looks at them with a jaundiced gaze, and I smile. "They'll have to hock one of those necklaces if they want to keep you in the style *you're* accustomed to."

His grumpy expression eases, and he chuckles. Then, looking over at them, he reaches out his hand and hauls me close. I end up half crouched over him on the sunbed.

"Whoa," I say, nearly falling off in surprise.

"Hush, boo," he says. "You are my new husband."

"And decoy material. Oh look, I didn't know anyone could move that quickly in heels that high." I register the sun-warmed heat of his skin and the scent of his lemony cologne. "You can let go of me now, Handsy McHanderson."

He smiles, lying back lazily. It's like having a sleepy lion underneath me. "Is that any way for a newlywed to behave?"

"It depends on the newlywed," I say wryly. "Maybe I'm the bad-tempered sort."

"Not you," he says, his fingers starting an absent-minded caress of my arm that makes heat coil in my belly. "You're the sunniest person I've ever met."

"That's rather sad," I say as he lets my arm go. Almost immediately, I want it back on me. "Everyone needs cheery people around them."

"Not many of those in my family."

I settle back cross-legged on my lounger. Taking a sip of my Coke, I watch him. "So, who is your family? I know they're insanely wealthy and live in Venice but not much more."

He takes a sip of water from his bottle and gazes out over the pool. I wish I could see his eyes behind those glasses.

"It is a long story."

"They're the best kind. Makes the gap between library visits longer."

"You sound knowledgeable."

"I am, but then my local library has the best-looking librarian in history. It makes *all* my visits thrilling."

I think he looks a little disgruntled, but his expression clears, so I was obviously wrong.

"My mother and father met when they were eighteen. He was working over here in one of my family's hotels. I think my grandfather gave him one of the lowest paid jobs so he would learn to be humble. He didn't expect them to fall passionately in love." His mouth quirks. "Needless to say, he did not repeat that work experiment with me."

"It's a shame. You could do with some humbleness."

He shrugs and I look at his broad shoulders. "You're going to burn. It's very hot now."

"I doubt it. I don't burn easily."

I wonder if there's a hidden message under that innocent statement, but I doubt I'll ever know. I stand up. "Budge up, Mateo."

"Pardon?"

"I'll put some cream on your back. Your shoulders are a little red."

He makes a moue of displeasure but rolls over. I settle myself next to him on his sunbed, feeling his skin hot against mine. This close, I can smell his lemon scent. I inhale, trying to fix it in my sensory memory.

He turns his head. "Are you putting cream on me during this millennium?"

"I bet you have a problem heading a hotel empire when you're so meek and mild," I observe.

His laughter is very sexy, and I swallow hard as I pour sun cream into my hand.

The scent of coconut rises, and I rub my palms together before spreading my hands out on his shoulders. They're wide, the skin golden brown and sun-hot to the touch. This close, I can see a couple of scars and a scatter of some curiously innocent-looking freckles. I swallow hard. *Maybe this isn't such a good idea*, I think, but my hands move independently of my brain, spreading the cream over his skin. My cock stiffens and I move back slightly so he won't feel it.

"So what happened?" I say quickly, my voice a little too high.

He's silent for a second, and when he does speak, his voice is hoarse. "What?"

"You were telling me about your family."

"Oh." He breathes in sharply.

"Oh, sorry," I say. "Did I scratch you?"

"No." He clears his throat. "Not at all. My mother got pregnant, and my father married her when my grandfather ordered him to, which is probably not the best start to marriage that I can think of."

"Can you think of many?" I ask idly, most of my attention on rubbing him and feeling his muscles.

"Good grief, no. Anyway, they lasted for about as long as her pregnancy. By the time I was born, he was in the throes of an affair with the woman who was to be my first stepmother."

"The first? How many wives has he had?"

"Three, but who's counting?" I chuckle, and he carries on talking. "By the time I was christened, the marriage was over, and he moved out and was ordered back to Venice."

"So, where did you grow up?"

"Here on the island until I was sixteen. That was the agreement my mother struck with my grandfather."

"Not your father?"

He gives a wry smile. "No. All decisions were made by my grandfather and still are to a certain extent. I don't think he'd ever met anyone like my mother. She's fierce about her family. Anyway, they achieved a grudging sort of mutual respect, and my mother was allowed to keep me with her on the island until I was sixteen, provided I holidayed in Venice. My father arrived on the island on that birthday and took me back with him permanently to Venice."

My hands stop moving. "And how did you feel about that?"

He rests his chin on his folded arms, looking ahead of him, his busy eyes probably cataloguing more hotel misdemeanours. "I didn't want to go. I was leaving everything I knew. My father was a stranger, as I'd only spent holidays with him, and even then, those times spent with him were consumed by whatever drama his wives were giving him."

"Were you sad? Did you miss your mum?" I ask anxiously.

He chuckles. "It's very nice of you to be concerned, Wren, and yes, I did miss her, but I was sixteen and left mostly to my own devices in a wonderful city with a lot of money at my disposal. So, I very quickly got over my homesickness."

"They left you alone?"

He looks bemused. "Of course. As long as I appeared at family dinners and went to school, I was left to do what I wanted."

"Blimey. I sort of imagined families having a little more involvement."

"Perhaps normal families do, but not very rich ones, I find." He pauses. "Have you finished?" he asks in a strained voice.

I become aware that I've stopped rubbing cream in and that my hands are just idly caressing him. "Sorry," I squeak. I rub the cream further down his back, heading towards his slim hips and the swell of his buttocks.

He jerks away and sits, pulling his towel into his lap. "I think I'm done, thank you," he says in a rush.

"You sure?"

He clears his throat. "Oh yes, definitely."

I bite my lip. "Okay," I finally say. "Let's get back to hotel investigation."

"Let's," he says, nodding as enthusiastically as if his life depends on it.

Men are strange, I think with a sigh.

CHAPTER SIX

Wren

Mateo is a little less enthusiastic about hotel investigation when we sit down for dinner that night.

"This wine is warm," he says, swirling it around in his glass and looking at it as if it's poison.

"Well, it is a warm night," I say. "And getting warmer as we're so close to the kitchen."

"If we get any closer, we'd be in the chef's lap."

"Kinky," I say cheerfully. "Although it might get us better service."

I bite back a smile as the door to the kitchen opens and slams into our table again, making everything on it rattle and jump.

"This is outrageous," Mateo says, his frown filling his face.

"This is life according to the non-jet set." I sit back so the harried waiter can put down my plate of meatballs in a tomato sauce.

"Thank you," I say to him, but he completely ignores me, sliding Mateo's plate over the table in a way I last saw on a bar counter in a Western film. Mateo puts out a hand to stop the plate from sliding off the table, and I snort and hastily cover it up as a cough as both Mateo and the waiter glare at me.

I pick my fork up. "I'm starving," I say as the waiter stalks off.

"I wanted you to have paella," he says, looking at my food sulkily. "You like that."

I'm immensely touched but decide I need to cheer him up. "Well, this is just as nice."

I take a mouthful and gasp for air after rapidly chewing and swallowing. The food couldn't have been saltier if they'd dipped it in the sea.

His mouth twitches, his eyes full of humour. "Even your perennial cheerfulness is suffering in this place."

I put my fork down. "It's been defeated by the food," I say, after swallowing another mouthful reluctantly. I grimace as I glance across the table at him. "You sound like perennial cheerfulness is a crime."

He looks startled. "Not at all. I like it." I raise one eyebrow, and he chuckles. "I really do. I must admit I'm not totally used to it, but I find it very admirable."

"Why? Because I had such a *bad* childhood?" I hold my hand to my forehead, watching his smile with pleasure. I like to make him laugh and smile.

He takes a sip of his drink and refills my glass. "The only way to get through this meal is to drink copious amounts of wine. Even they can't completely destroy this vintage," he advises me, and I take a sip.

"I think my background might be an actual bonus here," I tell him. "The only wine I've ever bought was a cheeky little Liebfraumilch that had a screw top and cost three quid from the corner shop, so this is delicious."

He makes a moue of disgust, and I laugh. "I *am* cheerful," I say, taking another sip and returning to our conversation. "I find it's better to be like that."

"Why?"

"Because then you're not crying," I say simply. "And people behave a lot better to someone who smiles. Tears seem to bring out the bully in a lot of people."

His brow furrows, and then becomes a ferocious scowl. "I can't stand the fact that you know that from experience," he says through gritted teeth.

I shrug. "We've all had bad experiences, Mateo. At least I never had a notion that I had a family. I always knew that everything was down to me."

"I would so like to see you with someone who proves that lonely little statement false," he says fervently, and I smile at him.

"I'm sure there will be someone someday," I inform him. "I do have a very endearing nose."

"You're very endearing, full stop," he says. His eyes widen, as if he can't believe what just came out of his mouth.

Luckily, the moment is broken when the door slams into the table again, and the salt and pepper pots jettison themselves over the edge. He grunts, and I start to laugh, holding my side.

"Your face," I gasp.

His smile is wry. "I have to say that this must be the most unusual meal I've ever sat down to."

"What? Do you mean you don't treat all your men to the best table where the door is in danger of giving them a concussion?"

He shakes his head. "Good grief, no. They'd have a fit of the vapours."

"Do you know that having a fit of the vapours was originally ascribed to women? They thought that things like hysteria and mania were caused by fumes coming from the womb."

"How do you know that?"

"A library card can be a dangerous thing in the wrong hands."

"Ah yes. Your library with the handsome librarian."

"Charlie isn't just handsome. He's stunning," I say with a dreamy sigh.

When he scowls, I ask, "So, what do your dates normally look like? Do you take them to the opera or kidnap them to fulfil a family vendetta?"

He raises his eyebrows, and I grin. "I told you I read a lot of Mills and Boon. They've given me very torrid expectations of romance that are by no means set for fulfilment while being gay in the twenty-first century."

"Should I give flowers during the kidnap? I ask because you seem to be the authority on the subject."

I burst out laughing. "That would be ridiculous. You wouldn't have a vase to put them in." I smile at him. "Go on, tell me how the other half lives. Do you charter a plane and take them to Sorrento for dinner?" To my astonishment, he grimaces. I laugh harder. "Oh my God, you *have*."

"Once. In my defence, I was a lot younger, and he was holding out on me."

"He hadn't shagged you after months of dating?"

"Days," he says, topping my glass up. "I don't hang around that long."

"Really? So, how long do your relationships last? I bet food has a better stab at attaining the sell-by date in your fridge than men do in your life." He glares, and I wave my glass around. "Please tell me more. This is absolutely *fascinating*."

He rolls his eyes and sighs but still elaborates for me as I guessed he would. "I date men my own age, but dating doesn't really sum it up. We keep company while we're having sex. It's not monogamous, and then when it ends, we part company in a pleasant way."

"Do you buy them something? I bet that helps the pleasantness," I ask idly. I must be drunk because I'd never be this free speaking ordinarily.

He bites his lip, his eyes dancing. "Well, that's put your finger on it."

"Which you don't once it's finished."

He shakes his head. "No. Definitely not. I never go back. Once something is finished, I always move on, and I never waste time on regrets."

"What are your men like?"

He takes a big gulp of his wine, probably to survive my line of questioning.

"They're usually worldly and good-looking. They dress well, they're cultured, and they can accompany me to functions."

Nothing like me, then.

I quickly dismiss the melancholy thought. He's never going to be mine. I'm just along for the ride this week, so I should sit back and enjoy it.

"And they never fall in love with you?" I ask disbelievingly. I think he'd be very easy to love. He's clever and kind and has a strong protective streak that very few people probably see.

"*No*," he says in a revolted tone. "Absolutely not. And I don't fall in love with them."

"And is that how you want it?"

He sits back in his chair. "It certainly is. Does that surprise you?"

I consider the question for a moment. "No," I say, taking another swig of my wine. When he reaches over to refill it, I realise with a shock that I've drained the glass. "No," I say, picking up the thread of my thoughts. "You seem like you'd hate being that out of control." He gazes at me for a long second, and then I give him a crooked smile. My lips feel a bit numb. "So, do you have many friends?"

He nods. "I have three very close friends from my school days in Venice. Bruno is married, and I'm godfather to his two children. I don't see as much of him as I used to for obvious reasons. Then there are Enzo and Leandro. I have known them since I first lived in Venice." He looks at me. "Do you have many friends?"

"Not really." I wriggle in my seat. "I moved around so much when I was a kid that I never formed friendships like the other children. Plus, a lot of parents seemed to view foster kids as being a bit suspicious. As if we were going to invite them round and spark up a doobie."

He looks cross. "That's very narrowminded."

I shrug. "Well, they weren't that wrong. It was a foster parent who rolled me my first joint." He looks stunned, and I start to laugh. "It was the last, too. I was moved on pretty sharpish when he got caught by my social worker. Shame really. He was mega relaxed about housework, and we always had crisps in the house."

I grin at his floored expression. "Let's have some more wine," I say happily. "I *love* wine."

He sighs in a gloomy fashion. "This isn't wine. It's liquid torture."

Mateo

. . .

I manoeuvre my chatty dinner partner into the lift, sparing a scowl for the receptionist sitting behind the desk filing her nails.

"Ooh, it's very shiny in here, isn't it?" Wren says, staring into the lift's mirrored wall and making a duck face. I try to repress my smile, but I'm not entirely successful.

"My lips feel numb," he informs me, poking at a spot on his face.

"That's your cheekbone," I say, and he gives a disgusting snort of laughter.

"Fa la la," he sings tunelessly, swaying to the beat of whatever random song is in his head at the moment.

He sways too far and lurches, so I put out my hand to steady him. The lift doors open, revealing a couple. The man is tanned to a shade I last saw on my mother's mahogany sideboard, and the woman is so thin she'd vanish if she were turned sideways. Her face has that peculiar frozenness only attained by copious amounts of Botox.

I nod to them, fully expecting them to give me a warm greeting back. I haven't accounted, however, for the outfit that Wren made me wear tonight. The tight black shorts and purple vest with the word *Diva* inscribed on it in rhinestones are not the most flattering outfit I've ever worn, and after a stunned silence, they both look at each other and immediately edge over to what they deem to be a safe corner of the lift. Somewhere our commonness won't touch them.

I'm astonished to feel laughter coursing through me. This little game of Wren's is proving to be unexpectedly entertaining. I look at his thin, high-boned face and that mess of shiny brown hair. Like him, I suppose. Wren is proving to be a delightful surprise in my life. I don't think I've laughed so much in years as I have with him, and it makes me realise how dull my life has become.

As the lift ascends, his drunken daze clears, and he becomes aware of the couple. "*Hello*," he says as excitedly as if seeing Santa Claus for the first time.

The couple steadfastly look everywhere than at my charming companion, but as I've already realised, Wren is made of sterner stuff. "Did you have a nice meal?" he slurs. "We didn't, did we, Bernie Boo

Bear?" he says, throwing his arm around my neck and dragging me, so I half fall into him.

The woman sniffs and looks intently at the lift panel in front of her, as if praying for a swift end to this nightmare.

"It was awful," he says in what he obviously thinks is a whisper but is very loud. "I had calamari to start. Even the squid was embarrassed."

I can't restrain my laughter, and he turns a face full of humour to me. His eyes are bleary, and he's completely right about his nose, but god, he's pretty. All shiny hair and effervescent spirits.

The lift doors open, and I usher him out. "Have a nice night," he says kindly. I'm coming to realise it's an integral part of him. "Don't let the bed bugs bite."

"There are no bed bugs in my hotels," I say after the lift's doors shut behind us.

He chuckles. "As far as you know. Did your shaggable hotel inspector tell you how to find bed bugs?"

"No, but I'm fairly sure I've dated a few."

He giggles and reels into the room as I open the door. I follow him in and shut the door behind me, watching as he flits about the room. My gaze intensifies as he starts to take his clothes off, strewing items of clothing wherever he walks.

I tell myself sternly to look away because he's drunk. *And far too young for you,* I remind myself, but it doesn't seem to make a difference, and my eyes track his progress, itemising his long slender body, his ribs showing under satiny olive skin that glows in the lamplight. He peels off his shorts, revealing the long length of his hairy legs with their curiously elegant feet. For how slender he is, his shoulders are broad and covered in freckles.

He reels into the bathroom and starts to clean his teeth, calling something through a mouthful of foam.

"Sorry?" I say and stop to clear my throat. Out of his sight, I press my hand to my cock, willing it to calm down. I hear water running, and then he appears again clad in just a pair of bright pink briefs, patting his mouth dry with a snowy white towel. I kiss goodbye to calming my cock.

"I said which bed do you want, Mateo?"

I shake my head, trying to get my brain back into gear. "I'm not bothered. Take which one you want."

"I think I'd like the one next to the window," he says. "I can see the sea when I wake up."

There's a yearning in his voice that touches me. "Didn't you have that in your hotel room earlier in the week?"

He pulls the covers back and slides in with a throaty sound of happiness. "No. I let Owen have that."

"Why?"

He comes up on his elbow, one hand cradling his head. "He wanted it."

"And don't you get what *you* want?" I ask crossly, peeling off the vest that feels like it's strangling me.

He snorts. "Not as often as you do, that's for sure."

"I wish that wasn't so."

He lies back on his pillow. "Don't be. I don't think it's very good for people to have what they want all the time. It leads to them becoming Josh."

I start to take off my shorts but feeling his gaze on me, I look up. He's watching me, his big brown eyes dark and slumberous.

"You're very good-looking," he says huskily.

I sway as I'm overcome with the most powerful surge of lust I've ever felt. I want to climb into that bed and take that pouty mouth and feel its pillowy softness under my own. I want him naked underneath me.

I take a step towards him, and then I make myself stop. Because wouldn't that just make me Josh? I have anything I want whenever I want it. It wouldn't be good for Wren to become just another thing I take and leave. So, for the first time in a long while, I put someone else's comfort ahead of mine and make myself step back.

He raises one eyebrow. "Don't be a minx," I advise him, and he chuckles.

"I like the sound of that. I've never been a minx before."

"It doesn't sound like you've had many opportunities," I say crossly and head into the bathroom to clean my teeth. When I emerge, he's still awake, staring dreamily at the view. The night is dark, but boats bob in the bay, casting a net of sparkly lights that echo the stars in the velvety blue sky.

"Look at the sky," he says dreamily. "It looks like someone flung a paintbrush at it."

I climb into bed, and he turns to me. His hair is a rich russet brown on the white linen of the pillowcase. "I don't think I have had a lot of opportunities," he says, and it takes me a second before I pick up the threads of our conversation. "Maybe I *should* be a bit wilder."

"I'm quite surprised you weren't. A lot of kids in your circumstances would have acted out."

"I couldn't. I figured early on that it was better to be the good boy. Then I might not be moved on so quickly."

"What was it like?" I say, switching off the lamp and rolling on my side to face him. The room is now lit by starlight, and although we're in two separate beds, it feels intimate in a way I've never felt before. It's a night made for confidences.

He sighs. "It wasn't brilliant, but it wasn't terrible, if you know what I mean?"

"I don't. I can't."

"No, I don't suppose you can. I was never abused."

I think of the couple who made young kids clean their house in the early hours and grit my teeth. I'd like to find them and give them a piece of my mind.

Wren stares at the ceiling, his lips pursed in thought. "It's just that I was always a cuckoo."

"What do you mean?" I ask, bewildered.

"I was like a cuckoo. They never really have their own homes, do they? They're left in someone else's nest. I remember reading about them in primary school and thinking, 'That's me. *I'm* a cuckoo, and there is nowhere that is really my home.'"

I swallow hard, feeling my eyes burn. "I'm sorry," I say hoarsely.

To my astonishment, he chuckles. "Don't be," he advises me, giving me his wide smile that shows off a chip in the incisor. "Plenty of people have a worse time than me. I was fed and warm, and I had a roof over my head and a bed."

"That shouldn't be the sum of your expectations."

"It sort of is in foster care. You don't wish for things because it just makes you unhappy when you don't get them."

"And you don't like that?"

"Does anyone?" he asks in amazement, and I think of my men, sulky and pouty at the slightest inconvenience.

"Then I'll wish *for* you, Wren. I wish for you to have everything that you want," I say fiercely, and he stretches his hand out to me. His palm and long fingers look unbearably innocent, but I slide my hand into his without a shred of hesitation. He clasps my fingers.

"Thank you," he says softly. "That would be nice." He sighs. "I just wish..."

"What? *Whatever* you want, you can have."

He rolls his eyes. "Mateo, I hope you're usually a bit more cautious."

"I usually am, but you're Wren, and I want the best for you. So tell me what you wish for." I imagine him wanting clothes or a watch or something that I am going to go out tomorrow and get for him whatever happens and whatever the cost.

"I wish my first time would be with someone like you. You feel safe, and you're incredibly hot."

I really should be getting used to the fact that Wren consistently surprises me. Now, is no exception. There's a very long silence that he doesn't appear to notice, as he's humming softly to himself.

"*What?*" I croak. "What first time? Do you mean on your first holiday?" I say almost hopefully.

He turns on his side. "No," he says sleepily. "My first time having sex. I hope it's with someone like you."

"You're a—?" I cough. "You're a virgin?"

"I am."

"But *how?*"

My astonishment is obvious, but he doesn't look embarrassed. For someone who has nothing and no one, Wren is surprisingly sure of himself.

"I never felt safe with anyone enough to do that," he says with a simplicity that completely slays me. He smiles at me, his eyes dark and mysterious in the moonlight. "But I feel safe with you, Mateo. You won't hurt me."

"I might," I say hoarsely.

He shakes his head. "You're talking emotionally. I'm talking physically."

"So, you've never done anything?" My voice has lowered as if I'm talking to a skittish foal, but he laughs raucously.

"Of course, I have. I'm not untouched and about to get my monk-hood. I've just never had penetrative sex." His words are slurring together now with sleep and drink. "I've never felt safe enough or attracted to someone enough to let them in my body." He stops talking for a second, and then his next words pack a punch. "But I do with you," he says huskily. "You're *beautiful*."

I'm very far from that, but I presume this is the wine talking. "I would be the worst person to have sex with. You need someone young. Someone who will want everything you have to give, Wren. Someone who will care for you and protect you."

My words trail off as I realise that he's fallen asleep, his long eyelashes brushing his cheeks. I can't work out whether I'm trying to convince Wren or myself that it would be a mistake. All I know is that when he said he wanted me to take his virginity, a wave of possessive-ness roared through me, and my breathing is still shaky from it.

Sleep is a long time coming that night.

CHAPTER SEVEN

Wren

I wake up the following day to a sharp pain over my right eye and the knowledge that there is some sort of fiery laser shooting at my face.

"Ungh," I mutter. "Make the light go away. Ish too hot."

A warm, rough voice with a Spanish lilt comes from my right. "How fickle you are, Wren. Just last night, you were prepared to do battle for that bed."

I squeeze one eye open cautiously. Mateo is lying on his side in his bed facing me. He looks like a very sexy pirate—stubble on his cheeks and a hairy chest and his dark silky hair everywhere. Although Long John Silver never wore Calvin Klein boxers and had a manicure that Kate Middleton would be proud of.

"I'm pretty sure I'd never have battled for a bed and a view," I mumble. "It all sounds far too energetic for someone who drank five bottles of wine."

He chuckles, the sound very intense in the quiet room. "It was four glasses. You're very much a lightweight."

I smile and close my eyes, listening to the sound of the breeze coming through the open balcony doors. "What time is it?" I finally ask.

I hear movement as he reaches for his watch and then an exclamation of surprise. "It's ten o'clock in the morning."

"And is that the end of the world?"

"It's unusual. I haven't slept this late in years. I'm normally up at five."

"That sounds very hearty. We're on holiday." I open one eye again. "Well, not really. We're on a fake holiday. But even fake people have to have fake lie-ins occasionally."

"That's appallingly convoluted."

"And that's a very big word for a hungover person to understand."

"I'll get you some tablets." He climbs out of bed, and I force both eyes open, all the better to get a sneaky peek at him in those briefs. They're white boxer briefs and very snug, clinging to his tight buttocks.

He rummages around in the bathroom, and I squeeze my eyes shut virtuously as he comes out. I'd love to see the front, but I might disgrace myself and drool.

"Here you are," he says.

I sit up, taking the tablets and a bottle of water from him before he climbs back into bed in a flash of olive skin and long legs.

"Did we have a nice time?" I ask after I've taken my life-saving treatment and settled back into the warm sheets. I bite my lip, feeling suddenly worried because my memory of the night is very hazy. I hope he didn't have to put me to bloody bed. That would be the ultimate in humiliation. "Tell me I was good company at least."

"Oh." He stops and clears his throat. "You don't remember?"

Alarm sweeps through me. "Remember what?" I ask, sitting up and immediately putting a hand to my head to stop it from blowing up. "I don't recall much past the second bottle of wine. Oh my god, what did I do? Did I strip off in the restaurant?"

He stares at me. "Do you *usually* do that?"

"Not to my knowledge, but there's a first time for everything."

He bites his lip, a glint of humour appearing. "How philosophical."

I wonder if his strange mood is because I let him down. "We were supposed to be working, and I got drunk. I'm so sorry. You can dock my pay for the day."

He looks at me as if I'm not making sense and then waves his hand cavalierly. "I'm not fucking docking your pay," he says in a disgusted voice. "The dinner alone was punishment enough, if that's what you're looking for."

"Okay, Gordon Ramsay." I pause. "So, what did I do?"

"You didn't do anything." He looks at his watch. "Oh dear, we've missed breakfast," he says in a blatant grab at distraction. "I'm sure that's a major tragedy."

I narrow my eyes at him. "I obviously did something. You'd better tell me now, Mateo, or I might not be able to work for you anymore. Not that it really feels like work anyway," I say in a spirit of honesty.

He looks panicked, which surprises me. I'd have thought he'd have had enough of me by now. "It was nothing," he says reluctantly. "You just got very chatty and told me things that you might not want me to know if you were sober." I open my mouth, and he puts up a hand to stop me. "I want you to know that I'll never tell anyone what you revealed. It's between you and me."

I eye him. *What the hell is he on about?* "Did I tell you about the murder?" I say earnestly. "It was just the one, and there's no need to worry. They'll never find the body."

"What?"

I start to laugh. I can't help it. "I'm *joking*. I have no idea what I talked to you about, but it can't be that embarrassing. I haven't done that much in my life." Realisation dawns in sickening full colour. "Oh my god," I groan. "I told you I was a virgin."

"Wren, it doesn't—"

"Oh my god," I say again, tunnelling under the covers, pulling them over my head. "I was wrong," I call through the cotton. "It *is* that embarrassing."

The covers peel back, and Mateo's face appears. This close, I can see the tiny starburst of lines around his golden eyes. "There is nothing to be ashamed of," he says firmly.

"I think there might be."

He shakes his head. "I was very flattered."

"Why were *you* flattered?" I groan and squeeze my eyes shut. "What did I say?"

He pets my cheek. "Wren, look at me," he insists, and I crack open my eyelids. "You said you'd like me to be your first." I start to speak, but he puts a finger over my lips. "No," he says fiercely. "Don't regret that. I think it's quite the nicest thing that's ever been said to me."

"You need to get out more."

"And you need to relax the wisecracks a little bit." He gives me a lopsided smile. "I was flattered, but I'm very aware that you were drunk, so I never took it as a serious offer. You'll meet someone your own age who wants a relationship, and it will be wonderful, Wren. Sex is amazing with someone you care about."

"How do you know?" I ask gently. He looks flummoxed, so I take pity on him. "Thank you, Mateo," I say.

He sags in obvious relief. "*De nada.*"

He goes to move away, but I grab his arm to stop him. "It's very nice of you to mentally set me up with a nice young man who'll take my virginity very carefully. There are probably candles and champagne in your vision, too, yes?"

He glares at me, and I grin, taking a deep breath. *Am I going to say this? Am I going to put myself out on the ledge like this?* This is Mateo, though, and I'll only know him for another few days. *You bet I am.*

"The thing is, Mateo," I say. "I meant every word of it."

"*What?*"

I smile at him. "I would love you to be the one to first have sex with me."

I wish I had a camera to record his gobsmacked face.

———

He's still struggling as we drive along the coast road. We pass little coves, the sand white in the bright light. The sun is already hot, sparkling on the sea and turning it translucent close to the shore. My hair whips around in the wind, and I bless my sunglasses. My hangover has retreated, but I need to eat, so Mateo is driving us to a small beach bar he knows that makes fantastic breakfasts. Well, he's doing that and panicking.

"You should think more thoroughly about this," he says for the fifth time in the last ten minutes.

I sigh. "Mateo." He glances over at me and then back at the road. "It's just sex. I might never have had penetrative sex, but I have done a lot of other stuff. I'm not going to come to bed wearing a nightcap and a Victorian nightdress and then cry afterwards at your brutish ways."

"Mills and Boon?" he asks.

I chuckle. "No. Harlequin Historical. They had a special section for them at the library." He can't conceal his smile, and I shrug. "I like you," I say. "And not in an 'Oh my god I must marry this man' type of like. I just think you're a brilliant person. You're sexy and funny, and I know you won't hurt me. I can't think of anyone better to make my first time a good memory. But that is all it will be." He looks at me in query. "A first time. Hopefully, I'll have many other times with other men. The thing is, I'm an honest person, Mateo. I'd like to have sex with you, so I'll tell you that. It doesn't mean you can't say no. You have done. So, no hard feelings. It's hardly affecting world peace."

He shakes his head. "I have never met anyone like you in my life."

"You keep saying that and I'm unsure whether that's bad or good this morning."

"Neither am I."

"Ouch." I start to laugh and see his lip twitching. I pat his arm. "No harm done. We can still be friends for the week. If you want to," I add quickly. "If I haven't made it awkward."

"You haven't."

We arrive at a bustling seaside resort. The streets are lined with little shops selling sunglasses, touristy mementos, and beach stuff. People are everywhere, walking in and out of the shops and heading to the beach. I spy a few red shoulders and faces and cringe in sympathy. The sun here is no joke even though it's the end of the season. The first couple days I'd been here, I'd been gratified to find that I didn't burn, but Owen hadn't been so lucky and had worn a red nose that made him look like a pissed-off cockerel.

"This is Can Picafort," Mateo says.

I gaze out of the window. "It's lovely."

We turn onto a road alongside a long stretch of sand. The beach is busy at this time of the morning, full of rows of sunbathers and children running around.

We pass bars and restaurants and a few hotels. One of the buildings catches my eye. "Ooh, can we eat there?" I say excitedly, pointing to a small hotel.

It looks old and is painted a soft pink with a long patio running on one side that is full of old tables and tiki umbrellas nodding cheerfully in the summer breeze. Anyone sitting there would have an uninterrupted view of the beach and vast expanse of sea. A second glance, however, shows that the pink paint is peeling, and the hotel sign is illegible.

"Why?" he asks in blatant incomprehension. He's probably never considered stopping at a place where the drinks cost less than a second mortgage.

"It's got such a lovely view."

"Are you sure?" he asks. "The beach restaurant I mentioned isn't that far."

"No, that one. It's very pretty," I say, seized by this strange sudden longing to sit on that patio.

"Okay, then." He immediately pulls the car over into a parking space on the side of the road. "Come on. Let's go and get some breakfast."

"You do things for me far too quickly, Mateo. It's a problem."

"I don't think I do. I think the problem is that fewer people do the same."

We get out of the Jeep, the salt-laced breeze hitting our faces, and I pause as he grabs my arm gently.

"Were you serious?" he asks. His tone is intense, and my heart starts to beat heavily. "You would trust me to be your first?"

I swallow and say simply, "Mateo, I can't think of a single person I trust more with that."

His eyes are shielded by his sunglasses and it's hard to read the expressions crossing quickly over his handsome face. Then he smiles, nods as if I've confirmed something for him, and walks off.

"Wait. That's *it*?" I shout after him. His chuckle floats back to me and I start to laugh too. "You're a gigantic fucking tease, Mateo Rossi."

He gives me a little wave over his shoulder. I hasten to catch up with him feeling like I'm full of sunshine today. Like it's sparkling along my skin and tickling my veins and arteries, making everything golden.

But inside the hotel, we're greeted by a gloomy atmosphere. The windows could have done with a good clean years ago, and the wallpaper is a very dark tropical print with prowling lions and tigers.

"Good grief," Mateo mutters.

"Don't look at the wallpaper," I advise him. "Look at those high ceilings and the beautiful flooring. A coat of cream paint and a sander on the floorboards, and it'd look very different." I bite my lip. "Not that you'd be the one doing the actual painting or sanding."

He cocks one eyebrow. "You think I can't do construction work?"

"That is not construction work, so I'm going with no, you can't."

"I'll have you know I took part in building houses for the homeless."

"Hadn't those people suffered enough?"

His laughter is interrupted when a young man comes through a doorway behind the reception desk. He's thin and gangly and wearing bright pink shorts with a white T-shirt. His hair has been dyed a rainbow colour and, as he steps behind the desk, I can see his eyeliner is smudged.

"Can I help you?" he asks with a strong Welsh accent.

"Yes, please," Mateo says. "We'd like a table for breakfast."

"Really?"

Mateo's eyebrow rises. "Yes," he says a lot less confidently.

The young man shrugs. "Okay, then. On your own head be it." He comes around the desk and gestures to us. "I'll show you to your table."

Mateo's flabbergasted expression makes me snort as we troop after the young man.

We perform a creative two-step to avoid bumping into him when he reels back from the sunlit patio.

"Fucking hell." His voice is loud and very pained.

"Pardon?" Mateo says in a frigid tone. I bite my lip to stop a laugh from coming out.

"Oh, sorry," the young man says. "Mind my language. It's the fucking sun, you see."

"Hmm." Mateo's manner suggests he doesn't want the young man to elaborate.

Unfortunately, he can't take a hint and leans in confidingly. "It's fucking hell on my head, I tell you. When I accepted multiple lemon drop shots last night from Pedro, I didn't expect to work today. The labour I'd hoped to do was moving between the sheets. Know what I mean?" He cackles and nudges Mateo, who looks as if he's been poleaxed. "But James, the bloody idle fuckwit of a chef, wouldn't know work if it bit him on the arse so here I am with my hangover."

"Oh dear," Mateo says faintly. "I'm sorry you're suffering."

He winks at Mateo, who responds by looking slightly stunned.

"No problem. It was worth it. Pedro is a bloody animal between the sheets." He gestures at the patio. "Take a seat, and someone will bring you the menu."

"Ooh, can we have the table over there by the sea?" I ask excitedly.

He smiles at me, and I notice clear tanned skin and a sweet face under the smudged eyeliner and bright hair. "You can definitely have that one," he says kindly. "Best seat in the house."

He whisks off, and Mateo pulls out my chair for me. I'm getting far too used to his manners, because it only takes me a second before I slide into the seat.

His gaze stays fixed on the chair. "Plastic," he whispers in a tragic voice.

"Lovely," I inform him. "You'll lose weight sitting in these."

"How?"

"When you get sweaty and stand, it'll rip off your outer epidermis."

He shakes his head and helps me push the chair closer to the table.

"Ooh, a gentleman," the young man says, coming towards us. "I've not had much experience of those. It's a bit like seeing Stephen Fry in the wild."

I laugh, and Mateo has a wry grin on his face. "So, when you said someone would be bringing us the menus, you meant you?"

He hands us two plastic menus. "It's a bit of a theme around here. I'm Alfie. When I came to Spain, I thought of the sun and Spanish men. I didn't realise I'd be doing more work than an oil rigger on a bad day."

Mateo looks down at the menu. "I think I will have the tortilla," he says. "Wren, is that alright for you or would you prefer something else?"

Alfie whistles through his teeth. "Ooh, I wouldn't do that," he says in a tone of doom.

"Why?" Mateo asks in a weary voice.

"Well, Fen, the second chef, isn't in a very good mood this morning. She lives with James the main chef you see, and they had a right bust up last night. She threw half the latte glasses at him and then—"

"And does that impact on the tortilla?" Mateo interrupts.

"In ways you don't want to know about."

There's a long beat of silence as Mateo looks calmly down at the menu. "How about the omelette?" he suggests. Alfie winces and Mateo sighs. "Okay, not that."

Alfie laughs and then cringes dramatically with the movement. "Fen's never really managed the difference between scrambled eggs and an omelette."

I snort, and Mateo shakes his head and hands the menu back. "It might be easier if you just tell us what we *can* have."

The waiter looks at me, and I say, "That's fine with me. I love a surprise."

"Well, you're obviously a glass-half-full type of boy. I like that in a man."

"Are you the same?" I ask.

He rolls his eyes. "Definitely not. The only use for a glass half full is to drink the contents." He tucks the menus under his arm. "Fen will have buggered off for a kip by now anyway. So, I'll nip out and buy you some pastries from the bakery next door. They're lush, they are."

"Would it have been simpler if we had gone to the bakery first?" Mateo snips.

"Course not. You'd have missed my charming personality," Alfie says blithely. "I'll make you some drinks. I'm a dab hand with the coffee machine, I am. Fresh orange juice?"

"Is it actually fresh?" Mateo says in a voice of doom.

"Fresh from the supermarket."

I laugh, and Alfie grins at me.

An old couple comes out onto the patio and stands blinking in the bright sunshine. "Ooh, Mr and Mrs Sampson. Lovely morning, isn't it?" Alfie calls. "Come and have a sit down and I'll get the kettle on and make you a nice cup of tea, and you can tell me all about your visit to Palma."

"Thank you, Alfie, dear," the old lady says gratefully. He shows them to a table, pulling their chairs out and chattering, while they smile at him, coming alive under his happy personality.

"He's good," I say.

"How do you get that?" Mateo asks.

"Well, we're still here, aren't we? You'd have been down the road like your backside was on fire as soon as you saw the wallpaper, otherwise."

He chuckles. "You've got a point."

I look around the patio. "This is a gorgeous spot. I thought it'd be full."

"It used to be," he says, his sharp and intelligent eyes taking in all the details. "It used to be the place to stay in Can Picafort, but then the owner's wife left him, and the place started to slide downhill. It's prime real estate."

"It could be lovely."

"How?" he asks, waving an elegant hand. The sun shines on his battered watch. I like it more and more each time I see it, because it's a clue to who Mateo is. "Tell me what you'd do."

"Well, I'd rip the concrete up out here and lay nice flagstones. I'd repaint in a colour scheme of sand and pink with some bright jade. Then I'd get rid of the seventies plastic furniture and put out some nice wood tables with coloured chairs. You could have some of those expensive cushioned wicker sofas over there, with low tables for the people who just want a coffee or a drink, and I'd make sure there were lots of bright cushions on them so they look really inviting. I'd put a pergola over the eating area so it's nice and shady and thread pretty lights through it so it attracts the night-time crowd. And the staff would wear cool uniforms that aren't too fussy." I look at him. He's watching me intently.

"You've put your finger on it," he says slowly.

"Was it as good for you as it was for me?"

He chuckles and then looks up at the hotel. "There are a lot of hotels around here. A place like this should be different—a bijou place where the service is excellent, the design a little quirky and not have the feel of a chain. I'd put in a fantastic chef who was experienced with fish and seafood and not afraid to take chances, and a morning chef who could make artisan pastries. The patio is a big pull. Lit by candlelight and with good music playing, it would sell itself at night. I remember from a previous visit a few years ago that the bedrooms are a good size. I'd make each room different but extremely high spec with only the best fixtures and fittings."

I stare at him. "It sounds like something you've thought about before."

He seems to come back from his place of deep thought. "I was very interested in doing a smaller line of hotels at one point. A portfolio that would be separate from our big commercial hotels."

"And what happened?"

He gives me a wry look. "My father rejected the idea, and my grandfather backed him up. They think we should stick to the big money spinners. They're blander and less likely to offend people."

"Unless Felipe serves you."

He scans the patio as if seeing all the changes he'd make.

"Look at you," I say softly, and he raises an eyebrow. "For the first time since I met you, I'm getting a glimpse of the real hotelier who lies under your skin."

"I'm the same person I've always been."

I shake my head. "No. You have real passion when you talk about smaller properties and doing something different." I smile at him. "I hope you get to do that. Everyone should have passion for their job."

"Do you have that with your job?"

"God, no. I work in a call centre dealing with car insurance for people who could win awards in rudeness. I'm shouted at from morning through to night, and the only respite is examining the very creative ways that people can claim insurance. Last week, a woman tried to claim that her lounge was destroyed by a river flooding its banks."

"And why was that a problem for you?"

"She lives on a hill thirty miles away from the nearest river."

He laughs.

I say, "The only passion I have at work is to get out of the door at five at night, but that doesn't mean *you* shouldn't have job satisfaction. You're one of the bosses, so it's achievable."

Before he can respond, someone says "Mateo" wonderingly, and we both turn to find a man standing on the patio next to us. He's tall and slender with dark, grey-flecked hair cut expertly to flop on his forehead. Dressed in slim grey trousers and a pale pink shirt, he looks sleek and expensive.

Mateo immediately stands up and hugs him. "Frederico. What are you doing here?"

Watching them—the close and easy way they embrace—I somehow know this is one of Mateo's men. As they step apart, Frederico gazes at Mateo with a lazy appreciation that seems to indicate he knows what he looks like naked, and it's a pleasant memory.

Something hot pangs in my stomach. They begin talking about a mutual friend, and I observe Frederico, realising he's what Mateo looks for in a man. I am nothing like him, with my messy hair, cheap clothes, and habit of blurting out anything that comes into my head.

Embarrassment coils in my chest as I remember asking Mateo to be my first. He must have been mortified if men like Frederico are his typical partners.

I become aware that they're both looking at me.

Mateo smiles. "This is Wren," he says to Frederico. "A very good friend of mine."

I note how wide and warm Mateo's smile is when he looks at me. Completely different from the one he'd given Frederico, which was contained and polite. My spirits lift a little.

"Hello," I say. "Nice to meet you."

"Likewise," he says, barely glancing at me.

A frown crosses Mateo's face.

"What are you doing in here?" Frederico asks far too loudly. "It's a complete dump. The last place on earth that I thought I'd find you."

Alfie, our waiter, approaches with a plate full of pastries and our drinks. He carries them with the ease of long practice, sliding the plates onto the table.

Frederico is still talking loudly about the shortcomings of the hotel. Alfie darts a glance at me and makes a quick wanker gesture. I burst out laughing, and Mateo and Frederico give me startled looks.

Mateo's gaze lingers on Alfie, and to my surprise, his expression darkens. I thought he liked Alfie.

The next second his expression smooths, and he says kindly, "The pastries smell nice." He's right. The air fills with the smell of warm dough and sugar.

"You got pastries?" Frederico exclaims crossly. "I couldn't even get coffee."

"Perhaps it was the way you asked, mate," Alfie says sweetly, adjusting his red plastic sunglasses. "When you speak to people like they're dogs, you might end up with a few fleas."

"Isn't it lie down with dogs and wake up with fleas?" I ask.

"I'd be happier lying down with Nigel Farage than him," Alfie says dismissively. "At least Nigel likes a beer."

Frederico glares at him.

"Why are you here, Rico?" Mateo asks.

"I'm here to make an offer on the hotel on behalf of my company." Frederico turns his annoyed gaze on Alfie again. "But this person informed me that the owner is still in bed."

"He won't get out unless you're a blonde with size forty double-D boobs," Alfie says cheerfully. "When he sees them, he's out of bed quicker than Lewis Hamilton when he sees a green light."

Frederico shakes his head and leans in to kiss Mateo on his cheek. "I'm sure I'll see you around," he says coolly. "I can't do business this way. Bye, darling."

He slinks across the patio, and none of us speak for a few moments after he leaves.

Alfie is the first to break the spell. "And you slept with *that*?" he says chattily, setting Mateo's glass of juice in front of him.

Mateo flushes slightly. "I wasn't aware that a sexual resume was required to eat breakfast here," he says in a frigid voice.

If he expects Alfie to be cowed, he's onto a loser. "Awesome," Alfie breathes. "Classy *and* cutting. It's a lethal combination."

I'm laughing and Mateo is shaking his head when a couple of new men arrive on the patio. "Ooh, Jerry and Mike," Alfie calls. "You're just in time for coffee. You look like you need it."

He bustles off, leaving us in silence. I take a bite of my pastry, closing my eyes in happiness at the taste of honey and almonds. When I open them, Mateo's eyes are dark and focused on my lips. I run my tongue over my lips, and he shifts in his seat. Our gazes hold for a moment, and then he gives me a crooked smile.

"Minx," he says affectionately.

I grin at him, my pulse thrumming in my wrists and echoing in my cock. I put my pastry down. "So that was one of your boyfriends?"

He grimaces. "Not a boyfriend. He was a lover for a short time."

"Are you okay?" I ask sympathetically.

"Why would you ask?"

"Well, it isn't easy to see old lovers."

"It is for me," he says baldly.

"I'm not sure why I'm speaking so knowledgeably on the subject anyway."

"Have you ever had a boyfriend, Wren?"

"I had a friend who I experimented with. He was in the same foster home for a while, and we explored stuff. I had a boyfriend when I was nineteen. He was quite a bit older than me and told me I was frigid when I wouldn't let him fuck me."

"What the hell?" he breathes, rage in his eyes.

I pat his hand. "I always thought if someone told me I was frigid, it would be dramatic like in the books. But unfortunately, it was just embarrassing to have that conversation when he still had a condom on, and his penis was slowly wilting." I snort. "Like a tulip stood in a vase for too long."

He doesn't join me in my hilarity. He straightens in his chair, his back ramrod straight. "Did he hurt you?"

"Course not. But you can see why I thought you were a good bet.

You're not going to get involved, and I'm certain you won't use guilt-tripping and gaslighting to get a shag."

"I have *never* done that," he says stiffly.

I pat his hand. "Well then, that's why I asked." I scrutinize his features.

"What?" He groans. "I'm pretty sure I am going to regret asking, but why are you staring at me?"

I grimace. "I think maybe I'm the one guilt-tripping, now I think of it, Mateo."

"How?" he says in abject astonishment.

"Well, telling you bits about my childhood. I don't want to think that you'd do me as some sort of sympathy shag. That would not be erotic in the slightest."

"Wren." His gaze holds mine. "I have never fucked anyone for sympathy, and I never will. If I fuck you, it will be because of your big brown eyes, that mass of hair, and full lips that would look good wrapped around my cock."

I gasp, my dick stiffening.

He gives me a wicked smile. "It would feel like fucking heaven to have those long legs of yours wrapped around my waist and your arse around my cock."

All I can hear is our rushed breathing and the waves breaking on the sand. Then I make myself sit back. "Cheeky. And you call *me* a minx."

CHAPTER EIGHT

Four Days Later

Wren

The taxi pulls off the main road and up a long drive before stopping outside an old house. It's made of a warm honey-coloured stone and the windows twinkle in the early evening sunshine. A wind chime tinkles, adding its melodic sweetness to the atmosphere.

"This is it?" I double-check with the driver.

"This is the address Senor Rossi gave me."

"Well, that's a relief. I wouldn't want to skip up to someone else's house. I'd be like Red Riding Hood but without the cape. It's far too hot. And I'd definitely jettison the pigtails." I pull out my wallet. "How much?"

He shakes his head immediately. "Senor Rossi phoned and paid for your journey."

I roll my eyes. "Did he? Quelle surprise. Well, let me give you a tip."

He accepts the note with an alacrity that tells me I've got the currency wrong again, and after I slam the car door behind me, he waves and accelerates off. I look up at the house nervously and run my hands through my hair, probably messing up the style I spent ages on. I climb the steps and knock on the front door, inhaling the sweet scent of flowers and earth still warm from the sun.

I wipe my damp palms on my trousers as I hear footsteps, and then the door swings open, and Mateo is there. I've spent the last four days with him motoring all over the island, laughing and talking, but every time I see him, it hits me how gorgeous he is. Tonight, he's wearing a black suit with a white shirt and a slim black tie, a colour combination that makes his olive skin glow. His shoes are so polished that I could check my hair in them if I wanted. He looks very expensive. I take a subtle breath. Even his lemon scent smells like extra money tonight.

He grins at me, his teeth white in his tanned face, the lines at the corners of his eyes elongating in a dreadfully attractive way. "You found it alright?" he says, gesturing me into the house.

"Well, the taxi driver did. Even if I'd been given a compass, I'd still be driving around lost."

He chuckles and looks me up and down slowly and thoroughly. By the time he gets to my face, I feel as if he's stripped me naked. I attempt a casual stance but can't help the flush on my cheeks.

Bloody hell, he's potent. A fact that has become apparent over the last few days. I don't know whether it's my offer for him to deflower me, or if he's just easier with me. Whatever it is, I'm finally seeing Mateo unleashed with no need to show caution around me. And it's becoming glaringly obvious that I've developed a huge crush on him. Every time I see him, my palms sweat, and my breathing becomes erratic. It's never happened to me before, and something tells me to keep my feelings hidden from Mateo because he's never going to want to sleep with me if he thinks I'm in danger of picking out china patterns.

"The suit arrived on time. You look amazing," he says huskily.

I look down at the light grey suit I'm wearing. It had arrived at my hotel room door this afternoon an hour after he'd dropped me off. We'd spent the day dismissing a hotel on the south side of the island as being wildly inappropriate.

When I'd heard the knock on the door, I'd thought it was Mateo, my heart pounding as it always does when I think I might see him. But it had been the concierge delivering me a suit.

I run a hand down my shirt front. It's blindingly white and the red tie looks like a splash of blood against it. "That's probably because it's a Tom Ford suit," I hiss. "How much did this cost?"

He waves a careless hand. "It was nothing."

"It was a lot more than that." Frustration bubbles in my chest—I'd been feeling it ever since I'd opened the bag and seen the suit. "I thought our relationship was something different."

He shifts his weight from foot to foot, his gaze landing anywhere but on me. As if he thinks I'm going to pull out a marriage license and an angry stepfather with a gun. "In what way?"

"Well, I thought this was my trousseau," I say earnestly.

He blanches and I'm quiet for a few moments just to torture him.

"Oh, don't be ridiculous," I say, flashing my eyes and flipping my tie jauntily. "My trousseau would definitely include lots of filmy peignoirs and slippers with feathers on them."

When he grins, I grimace and say in a stern voice, "I'm not one of your blokes, Mateo. I don't want you to buy stuff for me. You're already paying me a wage that would keep me in bonbons and mink for a year. I don't need or want anything else. I sort of think of you as a friend, which is probably a bit silly."

His lips curve and the tension leaves his shoulders. "It's not silly at all. I think of you as a friend too." He smiles coaxingly. "Look. You are coming to a family wedding with me, yes?"

"Yes, and I still don't know why."

"Because we are friends, and if you come, I know I will laugh a lot and not be obliged to make very earnest conversation about portfolios and the performance of my shares."

"I wouldn't think so, considering the first image that forms in my head about share performance is one that involves jazz hands."

He gestures wildly. "There. You *see*. And as you are my guest, I had to buy you a suit. You can't attend the wedding in a swimming costume, and I know you wouldn't have packed a suit for a summer holiday." He raises his eyebrows.

What can I do but nod? Of course, I hadn't brought anything formal to wear on this trip.

He nods. "That is good, and you will, of course, keep the suit."

"Oh my god." I look to the ceiling for calm. "You do this a lot, Mateo. You push until you get a little bit, and then rather than backing away, you immediately bulldozer forward for everything else."

A husky laugh sounds from the other side of the entryway. I turn to see a woman approaching. I'd guess that she was in her late fifties and she's beautiful, her dark, grey-flecked hair pulled back in a complicated style that emphasizes her huge brown eyes. She's wearing a filmy orange dress that flatters her olive skin and slender figure. I know, even before she speaks, that she's Mateo's mother.

"I see you know my son."

Mateo gestures to her. "Mama, come and meet Wren."

"Such a lovely name," she says, giving me a grin that echoes Mateo's full-wattage smile.

"Wren, this is my mother, Valentina," Mateo says.

I hold out my hand, but she steps forward and pulls me into a hug. I draw in a quick breath. Her embrace is soft and warm and scented of perfume, and I stand awkwardly, not entirely sure how to respond. I settle for patting her gently on the back, and she pulls away before I can become too uncomfortable.

"Such a handsome boy, Mateo," she says.

I'm completely charmed. "Thank you. I think it might be the suit."

She shakes her head. "I think it is not the suit. That just shows off your pretty eyes and hair." She threads her arm through mine, and I grin at her.

I glance at Mateo. He's watching us with a wide, warm smile on his face, looking as though he's seeing something he likes very much.

"Are we ready?" he asks, his expression clearing.

His mother rolls her eyes. "As I can be."

"Mama," he says chidingly.

"You and I both know how the evening will go. My brother will make an incredibly dull speech that will go on for far too long, and his wife will express her sadness that your gift isn't expensive enough.

Meanwhile, the happy couple will argue, which is what they have been doing since the moment they met."

"Marriage," Mateo says with a shudder. "Who would do that?"

"Well, David Foster likes it well enough," I observe.

His mother laughs. "Unfortunately, he won't be there. Too bad, as we'd have someone to play the piano." She winks at me. "I hope Mateo warned you about the evening."

"No. He mentioned it two hours ago as he dropped me off at the hotel. Then he vanished and sent me a suit and a taxi. It was hardly the sort of evening that Cinderella would approve of."

She grins. "That is because he's very unused to someone like you, Wren. He's used to his robot men."

"Really?" I say delightedly.

"*Mama*," Mateo groans.

"Oh, pah! They are robots. They do what you want with no emotion, and then they're gone to make way for the next on the production line." I laugh, and she smiles at me. "Life isn't calm, is it, Wren?"

"Not so I've noticed," I say, winking at Mateo and his disgruntled expression.

"Then you know what I'm talking about. Love is wild, and life should always have passion in it."

"Well, after reading a foster parent's Mills and Boon collection, I'd certainly agree with you. Mateo should at least be making an arranged marriage with a complete stranger or buying a company and sacking everyone while twirling a moustache."

She shakes her head. "Mateo struggled with growing one of those when he was seventeen. It looked like a tiny mouse."

"Oh god," Mateo whispers.

She chuckles huskily. "We have so much to talk about, Wren. I am a romance fanatic too. I read them all the time."

"Lovely," Mateo mutters, looking around. "Where are my damned keys?"

"Where you last dropped them, darling. You tend to lose things when there are no servants to hover behind you." I laugh, and she smiles at me. "As my son has neglected to tell you anything, I shall tell you a little before we leave. We are going to a party to celebrate my niece's wedding tonight. My brother is the father of the bride and he and I do not get on. He is very wealthy—a self-made man and known on the island. But he can never get over the fact that I married into a far wealthier family. He feels overshadowed. He disapproved of me getting pregnant, and then he disapproved of me getting divorced. He then had sixteen years to happily disapprove of the way I raised my child. I really should have been given a thank-you card from him for all the times I've made him feel superior."

"Well, I think you've done okay with Mateo," I say, and she smiles, leaning into me a little.

"He's not so bad," she says, reaching up a slender hand and running it through her son's wavy hair.

He rolls his eyes, fishing his car keys out of a huge terracotta bowl on a side table. "Let's get this done. Yes?"

———

The wedding is being held at an expensive-looking club with a private beach. Music drifts from the open windows as we walk up the steps and into the building.

I whistle as we join the receiving line. "Wow," I murmur to Mateo. "No wonder you thought I needed a makeover." The men are all dressed in posh suits, the women in very expensive-looking long dresses. The scent of perfume is overpowering.

Mateo shakes his head. "I didn't want you to feel uncomfortable. But I don't agree with the philosophy that what matters is how things look." He gestures at the lavish décor. "This is the most expensive venue on the island, and they chose it to impress. If it costs a lot, they think it's good. If I were getting married, it wouldn't matter what it cost. The meaning behind the event is what should be important."

"You say that because, with your money, you could afford to hire a South American country for the reception."

"Only a small one."

"Scrooge."

His smile turns to a wince when his mother asks in an innocent voice, "Oh, are you thinking of matrimony, darling?"

I snort. "He's on the lookout for a suitable man. Get your confetti packet ready."

Mateo looks between the two of us and shakes his head. "I'm beginning to wish I'd never introduced the two of you."

His mother laughs and grips my arm. "You can't take Wren away from me now."

I fight the mushy feeling in my chest because while this is lovely, I will be going home soon, and I'll never see these people again. They're family to each other. Not me. The thought makes me sad, but it's a good thing to remind myself of.

Mateo's eyes look melancholy for a second, and then he shakes it off and pats my arm. "Let's get a drink."

I wrinkle my nose. "Are we leaving the receiving line? We haven't spoken to anyone yet. I've never done a receiving line before. What do you say at the end of one?"

"As little as possible," he says grimly. "My uncle is talking to one of his golf club friends anyway. We'll be here until tomorrow if we wait for them." He begins to stride towards the bar, confident and assured as always, everyone moving out of his way.

"Like Moses parting the Red Sea," I say disapprovingly.

His mother laughs. "If he'd been Moses, the Ten Commandments would have been filed away in a proper fashion and not in a box." She smiles at me. "Mateo has always been that way."

"Really?"

She nods. "Even as a small boy, he had something about him—an inner confidence and an expectation that life would run his way."

"But he has a very warm personality too. It draws people to him."

I look down to find her staring at me. "You see that, then? Interesting."

I flush. "Why? Doesn't everyone see it?"

She shakes her head. "Surprisingly, no. Oh, he's very personable. Funny and clever. But he doesn't give a lot of himself away." She looks over at her son. "Hmm," she says. She grimaces at her brother who is still talking loudly. "Let us go and find a seat. I want to be sitting when my brother comes over. He is so boring that otherwise, I might fall over."

I laugh, and she steers us over to the patio, finding a table next to the beach. The sea is breaking onto the sand less than a foot away. I pull her chair out for her, inhaling the salty air appreciatively.

She smiles at me. "Ah, you have fallen in love with the island. Mateo did say."

"It's so beautiful. I can't describe."

"You do not have to. It is my home and always has been. It has always kept me here. Mateo's father wanted us to move to Venice, and I refused. I think that Majorca may have cost me my marriage." She gives me an impish smile. "Not that I'm complaining. It was a good exchange."

I chuckle and sit down opposite her. "Didn't you want to move to Venice? I'd love to see it."

"It is a beautiful city. You would love it. I liked it to visit, but the month we spent there, I longed for my own home."

"It's on my list. One day I'll get there."

"I'm sure you will." She looks at me intently for a second and then shrugs. "Venice seemed to be another person in my marriage. It was always there in the background calling to Mateo's father. That and his family. And then the same call took my son away from me." She looks at the sea for a second, seeming melancholy.

"He mentioned that he left home when he was sixteen," I say cautiously. I'm not used to people sharing things so openly.

"He told you that?"

I bite my lip. "Was he not meant to?" I need to apologise for landing Mateo in trouble. But I relax when she shakes her head.

"It is absolutely fine, Wren. It is just that he does not often talk about such things. What else did he say?" she asks, leaning forwards.

I scratch my head. "Not much," I say quickly. "Just that he had to leave here and that he didn't want to go."

She sits back. "Then you know more than me, Wren Roberts." For some reason, that makes her smile, and I look at her in confusion. Her restless fingers pleat the linen napkin. "My ex-husband and I struck a deal when we knew that our marriage was over. Mateo was mine until he came of age, and then his father would come for him. The intention was to mould him into the man who would be prepared to inherit the family business."

I whistle, forgetting myself. "I bet that went down well."

She grimaces. "You guess right. Mateo is not one to be controlled, and his father found that out very quickly. Oh, he abided by the agreement. He went to Venice, he went to the right school, and I saw the wild boy I'd raised on the island—the one with masses of friends who was quick to laugh and talk loudly—slowly disappear to be replaced by this young man who said the right things, who was serious and focused." She shoots me a look. "But no matter what his father did or said, every holiday Mateo would book his flight and come home to the island, and after a few days, I would see my boy again. He's still there," she says earnestly. "He's just hidden under a pile of pressures and expectations." She touches my hand. "Be patient with him, Wren. Don't give up."

"Give up?" I say, mystified. "I won't know him for much longer."

"Then that makes me sad." She looks behind me and gives a bright smile. "Oh, thank you, darling. I am very thirsty."

"I suppose you are with the amount of talking you've been doing," Mateo says wryly. He sets the drinks down on the table. "Poor Wren's ears must be about to drop off."

"Lucky him," she says sourly. "Here comes my brother."

I look over and see a man who bears a slight resemblance to Mateo. However, while Mateo is handsome, this man is portly, and his cheeks are flushed. A woman walks next to him. She's plump with dark hair and dripping in jewellery that hasn't managed to take the sulky look off her face.

"Valentina," the man says to Mateo's mum when he stops at our table. "And, Mateo," he adds pompously. "We're very honoured to have your presence here."

Mateo curls his lip but shakes his uncle's hand and kisses his aunt's cheek. "Lovely wedding," he says with such blatant insincerity that I choke on my drink.

His uncle looks down at me. "And who do we have here?"

"Wren Roberts," Mateo says. "A friend of mine. Wren, this is my Uncle Bart and Aunt Mia."

I reach out a hand to shake, but his uncle rolls his eyes. "Rather young for you, Mateo," he says disapprovingly. "You will be robbing the cradle next."

My hand hovers in mid-air for a second before I lower it, and Mateo's face clouds. "I beg your pardon," he says icily.

"Well, you'd know all about that," Mateo's mother interrupts in a sweet voice, grabbing her son's hand. "Wasn't Mia seventeen when you met her?" She taps her chin. "It's so hard to remember. So many years ago, Mia. But then you're looking remarkably well preserved. I can never work out whether she is bored with your company, brother, or just unable to make an expression anymore."

I gaze from person to person, as though I'm watching a ping pong competition.

"How rude," Mateo's aunt says. "But only what I expect from the two of you. Money doesn't buy manners." She sniffs. "Or appropriate presents, I see. Your gift arrived this morning. I always think that a cheque is so impersonal."

Mateo's mother rolls her eyes. "What would have been appropriate for the happy couple would have been a boxing ring, but it was too cumbersome to wrap."

I can't help my laugh, and Mateo's uncle glares at me. "I'm unsure why we are airing our family matters in front of this young man. It's extremely inappropriate. Where on earth did you find this one, Mateo. Your taste deteriorates as you get older. Like your father."

"Maybe I struck it lucky when I found him, because he's a far better person than you," Mateo says. Gone is his savoir faire and composure. He's flushed with anger, and his voice is bitingly cold. "And Wren tries to teach me to be kind, but even his wonderful good nature would be thwarted by you, Uncle."

There's an awkward silence, and much as my chest warms at the way Mateo came to my defence, I also want to melt into the floor. I look anxiously over at his mother, expecting her to be glaring at me. But, instead, she's watching her son with a strange look on her face. It seems almost like relief, but then he looks down at her, and she shutters her face.

"I think one of your golfers is trying to attract your attention, brother," she says. "Either that or he has a problem with his swing."

Mateo's uncle looks over and visibly calms his temper. "It is Javier. Let us go and greet him," he says to his wife. "I think you'll like him."

"Of course, she will," Valentina says. "Javier would sell his mother for a new set of golf clubs. Just like you, Bart."

The angry couple vanishes, and I blow out a breath. "*Wow!*" I say reverently. "Families can be troublesome. I had no idea."

Valentina's face softens, and I'm pretty sure Mateo has told her the facts of my background. She pats my cheek gently. *Yes, he did,* I think wryly.

I look over at Mateo. "You alright?" I ask. His expression is turbulent, and his fists are clenched.

"He was so rude to you," he bursts out. "The cheek of the man. His own son-in-law was involved in a scam conning people out of their money, but he sees fits to cast judgement on *you*."

I'm bewildered by the rage. "It's okay," I finally say. "Don't worry about it. He wasn't that mean."

"The fact that you can say that with knowledge makes me even angrier," he says through his teeth and stalks off.

I stare after him. "Shall I go after him?" I ask his mother.

She shakes her head. She looks remarkably unfazed by her son's anger. Instead, she seems almost pleased.

"No, darling. Let him calm down."

"Well, you know him best," I say, subsiding into my chair.

"On the contrary," she says, sipping her drink. "I don't know *this* Mateo at all." She winks at me. "But I'm looking forward to making his acquaintance again, Wren."

I wonder if there's something in the water that is making everyone loopy tonight.

CHAPTER NINE

Wren

The next couple of days fly by, and before I know it, I'm waking up to my last day in Majorca.

I lie in the warm sheets, feeling the sun on my face and listening to the sound of the waves through the open balcony doors.

My last day.

I feel a pain in my stomach and roll over, looking blindly at the wall. By tomorrow night, I'll be back in my cramped little bedsit, and the next day I'll be sitting in my dingy cubicle at work, letting people shout at me over the phone. I won't hear the sea when I wake up. Just the sound of traffic and Mr and Mrs Tinton from the bedsit downstairs having a row. I won't see the blue sky and the sunlight on the sea. I bite my lip. I won't see Mateo.

Moisture wells in my eyes. I went along with his plans for this week, thinking only of the good memories I'd gain, and now I know the only thing I'll have gained is a broken heart.

I roll my eyes. I'm behaving like a heroine from one of those old Mills and Boon books. I'd found a sort of safety in reading them. A comfort because people met and fell in love, and they always ended up happily ever after. I'm a poorly hidden romantic, and I've always been convinced that maybe someday if I were lucky, I'd meet a man to whom I could give all my love. Unfortunately, that romantic nature combined with the fact that I have no one of my own has led me to hold on too tightly to people. I would give them all my affection when they'd never asked for that, and the result was that they'd skedaddle quicker than Boris Johnson from a hairbrush. I never seemed to learn the lesson and would do it with the next person and then the one after that and so on. Into infinity.

Mateo isn't the one for me. He won't be sad when I go home. He'll just move on to the next distraction. I hope he looks back on our time together well and remembers me affectionately, but just for once, I would like someone to want me to stay. I want someone to miss me when I go.

"Get over yourself, Wren," I say. I fling the sheets back and pad into the bathroom to start the shower. I've got one day and night left with Mateo, and I'm going to make the most of it. Today, we're looking at a hotel on the other side of the island, and he's promised me a picnic.

Half an hour later, a knock on the door makes my heart speed up. I race over and throw it open.

"You're early," I say breathlessly, noting Mateo's appearance. "That does *not* look like hotel inspection gear."

He's wearing a white T-shirt and a pair of khaki shorts faded by age. Battered leather deck shoes are on his feet and the ever-present watch fastened on his wrist. He looks tanned and happy, his golden eyes glowing in the morning sunshine and his hair ruffled from a ride in the Jeep.

He walks in and shuts the door behind him, sure of his welcome. He should be. I practically roll out the red carpet when he appears.

"That is because we are not viewing hotels today," he says.

"We're not? You said we were."

"Wren, it's your last day. Do you honestly think we're going to spend it working?"

"Yes," I say breathlessly, as if, with those words, he's confirmed that I'm leaving. As if the plane ticket in my luggage isn't enough.

"We're not doing that."

"Then what are we doing?"

He bops me on the nose. "That's a secret, but we'll be out for the whole day."

"Will you be kidnapping me for family revenge only to be forced to marry me?" I ask, unable to keep the smile out of my voice. I'm bubbling over as if I inhaled helium, and I'll float away with happiness because we'll have an entire day together uninterrupted by work.

"No." Chuckling, he looks me up and down. I'm wearing my jeans and a blue and white striped T-shirt. "No good," he says. "Exchange the jeans for your swimming shorts and wear your trainers. Bring a sweater too because it might get a little cool."

"I'm very intrigued."

"Good," he says and walks onto the balcony whistling.

———

Mateo opens the Jeep door for me, and I climb in, noticing a big red canvas bag in the back.

"What's that?" I ask, reaching for it but pulling back when he smacks my fingers.

"It's a secret," he says. His eyes are sparkling and he seems to be brimming over with excitement. I look at him in fascination because it's such a departure from his usual suave self.

He starts the Jeep and pulls out into the morning traffic. "Put some music on," he says over the noise of the wind.

I sync my phone, and soon the sound of "Golden Brown" by The Stranglers filters through the stereo.

He gives me a startled look. "I like this one."

"Don't sound so surprised, Grandad. This is *your* generation."

"It certainly fucking isn't, but at least it isn't Steps singing about indigestion in the city."

"It was heartbreak, actually." I slide my sunglasses on. "Music snob," I say for probably the fiftieth time this week. Mateo is not a fan of my music at all, but he puts up with it with good humour.

We drive through small villages with little stone cottages and then more built-up areas full of hotels whose paintwork gleams in the sun. Mateo slows the Jeep to steer around the tourists who seem to have the safety sense of lemmings as they wander along peering in shop windows. Once we're out of the towns, we drive long empty stretches of roads where where the only company is the odd seagull.

Finally, he comes into a resort, manoeuvring down streets lined with swaying palms and white buildings with a laidback seaside vibe. We arrive at the beachfront, and I catch my breath at the sight of a beautiful marina. Rows of yachts and smaller boats bob in the sparkling water, their paintwork almost blinding in the morning sunshine. Around the marina are set hotels and other buildings. People are everywhere, most of them walking at that slow tourist pace with a few locals dodging around them. The air is full of the cries of gulls, the snapping of the canvas sails, and the jingle of the rigging.

"It's beautiful," I say.

Mateo smiles. "This is Cala d'Or which means Golden Bay. It's appropriate for here. The marina is very busy."

A boat skims past us, its sails extended in the breeze. "Wow!" I say softly.

He inserts a card into a kiosk and the barrier to the marina's car park instantly rises as if he's said, "Open sesame."

"Where are we going?" I ask.

"Into the marina." He parks and switches off the engine.

"What are we doing here? Is there a hotel nearby?"

"No." He surprises me by lifting a hand and pushing my hair back off my face. Then, he looks intently at me. "I want to show you something."

"Is it your etchings?"

He laughs. "Sort of. Come on." He grabs the canvas bag from the back seat, and we climb out of the Jeep. I follow him as he moves off down a jetty. The boards under my feet are worn with age, and every-where is the slop of water. Mateo is obviously well known, as several people on boats hail him. I wonder if he has a friend who moors a boat here.

Finally, he comes to a stop, and I look around. "Is your friend here?" He gives me a blank look, and I explain, "I thought maybe you had a friend here with a yacht."

"In a manner of speaking."

"Where is the boat, then?"

"Behind you." He points to a boat sitting neatly next to the dock.

I know zero things about boats, but this one is charming. Its white and navy paintwork and teak decking give it a charmingly old-fashioned air, as if Agatha Christie's characters are going to turn up at any moment. Hopefully, not for a murder.

Written on the side in jaunty lettering are the words *Luna Azul*.

I glance at him and then back at the boat, and he smiles at me. It takes a ridiculously long time for me to cotton on. "Oh my god," I say. "This is *your* boat?"

He nods. His eyes are hidden by his sunglasses, but his grin is wide and white, and he looks as excited as a young boy. It's a look that suits him, but I'd be prepared to guess none of the Rossi employees have ever seen it.

"My baby," he says. "It means Blue Moon."

"Wow, she's a beauty." I grin. "Are we going out on her?" I ask excitedly.

He laughs. "Yes, I thought I'd take you out on the water, and there is something I would like to show you."

"What's that?"

"It is a surprise. I do not share it with many people, but don't get too excited. There is not much to see."

"You are the king of the enigmas," I inform him.

He laughs as we climb on board, and he shows me the boat's features, pointing out little details and using terms I have no hope of deciphering.

Everything is streamlined and seems to be created to suit a purpose. There's a tiny galley kitchen below deck with some cupboards and a small fridge, and there's even a little cabin bedroom that's walled in teak wood that shines glossily. A double bed is made up with a fluffy white duvet and pillows, a pale blue patterned throw flung carelessly along the bottom. I peek through a small porthole and then into a narrow bathroom with a shower, toilet, and washbasin.

I edge past him, where he's standing watching me with an indulgent smile on his face. I open a door in the bedroom and find a neat wardrobe which is empty apart from a few lonely coat hangers.

"This is brilliant," I say. "Look at all these little doors. *Magic.*" I pat the bed. "Should this boat be called the *Pulling Palace* rather than the *Luna Azul?*"

For a second, he looks unsure, my terminology taking him off guard. It happens sometimes. He's fluent in English, Spanish, French, German, and Russian but not always in twenty-two-year-old South London boys.

Then he laughs. "No." His smile slowly dies away. "I've never brought a man on this boat."

Pleasure warms me from the inside out. "Really?" I ask shyly.

"Really."

A silence falls that is somehow sweet, but when he starts to look a little awkward, I rush in with chatter. "It's a beautiful boat. Why is it called that? Were you a fan of Frank Sinatra?"

He chuckles. "It was a way of getting back at my father. He said I would come back to the island on a blue moon, meaning never. I make sure that I return every year."

"Have you had it long?"

We leave the cabin and climb the steep little steps to the deck. "A few years. I bought it when I had my first bonus."

"You bought a *yacht* with a bonus?"

He runs his hand through his hair, the chocolate brown strands drifting around his face. "Yes."

"Wow! The biggest bonus I've ever had was when Mr Simpkins bought everyone a drink at the Christmas party." I look around in wonder. "This is *wicked.* Even if I don't know anything about boats, I can tell it's epic."

"You don't know boats?"

I wrinkle my nose at him. "Well, a foster family did take me out on a dinghy at Blackpool once, but I don't think it quite equipped me for a day spent with a hotel heir on his yacht."

"With *me*," he says softly. "Mateo. Not Mateo Rossi. Just Mateo."

"Teo," I say softly. The word has been poised on my lips for a few days. I like diminutives and nicknames. They indicate a kind of familiarity and warmth that I've always longed for in relationships.

He looks pleased. "I think it is only my mother who has ever called me that, and I was a small boy then."

I flush. "Do you mind?"

"*No*," he says quickly and emphatically. "I like being Teo to you."

We stare at each other. After a moment, he says, "Well, I am going to give you a crash course in boats because you are going to help me sail this one."

"*What?*"

"It is easy."

"Not to someone who forgot to put the handbrake on in my driving instructor's car. He'd got out to look at the tyres when the car set off on its solo voyage. It got up to quite a fast speed when it rolled down the hill and hit the number forty bus."

He starts to laugh. "I am sorry. It isn't funny."

"No, the bus driver used several words I'd never heard before, and Mr Dixon didn't think it was funny either. I never had another lesson."

"You can't drive?"

"Well, I can drive, but not in a way that the London test centres recognise."

"Boats will be easy then, yes? Come and join me. You can cast off."

"Like knitting."

"Not exactly." He ruffles my hair. "Do not look worried. I am a good teacher."

He is good. He's patient and quick to laugh with me but never derogatorily. Not that I expected anything else. He's never been unkind to me.

And I love it. We take the boat far out to sea where the water is dark green, and when he calls to me, I release the sails, and they unfurl with a huge slap making the boat surge forwards, and I shout with glee.

He grins at me, his teeth white in his tanned face as he stands at the wheel.

"Good, yes?"

"Oh my god, it's *epic*," I shout.

I lift my face to the sun, feeling its hot rays on my face, and when I lick my lips, I taste salt on them. We sail over the water, passing other boats whose passengers Mateo greets with waves. Music plays dimly in the background, but my attention is given to the sails' creak and the rigging's musical jingle. Gulls glide around us, riding the wind and sending mocking cries at us. It's the loveliest thing I've ever done and yet also the most beautifully simple.

Finally, Mateo slows the boat and steers into a small cove. It's banded by cliffs, and the water is almost translucent, a clear mint green showing darker green patches of seaweed. Trees line the cove, and the air is very still. Mateo lowers the anchor in a grinding flurry of noise, and then quiet settles like a blanket on us. The only sounds are the lap of the water against the hull and the ever-present sound of the cicadas.

"Where are we?" I ask, looking around avidly.

"Do you like it?"

"Like it? Teo, this is beautiful."

He looks surprisingly pleased. "I thought we would take the dinghy and go ashore. I have something to show you."

I spread my hands. "What could be better than this?"

He gives me an enigmatic smile. "Wait and see."

He moves along the boat to let the dinghy down. It lands with a splash in the water. "Would you like to swim before we have lunch?" he asks. I nod eagerly and he winks. "Okay, bring the bag, would you?" he commands.

I pick up the canvas bag he brought from the Jeep and stagger. "This is bloody heavy."

"It takes a surprisingly large amount of food to fill you, Wren."

"I'm a growing boy," I inform him, passing him the bag.

He helps me into the dinghy, his warm hand keeping me steady until I sit. Then he rows us to the shore, his movements sure and strong, his biceps bulging. I surreptitiously admire the muscles rippling down his torso and the broadness of his chest. Then, I look up and find his mouth twitching. *Not so subtle, then.*

"Oh, shut up," I say, and he laughs.

We come ashore, and I help him pull the dinghy onto the beach and out of the reach of the waves. The sand is white and powdery under my feet. Waves hit the beach, offering a gentle susurration that complements the sound of the wind in the giant pine trees that line the cove.

"Come," Mateo gestures towards the trees. I follow him along a narrow dirt path into the welcome shade. The air smells of pine and sage as we climb higher and higher. The path ends and we stop.

"Wow," I say faintly.

We're standing on a big plateau that slopes away to the edge of a cliff. The remains of an old house are here. It's not much more than a foundation and a few walls made from the local stone, but they stand tall, as if guarding this peaceful spot. I tread carefully along the walls, very aware of Mateo following like a big dog at my heels. We pass the empty remains of what must have been a swimming pool, but my whole attention is on the view. All I can see is the sky and sea stretching into infinity. Birds caw and weave over us.

"This is beautiful," I say quietly. Something about the place calls for a whisper.

He nods, coming to stand next to me. His face is completely peaceful—as if the air here has sawed years off him. The wind ruffles his hair. "This is mine," he says in an equally quiet voice.

"*Really?*"

"I bought it many years ago."

"And you've never done anything with it?"

"Not yet. It is for when I am older."

"You won't stay in Venice then?"

He shoots me a smile. "No, definitely not. I plan to move here when I retire. The plans are being drawn up for the new house. I will build here, but at the moment, I am in no rush."

"I don't know why," I say idly. He raises an eyebrow in query. "I wouldn't leave this place alone until I was nearly too old to enjoy it. I'd live in it now."

He shrugs. "That is not possible, I am afraid."

There's no regret in his voice, but I still know somewhere deep inside me that he would move here tomorrow if duty didn't pull him back to Venice.

I turn back to the ruins of the house. "Is this what you wanted to show me?" He nods. "Thank you," I say softly. "I'm ever so glad you did, Teo. I shall like thinking of you here."

His face twists with some strong emotion, but then he smooths it out. "I have the picnic," he says. "I thought we could eat here on the grounds."

"Perfect. And you can tell me about what your house will look like."

And he does. He unfurls a blanket that probably cost more than my rent and sets out an extraordinary amount of food. My mouth waters at the sight of tapas, each tiny portion something that I've enjoyed this week. There are also delicate slices of fresh ham that we eat with fresh crusty bread. We finish off with *Leche Frita*, a dessert that I've come to love. It's made of cream that's cooked very slowly and then battered and fried. It's delicious. Mateo teases me that it's a child's dessert, but he still always buys it for me. The whole picnic has been geared to my tastes, and I'm very touched.

We lie on the blanket, grazing on the food and talking. His hands move a mile a minute, and his face is full of life as he sits telling me where everything will be. I'm envious because it sounds fantastic and also a bit surprising. I thought he'd go for something modern and streamlined like his hotels, but instead, he's using local stone, and the house sounds cosy and light.

Finally, I lie back, cushioning my head on my bundled-up hoodie. I'm just wearing my swimming shorts, and I lie basking in the late afternoon sun, feeling the sea breeze skip over me. Mateo lies next to me wearing his own board shorts. The sun plays on his skin, turning it bronze, and sweat glistens on the light smattering of hair on his chest.

"I think it'll be wonderful," I say, smiling at him. "I now have the perfect image of you. When I'm back in England, and it's grey and dreary, I will think of you in your cove with the sun turning everything white. You'll be sitting by your pool looking out to sea, and you'll look as relaxed as you do right now."

He doesn't smile. After a moment, he sighs. "I hate the idea that I won't see you after today."

I prop myself up on my elbows. "Me too, Teo. I've never known anyone like you."

"I think that line should be mine, Wren. It has been..." He pauses. "...an extraordinary honour to know you."

I swallow hard, my eyes burning. "Thank you for taking me under your wing and giving me such a wonderful week." I look around. "And thank you for showing me this. I have a feeling you don't show many people."

"You're the only one."

I gasp before I can help myself. "Why?"

He looks puzzled but then says slowly, "Because you're the only one I know who would appreciate this. Anyone else would think this is a rich man's folly."

"It's not folly to want your own home and peace," I say softly.

Reaching out, he takes my hand. "I wish the same for you."

I chuckle, squeezing his fingers. "I don't think mine will take this shape, but it will be just as much of a palace to me."

There's a long silence, and we both go back to staring out to sea. The sun is lower now, gilding everything in magic dust.

"I want to do something for you," he says suddenly.

"You've done more than enough," I say, startled. "Don't, for god's sake, buy me anything else, Teo."

He raises one eyebrow. "Says no man I've ever met."

"You should get out more."

"Ah, but what I could give you is free."

I wrinkle my nose in thought. *What is he talking about?*

"Teo?" I ask.

He rolls over to look at me. This close, I can see the darker, choco-late-brown flecks in his funny golden eyes.

"You asked me once to be your first, Wren," he says softly. "Do you still want that?"

My pulse starts to hammer, and my cock stiffens as I inhale his lemony scent and the tang of sweat. "Yes," I say slowly. "But only if you want that too, Teo. Don't do it just for me."

He starts to laugh, and I gulp when he takes my hand, guiding it towards his shorts and the erection tenting them. "I don't think that will be a problem," he says solemnly, catching his breath as my fingers spread out to touch him. He's big. "I've wanted you since the first time I saw you."

"*What?*"

"In the foyer laying down the law to those rich idiots. I wanted you then, and it's even stronger now. I need to feel you naked and under me. I want you desperately, Wren." He pulls my fingers back reluctantly and sits up, muscles rippling along his torso. "We should go back."

"Why?" I ask in astonishment.

"Well, because we have a nice bed on the boat. I want to make it good for you. I want you to love sex so much that it consumes you."

I swallow hard. "Why not here?"

"*Here?* In the ruins?"

I nod quickly. "Yes. Under the sun and sky, Teo. There's no one to see, is there?"

"No. There isn't anyone around for miles."

I lie back on the blanket and smile at him. "Then can we do it here?"

"Why?"

I pause to get my thoughts in order. "Because it's open and free. Out here, we're the same. We'll both be naked and just Teo and Wren. Back on that boat, you're the millionaire hotel owner, and I'm just a call centre operator. I want to be equals for once."

He stares at me, and the silence begins to thrum with desire as he looks me up and down slowly. My cock throbs and I reach down to grab it tightly. His eyes flare and grow slumberous as he watches. "You are like no one else, Wren. I've said it before, and I will no doubt repeat it."

"But that's good, right?" I say, reaching down and stripping off my shorts. I kick them away and lie naked in front of him. His eyes eat me up, looking greedily over my form and for the first time, I don't feel like scrawny Wren. Instead, I feel lithe and powerful because I made that hot desire show in his eyes.

"I also think you haven't kissed me yet," I say hoarsely.

He smiles. "What an incredible error of judgement." He leans over me, blotting out the heat of the sun and replacing it with a burn that runs through my veins.

CHAPTER TEN

Wren

His lips are soft against mine and I can taste the wine we drank. For a second, we both stay immobile, as if stunned this is happening, and then Teo groans and rolls over onto me, kissing me deeply, his tongue twining with mine. I kiss him back furiously, grabbing at his shoulders and spreading my legs to welcome him. His cock is a hard rod in his shorts and, as he continues to kiss me, his hips move, pushing our dicks together. The feeling is intense, miles away from the adolescent fumbling and frotting I've done before.

He pulls back, and I chase his mouth drunkenly, wanting more of those deep kisses but he stays me with gentle fingers on my chin. "I need to be naked too," he says, his voice hoarse and deep. My hips thrust involuntarily. I love the feel of his soft cotton shorts against my bare cock. It's naughty and a little illicit to be naked when he's not.

He moans but then stays my hips with a hand. "First things first," he says, standing.

I lie back, revelling in the afternoon sun and the sea breeze playing over my bare skin. Teo stands next to the blanket, a small smile playing over his lips. Lips that are swollen from my kisses, I note approvingly. I spread my legs, completely unashamed and feeling freer than I ever have before. His eyes darken, and he reaches into one of the canvas bag's pockets and pulls out a condom and a small bottle of lube.

"Always prepared, Teo?" I say lazily.

He slants me a serious look. "You should always expect that of your partners. They should care about your safety above and beyond a need to get off." He throws the objects beside me and then starts to slide down his shorts. The root of his cock appears beneath his taut abdominal muscles, and I prop myself on an elbow.

He grins at me and stops his striptease.

I make a moue of dissatisfaction. "Tease," I accuse.

He throws his head back and laughs, the robust, hearty sound echoing around our spot. Finally, he lowers his shorts completely and kicking them free he stands still so I can look at him.

He's intimidatingly big, with a wide, meaty girth, and his large balls hang lower than mine. I should be scared but I'm amazed to find that it turns me on. Apparently, I'm a size queen now. Who knew?

"You're big," I breathe.

He smiles at me. "Don't worry. I'll take care of you, Wren."

He settles down next to me in one long graceful movement, and it's apparent that we're very different. I would probably have tripped trying to get out of my shorts and knocked myself out. He urges me onto my back and lies at my side. His skin is hot and sweaty against mine, and he pushes his arm under my head so that his bicep cradles my skull. I approve of the position as it brings him even closer.

His gaze tracks my features, intent and focused. He lowers his hand and rests it on my chest, spreading his fingers as if he's holding me down. A fingernail scrapes my nipple. The sharp burst of pleasure makes me jerk in shock and his eyes flare instantly. He bends and runs his tongue over the disc and then sucks it. My dick thumps against my belly as if there's a wire connecting it to my nipples.

"Teo," I pant. "Oh my god. I've never..."

He raises his head, his lips full. "Never?"

I shake my head, and with one finger, he traces a path from my chest to my belly button. He circles it lightly, and I arch under his hand. It tickles but in a really intense way. After teasing me for a second, his finger moves down, following my happy trail until he reaches the hair at my crotch. He fans his fingers through it, and I groan and push up. My cock is throbbing painfully, and I move my hips in a circle, begging for his touch.

"Please," I pant.

His face is intent and focused. Sweat stands out on his forehead and his eyes look strained before he shutters his expression. For a long second, we stare at each other and then he moves, taking my dick into his hand and closing his fingers around it. My eyes slam shut and I cry out, pushing my hips up and shoving my cock into the perfect tight grasp of his hand.

I force my eyes open and cup his chin, needing to touch him too. Our gazes meet and hold for a long second. Then he bends down and kisses me and all the time he's stroking my dick. When he pulls back, I make a loud protest but subside when I realise he's grabbing the lube.

He pours a stream into his hand and then fists my dick again. The coolness of the lube is lovely when we're both so sweaty and hot and I arch into his hand. His grip is perfectly slippery, letting him pump me steadily. When I look at him, he's watching his hand on my dick as intently as if he's never seen a penis before. His hair is wavy and rumpled from my hands and sweat glistens in his chest hair. I want to touch him so badly. I hesitate for a second and then just think, *fuck it.* After all, this won't happen again. He's the hottest man I've ever known, and you bet I'm going to fucking touch him and do everything I've been dreaming about all week.

I run my hand down his chest, feeling the crinkly hair and the skin that's sun-hot and tight as a drum over his muscles. His frame is bigger and wider than mine, but it doesn't make me feel small or threatened. There's gentleness in every line of his body.

His eyes slide shut as I stroke downward to where that monster cock is waiting, rearing up from a neat thatch of hair. I run my finger over it, and he groans as if in pain as I stroke around the head. It's as round and juicy as a plum, and my mouth waters with the desire to take him in my mouth. But then he shuttles his hand up and down my own dick, and my thoughts scatter.

When he pulls back, I make a loud protesting noise and he soothes me, stroking my torso. "Turn over," he says, his voice hoarse, and I obediently roll over, his hands guiding me into a position with one knee bent and pushed up. After I hear foil ripping, I look back to see him pulling a condom on. He settles it with a gentle snap and then pours lube over his sheathed cock.

"You're big," I say again for the record.

"I am, and it's not too late to say no."

I look wonderingly at him. "You would stop?"

He frowns, his face darkening. "Of course, I would stop. Has someone—"

I interrupt what is probably going to be a long conversation, the answers to which will only make him madder. "Has it escaped your attention that I'm waiting for a good dicking?"

He bursts into such loud laughter that a seagull who'd been sidling up in the hope of raiding the picnic, is startled and flies away with an accusing squark.

When he's finished chuckling, he returns doggedly to his favourite theme. "I will stop at any time. I know I'm not small and it's your first time. Even if I have my cock inside you and you decide you don't like it, then you tell me, and I'll stop."

"You'll stop having sex with me?" I sound utterly scandalised and his lip twitches.

"I'll still make you come. Penetrative sex isn't for everyone, so there's no shame in saying if you don't like it."

"I'd like to try it at some point this millennium," I say waspishly, and he grins and salutes me. Then he lowers himself until he's kneeling between my legs.

He trails a hand down my flank. The touch is almost startling, and I flinch. Despite my brave words, I am a little anxious. Trust me to pick the super-monster cock to pop my cherry. He pauses to pour lube onto his fingers and I feel him touch my entrance. I tense, but he just kisses my shoulder, saying something in Spanish into the skin. I relax when he doesn't try to force it in like Trevor from Accounting who acted as if he was trying to find his pound coin in the change slot. Instead, Teo rubs over the wrinkled skin, and I shift jerkily as his touch stirs up nerve endings I didn't know I possessed down there.

"Teo?" I whisper.

He hums and carries on with the slow movements, tracing over my hole and around it. The feeling is tickly, but after a few passes, I find myself chasing his touch whenever he lifts away. Soon my entrance is slippery, and I'm panting which is when he slides the tip of his finger in. It's an incredibly gentle gesture, and even though I automatically tense, he waits until I've relaxed again to move it farther in, pausing to add more lube to the mixture. It's a very strange feeling and not one I'm convinced is pleasurable until he crooks his finger and pleasure explodes across my brain like a Catherine Wheel leaving sparks everywhere.

"Oh shit!" I shout far too loudly, but it must please him because he presses a fervent kiss to my shoulder.

I stare blindly ahead, panting and groaning as he continues to open me up. He's slow and gentle and stops every so often for me to indicate that I'm comfortable. He never shows any impatience, even though I can tell how turned on he is as he ruts gently against my thigh. I've never experienced anything like the level of care he gives me. Boys my age have been all about their own comfort which is why I've never trusted any of them enough to do this.

Eventually, when I'm a writhing, panting, breathless mess, I snap. "Teo, I need you to fuck me. I'm ready."

He pulls his fingers gently out and comes closer, fisting his dick. He moves, and I feel the first kiss of it against my entrance.

"Any time you want," he reminds me.

"I'll say if I don't like it." I crane my head back. "Will it hurt?"

His face is gentle. "Maybe a little. I think it hurts everyone their first time."

"Oh," I say in a small voice.

"But you're forgetting that we keep on doing it and it gets better and better. I promise I will go gently."

"I trust you."

He stares at me. "Yes?"

I nod. "Please, Teo."

He doesn't ask again. Instead, holding my hips, he pushes the head of his cock in. I cringe, grabbing hold of the blanket tightly. It hurts and my instinctive reaction is to shove him off me.

He stays still, a visible tremor in his body. "Breathe in and out," he instructs, his voice hoarse.

I do as he says, and the pain eases a little. I relax, and he slowly pushes until he's all the way in, his balls resting against my arse. It's an odd feeling, and the pain makes it unpleasant. My erection has flagged and I'm starting to think that maybe I'm one of the people who just don't like anal.

Then Teo moves and my thoughts scatter, because his dick rubs over the spot he found earlier. It lights me up even more now it's the thick club of his cock pushing against it, and I groan and lower my head to my hands, lifting my arse for him. "There," I gasp. "Oh there, please."

He grunts and starts to thrust slowly at first, and then a little faster. He pauses to add more lube to his dick, which makes the slide into me smooth and wonderful and suddenly, all my doubts over whether I like this fly away, and my cries and groans fill the air along with the sound of sweaty bodies slapping together.

I crane my head back to kiss him, but all we can manage are sloppy kisses and then panting breaths.

He's thrusting harder now, his fingers digging into my hips, no doubt leaving bruises he'll be horrified over later. I groan, my eyes staring blindly ahead. My cock throbs and I strain for the end.

"I need to come," I gasp.

He comes up on one arm, reaching in and grabbing my dick. His grip is slippery and firm and almost as soon as he touches me, I scream and come all over his palm and fingers.

Mateo shouts out something as I constrict around him and then pushes me down, lying heavily on me. The hair on his chest tickles, and his body is sweaty and hot. His cock is a hard pole inside me. He thrusts hard. "I'm coming," he gasps. "Wren." Then he cries out and I feel him pulse into the condom.

For a few seconds, we stay there frozen in pleasure and then he puts a hand between my shoulder blades, pushing me gently down as he pulls out. It's not pleasant, and I give a pained whine. He pets my hair and kisses my shoulder, offering comfort wordlessly, and then falls to his side. He immediately drags me into his arms, and I rest my head against his chest, feeling the frantic hammering of his heart. I let my thoughts spin away, lost in a drifting haze and only aware of the heat of his body, the sound of the sea, and the calls of the gulls.

We stay that way for a while, wrapped in each other on our blanket. The breeze blows over me, cooling my skin, and the sun sinks lower in the sky. Time is ticking away for me. Soon we'll have to go back, and all this will come to an end, but for a little bit longer, I lie with him and pretend that this is just the beginning, and that when he builds his house, it will be ours. It's ridiculous, but I haven't had much material to daydream with, so shoot me.

Eventually, though, he stirs and moves away. We both chuckle as our skin separates with a raspberry sound. He pushes my hair back from my face, his golden eyes absorbed as he looks down my naked body.

"Well, I'm not a virgin anymore," I say perkily. "Good job, Mateo."

He chuckles and watches me intently. "Was it good?"

I examine his face for a moment. "It was the best," I say simply.

He looks as if he wants to say more but then he gives a heavy sigh. "It is time to go back," he says.

My stomach turns over, but I force a smile. "If you say so."

"I wish it were not so, but the sun is going down, and I have a meeting later on."

My sweet, lazy mood vanishes abruptly. I know he didn't mean anything by that, but it feels a little like he just slapped me. He has meetings, and he's an incredibly busy man, but it's as if now he's had me and I'm going home, he's moving on blithely. And why wouldn't he? Nothing about him has been changed by our sex. Nothing at all. Whereas I feel as if I've changed permanently.

"Well, we don't want you to be late," I say lightly, standing up and concealing my immediate wince. I step into my shorts and pull them up my legs but stop as he makes a disgruntled sound. "What?"

He shakes his head and stands up himself, and I watch as he pulls his own shorts on. "I'm sorry," he finally says. "That was a careless thing to say."

I force a cheerful look on my face. "Don't be silly. It's not as if I expect you to stop your life because you deflowered me."

That has the desired effect, and he laughs, making me relax a little. I don't want to make myself a nuisance and spoil the week we've had. I don't want him to regret meeting me. I will never feel like that about him.

So, I keep the conversation light and snarky, and the journey back is full of laughter and conversation about nothing in particular. But despite that, it lacks the magic of the trip to his cove.

———

It's dark by the time we get to the hotel. It looms over us, all the lights making it look like one of those giant cruise ships. Mateo parks and switches off the engine.

I look at him in query. "I'll see you up," he says quietly.

I smirk. "Why? Did you think I'd have trouble walking after having your cock up my arse?"

He eyes me in disbelief, and I smile at him. This is it. The moment I've been dreading. "Why don't we just say goodbye now, Teo? I hate big goodbye scenes. They make me twitchy." I pause. "I mean in films, of course. No one's exactly ever rent their bosoms and wailed at me for saying bon voyage to them."

"Then you have known idiots all your life."

"You must have met some of my men."

"You sound like Bette Davis."

He opens his door and steps out, giving me a stubborn look so I make sure that he can see me rolling my eyes. His mouth twitches, but he waits for me and follows me through the foyer and into the lift. As usual, we're the subject of a lot of covert observation. The staff seem fascinated by us, and it makes me flush a little. Probably most of them think I'm just some random twink having a holiday romance with the boss.

The lift doors close, and I turn to face him where he's leaning against the wall, but he says nothing. Instead, he draws me to him, so I stand between his legs and, cupping my face between his palms, he kisses me. It's a sweet kiss with none of the passion of his earlier ones. Instead, it tastes of affection and melancholy, and when I pull back, I sigh and rest my head on his chest.

"I'll miss you," I say into the cotton of his shirt, inhaling his scent of lemon and light sweat greedily.

"I will miss you too," he says steadily, dropping a kiss on my hair.

The lift doors open, and we separate, but he grabs my hand and walks me the distance to my room as if he's an old-fashioned suitor.

When we get to my door, I turn to him. "This is it. Thank you so much for everything you've done, Mateo."

"*Teo*," he says stubbornly, a frustrated look on his face. "You call me Teo. Not Mateo."

"Well, Teo, thank you." I reach up and cup his strong jawbone, feeling the stubble under my fingertips. "Thank you for giving me such a wonderful week." I kiss him lightly. "And thank you for being my first."

His face shows a powerful struggle, and I stare at him, my heart beginning to pound heavily.

"Wren, I don't want you to—"

The door behind me flies open. "Where the hell have you been?" an angry voice says.

I spin around to see Owen standing there.

"Where have you been?" he demands again. His hair is messy, and he has a pillow line down his cheek.

"What are you doing here?" I gasp.

Before he can respond, I turn away, dismissing him.

Mateo is watching us, but to my frustration, he's once again wearing his polite, hotel-mogul expression.

"What were you going to say?" I ask urgently, but I already know there's no point, and Teo's following words prove it.

"It was nothing. Well, goodbye, Wren Roberts. Thank you for a wonderful week." He holds out his hand.

For a wild second, I look at it in disbelief. I want to scream at him to tell me what he was going to say before the interruption, but I can't.

I'm guilty of holding on to people far too tightly. I won't do that with him. So, instead of demands and clutching hands, I slide my hand into his and shake it gently.

"Thank you," I say, staring into his eyes. Then, I offer him a crooked smile. "I mean that."

He steps back, and our hands part. "Goodbye, Wren Roberts," he says, his voice smooth, his face shut down. "Good luck."

Then he turns, and I watch as he walks away from me. I stay there until he gets into the lift, aware of Owen's whiny voice, but all my attention is on Mateo. When the doors slide shut and he's lost to sight, I sigh and close my eyes. Then I turn reluctantly to Owen, who's still talking.

"Why are you here?" I say sharply, entering our room.

"Why shouldn't I be? This is my hotel room, too." His tone is defensive but then he sighs. "I felt guilty about you being here on your own, so I thought I'd come back and spend the last day with you."

"You're a bit late. It's eight at night, and we fly first thing in the morning."

"I wanted to be here for you."

I turn and look at him in disbelief, and he shifts his eyes away guiltily.

"Oh my god," I say, sighing. "What happened?"

"Nothing."

"Don't bullshit me, Owen. You're back for a reason, and I'm pretty sure it's not our ex-friendship."

He looks hurt, which winds me up.

"You're still my friend, Wren. My best friend."

"If I were that, you wouldn't have left me on my own." I settle down on the chair wincing at my sore arse. "What happened?"

He looks as if he's going to try to keep up the pretence, but as usual, everyone has to know Owen's pain so they can rally and comfort him. I brace myself to help, but then realise with a shock that I don't have to. He's not my friend anymore. Just someone I clung to as a familiar point in an often-turbulent world. I'm fine without Owen. I think I've concretely proved that over and over again this week.

He settles down on the edge of his bed. "Josh and I had a row. He got off with another bloke."

"And that was a big shock to you? He's the biggest wanker around. The only surprise is that people find him attractive."

"He is attractive," Owen says earnestly. "He's immensely popular."

"His parents' *money* is immensely popular," I correct him. I pick at a loose thread on my T-shirt, and as I move, I get a sharp whiff of lemon and spunk and feel my whole body clench with yearning. I become aware that he's still talking. "Sorry," I say, not feeling it in the slightest. "What were you saying?"

"What is the matter with you?" he says. "You're in a daydream. Is it that Mateo? He's very handsome." He looks towards the door, realisation slowly dawning along with a considerable dose of shock. "Hang on. Was that Mateo Rossi? The owner of the hotel?"

My brain scrambles for an answer but in the end, I don't need to say anything because he stands up in excitement. "Oh my god, it *was*. What were you doing with him, Wren?" He pauses. "Why was he thanking you for a good week?"

"It was nothing," I say quickly. "I just helped him out this week."

"With what?" He gives a mocking laugh. "Does he need insurance?" I look steadily at him, and he flushes. "Sorry. That was shitty." He bites his lip. "I hope you didn't do anything with him that you're going to regret, Wren."

"What? Like naked skydiving or ice skating on a glass floor?"

He rolls his eyes. "The man's a complete bastard."

"Oh really?"

He nods. "Completely. My dad did some work for him and came home with some tales. He always has men hanging over him. There's a new one every other week or so, but my dad says he's as cold as ice."

I think of Mateo laughing with me on the boat, his hair whipping around his face and his teeth white. Then I remember his gentle hands and the slow tender way he'd pushed into me.

"He isn't," I say. "Not at all. He's lovely."

He shrugs. "What am I thinking? That's ridiculous anyway. Sorry, babe. As if Mateo Rossi, the heir to the Rossi hotel empire, is going to be interested in you." He looks worried. "No offence, Wren."

"Why do people always say that after they've said the rudest thing possible?"

"Oh, come on," he says defensively. "I'm just being honest. He's way out of your league. You deal with insurance claims, for fuck's sake, while he deals with multi-million-pound contracts. You'd have *nothing* in common—"

There's a sudden loud banging on the door.

Owen frowns. "Who could that be?"

"Maybe it's the compassion police," I say idly. "Coming to arrest you for being such a complete cocksicle, Owen."

He moves to the door and swings it open, and then we both go still. Maybe even the world stops turning. Mateo stands in the doorway. His hair is a mess, as if he's run his hands through it many times, and his face is agitated and tumultuous.

"Teo." I jump to my feet.

"*Teo?*" Owen echoes. "What the hell is going on?"

Mateo ignores him. He strides over to where I stand in shock.

"Come with me, Wren," he blurts out, his voice loud and rough.

"*What?*" Owen and I say in tandem.

"Come with me to Venice."

I stare at him. My heart is hammering so hard I can feel it in my throat. "What are you talking about?"

He grabs my hands. "I want you to come with me to Venice for a month."

I swallow hard, disappointment twisting in my stomach. "For a month?" I echo, and he nods fiercely.

"Yes, come with me. Venice is beautiful in the autumn." He speaks quickly, as if he wants to get his words out before I can say no. Hope stirs. He wants to keep knowing me. "The number of tourists in the city lessen, and I can show you Venice the way I showed you the island. It's beautiful, Wren. You must see it." Temptation swirls, and he obviously senses it as he squeezes my fingers. "You can stay with me and see another city on your bucket lust."

"It's list," Owen says snippily, but we ignore him.

"I can't come and live on your money," I finally say.

His eyes flare. "It's not like that." I shoot him a sceptical look, and he grimaces. "It's not. I have so much money that you staying with me will make no difference. You have the money you earned this week, yes?"

"Yes, you haven't let me pay for anything."

"Then use it as spending money, Wren. You can look at it as a lovely holiday and go home in a month when the colder weather comes."

"Like a bird who's anti migration?"

"But not a cuckoo," he says fiercely. "*Never* that."

I draw in a sharp breath. "But why, Teo? This is completely out of the blue. You don't do this. You put men in compartments."

He opens his mouth as if words are going to come tumbling out but then draws a steadying breath. He guides me to the side of the room. "It's not like that," he says in a low voice. "I'm not looking for love or a relationship."

He looks at me to see if I'm hurt by that, but honestly, I'm not. How could I be? He's never given me any indication of a desire for a long-term relationship, and so while I might long for that, it's not something he's been guilty of encouraging.

A tiny voice tells me he's not offering me the same deal as his other men. I don't fit in his world long term. I'm just a messy-haired, chaotic person he likes and maybe feels a bit sorry for. Not a well-groomed man of the world who can meet him as an equal. I push the thought away, but it lingers there like a splinter under my skin.

"I just want to carry on with whatever this is for a little while longer," he says.

"Just so you know. This is less of a Prince Charming speech and more of a Prince Charles engagement interview," I say weakly, aware of Owen visibly straining to hear.

"Well?" he says, looking at me with fierce golden eyes. "What do you say, Wren? Want to come to Venice for a bit?"

"You can't be serious," Owen bursts out, reminding Mateo that he's still in the room. "Wren, this is crazy. You can't go off with him."

"Please shut up," Mateo says in an autocratic voice that makes me think of breeches and wet shirts.

"Why is it crazy?" I ask Owen.

His eyes are wild. "Well, what about your... what about your job?" he splutters.

"Oh, the job you were just taking the piss out of? I'm sure they'll miss me running the company, but hopefully, it won't fold in my absence."

Mateo laughs, but Owen glares at him.

"This man is a complete player," he says loudly.

Mateo straightens up abruptly

Owen skips back out of reach, saying in a high voice, "He uses men up and tosses them aside, Wren. So, you're going to jaunt off with him? You'll lose your job and your home."

"My rent is paid for the next three months," I say, thinking hard.

"So, you're actually considering this. Are you *mad*? He's just another rich twat."

I stiffen. "Shut up," I say sharply. He flinches, astonished. "You can stand there and say all that, but Mateo is *not* the one who left his best friend in a strange country on his own, Owen. He's the one who stayed with me."

"I can't believe you're thinking of doing it," he says incredulously. "Have you gone bonkers?"

I look back at Mateo. *Teo*. His eyes are glowing in the light, and he looks at me hopefully. "Well?" he says. "Are you thinking of it, Wren?"

The thing is, I know how mad this is. A lifetime of being disposable has taught me to cling on white-knuckled to stability. I never leap, and if I were ever to do it, I'd make sure I looked a thousand times first. And I know this isn't forever with Mateo. It isn't even half a year. It's just a month with a man who will never love me and who is vastly different from me. We might have come together as equals in that quiet cove, but it's not something we'll ever be in the real world.

I look at his warm eyes, wind-ruffled hair, and the soft curve of his mouth. I catalogue the strength of his body and those broad shoulders, and I think of leaving him now and not ever seeing him again, and it hurts me inside. I know at the end of the month, it will happen, but why shouldn't I grab for a little bit of happiness first, even if it's transitory? Why shouldn't I do something wild for once in my fucking life? Why shouldn't I make some memories like everyone else?

A reckless, alien feeling rushes through me like a river washing away my ingrained caution. I realise that I'm grinning wildly at Teo.

"You know, Teo, I've always wanted to see Venice."

His eyes flare, and he grabs me into a rough hug, holding me tightly enough to make me gasp. Owen's voice is like a stuck record in the background, but I ignore him, focusing on the strength of Teo's arms and the feel of his heart hammering against mine.

I'm a bird, I tell myself. *I will be free and easy and ride the wind, but I will never be a cuckoo to him. I will go home when winter comes, and I will never make him regret wanting to spend time with me.* I hug him back, closing my mind to doubts and focusing on the scent of his skin.

PART TWO

CHAPTER ELEVEN

Wren

I wake up slowly, aware of the sun hot on my eyelids and the softness of the duvet around me. It smells of lemon. Like Teo. The thought forces my eyes open, and I turn my head quickly, only to relax when I find his dark head on the other pillow. It wasn't a dream.

He's facing away from me and has thrown off the covers in the night, so his broad back is on display. It's covered in sleek olive skin with a few freckles dotted over the shoulders that are strangely endearing. His chocolate-brown hair is a mess on the pillow, and I can hear soft snores.

I snuggle up into the duvet, feeling the soreness in my arse. It doesn't hurt, but I definitely know he's been there, and I love it. Last night, he'd brought me from the hotel to the villa he's been renting while he's been on the island, and although I'd wanted to fuck again, he'd gently refused, insisting I wasn't ready. So instead, he'd run me a bath and unpacked my case for me while I soaked. Then he'd pulled me into bed, and we'd slept. I'd protested at the time but clenching my cheeks together makes me realise he was right. I am a bit sore.

I bite my lip, looking across the bed at him. There isn't a huge gap between us, but it feels like the Channel Tunnel at the moment. He'd told me last night that he wasn't a cuddler. He'd said it apologetically as if I was going to throw a fit, but of course, I hadn't.

The truth is, I'd love to snuggle with him. I like touching people. That makes me sound like a creeper, but I mean that I love to hug and be hugged back and being able to reach out and touch. Maybe because I haven't been able to do much of that in my life. But I had my own space invaded enough times when I was in foster care, so instead of pouting, I'd smiled at him and shrugged, which I sort of think will be my role over the next month. I have no right to demand anything from him, because he's been unequivocal on what this is. Besides, he's given me far more than anyone in my life has ever done before.

Nevertheless, I daringly move a little closer and reach out to lay my hand gently on his back. It's silky and sun-warmed, the muscle beneath lying dormant. I resist the impulse to hug him and just leave my hand there. But something about the touch must register, because he stirs, mumbling something and stretching. I let my hand drop away, watching the movement of the muscles under his skin.

He rolls to his back, his eyes still closed, and then in a motion that makes me jump, he rears up, looking around wildly. "Wren?" he says hoarsely.

His voice is sleep-warm, his eyes tired. He's rumpled and very unlike the usually well-put-together hotel tycoon. I decide I like him like this and smile at him.

"I'm here."

He stares at me lying on his sheets, and a warm look comes over his face. "You look good there," he says softly.

I squirm, feeling my dick harden. "Really?"

He must catch my mood because his eyes flare. "Very good."

He bends to kiss me, and I lift towards him only to grumble when he stops. "What is it, Teo?"

"Morning breath," he says apologetically.

I wrap my arms around his neck and drag him down. He succumbs, laughing as he falls against me.

I squeeze him. "I've got it too. Are you bothered?"

"Not even a tiny bit."

Then he kisses me, and it's sleepy and leisurely. When we come up for air, my dick is hard, and my cheeks are red. Mateo is in a similar state, his cock rigid against me.

"Are you sore?" he whispers.

I think of lying, but his raised eyebrow deters me. "A little," I say, my cheeks getting hotter

He rubs his thumb across one, the callused tip stirring nerve endings I never knew were there. "Don't be embarrassed," he whispers. "I love it."

I flatten my hands on his shoulders, rubbing my fingertips across his skin, feeling a dimple from an old scar. "Really?"

He nods. "It's sexy knowing I'm the only one who's been inside you."

"I want to fuck, though." I can't help the frustrated note in my voice.

He smiles wickedly. "We can't do that, but I'm sure I can add to your experiences." He lowers himself under the covers, wriggling down in the bed.

"I don't wish to rain on your parade, but someone has sucked my dick before," I say breathily.

A chuckle sounds from under the sheets. When I raise them, he rests his chin on my stomach, gazing up at me with a devilish look on his face. "I'm not going to suck your cock, Wren."

"Then what are you going to do?" I ask and groan as he spreads my legs and cups my arse, bringing me towards his mouth. He hovers there, his breath hot on my entrance. "Oh shit," I say reverently.

"You don't mind rimming, do you?"

He licks over my hole, bathing it in wetness and then pulls back to blow over it. Now my groan sounds like somebody is being murdered in the bed.

"Wren?" he prompts, his tone wicked.

"I don't mind," I gabble. "There aren't enough words in my vocabulary to tell you how much I *don't* mind rimming."

He laughs and runs his big hand over my belly. He drops a kiss on the sharp edge of my hipbone and then bends back to work.

I sink my head into the pillows and screw my eyes shut as he licks at my hole. It feels strange and as if it should be intrusive, but it isn't. I never realised how much sensation could be wrung out of one tiny area on my body, but Mateo is a master. He licks delicately at the wrinkled opening, taking care of the slightly sore tissue. It's ticklish, but in the best way, like my head might explode from the pleasure, and I can't help my groans from coming out. I jam my hand over my mouth and then make a protesting noise as he levers up in the bed. His face is flushed, his mouth swollen, his eyes at half-mast.

"Don't be quiet," he instructs me. "It pleases me to hear you, Wren."

I clear my throat. "Oh, I wish you could have a word with my boss. He's always telling me to shut up."

His mouth quirks. "If you are doing this in your workplace, I will have to change my knowledge of British employment law."

Before I can reply, he continues his torture, and the only thing I can do is shout in shock as he wriggles his tongue into the opening and then pulls back to spit on it.

"That should *not* be as sexy as it is," I say fervently, coming up on my elbows. "Do it again."

Keeping eye contact, he spits into my hole and pushes my thighs to my chest. "Keep them there," he says, his voice more heavily accented than usual.

I grip the back of my thighs. It should be undignified, but I haven't got time to think about that as he sets in licking and kissing my entrance and pushing his tongue in. "Oh my god," I shout. My fingers are going to leave bruises on my legs, but that'll be a problem for reincarnated Wren, because if Teo doesn't make me come soon, I'll expire on the spot.

I cant my hips and writhe on the end of his tongue. "That's so good, Teo."

He rises suddenly, his movements fierce and unrestrained. "Spread your legs," he barks, and I hasten to obey, grunting as he fists my cock and gives it a quick stroke. He grabs the lube bottle from the bedside table and pours a stream over our dicks. "Kiss me," he demands, leaning in, and I do. Other men are squeamish about kissing after rimming—I've heard Owen grumble about it—but I kiss Teo, fiercely eating at his mouth and loving the darker taste on his tongue.

He slots our cocks together, and as we writhe together, the friction makes my eyes roll to the back of my head. The pressure is just right and the slick feel of his skin and the perfect pressure of his cock against mine is almost indescribable. I'm suddenly overcome with everything—the light smell of his sweat, the tangy aroma of precome, and the faint trace of cologne. I cry out, wrapping my legs tightly around his hips and clinging to him like a monkey.

"Teo," I whisper, straining for more.

He pulls back, panting heavily, his eyes unfocused. He twists his hips, and I groan like I'm dying. "Oh god," I whine. "Teo, I need to come. Make me come."

He lowers his hands to my arse, cupping the globes as he begins to thrust. Our dicks slide together smoothly in the mix of sweat and lube. He rubs one finger gently over my hole and I'm gone. Stars explode behind my eyes, and I'm pretty sure the heavens sing as I groan and come all over him.

I've barely finished when he rears back and sits up on his haunches. "Teo?" I say questioningly. His eyes are wild and unfocused.

"Can I come on you?" he asks, fisting his dick and stroking himself while staring intently at me.

I blush. I must look a right sight lying here with my legs open and come sticking to me. But Mateo seems to love it, so I open my legs farther.

"Yes," I say throatily. My voice is hoarse from all my moaning and groaning, and I sound like a sex chat operator on their best day.

It obviously does the trick for Teo. He straddles my thighs, resting his balls against me as he strokes his dick with frantic motions. His eyes are avaricious, and he grunts.

I watch fascinated as the big red head of his cock peeks through his fist. Daringly, I cup his balls with one gentle hand.

"Wren," he chokes out. Screwing his eyes shut, he gives a truncated groan and come spurts out of the slit in his cock, flying over me and coating my cock and balls.

He falls to his side, finding my hand and squeezing it. We lie panting on the bed for a few minutes. A light breeze blows through the windows, bringing the sound of the sea as it cools the sweat on our bodies. Our come is sticky on my skin, and it's bloody fantastic.

"Can we just do that for the next few weeks," I ask fervently. Hearing his loud laughter makes me smile.

———

Later on, showered and dressed in shorts and a T-shirt, I sit beside Teo in the Jeep as it barrels along the road. I feel sleek and like every atom in my body is buzzing.

"Where are we going?" I ask again.

He grins at me, his teeth white in his tanned face and the sun glancing off his sunglasses. "We're going to Cala d'Or."

Excitement stirs. "Ooh, are we going out on the boat again?"

He shakes his head regretfully. "No. We don't have time, Wren. A friend closed the boat down for me for the winter as I'm leaving. Our flight is at three."

I bite my lip. "I can't wait to see Venice, but I'm a bit sad to leave Majorca."

"Me too." He reaches over and squeezes my hand. "But you'll love Venice. I promise."

"What's it like?"

"It will appeal to your dramatic little heart." He chuckles as I pinch his fingers. "It is beautiful and melancholy and full of a sense of its place in history."

"Very different from here."

"Here is bold and bright."

"So why are we going to Cala d'Or?"

"We're going to a little shop that I know. You'll love it."

"Will I? I'm not a huge shopper, Teo."

"Do you not like it?" he asks with concern.

"I don't know. I've not had much reason to shop in the past, unless you count Sainsbury's and charity shops."

"Well, you'll like this place. It's a lot better than Sainsbury's."

I wonder what he's buying for himself and then dismiss the

thought. We've got the whole day together. I don't care what he's shopping for.

"You know Sainsbury's?" I ask.

He chuckles. "Of course. I went to university in Durham."

"Really? What did you take? Was university nice?" I stop talking, feeling my cheeks warm. "Sorry," I mutter. "I just have so many *questions*, Teo."

He chuckles. "Ask me anything you want. Let me see if I remember all that long list." He laughs as I pinch him. "Yes, the university was nice. Durham is a beautiful city. I took Business Administration, but I think I really excelled in drinking in the university bar."

"Well, that answers something I've been thinking for ages." He looks at me enquiringly. "Your English is very good, but it's more the fact that you understand little cultural references to do with British TV and such. I've wondered where it came from."

"I came back with that and some excellent friends. You'll like them."

"I'll meet them?" I can't help my surprise.

"Yes," he says, looking at me cautiously. "Of course you will, if they visit. You'll certainly meet my Venetian friends. Do you not want to?"

"Oh no. It's not that at all," I say immediately, and his shoulders relax. "I suppose I just thought I'd be kept separate from your real life."

"My real life is going on right now," he says evenly. "And I think they'll like you."

"Do they meet your usual men?" I ask.

"Of course." For some reason, that depresses me. For a wild second, I'd thought he was stepping outside his standard rules for me. I shake myself and turn to the stereo.

"Let's put some decent music on," I say.

He gives me a sharp look but the sound of 'Big Log' by Robert Plant distracts him. "You like this one?"

"I love it. I listen to it a lot. It's beautiful."

"The song is also older than you."

I smile at him, feeling the wind whip my hair about my face and the song work its usual magic on me. "One of my foster parents loved

Led Zeppelin and Robert Plant. So, I bet my music tastes are a lot older than you'd think."

"Then why have we been listening to Madonna all this time?"

"Because we're gay, Teo," I say patiently. His chuckle warms my stomach.

I sit listening to the tune and watching as he steers the Jeep down the town's roads. Then I jerk. "Shit."

"What?" he asks, concern on his face. "What is it?"

"I forgot something at home."

He pulls the car neatly into a parking spot outside a row of very upmarket shops.

"What is it?" he asks, turning off the engine and turning to me. "Can I help, Wren?"

"My library books."

For a second, he looks like he's forgotten the English language. "Sorry?" he finally says cautiously.

I turn to him. "My library books are due back tomorrow. What am I going to *do*?"

He looks like he's fighting laughter, but he says solemnly, "And this is a disaster, yes?"

"Yes," I say chidingly. "Which you'd know if you'd ever had to pay Southwark Council's late fees."

This time he can't stop the smile, but he brushes back my hair. "Can you renew over the phone?"

I feel relief run through me. "Of course, I can. Why didn't I think of that? If I can borrow your phone, I'll ring Charlie."

"Charlie?"

I know I'm imagining the edge to his voice, so I just nod. "The library manager."

"Ah, the good-looking one."

"You remember that?" I ask, astonished.

"I remember a great deal about you," he says, looking slightly chagrined by the fact.

I grin at him. "Thank you."

"*De nad*a." He shakes his head. "You phoned your temp agency on my phone so easily this morning, but library fines throw you?"

"Well, I won't be bothered if I don't go back to the insurance company, but I definitely want to go back to the library."

"Because of this Charlie?"

"No, Teo. Because of the books."

"You love them so much?"

"I really do," I say fervently. "I've always been able to escape into a book since I was little. They're the best."

"That accounts for a lot," he muses.

"Why?"

"Well, you are well-spoken and use slightly old-fashioned words sometimes. It's because you're very well read." He smiles. "You will love Venice then. My grandfather has his own library. He will love someone who shares his love of reading."

"His own library?" I say wonderingly. "What must that be like?" He raises his eyebrow, and I elaborate. "To actually own your books and not throw them away."

His expression darkens. "You do not own books?"

"No." I hesitate, but I'm always honest with Teo. "It's not a habit that I got into. You see, when you're fostered, you can be moved on at a moment's notice, and when you do, you have one bin bag to store your stuff. Nothing more. It isn't possible to keep your books, so I got used to leaving them behind."

"So, that is the attraction to the library?"

I nod. "Wherever I was, I always joined the library. It's free and warm and full of staff who love books. Where can be better?"

He swallows hard and reaches out, cupping my cheek in his big hand. "I will let you have your attractive librarian, Wren."

"Thank you," I whisper. "But I think he's taken. His boyfriend is a banker and very hot."

He shakes his head, his mood disappearing. He pulls my hair gently. "Come on. I'm going to spend a lot of money."

"What are you buying?" I ask as I get out of the car. I look at the window display of the shop he's heading for. "Ooh, clothes. Are you buying yourself some new clothes, Teo?" I wink at him. "Will you be naked when you try them on? I volunteer to hold the coat hangers."

He shakes his head, holding the door open for me. I love his old-style manners. "Not me. You, Wren."

I stop dead, causing an older man behind me to mutter disapprovingly. I step to one side so he can go in, and I stare at Teo. "For me?" I echo.

He nods, ushering me into the shop. It smells of leather and money, and I cling to the feeling of Teo's hand at my back. The warmth manages to overcome the fact that I manifestly don't belong in this place.

I look around me with big eyes as an assistant comes over. He's slender and dark-haired, and he goes immediately to Teo, correctly identifying him as the one with the wallet big enough to shop here.

"Good morning, sirs," he says in English, giving us both a big smile. "Do you require any assistance?"

"Yes, please," Teo says and nudges me forward. "Wren needs a whole new wardrobe."

"I certainly do *not*," I say, but the salesman's delighted concurrence drowns out my protests.

"We are travelling to Venice to stay for a while, and he will need clothes suitable for the cooler weather there," Teo says briskly, looking around the shop.

"Casual or formal?"

"A mixture of both," Teo says, and they both turn and look at me appraisingly as if I'm a shop dummy they're going to stick in the window. "I think more casual, though," Teo muses. "I can't see you wanting to come to work with me."

"I can't see me wanting to come to Venice with you either," I say through gritted teeth.

The salesman reads the room and bustles off to find work for Teo's credit card.

"Pardon?" Teo says, startled. "What is the matter?" The smile falls from his face, and for a wild moment, I feel a stirring of sympathy for him.

"What did I say about spending money on me?" I whisper.

A couple browsing nearby take one look at my face and steer away quickly, and Teo takes my arm and guides me into a changing room that is the size of my room at home.

"I know you don't want that—"

"I don't want you to spend *anything* on me, Teo." I grip the hair at the back of my neck in a frustrated gesture. "I told you before that we're not about that."

"But this is different," he says earnestly.

"Different how?"

"Because I'm taking you to Venice."

"Is this the same as the suit?" I ask wearily.

"Yes." He grabs my arm, gently pulling me to him. "Yes, it is. Unfortunately, you cannot go to Venice in a swimsuit and skinny jeans," he insists. "My father says that the weather has turned cooler, so you need clothes that are suitable for that, and you have none here."

"I have them at home. I could ship them over." I'm not sure where I'll get the money for that, but I'll do it somehow.

He immediately shakes his head. "Please, Wren. Let me do this for you."

"Why does it matter so much?"

"I don't know, but it does." He spreads his hands in a helpless gesture, and the frustration is written suddenly all over his face. "I just know that I need to do this, and you need to let me."

I stare at him, silence falling. However, he doesn't break. Just continues to gaze at me entreatingly.

"Please, Wren," he says.

"Okay," I finally say. "But I'm buying you something too."

He immediately looks worried. "Oh no. There is no need."

"Oh dear. The shoe appears to be on the other foot," I say sweetly, heading out of the changing room with him hot on my heels.

"But I don't want you to waste your money on me," he protests, stopping as I turn around.

"Exactly, but just as you're having your way regarding my clothes, I'm buying you something too. What do you want?"

"Nothing," he says. He seems utterly confused, and I'd be prepared to bet my year's wages that his other men don't behave like me. I bet they accept everything gratefully. I bet they thank him in one of the fifteen languages they speak, kiss him, and don't make scenes in expensive shops.

I twist around and focus on a glass cabinet. "There," I say. I pull him over. It holds a variety of accessories, but what has caught my eye are the leather bands. They're plain and intricately woven bracelets in a variety of different colours.

"One of those," I say.

He looks strangely at me. "Why those?"

I nod to the assistant, who has rushed over at the scent of a sale. "They're like friendship bands." He looks confused, so I elaborate. "We used to make them at school. They were fabric braided together that we wore around our wrists." I refrain from mentioning that everyone else made one to take home for their mums or dads, whereas I just wore mine on my wrist—a gift from myself to myself. But I suddenly desperately want to give one to Teo.

"Please, could we try that one?" I say, pointing to a golden-coloured leather band. It reminds me of the colour of Teo's eyes. She draws it out, and I take it from her, fastening it around his wrist where it nestles next to his old watch. "Looks good," I say, smiling and looking up to find him watching me rather than the band. "Teo?" I prompt. "What do you think?"

He traces one long finger over it, and for some reason, I remember him doing the same to my cock. I have to shift position. When he looks up, his eyes are dark with emotion.

"I love it," he says, his voice fierce.

"Then you shall have it," I say lightly. I look at the price, and I'm proud of the fact that I don't faint because it's my rent for four months. Instead, I just smile at him. "We'll have that one then," I say cheerfully.

———

Later that evening, I settle in the back of a boat sailing down the river leading into Venice. *Canal*, I remind myself, thinking of what Teo told me. These are canals, and they wind their way through Venice, where cars are banned. It's wildly romantic in a faded-glory sort of way. Huge old buildings loom, decorated in muted colours of beige and rose. Some of them have crumbling brickwork and look in danger of falling into the water. I remember what I read on the plane about how Venice is built on more than a hundred small islands in a lagoon and that the lowering of the surface of the city has contributed to seasonal floods.

I roll my eyes. Oh yes. The plane. We flew here in Teo's company's private plane. It was a definite change from the budget airline I'd taken to Majorca, where they charged me massive fees for being so outrageous as to actually want to take luggage on holiday.

I didn't have much time to discuss it with Teo, though, as another man shared the flight with us. He worked for the company and had been in Majorca on business. He and Teo immediately fell into business discussions, and beyond an apology, Teo had ignored me. I tried not to let it bother me, and instead, I read the guidebook about Venice he'd handed to me, feeling a mixture of excitement and trepidation stir in my stomach like a nest of blackbirds.

I don't feel much better now. The boat we're in belongs to Mateo's family, and it's all gleaming wood and paintwork. The family crest is woven on a bright flag that flaps jauntily from the back.

I look down at the clothes I'm wearing—a pair of grey slim-cut chinos, a white shirt, and a dark grey jumper. I'm glad of the jumper, because, after my time in hot, sunny Majorca, the wind here feels a lot cooler. On my feet are a pair of white Nike trainers. I only had to cast a look at them on the shelf and Teo had immediately thrown them on the pile of clothes he was buying.

It was a salutary lesson in not coveting things because he will immediately buy them for me. My new wardrobe is packed away in a beautiful leather suitcase that he bought for me too. There are jeans and more chinos, T-shirts, jumpers, and even a pure wool black peacoat with a stunning ochre silk lining. *At least I look a bit more like I belong by Mateo's side*, I think and then still. *Is that why he did it?*

The new clothes have bothered me all day, but I'd convinced myself that he just wanted to buy me something. Now another thought occurs to me—was he worried about me embarrassing him? I swallow hard. *Is he ashamed of my appearance?*

I wring my hands together, and my finger brushes the leather strap around my wrist. I look down and touch it. It's made of a supple brown plaited leather, a thinner version of Teo's that suits my slender wrist.

When I'd unpacked the bags at the villa, I found this in a little velvet bag. I'd heard a sound at the door, and when I looked up, I saw Teo's smiling face. I'm not sure why buying me things pleases him, but it was an undeniable fact that he'd been happy at that moment.

"Teo?" I'd said, pulling the band from the bag. He crossed to me, taking it from me and fastening it around my wrist. "Why?" I asked.

He smiled at me. "Because I wanted you to wear my friendship bracelet too. I wanted it more than anything," he'd finished passionately, looking eager and young. "Do you like it?" he asked.

I'd hesitated, but when his face had clouded, I flung my arms around him. "I love it," I said fiercely, and he drew me closer, kissing me and pulling me onto the bed where we made love amongst the clothes.

However, no matter how much I love this bracelet, it means that I'm once again the recipient of his generosity like all his other men. When I bought him his, I had the upper hand because it was new to him.

I push the horrible thought away, retracing the leather before looking at Venice's scenery again.

We pass beautiful buildings and travel under old bridges. Tourists are everywhere, obviously heading out to dinner. Bells ring from a church nearby and are immediately echoed all over the city. It's a beautiful sound, stunning as it mingles with the chug of the boat's motor and the gulls that soar above, calling crossly as if telling us off for not having bread for them.

Teo takes my hand. "Alright?" he shouts over the wind.

He seems different somehow. More focused with a more intense energy than in Majorca. As the week passed there, I'd seen him relaxed and full of lazy smiles, but those smiles have gone now. Instead, he's straight-backed and alert.

"Definitely," I say. My smile seems forced, laced with worry, but Teo doesn't seem to notice. He pats my hand and goes back to watching the scenery drift past. *It's like he's next to me but not.*

"Here we are," Teo exclaims. "Home."

I gape at the three-storey building he's indicating. It's built of stone and marble with light green shutters at the tall windows. The second and third floor are dominated by long balconies with huge arched windows. The red roof tiles glow in the early evening sunshine.

"Wow!" I say. "And this is a palazzo, right?" He nods. "And that means a palace?"

"It does. This one was built in the fifteenth century. The place has been in my family's possession for hundreds of years. Legend says that one of my ancestors won it gambling."

"Blimey. I've played bingo online, but the most I ever got was a ten-pound Amazon card," I say faintly.

He laughs. The boat slows and steers to a stopping place at a jetty. A man stands there waiting.

I look up at the looming mansion, its windows like empty eyes watching me. I shiver. Beautiful and stunning as it is, it doesn't feel welcoming.

I startle as I notice a girl on one of the balconies. Her hair is long and dark, and she leans on the carved stone balustrade staring down at us. I try a smile, but to my shock, she grimaces as if I'm dog shit arriving in the boat and vanishes in a whirl of scarlet fabric and dark hair.

I blow out a breath, becoming aware of Teo standing on the jetty, his hand out. "Wren," he says. "Coming in?"

Am I? I wonder. Something roils in my chest, some premonition that tells me this isn't going to be a happy place for me. I glance at Teo. His eyebrows are raised in confusion, and I make myself take his hand. I jump lightly down to stand next to him.

He issues orders to the man who's been waiting and then turns to me. "Wren, this is Carlo. He has been with the family for many years. He organises the house and us. Carlo, this is Wren. My..." He hesitates. "My friend," he finally says. "He'll be staying with us for the next month."

The man is thin and cadaverous looking, like a skeleton in a uniform. Sparse dark hair clings to the angles of his skull, and his face wears a cool expression. "Of course, sir," he says. The wind gusts around us making me shiver. "I have put your guest in the Blue Room, sir," Carlo says, raising his voice so Teo can hear, but he's turned away to organise our bags.

"Oh please, call me Wren," I say, immediately giving him a smile.

His face freezes in disapproval of the idea. "I have put your guest in the Blue Room, sir," he says again when Teo turns back to us.

Mateo grins. "Oh no. He'll sleep in with me," he says, his words careless.

He doesn't pay attention to Carlo's attitude. He's already looking up at the house, ready to get inside and get on with his life.

But I'm paying attention, and every atom of my body tells me I'm not welcome here. I swallow hard, worry settling in my bones.

CHAPTER TWELVE

Wren

I follow Teo and Carlo into the palazzo, and my mouth promptly falls open. I've never seen anything like this. We're standing in a huge marble-floored foyer with expensive-looking oil paintings hanging on the walls. Someone seems to have a fondness for pictures of their ancestors posing with small pets. It's notable that in some cases the pets are better looking.

A huge, circular, ornate, stained-glass ceiling light throws colours down on us and a marble staircase winds around and up to the two floors above us. Lights shine in ornate sconces on the walls, and elaborate displays of flowers rest on small tables, giving the air a rich scent that mingles with the faint smell of the water outside. I'm pretty sure my eyes are the same size as a stunned cartoon character's.

"My grandfather?" Teo asks Carlo.

"He is at a dinner party tonight, sir. He sends his apologies and says he will see you tomorrow."

Teo turns to me. "I think we'll eat in our room tonight."

I look gratefully at him. If the rest of the place is like the foyer, I'll be fighting an acute case of "I don't belong here" for my entire stay.

Carlo gives a polite cough, and Teo turns to him with his eyebrow raised. "Excuse me, sir, but your father and the family have arranged a dinner for your return. Naturally, they are eager to meet your... guest."

"Dinner," Teo says with such patent dismay that my lip twitches.

"Yes, sir. At seven o'clock if that is convenient?"

Teo looks at me, and although I want to run out of here screaming, I make myself smile. "Sounds good," I say brightly. This is his family, and even though he's grumbled about his father, families are *very* important. I wipe damp palms on my chinos. I'm not sure I'll be what they're expecting given Teo's previous men, but I won't let him down.

Carlo inclines his head and glides away. Teo watches him go, a frown on his face. He turns back to me. "Don't trust him," he says. "He is my father's man."

"Oh, okay," I say nervously. I open my mouth to ask lots of questions, but he's striding away and I hasten to follow him. We climb the stairs and come out onto a long corridor. More ancestors peer down at us from their pictures. Doors stand open, revealing tempting glances of sumptuously decorated rooms. It's a bit like a doll's house I saw in a friend's house once. I'd been allowed over to play, but instead, I'd stood staring as raptly as a peeper at the rooms with their tiny occupants. Then my friend had run his toy car up the roof, and part of it had fallen in, making his sister scream louder than I'd thought was humanly possible. That had been the last time I was allowed to visit, and I hope I don't have such a catastrophic effect on this place.

Finally, Teo stops outside two ornate gilded doors. "Home sweet home," he says with a wry twist to his lips. He throws them open, and I walk into what appears to be an entryway to a suite. On a highly polished wood floor stands a round table with another huge display of flowers. I don't have time to examine the artwork on the walls, as he pushes me gently through another door.

I stand, speechlessly taking in another richly furnished room. It's dominated by the huge arched windows I'd seen from the boat. They lead onto the balcony that runs the length of the room. The walls are high and papered in a coffee-coloured wallpaper. A coffered ceiling is a sea of pure white with an ornately carved border. More old pictures hang on the walls in gold frames. The two huge white sofas should look out of place in such a period room but they somehow fit, and the whole effect is one of wealthy comfort.

I walk over and open the doors, letting in the cool breeze. The balcony looks over the Grand Canal, the water's jade colour a rich contrast to the colours of the old buildings opposite us. Boats zip along the surface with an air of bustling industry.

"I thought this would be your bedroom," I say faintly.

He chuckles. "No. It's my apartment. Well, yours as well at the moment. My father and his wife have another apartment above us, my grandfather has another, and my half-sister has her own suite of rooms in the east wing.

"Wow," I say, walking around the room, touching furniture with a gentle hand, marvelling at the fabric on the sofa and the highly polished wood of the cabinets. "I've never stayed anywhere that has wings."

"Come and look at the rest," he says, holding his hand out to me. I take it gratefully, feeling a little unsettled. I never imagined people lived like this. His hand is warm, and he squeezes mine reassuringly, and some of my apprehension lifts.

I follow him through the rooms. First, there's his study which has a huge desk and leather chair but no books, I notice disapprovingly. Then there's a small kitchen, although our meals will be cooked for us according to Teo. He shows me the phone to ring down to the kitchen.

"It's open twenty-four hours a day," he tells me. "Just ring when you're hungry."

I try to imagine myself doing that, and I just can't, so I follow him silently down a long corridor. The oriental carpet is an expensive antique judging by the faded colours. At the end of the hall, he opens a door and ushers me through.

"Our bedroom," he says.

"Yours," I correct him. "Wow," I say for probably the fiftieth time today. It's another bloody massive room. The walls are papered in an gold coloured paper that looks wonderful against the carved wooden doors. A huge bed is against one wall. It's made up with white linens, lots of pillows and a stunning golden-coloured eiderdown. Whoever lies in that will have a lovely view of the Grand Canal through the tall windows that lead onto another balcony.

"Look up," he says softly.

I do as I'm told and immediately gasp. The ceiling is painted in rich colours. Strange creatures caper over it. They seem to be attending a party and the artistry is astonishing.

"How old is that?" I whisper. A low voice seems appropriate.

"It's fifteenth century. An impoverished artist apparently came to stay for the summer and paid his way with his art. You'll find several more like this in the house."

"Well, at least if your bed partner gets bored, there's something nice to look at," I say pertly.

He roars with laughter, and I turn away to goggle some more. He motions for me to follow him and we walk through a dressing room and into a bathroom painted gold with a green and gold mural running across the walls.

I stand still, looking around.

"What do you think?" Teo says, looking at me as he leans against the sink.

"It's very beautiful," I tell him earnestly.

"It's a little over the top," he says with a shrug. "But I suppose it's just home."

"Only if you're just Louis the Fifteenth."

He grins, his face lighting up, and he reaches out to draw me into him. "You have a worry line right here," he says, poking me gently between my eyes.

"That's because I appear to be staying with King Midas."

"I know my ears are large but they're nowhere near donkey size." He smiles at my chuckle. "It'll be fine. You'll love Venice."

"What about your family?" I ask.

He stiffens slightly. "My relationship with my father and his wife and my half-sister is complicated. But that doesn't mean that they'll be rude to you. On the contrary, they've always been very pleasant to…"

"Your other men?" I say wryly. "You can say it, Teo. I'm aware that you weren't living life as some hot monk."

"I'm approving of the hot bit, but there is no way I would suit a tonsure."

"Your robes would definitely be designer, though. Like a Gregorian Gucci."

He laughs, pulling me close. He hugs me, and I rest my face in his chest, inhaling the scent of lemon and laundry detergent. It's immensely comforting.

A bell rings in the apartment from somewhere, and he steps back from me. "That will be the bags," he says and cups my face, playing his thumb over my lips.

I resist the urge to clutch him tightly and demand more reassurance. I'm not doing that with him. He likes me as a confident, happy person, so that's who he'll get. He doesn't need to be exposed to the darker side of me that doubts myself and just wants someone of my own. So, instead, I kiss his thumb and step back from him.

He studies me for a second and then heads out to answer the door. I trail after him, sneaking more glimpses at the apartment.

When I arrive in the foyer, another man wearing the same livery as Carlo is bringing in our cases. He says something to Teo, who chuckles and claps him on the back. He waves me over.

"Wren, come and meet Luca. He's been coping with my family for twenty years. Hence the grey hairs."

The other man chuckles. He's in his fifties with a cheery grin, and it feels so lovely to be greeted with a smile that it makes me realise how they've been lacking so far.

"Hi," I say, coming up next to Teo, who immediately slings an arm over my shoulder.

Luca watches us with his dark, bright eyes, but most of his attention seems to be on Teo, and he finally nods as if in approval of something. "I'll put these in the dressing room, yes?"

Mateo nods, but then his smile disappears as a woman pushes past Luca and enters the apartment. I stiffen. It's the girl from the balcony—the one who glared so rudely. Up close, she's even more beautiful. Her hair falls in silky waves to her shoulders, and her red dress is obviously very expensive. She has leather sandals on her feet with straps that wind around her slender ankles. Her lipstick and nail polish are the same scarlet as her dress. But what grabs my attention are her eyes. They're the same golden colour as Mateo's, and I realise that this is his sister. *Half-sister*, I remind myself. The distinction seems to matter to Teo.

"Francesca," Teo says. His tone is even, and his face shows no welcome.

"Mateo," she says. Her voice has a beautiful lilt to it. "Welcome home." She looks over at me and offers me a mischievous look. "I came to see the man who has Carlo in such a mood."

Teo's arm tightens on my shoulder as if he's protecting me from something, and I smile cautiously at her. I can't forget the face she pulled at me earlier, no matter how warmly she looks at me now.

Teo smiles down at me and it's a stark contrast to the way he is with her. "Wren, this is Francesca."

"You're Teo's sister?" I ask, opting for discretion.

She chuckles. It's warm and mischievous, and it disarms me a little. "I am for his sins." She looks between us. "It was a surprise to hear about you."

"Francesca," Teo warns.

"In what way?" I ask.

She shrugs but doesn't answer. Instead, she looks at her brother. "There's a family dinner in your honour tonight, brother."

"There's no need," Teo says stiffly. There's no warmth in his eyes as he looks at her. I wonder why. I always wanted a sister or brother. It seemed the height of luckiness when I was little. Well, to be honest, I'd have settled for a mother or father, but siblings would have been a massive bonus.

"Why not?" she asks. "Just be glad they are not killing a fatted cow or whatever biblical thing people used to do when the prodigal son arrived home to retake control."

I look between them. She's still smiling, but it's chilly, and Teo looks bored, a fact that is confirmed when he says in a brisk voice, "Well, if we are expected for dinner, then we must get ready."

She inclines her head gracefully and offers me another slanting smile before vanishing in a cloud of perfume.

Silence falls as Teo looks after her, something working on his face.

"So, that's your sister?" I ask.

"Half-sister," he corrects me.

"Is there a difference?"

He pulls me to him and kisses my forehead. "You have no idea. Now, shall we go and unpack?"

"By all means," I say, wandering along as he strides ahead of me. The cases have been set down in the dressing room, and I settle down on the chaise longue, watching as he opens his case.

"I would have thought you'd have servants to do that. They do in all the Victoria Holt novels I've read."

"What are they?" he asks, his voice full of wry amusement.

I settle back against the chaise. "She wrote gothic bodice rippers full of innocent young women who married rich inscrutable men who usually had mad wives in the attic or some other secret. They always lived in houses full of strange servants. I read them one month while I was supposed to be on the phone to insurance claimants. It took my mind off the customers who wanted to blame the people they'd run over."

He laughs. "Well, I have no mad wife." He removes a pile of shirts and opens one of the doors to reveal a long length of hanging clothes and racks for shoes. "Although I do have several very irritating family members. And as for the servants, my father tends to monopolise them as he doesn't seem to be able even to get dressed without seeking someone's help."

I brighten. "So, there won't be any servants in here?"

"Someone will be up to clean in the morning and take away any laundry and dirty dishes but that's it."

He opens another door, showing me a big linen basket. "Put any laundry in here. It will be cleaned and put back in your closet."

"Wow! It's like we have laundry fairies."

He laughs. His phone rings, but he hesitates before answering.

I nod at the phone. "You need to answer that."

"Do you mind?"

"Why on earth would I?"

He sighs and answers the phone, his face growing darker as he listens to the voice from the other end. When he ends the call, he looks at me apologetically. "I must do some work."

I make myself wave a careless hand, even though I wish he'd stay. He's my safe spot in this big echoing palace. "I know you do," I make myself say. "I'll just put my clothes away if that's okay."

"Of *course*." He opens a door to an empty cupboard. "This is yours."

I glance at the hanging rail and drawers. "Really? Your last bloke must have cleared everything away sharpish."

He looks surprised. "I asked one of the staff to clear this section for you. My men never stayed here." Unaware of the bomb he just dropped, he kisses my nose and vanishes to his study.

I stay still for a long minute, trying to tamp down my excitement. *It still doesn't mean anything*, I remind myself. *Not when I'm leaving in a month.*

When I've settled my stupidity, I set about opening my case and removing the contents, which proves to be a bit of a magical mystery tour for the next hour.

———

A few hours later, I stand on the balcony, looking down at the Grand Canal. It's surprisingly busy. Boats sail up and down it, and the air is filled with the sound of the water and people calling out. It's a bit like being on the side of a big road, and I suppose it is a road of sorts, as cars are banned in Venice. In the distance, rises the massive dome of the church called the Santa Maria della Salute.

It's dark now and lights in the opposite buildings make the occupants appear as if they're on stage. A boat passes, and the tourists take photos of the palazzo. It's weird to think I will be on some stranger's pictures on the other side of the world, and they'll probably think I belong here.

I look down at myself, hoping that I do look like I belong. Mateo wasn't around to ask for advice on clothes. I'd finally decided on skinny black trousers and a black shirt that shows off my tan. Still, when I think about the upcoming meal, the nerves take flight in my stomach like baby birds.

Footsteps sound, and I turn to see Mateo stop in the doorway. He takes in my appearance, and I feel suddenly shy and pull at my collar. "I can't imagine why you're staring at me," I say tartly. "Not with this view to hand."

He comes and stands next to me, looking out for a long moment. Then he turns back to me. "No. That boatload of tourists has nothing on the sight of you dressed like that."

"You like it?" I ask nervously.

"You look wonderful."

I bite my lip. I'm pretty sure now that the clothes he bought me were so that he wasn't embarrassed by me. I'm suddenly resolved that I'm going to leave them behind when I leave.

I've been quiet for too long, so I force myself to smile at him. "You look good," I say. He's wearing navy trousers and a pale blue shirt, and his hair is still wet from the shower he must have taken. I wonder where, because I hadn't seen him after he left for his study.

He grimaces. "It'll do. Are you ready?"

"That tone reminds me of when, in *Jurassic Park*, they enter the area full of grazing dinosaurs."

"Do you remember the little dinosaurs that spat in the man's face and blinded him with poison?" I nod. "They've got nothing on my stepmother."

"Ouch." I start to laugh. "Holy shit, what are we walking into?"

He shakes his head. "Come on, let us get it over with and then we can come back to bed."

I bite my lip and his eyes darken. "That's good," I say huskily. "I had a nice long bath after you left. I'm feeling a lot less... sore."

His eyes flare, heat mingling with amusement. "You are turning into quite the flirt."

"That's what comes from having a bath in front of a floor-length window," I say disapprovingly. "It was very decadent. Haven't you people heard of frosted glass?"

His laughter accompanies us out of the apartment.

As we descend the staircase, I note the place is lit up like we're on the stage. Lights burn in all the rooms.

"I wouldn't like your electricity bill," I say. "This corridor alone is giving me hives."

He guides me through the foyer, a hand at my back. "No, you wouldn't. There are rather a lot of noughts on it." He gestures to an open door. "In there," he says softly. "There will be drinks before dinner. Make plentiful use of them. You'll need the alcohol."

I rub my hands together. "Jesus, this sounds epic. Just so you know, I will be making notes in case I decide to settle down and write the next big bodice ripper."

I walk into the room, and my laughter disappears immediately. Like many other rooms in the house, it has floor-to-ceiling windows that look out over the water. But the space is so big, it's cavernous and, unlike Teo's comfortable furniture, the sofas and chairs here look antique and spindly. I have a mental image of lying splayed over the broken remains of one and immediately resolve to avoid sitting while in this room.

It's a little chilly, and I shiver slightly. His father was right about the weather turning cool. I think of the sunlit place we've been for the last week and have a deep yearning to be back there. It all seemed more straightforward. Easier.

A small group of people turn when we come in. They're gathered in front of a stone fireplace with a huge ornate hood on which is carved a coat of arms. A fire roars in it, and I feel its warmth as we near them.

The group consists of one man and two women, one of whom is Teo's sister. The other woman has white-blonde hair pulled back in a knot. Diamonds glitter at her ears and wrists, and she's wearing a pale blue dress. She gives Mateo a thin smile and an even thinner one for me.

The man with them turns, and I swallow a gasp. It's like seeing how Mateo will look in twenty years. He has Teo's dark hair threaded with attractive strands of silver. It's swept back from a craggy face and his golden eyes are like Teo's and his sister's. I wonder idly if they're all secretly lion shifters and then make a mental note to leave off the shifter romances while I'm here. The gothic atmosphere of the place is bad enough without me adding to it.

"Mateo," he says eagerly, holding his hand out to his son. Teo takes it and is drawn into an embrace. I watch them, fascinated by their dynamic. Teo looks immensely uncomfortable and a little irritable already, while his father looks emotional.

"It's *so* good to see you," he says, loosing Teo only to grab his face. "It's wonderful to see your face again."

"Thank you, Papa," Teo says woodenly and steps back. His father's hand falls away reluctantly.

"Everyone, this is Wren," Teo says, drawing me into the circle. His smile is much warmer when he looks at me, and I hoard it like it's a bag of gold. "Wren, this is my father Alessandro, my stepmother Elena, and you've met my half-sister."

"*Sister,*" his father says reprovingly. "She is your sister, Mateo. I wish you wouldn't introduce her in that manner." His cheeks are flushed, and he looks like he's on the fifth or sixth drink of the evening.

Francesca and Elena give me chilly nods, and his father offers me a dismissive tilt of his lips before turning back to Teo. "So, tell me what you have been doing," he commands, drawing his son nearer, his eyes eating him up.

Teo offers me an apologetic glance, but I nod encouragingly at him. This is his dad. He should spend some time with him.

"Champagne, sir?" A waiter offers me a flute and I accept it with a thank you. I take a sip. It's cold and very dry on my tongue, and I immediately want to spit it out. I resist the impulse and settle for nursing it slowly.

Elena and her daughter are watching me while whispering to each other. Elena's mouth curls as she looks me up and down. I offer them a polite smile and shift awkwardly, unsure what to do with myself. I'd love to go over and get to know them, but their body language is as closed as a door in Pentonville Prison, so I don't think I'll do that. Instead, I wander a few steps away and look at the oil painting on the wall. It seems to depict the downfall of some civilisation accompanied by a lot of blood and one rather enterprising man who is wandering along the bottom of the picture swinging someone's head in his hands rather jauntily.

Teo comes up next to me. I'm aware of his father staring at him with feverish eyes. "Do you like the picture?" Teo asks me.

I lean closer and point at the little man who is swinging the head. "I'm sure one of my foster mothers had a handbag like that. She got it off eBay."

He's taking a sip of his drink, and I'm extremely gratified to see him snort it down his nose. "Shit," he coughs. "That burns." I pat him on the back helpfully and grin at him. His posture relaxes.

I look past him to find his dad watching us. "You and your father have a fu—" I stop myself. "A good relationship, yes?"

He rolls his eyes. "Say what you were going to say. We have a *strange* relationship. He's a very emotional man. He feels everything very deeply and, according to him, is a victim of his own passions." He grimaces, showing what he thinks of that idea.

I wrinkle my nose. "I think he's more of a victim to the sherry, Teo. He's had three glasses since we came in."

He bites his lip to stop himself from laughing, but a snort escapes, and his face is full of humour as he turns back to his family. His father catches his breath and stares at him as if he's never seen him before.

A servant comes into the room and advises us that dinner is ready.

"You go in," Teo's father says to the group, grabbing Teo by the elbow. "I just need a word with my son. Start without us."

Teo raises his eyebrow at me, and I smile reassuringly at him. I will not be a burden he has to look after constantly, so I traipse in after his mother and sister.

The dining room is papered with navy wallpaper, and there are many ornate mirrors on the walls that take the light of the candles dotted about the room and on the table, magnifying it in a dazzling way.

The table is huge and could easily seat sixteen people. It's loaded with candles in silver candlesticks and glassware that twinkles. I take the seat that a man in uniform pulls out for me and look warily at the place setting, which seems to have five hundred knives and forks on it. *Great.* When I look up, Teo's stepmother is watching me, a glint in her eyes that doesn't bode well for me.

I brace myself, but when she speaks, she's very polite. "You are from England, Mr Roberts?"

"Please call me Wren," I say, smiling kindly at her.

She gives me a small smile. "Maybe at a later date," she says, and I flush with embarrassment.

"You have a beautiful home," I say eagerly. "I've never seen anything like it."

"Unsurprising," she says coolly, and I bite my lip. "You are from England?" she prompts.

"Sorry. Yes, I'm from London."

"And how did you meet Mateo?"

"I was on holiday, and he rescued me."

"How interesting," she says.

Luckily, servants enter the room with plates of starters, and I avoid having to tell her the story. I'm not sure she'd find it amusing.

A plate is placed in front of me. The rice dish smells lovely, and my stomach rumbles. Breakfast this morning seems a long time ago. I pick up the outside knife and fork, recalling them doing this in *Downton Abbey*. If it was good enough for the Dowager Countess, then it should be good enough for the Rossi family.

When I look up, Francesca and Elena are watching me, their faces frozen into similar looks of disapproval. I freeze with my fork halfway to my mouth.

"Sorry?" I say.

"We say grace at the table," Elena says in a cool voice.

"Oh god, I'm so sorry," I say, embarrassment flooding every vein in my body. I put my fork down. "How rude of me."

"Not at all." Elena smiles, and it isn't pleasant. "Maybe you would like to do it, Wren?" she says in Italian, putting a horrid emphasis on my name as if it's too common for her mouth to form the word.

"Mama," Francesca says chidingly, but her mother shakes her head.

"I'd like Wren to say grace for us as he's such a man of the world who Mateo has brought home." She rolls her eyes, and Francesca gives a light tinkling laugh that's as cold as ice.

I watch them, anger pulsing through my chest. *How fucking rude are these women. They think I don't understand them.*

I take a deep breath. *Am I going to do this?* I look at their hard faces. *You bet I am.*

"I would love to say grace," I say in perfect Italian. "It would be my pleasure." Then I bow my head and carry on in the language, saying the grace I was taught in the year I spent with an Italian couple.

It had been one of my favourite places to live. She had been motherly and warm and a wonderful cook, and he'd been kind and steady. However, she got pregnant, so they stopped fostering, and I'd been moved on. I say a big silent thank you to them for unknowingly preparing me for the Witches of Palazzowick. When I look up, my cheeks are flushed with anger and Elena and Francesca are staring at me open-mouthed. Then I hear laughter behind me.

When I turn around, I find Mateo and his father. His father's face is full of humour, but Teo is staring at me as if he's never seen me before, and I smile apologetically. What I just did was impossibly rude. However, his father laughs again.

"We should never make assumptions about people," he says to his wife and daughter. "How many times does my father lecture you both on this subject?"

Francesca rolls her eyes, but Elena smiles at me. "I am sorry," she says. "I didn't realise I had lapsed into Italian until you replied. I hope you don't think I was rude."

She was rude then and she's being rude now. Her eyes are cold, and her apology is blatantly insincere. But I mask my nerves and give her a broad smile. "Not at all," I say, sneaking a look at Teo as he sits beside me. *Is he angry with me?*

He pats my leg gently and picks up his fork gesturing at my plate. "Eat," he says. "We've had nothing all day."

But I can't. It tastes like dust in my mouth. My appetite is spoiled for the rest of the meal as I worry whether he's angry with me.

It seems to take forever, but eventually, we make our way up the stairs to his apartment. I pace silently at Teo's side, my stomach twisting with a mixture of anxiety and hunger.

When he closes the door behind me, I spin around to face him. "I'm so sorry," I say immediately. "That was so rude of me."

He bites his lip, and to my amazement, he starts to laugh.

"Teo?" I say, my mouth twitching at the infectious sound as my worry drains away. If he's laughing like this, I can't be in that much trouble.

Finally, he stops laughing, but his eyes are still full of glee when he says in Italian, "Well, you are a surprise wrapped up in astonishment."

"Sorry I was rude," I answer in the same language.

"You were glorious is what you were," he says briskly.

"How?"

"My stepmother's face. I didn't think she could still use her facial muscles to express shock, but I was obviously wrong."

"*Teo,*" I say reprovingly, but he just seizes me in a big hug.

"You weren't rude," he says into my ear.

"I was."

"No, you were standing up for yourself, and I approve. I was worried that they might be a little cool towards you, and I thought you would be sad, but now I am relieved. I know you can stand up for yourself, and that makes me happy." He smiles broadly at me. "How did I not know you spoke Italian?"

"It never came up," I offer.

"How do you speak it anyway? Your accent is perfect."

"A foster parent I lived with for a year. She taught me, and I kept my hand in by listening to Italian audiobooks and speaking Italian with a lady who works with me."

"Was that foster mother nice? You sound as if you liked her."

"She was lovely."

He relaxes and kisses me softly. "Come to bed," he says huskily.

All thoughts slip out of my mind as I follow him through the apartment like he's the pied piper of sex. He topples me to the bed with a lot of laughter that slowly fades as he takes me hard, driving into me with powerful motions of his hips.

Later on, while Teo sleeps, I lie wide awake staring at the bedroom wall where the reflection of the water plays in lazy, undulating movements. I look over at Teo, his words in the foyer ringing in my mind. He'd sounded so pleased that I was okay with his family. I bite my lip. I can't escape the thought that he will be happy if I get on with things and don't bother him.

He's a busy man, and this is his family. Maybe the rudeness at the dinner table was indeed an accident, as his stepmother had insisted, and the rudeness was all in my mind. Everyone will be less tired tomorrow, I tell myself. And then I can actually get to know Teo's family. I hope so. Families fascinate me, and I desperately want his to like me.

The worry remains a knot in my belly, but then Teo stirs, and before I can turn, he wraps his arms around me, bringing me back against him. "Wren?" he says, and I feel his breathing instantly even out. When I crane my head back, I see he's deeply asleep and a smile works its way over my face.

I clasp my fingers over his wrists, holding them tight against me. "And you say you're not a cuddler," I whisper before I finally drift off to sleep.

CHAPTER THIRTEEN

Wren

The first thing I hear when I wake up is gulls arguing viciously over something. I stretch in the warm tumble of sheets, feeling the sore spots on my body with satisfaction. It's odd to be twenty-two and only just finding out what my body is meant for. I slide my hand across the sheets, but my eyes fly open when I encounter cold cotton. I look around blearily. Teo isn't here.

I register the sound of whistling coming from the bathroom just as the door opens and he appears.

"You're awake," he says in surprise. "I thought you'd sleep for a long while this morning."

I sit up, the sheets bunching around my waist. The air is cool on my exposed skin, and I knuckle my eyes. When they clear, they register that he's dressed in a suit. It's dark grey and the cut is impeccable, clinging to those wide shoulders.

My heart sinks. "You're going to work." I can't help the flatness in my voice.

He immediately looks apologetic. "I'm sorry, Wren. I have to go in.

There is a mess in the office I need to deal with." He grimaces. "My father has been in my papers and caused a bit of a problem." He cups my face. His hand is warm, and I smell his lemon cologne. "Do you mind?"

I nestle into his palm for a second and then pull away, giving myself a good talking to as I do. I scrub my hand through my hair. "It's fine, Teo. You've been away for a while."

"I wish it had been a little longer," he says grimly.

I give him a sympathetic smile. He looks tired, and he hasn't even started his day yet. I reach out and grab his tie, pulling him down to me, where I smack a kiss on his nose. "Take it easy," I instruct him. "You can't solve the world's problems in a day. Make sure you have something to eat. You don't eat when you're involved in work."

His expression is hard to read. "How do you know that?"

I poke his shoulder playfully. "I observe, Teo. You should try it sometime."

He grabs me and kisses me, ignoring my loud protests that I have morning breath when he's cleaned his teeth. When he pulls away, he's lying over my naked body with my legs wrapped around him. I chase his mouth drunkenly, my dick hard.

"Shit," he groans, levering off me and falling to his back in the bed, staring at the ceiling. He scrubs at his eyes with his hands, and I notice his cock is tenting his suit trousers. "That was a mistake."

I come up on my elbow next to him. "You started it."

He chuckles and grabs me for another kiss, making it brief before he climbs off the bed. He rearranges himself with a pained grimace. I snort, and he shakes his head.

"You are a tease, Wren Roberts."

"It's only teasing if I won't put out." I pull the sheet back and fist my cock. "I'm ready and willing to do that, Mr Rossi."

"Oh god," he says and throws the covers back over me as I laugh raucously.

When I've finished laughing, he comes down over me, keeping the sheet between us as his hands rest on either side of my face. "You will be alright today, yes?" he asks, his voice anxious.

"Yes," I say firmly, even though my worry is creeping back now that we've stopped playing around. I remind myself that being on my own isn't a big deal. "Teo, don't worry."

"I have put money in your account."

I glare at him. "Which I will *not* spend."

"I want you to," he says forcefully. "I need to know you have money while you look around the city."

"I have money. I have my wages from you, which I have to say again is a wildly over-the-top amount. That'll last me ages."

"Not in Venice. You need a second mortgage for a coffee. Besides, I want you to be able to buy yourself something nice."

"I'm unsure why. I've told you I'm not a shopper, Teo. I'm going to walk around and see the sights. I have that guidebook you gave me on the plane," I say, the idea solidifying into a plan. "I'm going to wander and enjoy myself."

"Maybe I could stay with you," he says, his eyes torn. "I hate that I'm abandoning you on your first day. We were supposed to be together."

"I don't recall that being a plan."

"It was in my head," he explains, and I smile up at him. "I'll tell them I'm not coming in," he says.

At that moment, his phone rings and he groans. "That's Carlo to tell me the launch is ready."

"Then you'd better not keep him waiting," I say lightly. "He strikes me as someone whose dark side is pretty deep."

Teo glances towards the window as he grips my hand tightly, part of him already on that boat ride to his office, but the rest of him still here warm on the bed with me. He drops a kiss on my lips, but it's light and almost distracted.

"I have to go," he says.

I nod. "I know."

I watch him as he grabs a briefcase from the chair. His goodbye is perfunctory, and I'm pretty sure he'll have forgotten me before he gets to the bottom of the stairs. I fall back in the sheets and sigh. The room feels empty without him.

I lie there for a few minutes but then the sound of the gulls and calls from the boats on the canal outside stir my curiosity. I wind a sheet around me and pad over to the tall window, opening it and peering out. It's a little cool, but the sun is shining brightly so that sunbeams skip across the surface of the canal, and boats are making their way up and down it already. Bells ring in the city somewhere, and excitement stirs in me.

I'm in Venice. It hasn't sunk in so far because my attention has been wrapped up in Teo. But now, I let the knowledge fill me. I'm in a fifteenth century palazzo looking down on the Grand Canal, and I have nothing to do today except explore. I smile widely. I'm Wren Roberts. I don't need anyone to enjoy myself, and I'm not going to start now. I'm going to go out and explore this beautiful city, and I'm going to enjoy every minute. Whistling, I head into the bathroom, ready to tackle that complicated shower.

———

I come down the stairs intent on leaving the house before any of Teo's family spots me. I'll grab breakfast out and then explore the city. Unfortunately, my plans are foiled when I hear someone say my name.

I turn cautiously and find Francesca leaning against a door. "Are you going out?" she asks.

"Yes. I'm going to have a walk around," I settle for saying vaguely.

"Well, you must have breakfast first," she exclaims. "Come in and get something to eat. Venice needs a full stomach to explore on. There is a lot to see."

"Oh no," I start to say, but she moves to me, threading her arm through mine and looking up at me with a coaxing expression.

"Please," she says brightly. "I would like to get to know the man who Mateo finds so fascinating."

I follow her slowly. To do anything else would be rude. Besides, against the warnings of my brain, I actually find her very charming. Maybe we can be friends, I think as we walk into a small breakfast room. However, I wish I'd chosen to run away when I see Cruella de Vil sitting at the table. Or Teo's stepmother, to give her the correct title.

"Wren," she says in her cold voice.

"Good morning." I hover for a second, contemplating escape, but I want Teo's family to like me, which they won't do if I run and hide in Venice. So I slide into the seat opposite her. "What a lovely morning," I say cheerfully.

She puts down her slice of toast and dabs her mouth with a napkin.

"I suppose it must seem so when you have nothing to do."

I blink, thrown by the cattiness of the remark. "Yes," I finally settle for saying vaguely.

Francesca slides into the seat next to her mother, giving me a smile that has a whiff of anticipation about it. I give her a bland smile of my own and glance around the room. *Should I help myself from the dishes set on a long sideboard near me or wait to be served?* Ah, the problems of the guests of the super-rich.

A servant arrives and solves my problem. "Coffee or tea, sir?"

"Could I please have a green tea?" I ask timidly. I'm not used to being waited on by someone like this.

I can't help the apologetic tone of my voice, and Francesca giggles, but the man inclines his head. "Of course, sir. I will get you one." He glides back out of the room, and silence falls.

I'm starving because I hardly ate anything last night and the food on the sideboard smells amazing, but I'm damned if I'll ask them what I should do. Instead, I fix my gaze on the room as if I'm going to be pricing up the antiques soon. It's a pretty room with blue and white patterned paper and spindly white antique furniture. The crockery is blue and white and very delicate-looking.

"So, Wren, you are staying here in our home for how long?"

I look at Teo's stepmother with a start. "Oh," I say, hesitating. "I think a month, or at least that's what Teo said."

Her lip curls. "You call him *Teo?*" Francesca laughs, and I flush.

"Yes, it's a bit of a pet name."

"How nice," Elena says in a cold voice that suggests the exact opposite. "Well, I have to say that Mateo is not the first person I would think to appreciate a nickname."

Francesca rolls her eyes. "Snugglebunny," she says, and her mother laughs.

"Honeybunny," she says, her voice skipping icily over the syllables.

I can feel my ears burning. "I think he likes it," I say quietly.

"I suppose it must be a novelty," she says, stopping laughing. "Or maybe *you* are the novelty, Wren."

She says my name with such disdain, but I dig my fingernails into my palms to stop being rude. I can't do that. This is their home, and they are Teo's family.

"I don't know about that," I say softly, accepting my tea from the servant with a murmur of thanks. He looks slightly startled, so I'd imagine manners are in short supply with these two women.

"I do," Elena snaps. "His other men have been so different from you."

"Look at Rocco," Francesca says. "He was *lovely*."

"Ah yes, he owned his own business making luxury yachts," Elena says, smiling at me. "Mateo spent a very happy summer with him. I suppose the shared interests helped."

I swallow hard. I'm trying to think what shared interests Teo and I have, but I'm coming up blank while they're staring at me.

"And then there was Andreas," Elena continues remorselessly. "He owned the computer company that provided services for our hotels. I think I still have a photo of the two of them at the masked ball they attended last year. They were beautiful together." She looks me up and down. "Of course, that was a very *upper*-class function," she says in a sympathetic tone that doesn't contain her glee and her daughter giggles.

I unclench my hands and take a steadying breath. "I'm glad that we understand each other now," I say quietly in Italian. "I am only here for a month, and it may be less. I'm sorry that Teo has foisted me on you. It must seem very rude. I will try to stay out of your way during my visit."

I stand up, throwing my napkin on the table and leaving my tea, and then stride out of the room. My breathing is irregular, and stupid tears fill my eyes. I've been looked at dismissively many times in my life but never like that. Like I was shit on the floor that someone else was going to clear away.

"Wren," Francesca calls.

I duck quickly into the first open door I find. I close it gently

behind me and lean against it, taking a few shuddering breaths. I
knuckle my eyes, and when I've calmed, I open my eyes and gasp. An
old man is sitting in a high-backed leather armchair, watching me
curiously.

"Shit!" I gasp, and his mouth quirks.

"Good morning," he says calmly in perfect English. "You must be
Wren. I am Giovanni, Mateo's grandfather."

I gape at him and then remember my manners. "I am," I say
huskily. "Good morning."

He folds his arms, still watching me with bright, dark eyes. He has
a mane of silver hair swept back from a patrician face. He looks a bit
like the actor Christopher Plummer. "I suppose good might be a slight
misnomer for you, young man. From the looks of you, you have
encountered my daughter-in-law and granddaughter. It is the only
explanation for the look of despair on your face."

"How do you know?" I ask before I can think better of it.

He leans forwards and says in a mischievous voice, "You look as if
you have had a truck run over you before reversing and doing it a few
more times." He winces. "All accompanied by that ridiculous cackling.
They put the Macbeth witches to shame."

I straighten cautiously up from where I'm leaning against the door.
"I am sorry I've disturbed you, sir."

He waves a careless hand. "Not at all. I welcome your visit."

"Not so much a visit as an escape route."

He bursts into laughter that lightens his face, and I suddenly see
Teo in him. It makes me relax a little, and I smile back at him.

"Come in," he urges.

"Am I not interrupting?"

"Only the passage of time from morning to evening. Come and sit.
I do very little at the moment, and I welcome a visit. Let me meet the
young man who has the house in an uproar."

I wince. "Oh, dear. I'm so sorry."

"Why?"

"Well, I think Teo landed me on you all without any warning, and
nobody is pleased about it."

"Wren, when you have stayed here for another couple of days, you will realise that there is very little that makes this family happy."

"That's a bit sad."

"But commonplace here." His eyes sharpen. "You call my grandson Teo?"

I flush. "Sorry. I've been made aware that I shouldn't."

"Why ever not?"

"His other men wouldn't do that."

"Pah! Those other men. Like very appropriate ghosts in Mateo's life. They flit around complying with whatever he wants and then vanishing when he decides that he wants that."

"Teo's mum said they were his robot men."

He laughs loudly. "Ah, Valentina. How is my lovely former daughter-in-law?"

"She's wonderful."

He looks sad. "She always was. I wish the marriage had lasted. She was far better for my son than any of her replacements." He gazes into space for a minute, and I look around the room to give him some privacy. The contents make me gasp. It's high ceilinged and lined with floor-to-ceiling bookcases. Books are stuffed tightly into them and arranged in piles around the room.

"Oh wow!" I say delightedly and turn to find him smiling at me.

"You like books, young Wren?"

"Oh, I *love* them," I say fervently, and his smile widens.

"Then you may borrow whatever you want from them." He bites his lip, looking naughty. "I understand that the Italian will not be a problem for you."

I flush. "I didn't keep it a secret," I say quickly. "It's just that—"

"No one asked," he says sympathetically. "Welcome to the world of the retired pensioner. Good for you for shocking them." He gives a bark of laughter. "I wish I had seen it. My daughter-in-law's face was apparently a picture."

I start to laugh too, and when we've finished, we look at each other in total accord.

"Did you mean it about the books?" I say longingly.

He waves a hand. "Of course. Come in whenever you need. Take a pile. Nothing gives me more pleasure than sharing my books. No one here is interested."

"Not even Teo? He strikes me as being well read."

"Oh, Mateo hasn't allowed himself to relax and read since he came to live here."

"Why?"

"Duty and obligation, child. They make a heavy yoke."

"I'm sorry for that," I say softly. "I honestly think that books have saved me. They're my escape route. Any problems I have—an hour in a book makes them seem not so bad. They're like visiting other worlds." I stop abruptly, feeling embarrassed, but he looks kindly at me.

"Then, despite my family's material wealth, I would say that you are the lucky one, Wren." He waves a hand at the shelves. "Go, have a look. Take what you want. Discover some new worlds, young man."

I wander the shelves, pulling down books as titles strike my interest. There are so many different subjects. There are books on military history that share space with poetry books, while biographies nestle cosily next to crime books.

I pull down a couple of books on the history of Venice, a poetry book, and a crime novel I saw reviewed in the paper.

Teo's grandfather smiles at me when I turn. He's sitting watching me and looks entertained. "You have chosen some?"

"Yes, I'll take them up to my room."

He waves a careless hand. "No need." He rings a bell, and a servant appears, a little stooped old man with grey hair and a face like a raisin. "Antonio will take them for you."

"Oh, thank you but there's no need. I can run up with them," I say but the man shakes his head and takes the books from me.

Teo's grandfather smiles. "Antonio, this is Wren Roberts."

"Ah, the young man who has set the house on its end," he observes, his head cocked to one side.

Teo's grandfather nods. "Exactly. Antonio, I would like you to watch out for him. Elena and Francesca have their claws out, and I want Wren to be comfortable here. He has the potential to be very important, I think."

Antonio looks at me with more interest, and I shuffle. "Oh, I don't think so," I say and then turn red as my stomach gives a thunderous rumble. "Sorry."

Teo's grandfather stands. "Come," he says.

"Where? It's not back in the breakfast room, is it?" I say warily. "I don't think I can deal with aggression on that scale unless it's for One Direction reunion tickets."

He laughs. "No, we'll go out."

Antonio slants a surprised glance at him. "Signore?" he says questioningly. "You are sure?"

He waves a careless hand. "Very sure, Antonio. I think today I shall take young Wren out for breakfast at the restaurant around the corner. That will give him a true taste of Venice. Then I shall take him to the basilica and then on to my book dealer."

"Really?" I say. "Won't that be too much trouble, Signor Rossi?"

His brows come together, and I get a brief flash of the man who sits at the head of this family. One who is not used to being questioned. Then he smiles. "It is Grandfather to you."

Antonio goes still. He's watching Teo's grandfather with an incredulous look on his face, but he says nothing more before quickly leaving the room.

"Well, Wren, do you fancy an old man keeping you company on your first day in Venice?"

"I would like nothing more," I say honestly.

He takes the jacket that Antonio gives him after returning to the library. He shrugs into it and handles a carved walking stick.

"Then let us go. The best pastries will be gone if we do not hurry."

———

The sun is setting when I let myself into Teo's apartment. I toe off my Vans, sighing in relief as my poor abused feet protest. I hang my jacket in the coat cupboard and pad into the lounge only to jump and give a huge shriek as a voice says from the gloom, "Where have you been?"

"Fucking *shit*," I gasp and fumble for the light switch.

The light blares on, and the figure sitting on the sofa hisses and holds up his hand to his eyes. "Wren, good grief."

"Sorry," I say, smiling at Teo, pleasure running through me at the sight of him.

I've become used to seeing him all day, and I've missed him. His suit jacket is off, his shirtsleeves rolled up, showing his corded forearms, and he's clutching a glass full of an amber liquid.

"Why are you sitting in here like you're auditioning for *An Interview with a Vampire?*" I ask with a laugh, flinging myself onto him.

He just manages to rescue his glass, reaching out and putting it on the side table with a clink, and then he wraps his arms around me, burying his head in my neck. He inhales once and then stays there, his breathing uneven.

"Teo," I say worriedly. "Are you okay?"

He pulls back. "I am fine," he says, his voice very accented. "Where have you been?"

"Out with your grandad," I say excitedly, sitting up.

"My *grandfather?*" he asks, astonished. "You went out of the house with him?"

"Yes, we went for breakfast, and I had a chocolate choux pastry filled with more chocolate that was delicious. Your grandfather insisted I drink espresso to offset the sugar, and it was so strong that I'm still buzzing. Then we visited a book dealer who was completely epic, and then he took me to the basilica."

"Oh," he says softly. "I wanted to take you there."

"I'm sorry," I say anxiously. "I didn't know."

"How could you?" He shakes his head and smiles, but there's a thin edge to it. "It's not a problem," he says as if to himself. "So, you have had a good day with my grandfather."

"He's wonderful. So funny and clever. He told me to call him 'Grandfather.'"

"He did *what?*"

"He's lovely. You're very lucky. He's lent me loads of books to read."

"He has lent you his books?" he says in a cautious tone of voice.

"Yes, didn't you hear me? Antonio brought them up. I wonder where they are?" I go to move, and he grabs me.

"No, stay here. Tell me some more of your day and how it is that my grandfather has lent you books."

"You keep saying that. Is there something wrong?"

"Not wrong. Just unusual. He guards those books like they're his sheep."

"Well, maybe he thinks I'm a good shepherd."

He looks at me intently. "I'm beginning to think the same," he finally says enigmatically. He shakes his head as I go to move off his lap. "No, stay there," he commands. "Tell me everything."

I shoot him a doubtful look. "It's a bit of a cuddly position for you."

He smiles wryly. "I shall endeavour to bear it. Now come and hug me."

I do and then pull back. "I almost forgot," I say. "I bought you something."

"You bought me a present?" he says in an astonished voice.

I grin at him as I dig in my pocket. "Don't get too excited," I say, handing him the paper bag. "I saw this and thought of you."

"Didn't you buy something for yourself? That was what the money was for."

"You never specified that. You just said it was for me to spend, and I wanted to spend some on you." I tap the packet. "Open it."

He opens the packet, looking like a small boy for a second and pulls out the object inside. His lip twitches. "You saw this and thought of me?"

I look affectionately down at the lurid little keyring. On it is a gondolier with a rather malevolent look on his face. I touch it, and it immediately spins around so fast that it nearly takes the skin off his finger.

"You have to be quick with it," I advise him as he sucks the offended digit. "It's a fidget spinner keyring."

He bites his lip. "And I have it, why?"

"Because you need a bit of something bright on your keyring. You've only got that boring old silver thing."

"That silver thing is from Tiffany's."

"It's boring," I correct him. "This is great. Just don't tap it when it's in your pocket. It might take off something valuable."

"There is a lot that is valuable in there."

"Alright, Braggy McBraggerson." I grin at him. "Do you like it?"

He examines my face for a long second, his golden eyes intent, and then digs out his keys from his pocket. "I love it," he says, taking off the silver keyring. He tosses it at me carelessly. "Look after that," he advises me.

"Isn't it Tiffany's?"

"Yes, and the day that Tiffany's branch out into gondolier fidget spinners, they can go back on my keyring."

I grin at him as he puts the keyring on. "Don't look at it at night, though. It might give you bad dreams," I say, looking at the evil little face.

Teo snorts and then gathers me close. "Thank you," he says. "Now tell me about your day."

So, I do, and it's very far from my usual dull days at home. I've never had anyone wait for me at home, eager to hear about my day. It's novel and lovely, and it makes me talk and talk.

Eventually, I fall silent, and he kisses my hair. "So, did you see the rest of my family?" he says. "Was everyone nice to you?"

I think about telling him about his stepmother and sister—their disdain and rudeness and the antagonistic edge to their words and actions that have shown me there's plenty more where that came from. Some people need a person to bully. They enjoy it, and the position that I occupy in this house has put me in the ideal position of weakness to make me their target.

Then I remember that these are Teo's family. I don't have one, and I have no desire to damage his relationship with his. I know it's fractured. A blind man could see that. But I don't want to be the crack that breaks it entirely apart.

"Everyone was nice," I finally say softly, realising he's waiting for an answer.

His look of relief is my reward, even though the thought that I've just told him my first lie makes me feel dirty. Unfortunately, I sense it won't be the last.

CHAPTER FOURTEEN

One Week Later

Wren

I'm sitting on the apartment balcony watching the early evening rush hour on the canal when I hear Teo call my name. My heart gives an excited thud, and I call to him. "I'm out here."

I hear the sound of footsteps, and he appears. He looks shattered, lines of tiredness etched into his face by the side of his nose, and his lovely golden eyes are shadowed. I'm not surprised. For the last week, I've hardly seen him. He leaves at five in the morning and usually comes home at ten or eleven. I've missed him desperately, but I've kept my mouth shut. We're not in a relationship, so I can't tell him to come home early. I'm just a guest in his house. He's allowed me to stay here, so I can see Venice, and over the last week that's just what I've done.

"You look so tired," I say, springing up from my chair.

"I thought you were still out. I couldn't see you in the apartment," he grumbles, subsiding into the comfortable wicker chair with the bright red cushions. He does a double take. "Why is your chair tucked on one side of the balcony like this?"

I'd moved the chair so anyone coming into the lounge won't see me. It's my hiding place. And when I say anyone, I'm talking about his sister. She's a little like a cat, and I'm the mouse she's toying with at the moment. I can see now why Teo is so distant from her. She's cruel and bored, and it's a terrible combination.

She'll pop into the apartment and move about, touching things restlessly and telling me all about Teo's men. Then, while she's in full flow, she'll intersperse the commentary with remarks about my youth and unsuitability. It's all done with a charming air of mischief, as if she's confiding in me. At first, I didn't realise her game and spent the second day feeling very shitty. I'm a quick learner, though. Hence, my manoeuvring of the chair position. She can't see me from the apartment door, so I'm safe. I read out here and spend hours watching the life on the water. It's fascinating.

Teo's staring at me and waiting for an answer, so I say chattily, "It's tucked up out of the wind. It's getting cooler."

If he were his usual alert self, he'd spot my lie immediately. As it is, his eyes sharpen a little, but before he can say anything, the screaming starts again.

"What the *fuck?*" he says, sitting up straight as if he's been shot.

I laugh, pulling up the other chair and sitting next to him. I draw my legs up and rest my feet on the balcony and pick up my bag of crisps again. "I know. It's been going on all afternoon with intervals of blessed silence."

I munch on my crisps as he listens to his stepmother screaming through the open doors of the balcony above us.

Her tirade contains many swear words and a poisonous running commentary about his father's apparently diseased manhood. I snort. "I didn't know your dad's penis was ready to drop off. I'll be a lot more careful about walking behind him in future."

He grimaces. "It would do us all an immense favour if that was to happen." He looks at me as the screeching intensifies. "My stepmother is an angel in human form."

I start to laugh. "I have to say how impressed I am. She hasn't repeated one swear word in four hours. That's language a sailor would be proud of."

He rubs his eyes tiredly. "I'm sorry," he says. "I did warn you about my family. This outburst is because she's discovered he's having another affair."

"*No*," I say, leaning forwards. "Really?"

He looks at me, and his mouth tilts upwards. "You seem rather interested."

"Are you kidding? This is like *Dynasty* but without the shoulder pads." I listen to her scream something about how she's going to sever his cock, and I wince. "But with a shit load more family warfare. *Dynasty* had nothing on the Rossi's."

He starts to laugh and then holds out his hand. When I slide mine into his clasp, he squeezes it and pulls me forward for a kiss. His lips are dry, and he tastes of old coffee, but as usual with us, as soon as our lips touch, it kindles a little spark that doesn't take much to grow into a fire.

He might have been tired this week, but he's shown no sign of it in bed where he's fucked me into the mattress every night. He seems to love my body, spending ages kissing and stroking me. I count myself very lucky to have had him as my first lover. Today is no exception. Within seconds I'm in his lap, and he's kissing me furiously, his tongue in my mouth and his nimble fingers stroking the length of my stiff cock in my jeans.

I groan and pull away. He chases my mouth, but I edge back on his lap.

"Where are you going?" he says so sulkily that it's adorable.

I pinch his pouting lip gently, and his eyes light with humour. "No sex until after dinner, Teo."

He cocks his head as his stepmother screams about how she's going to kill his father. Then we jerk in surprise as a load of clothes comes sailing past our balcony, landing in the water below us. "I don't think they will be very congenial dining companions tonight, Wren."

I chuckle and edge off his knees. Once upright, I rearrange myself and glare at him. "Thanks for this."

He sits back and stretches his arms behind his head, giving me a smirk. "Your fault. If it were up to me, I'd be inside you now."

"On a balcony overlooking the Grand Canal? Teo, you're very naughty."

"My balcony," he says arrogantly. "So, I do what I please."

"I somehow think that might have been your yoga mantra for many years." I hold out my hand. "Come on. Get up."

He groans. "Can't I just stay here?"

"Well, we can eat dinner out here and listen to this. It'll be a bit like a television dinner with no visual."

Something shatters above, and he winces. "It is probably a good thing that we have no visual," he mutters. Then he pauses as if registering my words. "Wait. We are eating up here?"

"Yep. I cooked."

"You can cook?"

"You look as surprised as if I said I was a fire eater in the circus."

He eyes me appraisingly. "It is surprising, but I'm not sure why. Of course, you'd be able to cook."

"I'm pretty good. I got the ingredients while I was out today, so you're going to have a nice shower and dress in something you can slouch around in because, after dinner, we're going to snuggle on the sofa and watch something trashy on Netflix."

"You actually cooked for me?" He seems obsessed with the fact. "You don't want to go out for a meal or have the chef send something up?" He still sounds astonished.

"Nope. I actually like cooking."

"The kitchen is tiny up here."

I roll my eyes. "Teo, it's a luxury kitchen. I work with a hot plate and a microwave at home." I frown because he still seems discomposed. "Do you not want to do this?" I ask tentatively. "I just thought it would be nice for you." I wanted to coddle him a little, but I can't say that, and now I'm worried that I've overstepped.

However, he shakes his head and bounds to his feet. He draws me into a tight hug, kissing the top of my head. "No," he says. "I'd rather do this than anything."

"So why the hesitation?" I say into his neck.

He strokes my hair. "Because nobody has ever done this for me. I've never had anyone cook for me, apart from the staff and my mother when I was young."

I pull back to stare up at him. "*Really?* No one? None of your men cooked?"

He shakes his head solemnly. "Never. And I wish people would stop calling them my men. It makes it sound like I'm keeping a harem. I usually restrict myself to one man at a time. Does that make me boring?"

"No, it's sensible considering all the trouble upstairs. Before you'd know it, you'd be entertaining the tourists like your stepmother."

He chuckles. "Well, none of the men I kept company with ever cooked for me, so thank you."

"You're welcome."

A boat passes slowly below, playing Matt Munro's "Days Like These" loudly.

"Ooh. I love this one," I say.

He stares at me. "How do you know such an old song?"

"Your grandfather plays it all the time. The man on the boat is a friend of his and he plays it whenever he passes the palazzo."

As if on cue, we hear a window opening below us and his grandfather's voice sounds out, calling to his friend.

The music drifts over the water and up to us, and before I realise what he's doing, Teo draws me into his arms. He does a neat two-step before launching us into an over-the-top waltz.

"*Teo*," I say, laughing and snorting as he does a very elaborate dip.

"Do the heroes in your romance books do this, Wren?" he says, leaning over me, twirling an imaginary moustache with devilry in his eyes.

"Yes, before they deflower the heroine. They usually get caught and have to marry her. Then she'll either fall down the stairs or catch dysentery, and he'll realise he's in love with her."

He looks down at me, laughing loudly, and then he suddenly stops, and time moves as slowly as treacle. His face is full of some powerful emotion.

"Teo?" I say and then wish I hadn't as his expression clears, and he pulls me back up.

"Thank you for the dance," he says formally, calm once more.

I look at him uncertainly for a second and then dismiss it. "You're very welcome, and luckily for you, I'm not standing near any stairs." I move past him and smack his bum. "Get changed. I'll put the dinner on."

Half an hour later, he appears at the door of the kitchen. "I would come in, but I don't think there's room in here for two."

I look up from where I'm stirring a pot on the small stove. "Snob," I say affectionately. "I'm just about ready to dish up. Go and take a seat."

"Where?"

"The sofa in the lounge."

"We are eating in the *lounge?*"

"Do you have a hearing problem? Yes, the lounge. We're having dinner on our laps."

"Our laps?"

"It's like having a rather attractive parrot," I tell the room.

"Don't think I'm not noting the use of the word *rather.*"

"Don't think I haven't noticed that you're not doing as you're told."

He chuckles. "I'm going." He vanishes and then pops his head back around the door. "Shall I open some wine? What are you serving?"

"*Risotto al nero di seppia.*"

A broad smile crosses his face. "That's my favourite."

"I know. Your granddad told me. I got the recipe from Antonio. I think it's usually a starter, so I upped the ingredients." I poke the rice in the pan. "The squid ink made it black which looked a bit worrying, but it's actually quite nice."

"Antonio gave you his recipe? He must like you. That book is usually sealed tighter than a bank vault."

"He and your grandfather are good fun."

He hesitates and then shrugs. "I'll open the wine."

I edge my way into the living room a few minutes later, carrying a tray. Mateo is sitting staring into the fireplace, where a fire is burning merrily. He stands up quickly, taking the tray from me. He then hovers, looking rather hesitant.

I roll my eyes. "Sit down and put it on your lap. Did you not eat like this when you were at university?"

He settles back on the sofa. "No. We ate out most of the time." He inhales. "This smells delicious," he says eagerly, unrolling his cutlery from the napkin.

"Hope it tastes as good." I disappear to get my own tray and then settle down next to him. "I was going to set up on the balcony," I say. "But it's a little cold."

"And rather noisy," he offers as the screaming starts up again, accompanied by some smashing sounds as a musical accompaniment.

I take a mouthful of my risotto and nod in approval. "Not bad."

"Not bad? It's delicious," he says, forking it up with a lot of enthusiasm.

"Did you eat today?" I ask.

He considers that for a second. "My assistant got me a sandwich. I had a few bites."

"You need to eat."

He smirks. "I find my appetite is affected when I have to tidy up my father's messes."

Another crash comes from upstairs, and I grimace. "I wouldn't like to be cleaning up there tomorrow, although a large part of your father's wardrobe is now at the bottom of the Grand Canal."

He shakes his head. "I will give his staff a bonus."

I smile at him as he passes me a glass of wine from the side table. Then I aim the remote at the TV. "What do you want to watch?"

He looks at the screen displaying the Netflix menu. "I don't think I know any of these programmes," he says hesitantly. "I don't watch a lot of television."

"Then we'll watch the Real Housewives," I say decisively. "It'll make you feel right at home tonight."

"Must we?" he says somewhat desperately. "Surely we have enough with the desperate housewife in the apartment above us?"

"She's nothing on some of these women," I say with relish, starting the first episode.

He grimaces, but as the episode plays, he starts to pay attention. I hide a grin when I see him shake his head.

"That is not fair," he says passionately. "These women are very hypocritical. They've been talking behind her back for the entire episode." I start to laugh, and he closes his eyes. "What have you done to me, Wren?"

"I'm introducing you to new things." He looks a little sad. "What is it?" I ask anxiously.

"It should be the other way around." He takes the tray from me and puts both of them on the coffee table. "Leave it," he says when I make a move to take them into the kitchen. "They will be picked up tomorrow."

"That doesn't seem fair," I say, but he shakes his head, and I subside. "What did you mean?" I ask as he stands and grabs the throw from the back of the sofa. "What are you doing?"

He holds his hand out. "Come on. My turn to do something I've wanted to do since we came here."

"Ooh, is it sexual?"

He winks, and I let him take my hand, leading me out onto the balcony.

"It's a little chilly," I say, shivering. "I can't believe how quickly the weather has turned cold."

"It's nearly autumn, and they're predicting a cold one. You're lucky in a way because it can sometimes be very humid at this time of the year." He puts our wine glasses down on a little table and dropping my hand he moves over to a long cylindrical object next to the chairs. "But we'll be warm enough once this is switched on."

"There's a *heater* out here," I say, outraged as the canvas falls away. "I've been swaddling myself in a duvet all week."

He starts to laugh and then fiddles with it until there's a click, and it starts to glow. "What did you think this was?"

"I don't know—a lamp, a giant dildo. I don't poke my nose into things that aren't my business."

He drags the long chaise out. It's wicker with red cushions, and it's so soft. He sits back on it and then pulls me down, so I lie against him, my back to his front. Then he hands me my glass of wine and kisses my ear. "Now, let's lie and watch the canal. It's fascinating at this time of the night."

I do as he says, watching the boats. Their lamps are lit, and their reflections on the water shatter into a thousand glittery pieces as the boats glide by. Music plays on the air, and the church bells ring the hour.

"It's so magical here," I say softly.

He hugs me. "Tell me what you've been doing over the last week. I'm so sorry that work has consumed me."

"Don't be," I say, craning my head back to look at him. From this angle, I can see his strong jaw and his eyes looking out over the water. "I've been enjoying myself while you work. Doesn't seem fair."

"So, tell me what a day has been like for you?"

"Well, I go out exploring in the morning, visiting the places your grandfather recommends, and then in the afternoon, I visit with him. He's teaching me how to play chess, and we discuss books, and I show him my photos from the morning."

"He told me that he was teaching you chess. He's taken to you."

"You sound surprised."

"I am a bit. It's nothing to do with you. You'd charm the birds out of the trees. It's just that he hasn't been fond of company since my grandmother died."

"He hasn't spoken about her." I look curiously at him. "I've seen the portrait of her in the library, though. She was very beautiful."

"She was that. She was also bossy, hot-tempered and strong-willed, but they loved each other desperately. He resigned from the business when she became ill, and he has never made any moves about coming back. I wish he would. It is not good to sit alone all day."

"I think he wants company again. He's starting to become curious about the world."

"Well, thank you for keeping him company."

"I should thank him. He's very funny and entertaining as long as you do as he says."

He laughs loudly. "I've never heard a better description of him. Maybe that is me too."

I shake my head. "No, you're not like him. I think you have his drive and his determination to do the right thing and the hardness to see it through, but you're softer than he is."

"I think maybe you are the only person in the world who would say that, Wren."

"Maybe they just haven't got to know you," I say, patting him on the arm comfortingly.

A crash sounds from above, and he winces. "That's probably part of my inheritance hitting the wall."

"Will she leave him?"

"I think not. It's not the first affair he's had, and it won't be the last. I used to feel a little sorry for her, but she was his mistress before she became his wife, so she knew his tendencies well. She likes the money and prestige too much to leave. He says he's driven by the heart, but I'd categorise it as poor impulse control and weakness."

"Yes, I suppose you would."

I reckon he lives his life the way he does in direct repudiation of his father's lifestyle. It's why he keeps the men at arm's length. However, it's not my place to say anything, so we listen to his stepmother scream for a bit longer.

"Will she get a lot of money if she goes?" I finally ask.

He kisses the top of my head. "Yes, but nothing else. She signed an ironclad prenuptial agreement. She will have a large sum of money settled on her, and she and her daughter will be comfortable for life, but she cannot touch the business."

"Her daughter? You never say your sister."

"I prefer to forget we are related."

"I'd have been horrified by that statement before I met her," I say idly and then realise my mistake as he stiffens.

"Has she been horrible to you, Wren? She has a nasty tongue and can be spiteful."

"Shh," I say, stroking his arm as he sits up, his face agitated. "No, she's been fine."

Only because I've stayed out of her way, but he doesn't need to know that.

"Let me tell you what I've seen of Venice so far," I say to change the subject.

He acquiesces, holding me close against his body as I describe the beautiful little square I found this morning.

A bell ringing interrupts us, and we both jump, so absorbed were we in the discussion.

"I will get it," he says, standing up and heading into the apartment.

I look out at the night. It's quieter now. Venice at night always seems a little melancholy with the mournful slap of water against the crumbling buildings. As if it's a magical place that is slowly sinking into the water and will vanish soon, never to be seen again by the world.

"Wren." The shout of my name distracts me, and I unravel myself from the blanket and walk into the lounge only to stop dead. Two of the staff are bringing in a huge box and putting it on the floor. Mateo thanks them, and they smile as he slips them some money.

He locks the door after them, and when he comes back, he grins at me, looking young and eager, his eyes shining. "I've been waiting for this," he says excitedly. He gestures at me. "Well, open it then."

"Open what?" I ask.

"The box. It's for you."

"For me? That box is huge. What have you done, Teo?" I groan.

"No." He puts up his hand. "Not with that gloomy, fun-stealing attitude tonight, Wren. I bought these for you, and I have to say it has made me happier than anything I've shopped for in the past."

"First this one, though." He hands me a parcel wrapped in gold paper and tied clumsily with a bow, and I know somehow that he wrapped this. I look up at him, and he smiles. "Well, open it."

I give in and tear open the paper, laughing breathlessly and ripping it apart in my eagerness. I go quiet when the paper falls off, and a box slides out. It's an iPad.

"Teo?" I say uncertainly.

"No," he says in an authoritative voice that makes my balls tingle. "My money, so my decision to give this present to you. I've opened an account with Amazon, and I've downloaded some books onto it already. See that icon." He points to it. "Tap on it." I do and gape as it opens, revealing a multitude of book covers. I scroll down. There must be hundreds of books here.

"Oh my god," I say.

He chuckles. "I downloaded all the top one hundred bestsellers in fiction and non-fiction because I know you love reading those too, and I think you'll enjoy some of the thrillers. Then I downloaded the top one hundred romance titles." He grins. "I must say I've never been so close to so many heaving bosoms." I give a watery sniff, and he winks. "I've also downloaded the top one hundred gay romances. They might be more your speed now."

Before I can say anything, he hands me a silver letter opener. "Open the box now," he urges, sitting in a nearby chair. "I shall watch because I want to see your face."

I kneel by the box, sliding the opener along the packing tape. It parts cleanly, and I open the flaps and go still immediately. "Teo," I breathe.

"Go on," he urges, sitting forward in his eagerness.

I pull out the books, setting them in neat piles on the blue and gold oriental rug. There are children's books—hundreds of them. I see titles of books I once owned and had to leave behind, like the Harry Potter series and all of Rick Riordan's books. They share space with books I haven't seen in years from authors like Barbara Sleigh and Jill Murphy. I pick up a copy of *The Lion, the Witch, and the Wardrobe* and gaze at the familiar cover. I remember a teacher reading this to us in primary school, and I'd fallen deeply in love with the story. I'd had to wait ages for the school library to get me the whole series, but the wait had been worth it.

"Oh my god," I say faintly. I can barely see him through the tears in my eyes, and I scrub at my eyes. "Teo."

"You like them, yes?" he says. "I bought all the children's books I could think of, and then I rang an English bookshop, and they sold me more titles. I've been waiting for them to arrive. They are yours, Wren. I wanted you to have your own physical copies of these books. And when you go home, I shall pay to send them with you, and I have engaged a craftsman to make a special bookcase for you. It will fold into its own packing case so when you move, you can take the books with you. I don't want you ever to leave a book behind again," he says fervently.

A tear slides down my face, and he checks, looking worried. "Have I done the wrong thing?" he asks anxiously.

I choke back a sob, climbing into his lap. "Teo," I say into his neck. "It's the most wonderful thing that anyone has *ever* done for me."

He rocks me, his big hand clutching my neck in a protective embrace. "Well, that is just sad," he says softly. "But while you are here, you can maybe let me look after you a little. It is something that I want to do."

I stare at him, and, in the space of my next breath, I realise that I love him. This man sitting here with tired eyes has been hard at work from morning until night, but he still found time to do something so sweet for me—so alien to everything I've experienced before. How could I not love him? He's wonderful—kind and calm and funny and sexy.

I love you, I think passionately, wishing that the words could come out and that I could say them with every atom of my being.

"Are you okay?" he asks anxiously.

My stomach twists. I might be in love with him, but I am still something temporary for him. He's talking easily about when I go home, while the mere thought of leaving him breaks my heart. I'm someone he can indulge and spoil and then send on his way. And now I know where I'm similar to his other men. We're all disposable.

I realise he's watching me, and I wipe my face. "Thank you," I say.

But I'm not just thanking him for the books. I'm thanking him for showing me how it feels to fall in love, and although the ending won't be like my romance novels, I'm still intensely grateful that I've been gifted Teo for this short time. I will never forget him.

CHAPTER FIFTEEN

Wren

I come awake slowly. I've never been a morning person, and so I snuggle into the covers, enjoying the feeling of soreness in my arse. I stretch my legs out, and my eyes fly open when I encounter a hairy leg and a warm body.

"Teo," I gasp.

He looks over at me. He's propped against the pillows, looking at something on his iPad. His hairy chest is on full view, his skin a lovely olive-brown against the white sheets. His hair is morning messy, and he's wearing a pair of tortoiseshell-framed glasses that are incredibly hot on him. He removes an AirPod from his ear and looks at me quizzically. "You were expecting someone else?"

I laugh. "No. You're just usually either in the shower and getting ready for work or you've already left by the time I wake up."

He winces. "I have been a terrible host."

"Don't be silly," I say sleepily, snuggling up to him. "You have to work."

"Not as if it's going out of fashion." He drops a kiss on my head, and we lie for a while as I enjoy the heat of his big body against mine.

"What are you doing?" I gesture at the iPad. He groans, and I crane my head to look at him. "Teo?"

He bites his lips, his eyes warm and merry. "I was watching another episode of Real Housewives."

I start to laugh. "Oh my god, I've created a monster."

"I would say that is the cast. I've never seen such a lot of harpies."

"Just wait. The first series is a bit tame."

He shakes his head. "Society is going to the devil."

"Can you imagine your stepmother on the programme?"

"She would rule the world, or they'd know pain." He rubs his nose. "Not such a good idea to show my father in full flow though. We would be bankrupt in a few days."

"Is it that bad?" I ask, smoothing my hand over his chest.

"Define bad."

When I groan, he chuckles and says, "Ah, that is a problem for future Mateo. Not today's Mateo."

"What are you talking about?" I look at the clock and sit bolt upright. "It's eight o'clock. Aren't you normally at work by now?"

He lies back, putting his hands behind his head. The position displays the dark tufted hair in his armpits that I find oddly fascinating. It's thick and soft, and I like to bury my nose there after he's showered because it's the essence of him.

"Usually," he says, dragging my attention back to the conversation. "But not today, Wren."

"What's happening today?"

"I am playing hooky, or so I think the expression says." His grin is like a child's. "I'm taking you out for the day."

"*Really?*" My excitement must show on my face because he chuckles.

"Yes, the whole day."

"But won't the entire Rossi empire crumble?"

"Who cares today." He sits up, throwing the covers back and bounding out of bed with his usual energy. "Come on," he calls. "Shower with me. I want to suck your cock."

"Oh. Well then," I say. "Why not?" And I rush to meet him.

———

An hour later, we creep down the stairs. He's dressed in jeans, a white T-shirt, and a navy jumper, and I'm wearing something similar, but my jumper is red. He carries our jackets in one big hand.

I whisper as I follow Teo, "This really is playing hooky. If we get caught by your father, will you have to sit on the naughty step?"

He looks back at me and grins. "I wish. No, we will have to stand for an hour while we are lectured about how I am avoiding family duty and how my first impulse should be to do good for the Rossi name." He rolls his eyes. "As if he didn't cover that with glory by smashing the china cupboard and relating our business across the Grand Canal."

"It was quite entertaining," I admit as we slip out of the palazzo. "I ate my crisps and listened for hours. If you hadn't come back when you did, I was going for popcorn."

The breeze hits us as we leave the building. It's fresh and cool as I lift my face into it, feeling the sun warm on my eyelids. When I open my eyes, Teo is watching me, wearing the same strange expression he had on the balcony last night.

I raise my eyebrow at him. "Okay?"

"Yes, fine," he says quickly. He guides me towards the launch that is waiting, the flag snapping in the breeze.

Teo jumps in, putting out a hand to help me in and then smiles at the driver or captain or whatever they're called. After exchanging greetings with us, he starts the engine, and we ease out onto the water.

The canal is busy this morning. Boats nip by, easing around the big *vaporettos,* or water buses. The sun sparkles, but the wind is cold, and I'm glad Teo told me to bring my jacket.

I ease into his side, and he throws his arm over my shoulder as he looks ahead. His eyes are covered by his sunglasses, as are mine, but I can feel his contentment.

"Where are we going?" I ask.

"Burano."

"Where is that?"

"It is a little island on the lagoon."

"I love that word."

When he gives me a curious look, I explain, "Lagoon. It makes me think of fantastical monsters."

His expression has a softness to it. "If anywhere had that, it would be Venice, and you would be the one to spot it." I look in query at him. "You have a way of seeing magic in the most mundane circumstances."

"It certainly is a magical city," I say, looking back at the city, the spires and domes gleaming in the sun.

"You are enjoying your time here, yes?"

"I am. This summer has turned out to be rather unexpected in all ways."

He hugs me. "I am glad."

We stand there, feeling the wind in our faces, talking idly, and after ten minutes, Teo opens a basket that's been placed on a seat. Inside are two thick mugs and a thermos that he uncaps. Then, gesturing for me to hold up the mugs, he pours coffee into them. After handing him one of the mugs, I inhale the scent and wrap my cold fingers around mine.

He smiles at me and unwraps a linen parcel. Inside it is the *fugassa* that I've come to love. They're little cakes that are flecked with almond icing and they melt in your mouth.

"My favourite," I say.

He chuckles, looking at me indulgently. "I know. Antonio told me. He makes them especially for you." He eyes me. "You have done something to my household."

"Good or bad?"

"How could it be bad when it's you?"

"You have no idea," I say, taking the cake with a thank you and biting into it happily. It's as light as air.

"I think I do," he says calmly, placing his mug on a little shelf before reaching for his own cake. He leans against the side of the boat, looking at me. The wind blows his dark hair about. "You have a softness, Wren, and a real warmth. I felt it the moment I met you, and others respond to it."

I flush under his clear regard. "Thank you," I finally say.

He points a finger at me. "Good. Well done."

"What do you mean?"

"You usually deflect praise. So, it is nice to see you accept it as your due."

"Shut up," I say affectionately and pass him his cup. "Drink your coffee."

He grins, his teeth white in his tanned face. "I will do as I am told," he says meekly. "Now, tell me some more about these errands my grandfather has sent you on. Knowing how bored he is, he could be arranging a political coup. I don't wish for you to take home a prison sentence as your souvenir from this holiday."

I laugh, and we fall into conversation as we watch the island coming closer. I nibble on my breakfast, leaning into him and trying to memorise the warmth of his body against me and his fresh lemony scent so I can take this memory out again and again when I'm back in London and far from him. The thought saddens me, and that's not an emotion that has a place on this day, so I snuggle into him.

"Alright?" he asks.

I nod enthusiastically. "Never better."

He kisses the top of my nose as we stand entwined, and if the day ended now, it would still be the best one I've ever had.

———

Burano proves to be beautiful, and we wander for a while looking into the shops and passing squares where old ladies sit embroidering lace that Teo says the island is famous for. The women chatter, calling to the tourists in shrill voices to come to see their shops. Little houses are set along the canals, and they're the most fantastical colours. I spot reds, yellows, purple, and a bright blue that echoes the colour of the sky this morning. It's busy with locals walking to work and the first tourists decamping from the *vaporettos*.

Teo and I stroll along hand in hand, and I sneak peeks at him every so often. He looks so different this morning, more like the Teo I knew in Majorca. He smiles more, and the lines of stress have vanished from his face.

Just as I'm thinking it, he looks down at me and smiles. "Have I something on my face?"

"Yes. A smile," I say tartly. "I haven't seen it in a while."

He looks puzzled. "Surely that can't be so, Wren. I always smile when I am with you."

I consider that for a startled second and realise he's right. He *does* smile with me. The thought makes me happy and so I immediately divert the subject. "The house colours are so vibrant, Teo. It feels like an artist's community. Free from rules."

He gives me an indulgent nod and goes along with the change in subject. "Not as much as you think. Originally, they were painted so that you could delineate your own house from your neighbours', but legend also says that the fishermen painted their homes so they could see them from the sea."

"That's lovely."

He shrugs. "But nowadays, as with so much else, bureaucracy has taken over. For example, if someone wishes to paint their house, they now have to contact the government, and they will tell them what colour their house may be."

"Not so romantic," I say, wrinkling my nose.

He chuckles. "And probably better for it. Romance is not conducive to a successful life. Rather, it leads the other way. To chaos and mess." He eyes a little cafe next to the canal with bright orange umbrellas looking jaunty and cheerful. "Shall we have coffee?" he asks, steering me towards it. "I know it's at least two hours since you had one of your horrible drinks."

"It's hot chocolate, not raw sewage."

"It is a froufrou drink," he declares and smiles at remembering the phrase.

I look back at a yellow house. "Reminds me of a children's programme called *Balamory*. They had a policeman character on there who scared me shitless. I wonder how many children chose a life of crime as a reaction to him."

He laughs, and I follow him into the café. After he pulls out my chair for me, he slides in opposite me, and while he looks out at the canal and a boat gliding past, I take the opportunity to gaze at him. He's mentioned love and chaos before.

As if sensing my regard, he raises his eyebrows at me, his mouth twisting wryly. "Ask away, Wren."

"How did you know?"

The affection in his expression makes my chest warm. "You are like a tuning fork where there is information to be had. You quiver, and somewhere a little bell rings."

"You make me sound like Tinkerbell. Are you trying to say that I'm a gossipmonger?"

I sit back as he gives the waiter our order. When the man has gone, Teo smiles. "Not at all." His mouth tilts. "Well, maybe a little bit." I laugh, and he taps my hand. "You have a thirst for knowledge. It is a good thing."

"So, tell me why you equate love with chaos. Is it just your father and his relationships?" I'm curiously bold this morning. Maybe because my time here is drawing shorter. A week has already gone by, and where before a month seemed an eternity, now, it seems far too small a time to be with Mateo like this.

The waiter delivers our drinks. Teo takes a sip and makes his happy coffee face. Then he sits back, and I know I'm going to get an answer.

"You have seen my father." He grimaces. "You have heard him."

"He is *loud*," I say reverently.

He chuckles, but there isn't much humour in it. "Elena is his third wife."

"You've mentioned his multiple wives. What happened to his second? Is she locked in an attic somewhere?"

He spreads his arms. "Am I to be allowed to answer just one question before you ask twenty more?"

I seesaw my hand, enjoying the light in his eyes. "Probably not."

"My father met his second wife when he was married to my mother. She was the granddaughter of one of my grandfather's friends and only eighteen at the time. It caused rather a stir in society and is probably why my father was in such a rush to get divorced. He gave my mother everything she asked for, which meant she could keep me on the island until I was of age, simply because he needed to marry the other woman."

"Why the rush?"

"She was pregnant."

"So, you have another brother or sister? You've never mentioned them."

"I have a half-brother who wants nothing to do with my father. He runs his mother's family's company. We see each other at social events and nod."

"*Dynasty*," I say reverently. "Pure *Dynasty*."

"I would not be Crystal, I'm afraid. I am too unforgiving, and her hair never moved."

"You've watched *Dynasty*?" I say, smacking his arm. "All this time, you've been taking the piss out of me, and you actually know the programme. And yes, her hair never moved. It was like magic."

"Or twenty cans of hairspray. Sections of the rainforest wilted as soon as she came on set." I laugh, and he smiles at me. "An old friend from university watched it. Some images sink into your mind, and it's impossible to get rid of them. I probably misplaced a precious piece of knowledge for that *Dynasty* fact. How did you know it anyway? Aren't you a little young?"

I wave a hand. "One of my foster mothers had the old DVDs and watched them all the time. She wanted passionately to be Alexis, but shoulder pads and power suits hadn't come to Bermondsey." I lean forwards eagerly. "So, what happened after he married?"

"My grandfather was very cross with him. He disapproved of the deal my father had struck regarding me, as he felt that the heir to the Rossi business should live with them in Venice where it all started."

"You're the sole heir?"

He nods. "It all goes to the firstborn child. My siblings have already received the first part of their financial settlement and will get another one on my grandfather's death. The will cannot be contested. I'll get the business."

"You don't sound very happy about that."

He shrugs. "Maybe because part of me isn't happy. It is a great burden, but I cannot say that to many people because who has sympathy for a rich man in the world we live in?"

"You're still a person," I say fiercely. "You are allowed to have problems."

"Ah, Wren, but we do not speak of them."

I stroke his arm and smile when he grabs my hand and squeezes it. He's such an affectionate man, quick to touch and hug. "So, your grandfather was unhappy?" I prompt.

"Yes. He insisted that I stayed with them every holiday despite my objections. But it was good that I did. I found that I loved my grandfather, and he spent a lot of time with me, showing me Venice and teaching me the family history. I learnt much about duty and obligation from him, which is good because that lesson was lacking from my father."

"How long was he married to her?"

He considers that for a second. "Ten torturous years," he finally concludes. "And if you think the row was interesting last night, you would have been endlessly entertained throughout their marriage."

"Ouch."

"They argued from morning to night over money, her son's position in the family, her affairs, his affairs. It never stopped. Majorca was an oasis of peace whenever I went home. Finally, she left him for another man, and he tried to kill himself."

I gasp. "*What?*"

He grimaces sadly. "He took tablets, and luckily he was found in time, but even while he recovered, we were treated to an endless emotional rant about how he had lost the love of his life. Then just two weeks after he came out of the hospital, he met and married Elena."

"A two-week courtship explains a lot," I say fervently. "You couldn't hide her true personality for a longer period of time." He laughs, and I squeeze his hand. "I'm sorry about your dad," I say.

His mouth twists as if tasting something bitter. "I don't think he really wanted to die as he'd arranged to be found. At first, I was sympathetic and raced to his bedside. His period of recovery was the longest I had spent with him. But then I saw more and more of who he was. He treats women terribly. He is feckless, arrogant, dramatic, and *weak*." He says that last word with a great deal of emphasis. "He nearly brought the company down with his laziness and his affairs and scandals, and it was only with a lot of side-stepping that my grandfather and I managed to right the ship."

"Is that when you entered the business?"

He nods. "I was called to Venice and expected to pick up his slack. It took me nearly five years to clean up the mess he had made, by which time he was back again making more. It is like the legend of Sisyphus."

"That sounds like something you'd need penicillin for." He laughs and I hesitate. "Maybe you should feel sorry for him," I say tentatively.

"Why?" When I bite my lip, he says, "Go on. I want to know what you think."

"Just because he's dramatic, it doesn't mean that he doesn't feel emotions. I know you don't want to live that way, and I respect that, but you should maybe be a bit gentler with him. He might have wanted to be found, but that doesn't negate the fact he took the tablets in the first place." He seems struck dumb, and I hesitate before going on. "He loves you, Teo. It may be over the top and too emotional for you, but don't doubt the reality of it. He watches you whenever you're in a room together. He never takes his eyes off you."

He sighs. "I know that. I feel it. It's just that..." He seems to struggle for words. "It's just a lot," he finally says. "Like being held in a chokehold until I cannot breathe."

"No one's saying you should run the father-and-son race at school, but it doesn't mean you can't be kind. Be kind and nice, and you can still avoid the excesses."

He looks intently at me for a long second. "You have a wise head, Wren, and you're very down to earth."

"It's the nose. It pulls me towards the ground. It's more powerful than gravity."

He smiles, and we sit in silence for a minute before I stir. "So that's why you don't want love?"

He looks at me sharply. "It is why I will never fall in love, yes. I do not want ever to be as uncontrolled as he is."

My heart sinks. I think of trying to persuade him otherwise. If only I could make him see that loving me would be entirely different from his father's way of loving people. Teo is obviously a very different man from his father, but maybe he's too close to the situation to see that. But I hold my tongue. He never asked for lectures from me, and he's gifted me with his honesty. So, the least I can do is not argue with his life decisions. I sit back, and he looks surprised.

Being Teo, he's astute enough not to question my silence. "Shall we go?" he says, throwing some money down for the drinks. "We have more to do today."

He resists answering my questions and steers me back to the boat waiting for us. I look at the lines of tourists waiting for the *vaporetto*. It's a different world, I think.

"Thank you for bringing me here. Burano was beautiful," I say as our boat sets off again, and I look back at the island. "It has a real community feeling to it."

He shakes his head. "Maybe in the past, but not so much now. The community is dwindling, though, as so many do. The floods get worse every year, and so they are losing the youngsters to the mainland."

"That's sad. A little bit like the small villages in the south of England where Londoners are buying second houses and pushing up the prices so the local people can't afford to live there. Such a shame. I hate to think of families being torn apart."

He leans against the boat's side, watching me. "Family is very important to you, yes?"

"Probably because I haven't had one. I have very rosy-coloured views of them. I dare say, if I'd been brought up in yours, I'd be cynical and world-weary too."

"I am surprised we have not accomplished that in your short time of knowing them." He lifts a hand and strokes the hair back from my face. "I hope you make your own family, Wren, and it's everything that your rose-coloured spectacles expect."

I grab his fingers and kiss them. "I'm sure it will be. Now tell me where we're going next."

"Murano. The island of glass."

"That sounds very exciting."

"Alas, there will be no dragons or men made of glass."

"Well, that's rather disappointing, but I'll endeavour to get over it."

"It's called the island of glass, because in the thirteenth century all the glassmakers of Venice were made to move to Murano and the island became famous for their art. At one point, Murano produced most of the glass in Europe. Aventurine glass was invented there."

"What is that? It sounds like something from *Doctor Who*."

"It's a type of glass that glitters. It can be carved into figurines and beads."

He tells me lively stories all the way to Murano, and I hang on his words. The island proves to be a little different from Burano. The houses are similar in architecture, but while Burano's houses were painted in bright, sunny colours, the colours here are umbers and reds and mustards that make the green water of the canals glow.

It's busy too. People are everywhere, the tourists out in full force, and we squeeze down the narrow paths with the canal on one side and shops on the other. These seem to primarily be selling either glass or jewellery interspersed with little cafés where people sit eating lunch and talking loudly in a variety of languages.

I stop dead by one shop and stare into the window. "Wow!" I say faintly. It's a display of hot-air balloons made entirely from glass. The colours and patterns on the balloons glow in the bright sunlight as the balloons lift upwards to a glass sky and fluffy clouds. "That's so beautiful."

"The artistry on this island is unbelievable," Teo says. He steers me past the shop and down a little alley.

"Where are we going?" I ask as we come out into a square. A table and chairs made of purple-painted iron sit under an old tree from which hang glass ornaments that catch the sun.

"This is the studio of a friend of mine." He points to a set of bright red double doors. "He's famous for his glass. He did a stunning installation in our flagship hotel in Venice. It's a huge octopus that hangs over the foyer. I'll take you to see it before you go, but I thought you might want to see how glass is made here using the old methods."

My heart hurts at the casual way he mentions me leaving, but I say nothing as he steers me through the double doors and into a huge stone-walled workshop.

My eyes flit from one thing to another in a room filled with colourful chaos. Glass tubes of every colour are piled into buckets, and a massive table is covered with tools and plates full of little glass eyes that seem to watch us as we pass them. Shelves are mounted next to the windows on which fantastical glass figures stand, the sun shining through them and leaving colourful stripes over our hands and faces.

Pipes run along the ceiling, dust is everywhere, and the windows are dirt-smeared. However, the shop has a bustling and industrious atmosphere. I'm fascinated and stop to look at a table full of glass flowers of every colour.

A figure leaning over a table straightens up and removes his goggles. "Mateo," he says, rushing forward. I tense as the two men fall into a warm embrace but then I relax as I look at them. This isn't one of Teo's men. If he were, they'd probably be shaking hands or exchanging calling cards or something.

The man steps back, and I see that he's muscular with broad shoulders and messy dark hair shot through with grey. He's very handsome, with a beaky nose and full soft lips, but what most people will see immediately is the scar on his face. It runs from his eyebrow down over his cheek, ending at his sharp jawbone. He was obviously cut very deeply at some point.

Warm brown eyes turn my way, and the stranger smiles. It's wide and white, pulling the scar tight. "This must be the famous Wren," he says, his voice more heavily accented than Teo's.

I bite my lip. "I'm not sure I'm famous, but yes, I'm Wren."

"Not famous?" he exclaims, throwing his arm over Teo's shoulders and pulling him in despite his muffled protests. "But you are living with Mateo in his apartment, yes?"

"Yes, I am. For a little while," I add quickly.

"But this is a miracle. And made even more so because legend tells me that you actually disagree with him occasionally. Unlike his men of the past."

"It's for his own good," I offer.

He gives a big, booming laugh. "Ah, it is good to know that some legends are true." He examines me closely. "You are as I thought," he proclaims, and I warm to him. He has an irrepressible air about him that speaks of mischief and mayhem.

"I'm not sure whether that is good or bad. Teo never lets on."

He looks at me intently and then smiles as if relieved. "Mateo talks of you constantly."

"Does he?" I ask, startled.

Teo groans. "Enough, Enzo. You are giving away all my secrets."

"No, my friend. You have many more." He looks at Teo. "Some of them aren't known to you yet, either."

"As usual, you are enigmatic," Teo proclaims in disgust. He straightens up and dusts off his jacket where Enzo has clutched him. "Always this dust too," he says. "It puffs out of you wherever you go."

Like a scarred dragon with smoke coming off him, I think fancifully to myself, watching them talk. Now that Enzo isn't looking at me, I can detect signs of tiredness in those stunning eyes, and his full mouth pulls down a little as if he's sad.

I become aware that they've stopped talking and are looking at me expectantly. "Eh?" I say intelligently.

Teo rolls his eyes. "Enzo is going to show you how he makes glass, if you would like."

"Ooh, I would," I say excitedly.

"That is good," Enzo says. He shoots Teo a wicked look. "Glass is so fascinating, isn't it, Teo? Sometimes when it is gifted to someone, it reveals more about the giver than the recipient."

"*Enzo,*" Teo warns. "Glass instruction," he orders.

Enzo gives a wry salute. "I hear and obey."

Teo's phone rings and he curses. "I have to take this," he says.

I nod, giving him a smile so he'll know I don't mind. How could I? I have a whole day with him.

I follow Enzo across the workshop to a huge table set back against a wall. It's filled with a clutter of glasses and jars holding pens and tools. He picks up a sheaf of papers.

"Everything starts with a drawing," he says, showing me one of the pages.

I look down at it and gasp. It's a figure of a little knight. His teeth are bared in a ferocious scowl and he brandishes a tiny fist. "That's *beautiful,*" I say.

Enzo shrugs. "It is adequate."

"It's more than adequate. I struggle to draw a stick man."

He chuckles and takes back the page. "I have been commissioned to make a chess set and board for a *very* special customer." Something about that seems to amuse him and I wonder who his customer is. "Most of it is done. I am just making the last of the figures." Teo's voice rises on the other side of the room, and Enzo glances over and frowns. "Trouble?" he asks.

"Who knows?" I'm not prepared to air Teo's business.

Enzo nods approvingly at me. "You are loyal, Wren. I like that in a person."

I look back at Teo who is pacing while he talks on the phone. "He deserves all the loyalty."

He puts the papers down. "He certainly does. It's nice to meet someone who recognises it." He gathers several sticks of jade-coloured glass from a nearby bucket and settles down at the table. He picks up two pairs of dark glasses, and chucks one to me. "Put those on," he commands. "And stand back."

I obey as he pulls on a pair of industrial gloves and picks up one of the glass sticks. Then he flicks the button on something that looks like one of the Bunsen burners we used to have at school. A powerful jet of flame shoots out.

"Wow!" I say, taking another step back.

He grins at me. "Powerful, yes?"

"It certainly is."

He cleans the glass with a cloth and then puts the stick into the flame. He shoots me a quick look. "I have to heat the glass until it softens and then I can fuse the other glass rods to it," he explains. He takes a huge pair of tweezers and begins to sculpt the glass. Within seconds, a pair of little feet appear. He works with quick, deft movements, his gaze intent as he handles the glass. He turns it constantly and soon a body is added to the feet.

"You're quick," I say.

He grins. "I must be so because the glass will cool and fracture otherwise."

"It's so delicate."

"It is indeed. I also have to be careful not to let the glass get too hot or it will melt too much."

"That's a lot of things to think about."

He shrugs. "I have been doing this for many years, so I am used to it." He points to a chair behind me. "Sit down. You can talk to me. It will not distract me."

I flush. "I think I've jumped the gun on that one."

He chuckles, his big hands working gently on the glass as the body gets a neck. "Mateo said you would have a million questions."

"Did he really?" I say darkly. "How helpful of him."

He laughs and stands up, holding the little body. He opens a nearby kiln and puts the figure gently inside. Then he shuts the door and clicks some buttons.

"What are you doing now?" I ask. "That's the first question. Before, I was just talking. My idle chatter exists to lull you into a false sense of security."

He grins at me, the scar pulling the skin tight on his face. "I am baking the glass so it doesn't cool and fracture."

He grabs another glass rod and begins to form a head under the flame. This time he uses a large pin to put in the tiny details of a helmet and wisps of hair.

"So, how long have you known Teo?" I ask.

He shoots me a quick glance and then returns his gaze to his manipulation of the figure's tiny head.

"Many years," he finally answers. I note that he hasn't expressed any surprise at my nickname for Mateo. Everyone else acts as if I've called him bad names. "We met at school when he came to live in Venice. We met on his first day there. I liked him immediately."

"That's easy to do."

A smile crosses his lips. "It is indeed. He has always been memorable. Very sociable and warm and welcoming." He sighs. "Which is why it was a shame to watch his family work on him and dim all that warmth and joy."

"It's still there," I say immediately.

He makes a conciliatory gesture. "Put down your hackles, little Wren. I meant no ill." He opens the kiln and retrieves the glass body. Then he begins to fuse it with the head under the flame. "You are right. It is still there but hidden now under a layer of what I term the

Rossi Tycoon Effect." I chuckle and he smiles at me. "I'm glad you can see him, though. He needs someone to do that."

"Oh well, I'm just a temporary presence," I say quickly.

He shoots me a glance and puts the figure back into the kiln. Then he starts to clear away the mess on the table. "I hope not," he finally says. "I think you might be good for Mateo."

"How do you know that? You've never met me before."

He concentrates on his work. "Ah, but Mateo has mentioned you and sometimes with him you have to listen to what he doesn't say first."

I'm dying to ask what he means, but it'll just get my silly hopes up, so I make myself grin at him instead. "So, what now, Enzo?"

"When the figure is finished firing in the kiln, I will examine it over a polarised light with a magnifying glass and check for stresses in the glass that could cause cracks. It's a good thing to do in life as well." He seems far away for a second, but then shakes himself and comes back to the conversation. "Then this little knight will join his brothers and sisters behind you."

I turn and gasp. A beautiful glass chessboard is set on a table behind me. The chequerboard is made of squares of navy blue and white glass, and on top are the glass figures of bishops and knights and pawns. Half are in the same jade glass that he just fashioned the little knight from, while the others are a violet colour. The set glows in the sunlight.

"Oh my god, that's *gorgeous*."

He pushes the glasses up into his hair. His face is sweaty and a little dirty, but his smile is sweet and also amused for some reason. "Thank you. It is very good you like it."

"Teo's grandfather is teaching me to play chess. He'd love this."

"I think not," he says wryly. "His grandfather is one for tradition and that would not include my glass." He checks. "Wait. His *grandfather* is teaching you?"

I smile at him and go back to looking covetously at the chessboard. I'm dying to touch one of the figures. "He's been very kind."

"He was a recluse the last time Mateo talked of him."

"Ah, but that is the Wren Effect." Teo's voice comes from behind us, and we both turn to see him watching us with a warm look on his face.

"Interesting, yes?" he says to me.

I grin at him. "It's brilliant. Enzo is *so* talented."

"He is that." He claps his friend on the shoulder. "Do you have a moment? Leah has a question about the Palma job."

Teo and Enzo fall into a discussion about an installation he's going to do in Teo's Palma hotel, and I drift around the workshop, looking at things with a curious eye but keeping my fingers to myself.

I'm staring at a beautiful phoenix perched on a cupboard when Teo approaches.

"Have you sorted everything?" I ask as he hoists himself up on a table, sitting and swinging his feet. He looks like a small boy, and I repress my smile.

"Yes, it's all sorted. Enzo will come out and stay with me in Majorca while it's being done."

I sigh wistfully, wishing I could be around then. They're fascinating together. But Enzo is part of Teo's life, and I am not. I notice Enzo has left the workshop. "Where has he gone?"

"To get us some lunch from the restaurant across the street. They do the most delicious *fritole*, and I know you love them."

My mouth waters at the thought of the sweet pastry fritters. "How do you know that?"

"Because you would eat them for every meal," he says patiently.

I laugh. "That's a bit of a giveaway. I could never become an international man of mystery."

"Not with your penchant for opening your mouth, no."

"Ouch," I say, laughing again and drifting closer. He opens his legs and draws me into him, and I put my hands on his thighs, smiling up at him. He looks down at the table, and I notice a small sage green box sitting there.

"What's that?" I ask.

He smiles. "It is for you. Open it."

"Teo," I warn him.

He throws up his hands. "I promise this didn't cost much."

I open the box and pull back the yellow tissue paper. "*Teo*," I breathe.

"Do you like it?" he asks anxiously, but I can't answer him as my throat is full of tears.

It's a small glass figurine of a cuckoo. I pull him from the box, and he sits on my palm. His tail and head are black, and his body is a clear mottled golden colour the same shade as Teo's eyes. The little bird stands with his head cocked, his eyes full of curiosity, and the lines of his tiny body suggesting naughtiness. It's stunning, and the craft that went into giving such a tiny thing a personality is astounding.

"This is for me?" I finally manage to say, my voice hoarse.

He strokes under my eye, and when his finger comes away, it's damp. "It is for you," he says, his voice deep. "I rang Enzo and asked him to make it for you. It's a one-off because he has never made one before, and I have made him promise to make no more." He gives me a smile that seems almost tender. "It's a rarity like you, Wren, and the bird has your graceful lines and the bright eyes you have for everything in the world." He pauses. "Do you like it?" he asks again.

I sniff. "Like it? I *love* it. I'll look after it."

He strokes my hair back from my face. "And maybe when you look at it, you will think of me a little, yes?" His voice is wistful, as if he can't imagine being so important to me.

But I know I'll think of him every day for the rest of my life.

I meet his eyes, and suddenly my feelings are too much for me to hold in. "Teo," I say breathlessly. "Teo, I—"

"Lunch is here," Enzo's voice sounds from behind us.

Teo looks at me anxiously. "What were you going to say?" he asks with an odd note of urgency in his voice. "Wren?"

I bite my lip as I look at him. Perhaps it's for the best. He doesn't need me dumping my feelings all over him. He's never asked for that.

"Oh nothing," I say lightly, stepping back. I put my cuckoo gently back in his bed and pull the tissue paper over him. "Just thank you, I suppose." I look up at him. "Thank you for everything."

He smiles at me, and I'm sure it's my imagination that sees disappointment and bewilderment in the line of his lips.

CHAPTER SIXTEEN

Mateo

I shelter in the cabin of the boat as I look out over the water. The entire city seems to be made of water today. The skies had opened in the morning, pouring rain down on the tourists and never stopping. Tendrils of mist coil over the canals, and I'm pretty sure we'll be gifted with one of the city's famous fogs that shroud everything in mystery. Wren will think it's magic.

My smile is impossible to contain when I think of him, but it's also tinged with a little worry. I have left work much earlier than usual, the thought of him at home drawing me like metal to a magnet. I should be at my desk, not racing across the city to be with him.

I curse under my breath and scrub my hair back. *What is this between us?*

I don't think I know anymore. Our relationship has shifted over the last month and become something nebulous just like the mist outside. When it first started, I was the older man who knew the world and wanted to show it to Wren, the younger man filled with curiosity. Now we have shifted somehow, and I don't know when it happened, but he has become the teacher while I've become the student.

He's wise beyond his years and a born observer, probably because no one in his life seems to have bothered with him.

Something wrenches in my chest. I wish so much for him. I want him to find love and make his own family. I wish him to see the world and all its glories. But at some point, that wish has shifted to include me in those visions.

I open the window, suddenly breathless as I remember yesterday in the glass studio when he'd looked up at me, the little cuckoo on his palm. His eyes had been full of secrets, and I'd wanted him to say the words on the tip of his tongue, but equally, I'd been passionately relieved when we were interrupted, and he'd backed away.

The whole thing has left me feeling like I have indigestion.

My phone ringing distracts me, but I hesitate to answer it when I see Leandro's name on display. He's one of my oldest friends. We played together, and later as young men, we hunted the city like modern day versions of the roistering nobles who made Venice their playground so many years ago.

However, lately, he has made me uneasy. His embraces are too tight, his eyes too avid. With a curse, I click to connect.

"Leandro," I say.

"Hello, stranger," comes his rich, low voice. "Could you send me a picture of you so I might remember what you look like?"

"Ah, it's not like that," I say, laughing in relief. "I have been busy."

"Ah yes. Enzo told me. Who is he?"

"He's Wren," I say simply, his name explaining everything. But the silence on Leandro's end tells me he wants to know more. "I met him in Majorca. He's staying with me while he sees Venice."

"For a *month*? It's not that big a city, Mateo."

"Enzo has been talking."

"He liked him. Said he was funny and a good person."

"He is," I say.

"You're too trusting, Mateo."

"I don't think that's true at all," I say, thinking of my mother's lectures on how cynical I have become.

"So, while you've been at work all day and night, what has this young visitor been doing? I would hope you've had the bedsheets cleaned regularly. There has likely been a lot of traffic through your bed while you've been absent. You know how young men are. Hell, think of what we were like at his age. You never passed up the chance of cock back then."

I'm stunned into silence, feeling as though he's struck me. There's a spiteful edge to his voice that has been there more and more over the years. "I beg your fucking pardon," I finally growl. "Wren is not like that."

There's a short silence, and then he chuckles. "Sorry, sorry," he says breathlessly. "I am looking out for my friend. Of course, he isn't out fucking other men. So, when am I to meet him?"

"Pardon?"

"I'd like to meet him. Enzo said he's going home soon."

My breath catches at the thought, but it's true. Autumn is in the air, and then Wren will go leaving me alone again. *Just the way I like it*, I reassure myself. "Yes, soon," I say, my voice tight.

"Then let me meet him."

"Why are you so interested?"

"Because Enzo says this one is different." His voice is tight. "I want to check you're not getting involved, Mateo. Remember your promise. It's been important enough to you over the years."

"I do remember. I've never broken it. I'm not getting involved."

"Enzo says differently."

"Well, he would. He happens to be the romantic out of the three of us."

He scoffs. "I don't know why. Look at where that has got him."

Worry stirs for my best friend. It's been there since I saw him yesterday. "He looks terrible."

"Hardly surprising after what Vincent did to him. Enzo says he's living at the studio. That's not good for him either. He gets too involved in his art. He needs space and separation from it."

I relax fully because this Leandro is familiar. Of course, he's concerned for Enzo.

"Let us meet," I say impulsively. "I would like you to meet Wren before he goes home."

"How about *Agustin?* It's the club of the moment." When I hesitate, he quickly insists, "Come on. Let's go and show your Wren some Venetian nightlife before he goes back to dull old Britain."

With a sigh, I agree and say a hasty goodbye as the boat pulls up outside my home. I climb out of the boat, greeting Antonio with a wry smile. "There is no need to stand by with an umbrella, Antonio. I will not rust with a little rain, and you will catch a cold in this damp weather."

"I have waited like this every day for the head of the Rossi family, Mateo. At the moment, that is you."

"At the *moment?*" I say humorously, taking the umbrella from him as he is far too short to hold it over me. I hold it over the two of us. "Do you know something I do not?"

He gives one of his enigmatic shrugs. They've always fascinated me. Some days I think they demonstrate he doesn't know everything, but then on other days, I am convinced he is omniscient.

When we get to the lobby, he vanishes without giving me an answer. I have one foot on the stairs and I'm loosening my tie when someone rises from one of the ornate chairs in the foyer. I groan inside when I see my half-sister.

"Mateo," she says, her voice full of its usual lively tone that covers up what a hard witch she is.

I incline my head but don't come down the step to her. "Francesca."

"You are home early. Something drew you here?"

"I was finished," I say stiffly. "I'm unsure why I'm accounting to you for the way I spend my time, when I don't believe you've ever done a day's work yourself."

"Ouch," she says, giving her usual lilting laugh. It's the same chuckle she gave when torturing the dog she had as a child, so it always leaves me wary. I think of the dog and repress a grin. He finally bit her and was taken to live in the kitchen under Antonio's watchful eye. After that, he took to hiding in dark corners and jumping out at her like a canine terrorist and was the recipient of many treats from me. I hope it fucking hurt when he bit her.

I keep my expression blank. Emotions are catnip to Francesca. "Can I help you?" I ask, moving up another couple of steps.

"Oh, are you going to see Wren?"

"More than likely. It's inevitable given that he's staying in my apartment."

"Is he? I hardly know. We never see him."

"Then he is the sensible one," I say, inclining my head to her. "Good afternoon, Francesca."

"You might want to ask where he's been lately, Mateo."

Against my will, I look back. She's leaning against the balustrade, her expression filled with faux innocence.

"What are you talking about?" I say sharply. "Do not try to look like an innocent young woman, *mia cara*. It's many years past you."

Her expression sharpens, becoming hard. "I'm simply saying you might want to enquire what your house guest has been doing while you are at work."

The words echo Leandro's words uncannily, and despite myself, doubt stirs. *Do these two know something I do not?*

She smiles. "When I was out this afternoon, I saw your little Wren talking to another young man. They looked very absorbed in each other." She shrugs. "While the cat is away, the little British mouse will play, Mateo. *Ciao.*"

She vanishes back into the shadows of the house, leaving me standing on the staircase staring after her. After a few seconds, I shake myself and climb the stairs.

When I enter the apartment, at first, I think he isn't here. The place is silent and cloaked in shadows. Then I hear the hiss of the shower and make my way into the bedroom. Wren's clothes have been discarded on the marble floor, and when I bend to touch them, they're soaked through. No wonder he is in the shower.

For a second, the thought occurs to me that maybe he's washing off the scent of another man. Then I shake my head in disgust. He isn't like that, and even if he was, he owes me nothing. He is free to fuck other men. As many as he wants. My gorge rises at the thought, and I rub my forehead. I'm tired, and the thoughts whirl in my head like a cyclone.

I drift over to the soft chair in the corner of the room. It's situated by the window, and I lower myself into it, feeling it cushion my tired body. The balcony doors are open, letting in the scent of the rain, and, with the sound of the shower a comforting hum, I let myself drift.

I'm nearly asleep when he appears at the door. He's naked and rubbing his hair with a towel. Steam rises from his wet body, and when he looks up and sees me, delight fills his face, making my half-formed suspicions fall away.

"Teo," he exclaims. "You're here."

I don't get up, resting my head back on the chair and feeling my body sink into its depths. A smile crosses his face. It's slow and wicked, and he drops the towel to the floor and steps towards me. The sheer curtains billow out in a breeze, and, as he moves through the shadows, he seems magical. Like a legendary merman come to land to lure willing lovers.

I'm fascinated by the change in this young man. When I first met him, he was diffident and a little shy. Now temptation is in every inch of his body.

He is beautiful to me. His hair is a rich brown tangle, longer now and softening the line of his jaw and the beak of his nose. His lips are soft and pink, and his eyes full of slumberous intent. He's still thin, but it gives him a litheness that's as charming as he is. His penis is rising as I watch it—a slender, pale shaft nestled in a cloud of dark hair.

He reaches me and stands at my knee, and when I inhale, I can smell the scent of my shower gel on him. It's curiously erotic, as if I've covered his skin with myself. I trail a finger down his flank. A shiver runs through him in a tiny shudder, like the waves breaking on the shore.

He looks down at me for a long second and then climbs onto my lap, straddling me in a languid, sensual movement. I lift my hand and brush his wet hair back. "Your clothes are wet," I say, my voice shockingly hoarse.

He smiles. "That's because I got stopped in the rain. Someone was asking me for directions. Can you believe it?" He strikes a pose. "I look Venetian, Teo."

"You do." I hesitate, and something urgent compels me to ask. "Who asked you for directions?"

He waves a careless hand. "Some tourist."

"Old or young?"

He gives me a quizzical look, but he's not suspicious of my questions because Wren doesn't know his own worth. He wouldn't be able to conceive that someone would be jealous over him.

Am I jealous? The emotion is ridiculous, but I am indeed jealous of that stranger. Leandro and Francesca's words may have lodged in my head, but I'm responsible for allowing the feelings to flower.

Wren brings me back to the moment, a talent that he's proved very adept at. "He was the same age as me, I guess. He wanted to know where the Doge's Palace was. I did my best to give him directions, but I'm not terribly good at it. He's probably in Rome by now."

His face is so young and honest, and the last doubts drift away, leaving me with a feeling of deep shame. He's the most honest person I've ever met. If he were going to cheat, he would leave me first.

Leave me? As if I own him?

Seeking to escape my thoughts, I bury my fingers in the soft, damp hair at the back of his neck. "Kiss me," I say in a guttural whisper.

His eyes flare. He's still straddling me, so he only has to bend slightly, and his mouth finds mine. His lips are full and soft, and I can taste the toothpaste on his breath. I open to him, sighing as his tongue enters my mouth. His kiss is languid and his hands are gentle when they clasp my face. That, combined with the distant sounds of the rain and the soft breeze, makes it all seem part of a dream. A hazy imagining. Maybe I will wake soon and find that I dreamt him.

Rejecting that thought, I raise my hands and grab his shoulders. They're bony, but the skin is satin smooth, and I drag my fingers over him as he sucks gently on my tongue. Of course, once I've touched him, I need more. With Wren, I'm always consumed with the need for more. Maybe because he will go soon and leave me alone and I'll no longer be able to reach out and touch him whenever I want. I won't hear his contagious chuckle and have conversations that meander more than a garden path.

I clutch him tighter, and he pulls back, smiling sleepily at me. His warm, brown eyes are dark with lust, a flush riding over those high cheekbones. "Teo," he says and the sound of my name on his lips makes feelings course through me that I have no intention of contemplating. Instead, I smile up at him.

"You have me in your power, Wren." I'm shocked at the hoarseness in my voice after just a little light kissing, but I shouldn't be. Wren has the ability to rev my engine better than any of the experienced partners I've had in the past. I lean back into my chair. "So what are you going to do with me?"

His eyes light up, and I want to smile. He has changed since our first time together. He's surer and more confident of himself and his body, his movements imbued with an innate sensuality that was just waiting to come out. I feel curiously honoured to have been the person who introduced him to that.

"Come back." The words startle me, and I look up to find Wren watching me. "You were far away," he says.

I brush my fingers down his face, tracing down the elegant line of his throat and over the smooth lines of his chest. He shudders as I brush his nipple. The tiny copper disc tightens, and he gives a short moan. So, of course I lean in and suckle on one, running my tongue around it and feeling it pebble. He grabs my head and holds me there, panting lightly. We've found to our delight that his nipples are extremely sensitive. Once, I made him come just by suckling on them.

But that's not my goal today, so I keep the suction light. It becomes considerably difficult when Wren starts to grind down on me. His cock is hard, the hood peeled back to display the juicy head like a little plum. Even as I glance at it, a bead of precome pearls on the slit. I reach down and catch it with my thumb, bringing it to my lips and sucking it. I close my eyes for a second to savour the tart taste of him but open them quickly when he levers off my lap.

At first, I think he's changed his mind about sex, but he races to the bedside table and fumbles around in it. When he turns, he holds up a foil wrapper and the lube, a wicked expression on his face.

"Let me see you," he says throatily. "Take your clothes off."

I immediately stand up, shucking my suit jacket and throwing it over the bed before starting on my shirt. He watches me, his eyes dark and his breathing fast. When every last shred of clothing is lying on the floor and I'm naked, I spread my hands.

"Now what?" I ask.

It takes him a second to realise I've spoken, as his eyes are fixed on my cock. I fist it with my left hand and then shudder as a light mist of rain blows over me from the open window.

He raises his head and gives me a sultry smile. "Sit down," he commands.

I hasten to obey, spreading my legs and holding my cock in my hand as I watch him drift towards me. He places the lube and condom on the side table and then lowers himself to sit in my lap but facing away. I gaze at the long line of his spine and the swell of his buttocks.

"Now what?" I ask again hoarsely.

He directs a wicked look over his shoulder before bending over. It's a slow, graceful movement like cream being poured from a jug. My mouth goes dry as he reaches back and pulls at his left cheek, displaying the pink-copper whorl of his hole.

"Now you get me ready," he says huskily.

I run my finger down the bumps of his spine, watching as goose-bumps appear on the silky skin. I grab the lube and coat my fingers. Then I put one finger to his hole, tracing the tiny opening.

He sucks in a breath and leans forward a little, both hands grasping my knees. I'm fascinated by the movement of his ribcage as he breathes. The bones are so delicate under his skin. I'm consumed with the need to throw him down and take him hard, pounding into him and hearing those abandoned little cries he gives. But this is his show, and so I prepare him slowly, one finger at a time until I'm three fingers deep, his hole spread almost obscenely around them. I'm mouthing his back, kissing the skin and breathing harshly.

He sits forward, writhing lewdly on my lap, his head bent low as he utters staccato little cries. I crook one finger, sliding it over his prostate. He arches up immediately, his whole body becoming a straight line in my lap.

"Yes," he groans.

I pulse my finger against the little nub inside him. He reacts as if he's been struck by lightning, grunting and leaning back into me so he can take my fingers more deeply. Then he stiffens and stands, staggering a little.

I steady him with my free hand. "Alright?"

He nods and reaches for the condom. His cheeks are flushed and his eyes dark and mysterious in the dim light. "I'm ready. I want you. Teo."

I lean back, watching as he rips open the foil packet and slides the condom over me. I shudder and tip my head back groaning as he pours lube over my cock and then climbs back into my lap. This time he's facing me, and he wastes no time in kissing me.

He pulls back too soon. "God, I fucking want you," he mutters, kissing a path from my nipple to the line of my jaw. I grab our cocks together and fist them as he undulates his hips, providing friction with sinuous snaps of his hips. He kisses me, greedy and all over me like a storm in the shape of a dark-haired young man. His hands clutch and his teeth are sharp, and then he pulls back and lifts up, using my shoulders for balance. I hold my cock ready, and then we both cry out as he positions himself and slides down in one smooth motion.

I grind my teeth and grunt as he bottoms out. My hands shoot out, stopping him. "Careful," I grit out.

He slaps my hands away. "I'm okay."

He proves it by lifting up until my cock nearly falls out and then shuttling down. My guttural shout acts like a match to accelerant, as he bends to kiss me furiously, eating at my mouth and panting as he sets a steady rhythm until he's bouncing in my lap. The tightness and the heat of him even through the condom are incredible and I grab his hips. It's a hard enough grip to leave bruises but he seems to revel in it, riding me with supple snaps of his narrow hips. I lower my hands, filling my palms with the full globes of his buttocks, helping him to lift and fall.

The wind continues to gust, blowing the curtains back. They're damp with the rain as they drift over our bodies, but the real storm is in this dim room that is filled with the sounds of our cries and groans. I clutch him tight, fucking up into him and bouncing him on my cock. It's the last straw for Wren. He cries out, his head thrown back and his lovely neck exposed as he strains for the end.

"I need..." he pants. "Teo."

"Do it. Come," I shout.

He shudders all over before come spurts from his cock, raining hot spunk over my abdomen and chest. His hole tightens like a fist around my cock, and I give a low, guttural groan as lightning shoots through my body, and I come in pulses, filling the condom. I ride out the orgasm with a few more thrusts, and then slump back into the chair. Thunder rumbles in the distance, and Wren slumps into my arms, his head on my shoulders.

For a long few minutes, we sit in the shadows, our hurried breaths mingling with the sound of the rain and the mournful noise of a boat's horn.

He nestles into me. "Teo," he says throatily. "Oh, Teo." He hugs me so tightly I gasp and tighten my grip on him when he pulls back.

"I *love* you," he says.

The fierceness of the declaration stuns me. It's open and so fucking honest. Just like Wren. And I reel, feeling like he just struck me in the heart. Emotion fills me. Part of me wants to shout to the heavens that he's mine, that he loves me. The other part immediately whispers in my ear, telling me what a fool I will be if I give in to this passion. It reminds me of my father's weakness and my vow to renounce all passionate attachments.

I wait too long. And as the silence grows, Wren pulls away, shuttering his eyes, all the fierce passion disappearing into the air like mist.

"Wren," I say hoarsely, grabbing him before he can walk away. "I... I... thank you," I finally say fervently and incredibly stupidly.

It isn't what I meant to say. I'm not sure what I was going to say, but these words are not good. How can they be when they can't reflect the turbulent feelings he stirs in me, the desire to grab, to hold on tight and never let go of him?

But that's not love. It's dominion over a possession. I've seen enough of it in this fucking family to recognise that.

He smiles, and strangely there is only a little sadness in the curve of his mouth. "It doesn't matter, Teo," he says.

And it's now that I finally see how courageous Wren is as he faces me. "There's no obligation to return that feeling. I wanted you to know, and now you do."

He climbs gracefully from my lap, and I clench my hands into fists to stop myself from holding on. I don't have that right. But watching him walk away from me into the bathroom, I wish passionately that I had said other words—the ones that are still hovering on my lips.

CHAPTER SEVENTEEN

Wren

The evening isn't going well. It should be. We're sitting in a very posh restaurant in a crumbling old palazzo that looks down on a moonlit canal. The food is delicious, and there's a waiting list of months to get in. I've already spotted a chart-topping singer with his entourage, and a very famous actor who's supposedly eating here but instead is nibbling on a woman's neck who isn't his wife.

"Ah, the city of love," Enzo says, following my gaze. He's sitting beside me dressed in black trousers and a black shirt. He'd look handsome, but tiredness is in every line of his body and pulling his face and the scar down, so it looks tight and angry.

I smile at him. "I thought that was Paris."

"How can that be when there is Venice?" he proclaims in incomprehension. A true Venetian.

"I wouldn't know. I've never been there."

"No?" he says, topping up my glass with the very expensive wine we're drinking. We're on the fourth bottle, and I feel faint after seeing the price. I could eat for a couple of months on that money. "Well, Mateo should take you. It's beautiful."

I pick my glass up to take a sip. "It's not like that. I'll be going home soon."

"Really? Why?"

"Because real life is intruding, Enzo. I was only supposed to be staying to see Venice, and I've done that. So, it's time for me to go home."

"Your words are very sensible, but your voice says otherwise, my friend."

I put my glass down. "No matter what my voice says, it is time. I need to go back to my life rather than playing in the fairy-tale castle."

"If the Rossi house is in a fairy tale, a witch would live there."

"Two of them already do."

He laughs, draining his glass. "Ah yes, the Rossi women. They never met a stake they shouldn't have been burnt at."

"Oh, Jesus," I say, coughing as I inhale my wine.

Teo breaks away from his intense conversation with his other friend and looks across the table at me. "Okay?" he says, giving me his wide, warm smile.

"Went down the wrong hole," I say, banging my chest.

"Not a problem that I suppose you've had before," the fourth member and current fly in the ointment of our party, says. *Leandro*. One of Teo's best friends and the reason why this evening isn't going well.

He's stunningly beautiful—tall and slim with longish black hair. His eyes are big and dark in a starkly beautiful face. And he wants Teo. Badly.

I watch as he draws Teo back into the intense conversation they've been having for the last twenty minutes. Teo shoots apologetic glances and keeps trying to draw me into the conversation, but it's utterly useless, as it's about the stock markets. I know about as much about stocks as I do about the inner working of the Italian parliament. Another conversation Leandro and Teo have been having.

I consider introducing the subject of Southwark Library and how I'd once picked up a drag queen's handbag. Marlena Dicktricks had declared me to be the most beautiful twink in all of London. I abandon the idea and gaze idly around the restaurant.

My gaze strays to the couple at the next table. I've been noticing them throughout the meal.

They're married to each other, judging by the gold bands on their fingers and their closeness. They look beautiful together. The older man is tall with shaggy black hair and a mischievous look on his face, while his companion is slight with a sharp face and messy dark hair. Enzo told me that the older man is a very famous retired war journalist, but he hangs on his companion's words, and they've been sharing a lot of laughter. It makes up for the fact that precious little laughter is happening at our table.

"You are fascinated with them?" Enzo asks, once again trying to top up my glass.

I shake my head, and he adds wine only to his own glass. I eye the signs of strain around his eyes.

"They're one of those couples who's impossible to ignore," I finally say.

"Why?"

"They're so obviously together. There's a connection there that's almost visible. I would like that in my life."

He watches his finger tap his wine glass. "Sometimes the connection lies," he says.

For the first time I notice a pale strip of skin on the ring finger of his left hand. He catches my gaze and gives me a sad smile. "Sometimes happy ever after means just for a bit."

"I'm sorry," I say quietly.

He shrugs. "No need."

I look back at Teo and Leandro, their dark heads close together as Leandro draws something on a napkin. Enzo follows my gaze and says, "That means nothing."

"Whether it does or doesn't, it's not exactly anything to do with me." The words feel like crushed glass in my throat.

"You think so?" he asks with evident surprise.

"I know it."

I glance at Teo again, and, as it's done so often in the last day, my impassioned words of love for him come back to me. I remember the horror on his face and the gentle way he'd tried to let me down. But I'm resolved not to feel bad about my admission. I'd said how I felt. Something I always try to do. I want to be honest in my relationships because I've had years of people lying to try and make things better. And I don't blame Teo for not saying it back. It would have been worse if he'd said it, and I'd known he didn't mean it.

Teo's thank you might have stung like a bitch, but it was honest and kind, and that is all I can ever ask of him. Nevertheless, I need to go back to London soon.

As if sensing my gaze, Teo glances up. Once again, his eyes soften and warm, and I want to shout at him not to do that. Not to look at me as if I was precious and special when it's all a lie.

"Have you eaten enough, Wren?" he asks.

I grin at him. "I'm stuffed."

"I bet you are. One reason for you being in Venice," Leandro mutters, shooting me the dismissive look he's been giving me all night, as if I'm so insignificant.

Every time Teo has spoken to me, I've seen the incredulity on Leandro's face. Teo misses the comment because he's summoned the waiter for our bill, but Enzo and I glare at Leandro. Undeterred, he gives me a spiteful sneer.

"Ready for the club?" he says, standing up and holding out Teo's jacket for him. Teo slides his arms into the sleeves, and Leandro brushes the hair back on his collar and says something low that makes Teo laugh.

Leandro shoots me a smug smile but frowns as Teo immediately turns and helps me on with my jacket.

Teo looks down at me intently, the corner of his mouth tipped up. "Are you enjoying yourself?"

No, I think. "Yes," my mouth says. "What a lovely restaurant, Teo."

"Not something you'd be used to, I suppose," Leandro says carelessly.

Teo glares at him. "That was bloody rude, Leandro."

"*Sorry*," he says immediately. "I'm so sorry, Wren. I didn't mean to be rude." Enzo huffs, and Leandro glares at him before turning back to me. "I just meant that there is a very obvious gulf between you and Teo. It must raise its head a lot." He turns to Teo. "You should be more careful," he scolds. "And look after your young man."

I frown at his emphasis on the word young.

"Let's go to the club," Teo says briskly.

––––––––

The club is buzzing. It's set on a side street in Venice and has four floors. Apparently, the top floor has suites for people who really want to make a night of it. A restaurant is on the ground level, and the nightclub is in the basement. On the walk over, Leandro mentioned he was a member of the club and that the waiting list is huge.

I follow as we fight our way through the crowd, forging a path towards what Teo explains are the private rooms. He clutches my hand tight, looking back occasionally to smile at me. Each smile warms me, but I catch Leandro glaring at me.

The private room is huge with sofas dotted around the room. Torches flicker on the wall and candles burn on the tables.

I fall onto one of the squashy sofas, watching as Leandro manoeuvres Teo onto another one, using another of their intense conversations to get him there. The door opens, letting in the heavy beat of the music, and a group of men and women pour in, talking loudly in Italian. They greet the three men enthusiastically, submerging them in hugs and kisses while talking and laughing loudly.

I edge back farther into the corner of the sofa, lifting my legs to avoid being kicked in the shins by the crowd that becomes bigger as more people flood in.

Leandro is suddenly there leaning over me. "Excuse this," he says. "These are all Mateo's friends who haven't seen him in a long time."

I get the feeling that's supposed to be my fault. "That's fine," I say mildly. "I'll be here."

He rolls his eyes. "I'm sure you will cling on as long as you can."

Ah, the gloves are off.

I give him a big smile that I know will irritate him far more than me losing my temper. Angry words are what he wants, and I won't give them to him. Better men and women have tried to manipulate me in the past, and they didn't win either.

As predicted, his expression clouds. "Mateo is well known here," he says sulkily.

"Oh, yes?"

"It is one of the best gay clubs. There is a fantastic room at the back. Mateo and I have been in there many times."

"Lovely."

His look is taunting. "It was. We have always shared men. Mateo does not believe in monogamy."

"Interesting," I say faintly, but I don't conceal my flinch well enough, and he edges closer, coming down on the sofa next to me, his expression pleased.

"Yes, we shared his men many times. No ties. No promises. Just pleasure for pleasure's sake." He winks at me. "Maybe we will share you tonight, Wren. It's an experience you shouldn't pass up."

"It's an experience I'll be happy to pass up," I say steadily. "I'd rather experience heart failure. You and Teo together wouldn't be my scene, I'm afraid."

"Ah, but you are very young."

"You say that as if it's a fault."

"In Mateo's world, it is."

The stark simplicity of his words and the knowledge that it's true strikes me dumb, and he opens his mouth to say more, but Teo comes over to us.

"Wren, you are okay, yes?"

I nod and force a smile that he doesn't seem to see is worn thin. I hadn't realised in the restaurant, but now I can see that he's very drunk. I remember the seemingly endless bottles of wine, so it's hardly surprising. He's swaying slightly, his face flushed. I've never seen him this way, and I feel a little uneasy. I've come to see him as my protector, and now that he's not sober I feel a little like a tiny sheep abandoned amongst a nightclub full of wolves. At the thought of the most prominent wolf, I sneak a look at Leandro. He's ordering a huge round of drinks with a happy expression on his face.

More and more people push into the room. Someone calls to Teo, and he laughs, letting Leandro lead him away. I feel invisible, and I'm happy about that, especially when Teo's sister arrives. She's hanging on the arm of a slim and very pouty young man wearing head-to-toe velvet. Not something easily managed unless you're a toy rabbit.

Her gaze roams around the room and settles like a tractor beam on me. Her stare takes in the fact that I'm sitting alone in the corner and then turns slowly to the centre of the group where Teo is the focus of attention as he holds court, a drink in his hand. Her lips curve happily, and I've abruptly had enough. I'm not sitting here waiting for her to come over and tell me again about what a poor idiot I am.

I struggle out of the clutches of the sofa. One glance tells me it's useless to try and get through the crowd to speak to Teo, and I don't want to be at the centre of this crowd's gazes. I find Enzo standing near the door, talking to a slender blond man. He's beautiful with a very discontented slant to his mouth, and the two of them are arguing not so quietly. I catch the word "divorce" as I near them before Enzo looks up and spots me. He gives me a strained smile.

"Wren, are you alright?"

"I'm going for a walk around the club."

He looks concerned and opens his mouth, but the blond man makes a move as if he's leaving. Enzo's attention abruptly shifts, and he grabs his companion's arm gently to stop him, his attention severed from me as if I don't exist.

I cast a glance over my shoulder. Leandro is looking directly at me. His arm is over Teo's shoulder, and as I watch, he gives him a sideways hug and directs a look of triumph at me. I stick two fingers up at him and have the satisfaction of seeing his mouth drop open before I walk out the door.

The club is even busier than when we came in, the dancefloor packed. I edge to the balustrade and watch for a while, leaning on it and enjoying the feeling of being on my own rather than in a group and completely invisible.

The DJ starts to play "Mi Gente" by J Balvin and Beyonce, and my foot taps as I hear the beat. I love this song, and I adore dancing. I also don't need a partner to enjoy myself. Even as the thought creeps into my head, I'm moving, pushing my way through the dancers until

I'm near the centre and just another anonymous person moving to the beat.

I dance for ages, sometimes with partners, but I brush away any hands that want to touch. I don't mind dancing with someone, but I'm not getting physical with another man while I'm still technically with Teo. My thoughts stray to that back room, and for a second, I wonder whether Teo is there now. He doesn't seem to have noticed that I'm gone, and he's very drunk. The thought wrenches at me. So, I let the music take me away from this Venetian nightclub where I'm nothing and smile my refusals as men try to tempt me towards the back room.

I'm drawn back to harsh reality when someone comes up behind me. The man dances close, shoving his hard cock into my back. I spin around and stop dead in the middle of the floor as I look into Leandro's face.

I shove him, but the dense crowd moves and pushes him back into me. "What the *fuck* are you doing?" I say, outraged.

He grins and wraps his arms around me, letting the movement of the crowd push us together, his cock poking into my stomach. I struggle against his octopus-like grip, but he's bigger than me and easily resists me. You couldn't get a piece of paper between us, and he buries his face in my neck.

"You know you want me," he shouts into my ear. "Let's go and fuck. Mateo says it's fine."

For a second, I believe him. It's not surprising. They're in a club, and apparently, they've done it before many times. I freeze, and he takes the opportunity to grab my arse and grind against me.

I go to shove him away, but in the next second, he's gone. I watch, stunned, as he's thrown across the dancefloor, landing with a thud. Dancers shriek and scatter in all directions, and it's a confusing mess as I'm pushed and shoved. I turn and gasp. Teo is standing there. His hair is a wild mess, his face flushed, and he's dishevelled, his shirt hanging out of his trousers. He's so far from the perfectly put-together man I know that I just stand and gape at him.

His face twists in rage. "Is this why you disappeared?" he shouts in my face.

I flinch as if he's slapped me. I can't speak for a second, and he takes advantage of the silence by shouting some more. Unfortunately, he's lapsed into Italian that's so fast I can't grasp what he's saying beyond the knowledge that he apparently thinks I'm perfectly capable of shagging his best friend.

I'm so hurt that I physically ache. But the hurt flames into anger, and I shove him.

"Not *me*," I shout. "Go fuck yourself and don't lump me with your other men. I was dancing on my own. It was your best friend who decided to come over and get his grind on. Apparently, you do this all the time, and he thought you could double team me the way you've done your other blokes."

"What?" The music dies, and out of the corner of my eye, I see some bouncers approaching. I put my hand up to alert him but it's too late as at that moment, Leandro gets up and staggers over to us, only for Teo to cock his fist back and plant one right in his face. Leandro's eyes roll up and he falls straight back over like a bowling pin.

I'd like to have savoured the sight, but unfortunately, the bouncers descend on us, and I'm caught in a tight hold and marched out of the club with Teo and his twat of a friend. The last thing I see is his sister smirking at me.

"Go fuck yourself, you horrible old bint," I shout at her, and I'm cuffed around the ear by one of the bouncers for my pains. "Ouch," I say, aggrieved. "If you knew her, you'd say exactly the same."

We're flung into the cool night. It's still raining, and the drops are cold on my face, quickly soaking my shirt and running down the back of my neck.

I shake away the feeling when Teo lunges at Leandro, who has his hands up and is saying something in a low voice. I've got a feeling he's blaming me, and I obviously should play the lottery because he raises his volume, confirming my suspicions.

"It was Wren," he shouts. "For fuck's sake, Mateo, think what you're doing. *Ouch!*" he says as Teo shoves him against the brick wall. "He came onto me," he protests, grabbing Teo's shirt, so he falls against him. "And I thought why not. He's nothing after all. Just some boy you picked up, and you'll send away just as quickly."

"Shut your fucking mouth," Teo says in a guttural voice.

The bouncer on the door says something warningly, and I rush towards them. I'm thinking of separating them, which is foolish when they're both much taller than me. But luckily, Enzo appears, grabbing Teo from behind and pulling him back.

"No," he says sharply. "Mateo, think, man. You are being watched out here. There's a journalist over there."

Teo ignores him and snarls at Leandro. "You don't talk about Wren. You don't see him. You don't even *look* at him," he shouts before lurching at him again.

"Fuck off," Leandro shouts, holding his eye that's swelling rapidly. "If you let some little tart come between us, what does that say?"

"It says we are no longer friends," Teo shouts.

I hear the clicking of a camera and groan.

"You would let him come between us?" Leandro stands, seemingly struck dumb. "That little whore."

"Every time," Teo shouts and lunges at him.

Enzo curses and manages to restrain him. "Wren," he shouts. "Come and try to talk some sense into him."

I rush over. "Teo," I say, grabbing his face. His eyes are blind and full of rage, but when he sees me, they gentle immediately.

"Wren," he says as if seeing me for the first time. "You are okay, *cuore mio?*" His hands come up to hold mine. "He didn't hurt you, my Wren?"

"I'm fine," I say. His breath is hot and smells heavily of brandy.

"I'm so sorry for blaming you," he mutters. "It was only for a second and no more."

Enzo makes a pleading sound, and I rally my thoughts. "Please, can we go?" I say, holding Teo's gaze. "I want to go back to the palazzo."

Instantly he nods. "Of course," he says, the ever-present gentleness in his voice almost shocking after his violence.

He looks around as if expecting a fairy-tale carriage to be plucked out of thin air and waiting for him. I roll my eyes. That's probably what he's used to.

Enzo lets him go cautiously but then relaxes as Teo does nothing more than sway on the pavement. "The launch is here," Enzo says to me. "Will you be alright on your own with him? I have to stay here and do some damage limitation. This will be all over tomorrow's papers as it is."

"I'll be fine," I say immediately. "Teo wouldn't hurt me."

"And at some point, it would be lovely if the two of you put your heads together and realised why that is," he mutters. He grabs Teo, guiding him over to the boat. We help him on board; he's docile now, moving when we instruct him. The cold air is sobering him up a little.

When he's sitting on the cushioned bench, Enzo and I heave a sigh of relief. "Well, goodnight, Wren," he says. "It has been an enlightening evening."

"It's been a bloody awful one."

He barks out a laugh. "Sometimes, they reveal the most." He claps me on the shoulder gently. "Are you sure you will be okay?" He says something to the man at the wheel of the boat and then looks back at me. "He will help you at the other end, but hopefully, Mateo will have sobered up by then."

"Of course."

"Goodbye, for now, Wren Roberts." He sketches a slight bow before returning to the club.

The journey home is quiet as Teo leans against the side of the boat with his eyes closed. I sit close, ready for him to vomit or fall overboard, but nothing happens, and he's able to get off the boat himself.

However, his gait is unsteady, and I hover behind him as he makes his way upstairs. When we finally get into our apartment, I sigh with relief. Teo staggers towards the bedroom, shedding his clothes as he goes. I follow behind him, picking the same items up and putting them over my arm, watching him end his progress by falling face-first onto the bed stark naked.

He lies there for a second with his eyes closed and then he groans. "The room is spinning," he grumbles in Italian.

I throw his clothes over the chair and lean over him, stroking his hair.

"I'm sorry," I say.

His eyes come half-open "Why?" he slurs, visibly losing the battle to stay awake.

"It's my fault, Teo."

"It is not," he says firmly but then groans and closes his eyes again. "You did nothing wrong at all. It is *my* fault," he mumbles. "Emotions like this are not good. Not good at all." He shakes his head. "I was like my father tonight."

"What do you mean, Teo?"

"I let emotion cloud my judgement," he says fretfully. "I cannot live like that, Wren. It feels sticky and uncomfortable. I must have balance."

"I'm sorry," I say again, but Teo is sleeping with the suddenness of a child.

I make my way out to the balcony and collapse onto a chair. A mist rises from the water, causing everything to look hazy and nebulous. Even as I sit down, the rain changes to a downpour, making the world beyond the balcony vanish behind a sheet of water.

I look back at Teo's sleeping figure and finally let my hopes die away. They weren't big or grandiose. I just wanted someone who would be my best friend and never abandon me. I wanted it to be Teo because I love him deeply, but that is also why I must leave.

Look at what my love has brought him—brawling outside a club that will likely be splashed over the front pages of gossip magazines. I think of his family's sneers, and I groan. It seems they were right all along.

Even Leandro was right. I am a bauble on Teo's tree, and he feels protective towards me. He will defend me and look after me, but he'll never allow himself to feel passionate love for me—not the way I feel about him.

I feel like a tiny, vulnerable fish moving through a foreign sea with obstacles everywhere. It is time to go home.

I stay sitting on the chair watching Teo. It's not just to make sure he's okay, but also to fasten his sleeping face in my mind so I'll never forget it. I listen to the clock on the wall as it ticks away my time with him. There are only hours and not days left now.

CHAPTER EIGHTEEN

Wren

I'm sitting on the balcony when Teo stirs. I look over and watch as he stretches and makes a pained, displeased sound. Despite myself, I smile a little. It's such a universal hangover sound, and it seems strange on Teo. He sits up, rubbing his eyes. "Wren?" he says immediately, looking around.

"Out here," I say quietly.

He throws the sheets back and gets out of bed, swaying slightly before walking out to me.

"*Mateo*," I gasp. "You're completely starkers."

He waves a dismissive hand. "If someone is taking the time to spy on me, then they will see what they see."

"Which is fine and very laudable if you weren't standing on a balcony in front of thirty thousand tourists."

"Always the exaggeration." He looks at me through red-rimmed eyes. "You are okay?"

"I'm fine," I say steadily. "Why?"

"You are up early, and you look pensive."

I shrug. I only caught an hour or two of sleep. I was too occupied by trying to fix his image in my head. "I was awake early," I say. I grab the throw that sits on the back of my chair and chuck it to him. "Here, put this on before you scandalise someone." I bite my lip. "Not that it's going to be a huge problem this morning."

"Why?" He narrows his eyes in obvious painful thought and then collapses into a chair. "Shit," he says. "I forgot."

I eye him sympathetically. "It's all over the Italian papers, Teo. My Italian isn't brilliant for reading, but the photos and the headlines on Google say a lot."

"But are you okay?" he asks earnestly.

I blink. "Did you hear me? It's all over the press about you brawling with Leandro."

He shakes his head. "You had a bad night. I'm sorry."

Against my will, hope stirs. Surely, he cares for me if this is his first thought. Not his family, not the scandal. Just me. I think of my plans, and for the first time this morning, I waver. I open my mouth to say something, but we both turn as the bedroom door opens and footsteps come towards us.

Teo looks behind me and groans. "Am I not suffering enough with this hangover that I have to talk to *her*?"

I wince when I see his sister. "You're out of luck. She was at the club."

He doesn't have time to answer because she appears on the balcony. "Brother," she says.

"Why are you here in this way, Francesca? Do you no longer knock and ask to be let in?" he demands in sulky tones, and somehow despite smelling of booze and sitting on a balcony naked apart from a blanket, he looks like a king addressing a subject.

I roll my eyes. It must be his secret superpower.

His sister hands him a cardboard cup. "Triple espresso the way you like it," she says. "I popped out to the little cafe on the corner for you."

He takes it warily but gives a pleased sound when he sips it. I can almost see life flowing back into his veins. Italians and their coffee. Finally, he puts it down and looks at his sister, who has arranged herself prettily against the balustrade. "Why?" he says. "And don't say it's because you are kind because no one would ever believe that."

I snort, and he looks to me with a smile, completely missing the poisonous glare his sister gives me.

She drags his attention back to her, by saying, "I thought you might need a bit of extra stimulus this morning, especially considering what's in your diary."

He looks blank for a second, and then horrified realisation dawns. "*Shit,*" he shouts, standing up and nearly losing his grip on the blanket. "Shit, shit, shit."

"What?" I ask.

"It's the board meeting this morning. How the fuck could I forget that?"

"Seven bottles of wine and countless mojitos," I offer, but he's already striding quickly into the bathroom and slamming the door behind him.

Francesca drifts over to sit on his vacated chair.

"What do you want?" I say wearily.

"Just to talk." Her voice is sweet and low. "You have seen the papers, yes?" I nod, and she leans forward, her attention solely on me. "You must see it is time to go, Wren. This—" She waves her hands. "—this farce will ruin him. Our father cannot have this strain. He..."

"I know about your father," I say.

"Mateo *told* you?" She watches me for a second, biting her lip. "This is no good for him or the family business, Wren. Falling out of clubs and fighting. It is not the behaviour of the future chairman of the Rossi empire. It cannot happen."

"I know," I say softly, feeling those earlier little hopes die away.

I'm not stupid. I know she has her own agenda, but everything she says echoes my thoughts from the night. By being here locked in this strange relationship we've fallen into, I'm hurting Teo. It's damaging his equilibrium and his stated aim of living his life calmly, and I don't want that. I don't want Teo damaged by his association with me because being with him, despite the end, has been wonderful for me. It's opened a new world, not of money but late-night soft talks in bed, laughter and attention, companionship.

And although the door will shut soon, I don't want him hurt one single bit. "I'm going," I say.

Triumph flares in her eyes, but she shutters her expression as Teo emerges from his dressing room clad in a dark suit with a white shirt and blue tie. His hair is wet and brushed back off his forehead, but it's already curling at the ends.

"I'll go," his sister says and leaves.

My whole attention is on Teo as he leans over me. I inhale the scent of his lemon cologne for the last time and smile at him. It takes more effort than I'd like, and Teo must sense it because his expression turns worried.

"You are alright, Wren?"

"I'm fine," I say steadily.

He brushes my hair back. It's far too long now. "I am sorry for last night," he says. "For my behaviour and Leandro. Did he hurt you?"

"Of course not."

His lip twists. "I think you would not tell me otherwise. Well, you will not see him again. He's dead to me."

"And that's the problem. You shouldn't lose your friends over me."

"*Why?*" he says incredulously. His phone rings, and he inhales sharply. "Shit," he says. "I have to take this."

I nod and watch as he paces the balcony, talking in rapid Italian.

Finally, he hangs up and swears under his breath. He strides over to me and leans over, fisting his hand in my hair and gently tipping my face. He kisses me, and I taste toothpaste as I kiss him back passionately because this is the last time. When he pulls away, concern crosses his face. "I have to go," he says regretfully.

"It's fine."

"I will be gone until tomorrow. The board meeting is in Rome, and there are other meetings I'll have to attend as well. So, I should be back sometime tomorrow evening."

"I know," I say, smiling sadly up at him. "You told me ages ago."

His business face slides back on, and he's once again Mateo Rossi standing on the balcony of his family's palazzo with the world at his feet. "I shall see you tomorrow then, Wren." He bends and kisses my forehead. "I will bring you back something nice."

"Thank you."

He looks confused. "That is not what you usually say when I announce that I am buying you something. Where are the thousand complaints and insistence that I should not spoil you one iota?"

"They're useless," I say, smiling up at him. "No, it's a thank you for everything, Teo. You've shown me things I've never known, and I'm not talking about Majorca or Venice."

"Then what *are* you talking about?"

I grab his hand and squeeze it, feeling his skin warm against mine for the last time. "You've given me so much you'll never understand, and I want you to know in your soul how grateful I am and that I'll never regret meeting you and having this wild adventure. Always remember that."

He stares at me, his brow furrowed, but the moment is broken when his father calls him from the bedroom door. "Mateo, we are going to be late for the flight. The boat is waiting. Come, let us go."

He swears under his breath. "Is my bedroom now St. Mark's Square?"

"That's a question your immortal soul should answer. I'll pray for you."

He laughs, and I savour the moment when humour fills his face, creasing his eyes and cheeks, his whole face alight. Then he bends, kissing me gently. "*Arrivederci*, Wren," he says, and then he's gone.

I sit for a while listening to the shouts and voluble Italian from below, and I watch the boat until it disappears into the fog. Then I get up and grab my backpack from where I stashed it at four this morning. Inside it are my clothes from the holiday, and I touch the pink T-shirt, hearing echoes of our time in the sun.

I'm only taking the clothes that I brought with me. The things he gave me I've left hanging in his dressing room. It will hurt him, but I can't help that. I want to leave his life taking only what I brought with me, and in the future, I can console myself with that. I'm not one of his other men. The only exceptions to that are the little cuckoo packed securely in tissue paper in my bag and my wrist band. I touch the leather strands as reverently as if they were a holy object and then put the envelope with Teo's name on it on the table in his dressing room.

I spent a lot of time staring at a blank piece of paper in the early hours of the morning, but in the end, once I started writing, the words came quickly. It's another sign that I'm doing the right thing. I touch his name on the envelope gently with the tip of my finger, and then, with one last look at the apartment to fix it in my mind, I close the door behind me and make my way downstairs.

The house is quiet, with no signs of life, and I've nearly made it to the door when I hear a throat clear behind me. I spin around and find Teo's grandfather watching me. His gaze is steady and knowing, and I sigh. Somehow the sound makes his lips twitch with amusement.

"Ah," he says. "We have a bird escaping the nest, I think, Antonio."

His manservant comes from behind him and sniffs disapprovingly.

"You were leaving, Wren, without saying goodbye?" Grandfather says, disappointment is evident in his voice.

"I was leaving you a letter, sir," I say, holding up the envelope in my hand.

"Ah." He puts his hand out, his bossiness very evident this morning. "Let us see it," he says autocratically. I take a few steps towards him and hand him the envelope only to watch open-mouthed as he rips it in two.

"I spent *ages* on that," I say crossly.

He waves a dismissive hand. "I'm fairly sure it was you telling me what an honour it was to know me. How wonderful I have been, and how you wish I were your own grandfather."

"I think that's a letter you'd send yourself," I say sulkily, and Antonio laughs.

Teo's grandfather smiles. "And I think I can guess what your letter to Mateo says too. How you are sorry to be leaving, but you are doing your best for him and that being with you is damaging him."

I scowl and then say snippily, "You should take that show on the road. You'd make a fortune."

"I already have several of them."

Antonio rolls his eyes. "I shall get the boat ready," he says and walks away.

I ask Teo's grandfather, "Are you going to stop me from going?" I flinch after he shakes his head. "Why?" I finally say. "Do you agree with me?"

"I find it a good practice not to agree with the younger generation until at least lunchtime." He purses his lips. "I am letting you go because I think it is for the best."

"Then you do agree with me," I say eagerly. "I *knew* I was doing the right thing."

"On the contrary, dear child, it's an imbecilic move." I exhale a huff of frustration, and he smiles. "But it might give my grandson the kick up the behind he desperately needs."

"What?"

He studies me and then says, "Because he is forty and still persists in believing that emotion is best weeded from his life." He grimaces. "Utter rubbish, of course, but that is his father's fault." He steps forward. "So, I will let you go, Wren, but only because I know I will see you again. Now hug me, child."

I step into his arms, feeling his gnarled hand pet my hair. "If it's the morning for giving advice, I think you should get out again and go back to work," I say into his shoulder. "It's not doing you any good hiding away in your study."

Incredibly, he chuckles, and I pull back to look at him.

His eyes are old and wise. "I don't think it will be long now, Wren." He steps back and offers his hand for me to shake. "Good speed on your travels, young Wren. I feel you are like a young prince who came into this house and woke us all up from an enchanted sleep."

"In the spirit of honesty, I have to say that some of you would have been better left sleeping."

He throws his head back and laughs uproariously. I step away, and he asks abruptly, "Where are you going?"

"To get a water taxi," I say patiently.

"Absolutely not. Antonio is waiting with the spare launch. He will take you."

"That's too much," I protest.

"Not for you," he says affectionately. "Goodbye, my young friend. I will see you soon."

He vanishes back into his study, and I look after him, feeling tears prickle my eyes. I'll miss his acid commentary and humour so much. Then footsteps sound above, and I make haste to leave the house as quietly as I entered it.

Mateo

The boat moves slowly along the water, and my father tuts impatiently. "We shall miss our flight if they are not careful. I wonder if your step-mother would be in a better mood with me if we manage to come back tonight. Let us try that. I grow tired of her recriminations."

I tune him out with the ease of long practice and gaze blindly at the cabin's wall. I'm thinking of Wren. Something is bothering me, worrying at the corners of my mind.

I know he's not angry with me, because he doesn't lie. But I can't help being mad at myself. I'd got so drunk last night. Drunker than I've been in years. I'd swallowed glass after glass, trying to stop the echo of his passionate declaration of love, but it hadn't worked. So instead, I'd fed him to the wolves, leaving him alone in the hands of Leandro. And then I'd blamed Wren for the repercussions. I think back to seeing him in Leandro's arms and the blind rage that had seized me.

As if on cue, my phone rings. I look down at it and curse, bringing my father's ruminations on the fickleness of women to an abrupt close. I connect the call. "What?" I say tersely.

"I've rung you three times already. So why didn't you answer?" Leandro's voice is inexplicably cheerful.

"The end of the evening should have given you a clue. If not, check the mirror. You have a black eye."

Incredibly, he laughs. "It won't be the last. But, anyway, that's just this morning's news. A politician and his five mistresses have already overturned us."

"I'm not bothered about the press," I say.

My father gives an angry grunt, but he knows I don't care about his opinions. I've already reminded him that throwing our possessions into the Grand Canal during a marital row isn't a way to keep the Rossi family name out of the papers.

"So, what is it? Wren, I suppose." Leandro's voice drips with disdain. "Buy him something pretty, and he'll soon come around."

"He isn't like that," I say coldly. "He's kind and clever and utterly disinterested in what my money can buy him. But you wouldn't know, because rather than getting to know him, you were incredibly rude to him, isolated him, and then tried to stick your tongue down his throat."

There's a silence. "I'm sorry," he finally says truculently. A moment later, he cajoles, "Come on, Mateo. He's just another one of your men, unusual as he is. We can't let him come between us."

"*Why?*" I ask. "He's important to me, and you knew it and still behaved that way. So even though you've already forgotten what you did, I can assure you that I haven't forgotten anything."

"What are you saying?" he asks, the first trace of unease entering his voice.

"I'm saying that we are no longer friends. Do not call me or text me or turn up where I am. These are all the things you do, but I'm no longer interested in being friends with someone who treats a man who's important to me with such disdain."

I click End on his protests. My father observes me with a jaundiced eye.

"He's your best friend, and you're giving him up for that... that boy. Leandro is not wrong in what he says. The boy is just another in a long line of men."

"Listening in on my conversations again?"

"It's hardly difficult when Leandro has such a loud voice."

I roll my eyes, and he starts up another tirade about how cavalier I've been lately and how he doesn't understand me and how I'm in danger of ruining everything and doing it all for a boy named Wren.

He says the name with such disdain, but as always, hearing Wren's name gives me a warm feeling. But the moment my thoughts return to Wren, I once again tune out my father completely.

What was it about him this morning? He's honest and open with his emotions, and nothing about him appeared angry on the balcony. He was his usual self with his wry smile and sad eyes.

Sad eyes? I sit bolt upright. He'd been sad this morning.

I feel sick as everything comes together.

I've been slow because of the hangover, but now it becomes obvious. He'd been sad. And he'd also spent a good amount of time thanking me.

I stand up abruptly.

My father stops talking and stares at me. "Mateo?"

"He's leaving," I gasp.

"Who's leaving?"

"Wren."

He huffs. "Good. The boy appears to have the good sense you are lacking. He knows it's time to leave because he won't get much more out of you. He's doing you a favour, Mateo."

"Turn the boat around," I call to Luca.

"What?" My father stands up too, holding onto the boat's side as it begins to turn. "Have you gone mad, Mateo? What are you *doing*?"

"I'm going back."

"Impossible. We have a board meeting in a few hours. Calm yourself and get a grip."

"I'm not going."

"*What?*" he roars. Luca jerks the wheel in surprise. "You cannot be serious."

"I certainly am. I'm going back to find Wren and apologise."

"You are apologising to that... that—"

"I wouldn't finish that sentence if I were you, father," I say icily, warning written all over me. "You haven't exactly earned the right to criticise others for their life choices, have you?" He blanches, and I shake my head in disgust. "It is perhaps better that we do not talk on the way back."

He subsides into his seat and looks at me as if I've gone mad.

It's not something I could disagree with, as half an hour later, I find myself racing through the palazzo, shouting Wren's name. Part of me is aghast to be breaking the habits of a lifetime like a fool, with no time for regrets. The other part is filled with a burgeoning sense of urgency that grows more intense as I burst into the apartment and find it quiet and still.

I know instantly that he isn't here. Wherever Wren is, there is usually music or the television, and the apartment lacks both. I tear into the bedroom, banging my shoulder painfully, but that too is empty and still, the bed made neatly and the room clean and tidy once more.

I race into my dressing room, opening Wren's wardrobe and sagging when I see his clothes hanging there neatly. I breathe in, inhaling his scent that always seems to contain coconut. It's as if he absorbed Majorca into his skin along with his sun cream and just smelling it makes me happy. I sink onto the chaise longue, still staring at the wardrobe. *He hasn't gone.* I feel relief, but it's still tempered with a strange anxiety, and I can't relax. I turn my head, and that's when I see it—a white envelope propped neatly against the mirror on the table.

I reach out, dimly noticing that my hands are shaking. On the front of the envelope is written *Teo* in Wren's neat writing. I trace the letters, not wanting to open it, but knowing I must. Finally, I tear open the envelope and read what is written on the thin sheet of paper.

Teo,

I think it's time that I went home. It's making your world much more difficult to have me in it, and that's the last thing I'd want.

Thank you for Majorca and Venice. I know you don't own them, but in a way, you did give them to me, and you did it in a way that I'll never forget.

I meant what I said before. I love you. I love the way you hug me so tightly. I've never had that before, so I didn't know how it would make me feel so safe. I have felt more alive with you than at any time in my life. I love you for the way you make me laugh and the way you listen to me. No one has ever really done that before, so it's a bigger gift than you know.

But that makes it sound like I love you for what you do for me, and that's very far from the truth. I love your humour, the tiny wrinkle between your eyes when you're concentrating, that hearty laugh of yours that echoes in your funny eyes—the kindness in you and your capacity for compassion. I even love your bursts of arrogance.

I don't regret my love. The only thing I regret is that it's made you uncomfortable, and I hate that. I don't want you to feel guilty for not loving me because that's not your responsibility. But I know you will because you wear responsibility like a hair shirt.

I hope you do fall in love one day, even if it isn't with me. I want you to have someone at your back protecting you the way you do everyone else. I would love to see you happy and fulfilled with the realisation that love isn't always chaos, and if it is, then it's the best sort of chaos that always brings brilliant things into your life.

Ti amo.

Your Wren

My eyes blur, and I curse and wipe them. This is what I've come to—crying over a boy and a letter.

Eventually, I stir and make my way downstairs. I don't know where I'm going, but I need to get away from my empty apartment. The palazzo has always felt like a tomb waiting to swallow me whole, and I realise with a start how this last month with Wren, none of that mattered. I would race into the house eager to see him and taking notice only of the lightness and simple joy I felt at seeing his messy hair and wide, unpractised smile. And now he's gone, and it is all my fault.

My grandfather interrupts my misery by strolling out of his study and waiting for me at the bottom of the stairs.

"Such a noise and racket this morning," he admonishes. "All this shouting and urgency. It rattles my old bones."

"Sorry, Grandfather, but I'm not in the mood."

"Ah, you've read his letter, then."

"What? You know he left a letter?"

"Of course." He rolls his eyes. "You know, in my day, we listened to other people and had proper conversations. But unfortunately, your generation seems unable to communicate better than cavemen."

"You saw him?" I gasp. "How was he?"

He shrugs, and I follow him into his study like a bird tracking crumbs of Wren.

I slump into the chair he indicates. "This is my fault," I say bitterly. "Maybe it is good that he has gone. I'm not good for him. We are not good for each other if he has to sneak out like a thief in the night."

"On the contrary, I think you're perfect."

I look at him incredulously. "And how did you come to that conclusion?"

"Wren is an old soul in a young body, which is the right way round if you ask me. He has somehow come out of a bad start with this engrained cheerful optimism. God knows how he's managed that."

"I think it's because no one was ever interested in him."

"Perhaps that's it. No one to interfere with the raw material."

I rub my eyes. "I never wanted to be like the people who discarded him."

"You're not, or if you wake up, you can stop being one." He studies me, his old eyes as keen as ever. "The family have been dreadful to him, Mateo."

"*What?*" I burst out.

"Catty and spiteful. What did you expect? Tell me you didn't think they'd be nice, Mateo, because I shall call you a fool."

I feel breathless, as if the walls of the palazzo have collapsed on me. "I was worried that they'd be catty, but I thought he could handle them. He did so well at the dinner on the first night, and he never said another word, so I relaxed. He seemed to be enjoying himself, and he loved being with you."

He looks sad. "I have enjoyed his company immensely, Mateo. Somehow, without making any effort to do it, you managed to stumble across the perfect person for you."

"And still managed to mess things up. How bad were they?" Dread fills me, making my limbs feel heavy.

"Nasty and vindictive. Your father largely ignored him."

"Not exactly a tragedy."

He huffs a laugh but then sobers. "But your sister and stepmother were bad. They constantly played on Wren's feelings of being unsuitable. I have done my best to keep his spirits up and kept him busy."

"Why didn't you tell me?" I burst out and then bite my lip. I don't throw recriminations at my grandfather. He's old and deserves my respect.

To my surprise, he doesn't react with anger but lowers himself to his chair. "I perhaps should have done," he admits. "But I did not like to interfere. He's a young man and should make his own way."

"Well, he's done that by making his way out of the building." I sink farther into the seat and the leather creaks comfortingly around me.

I look at the room. Books are everywhere, the apparent source of the teetering piles that have appeared in my bedroom lately. No wonder Wren felt at home in here. All that was missing was his pretty librarian. I swallow hard. I've failed Wren at every step when all I wanted was to keep him safe and happy.

"I don't know what to do." It's as if, with that simple sentence, I've rolled back the years, and I'm a young man again looking to this man for advice.

"Yes, you do."

I sigh, the knowledge seemingly deep in my bones waiting for me to confront it. "Yes, I do. He can't thrive here. The family won't allow it, and no matter what I do, I can't stop what they do when I'm not here. I can't stop their words hurting him."

"You will never be able to do that, Mateo."

The simple words stop me dead. "Then what is the point?" I say angrily.

He makes a tsking noise. "Such passion. It's good to see it in you, my boy. You've shut yourself off for too long, thinking that passion makes you like your father, when all along it's been weakness that has guided him in his relationships. You have never been weak." He reaches over and taps my hand. "When you love, you do it well."

I open my mouth to pour scorn on him but then abruptly shut it again.

Do I love Wren? How can that be?

But the answer is as easy as being with him. Of course, I love him. He's funny and kind and compassionate, and just being with him makes me happy. I try to be a better person just to see admiration in his eyes. I want to look after him, but that doesn't come from a mere impulse as I'd thought initially. It comes from love and a desire for him to have everything. That's why I try to give him things and see him smile. I want him to be happy more than I want my last breath.

My grandfather shakes his head. "Do not bother to deny it. It is written over every inch of you."

I groan. "But even though I love him, he's still gone. I'm not enough."

"Not the way you are at the moment, Mateo," he says plainly. "You think to compartmentalise him in your life. A shiny possession that you keep packed away and bring out to admire. He's not that and can never be so. You cannot stop the world from hurting Wren. He's a warm and curious young man, and people will be unkind to him. It's human nature for some people to see something shiny and want to besmirch it. But you can be there for him when he comes home. You can listen, and you can hold the world at bay for a while and strengthen his armour, so he goes out again with that indomitable sturdy nature that Wren has. His armour will get battered, but he will carry you with him, and that will give him strength." He looks sternly at me. "And you must allow him to do the same. A true partnership must have reciprocity. It won't work, otherwise. You have to let him in."

"I can't stay here," I say softly. Relief tears through me, and I see my life more clearly than I ever have before. "I love Venice, but this is your home. It's not mine, Grandfather. I don't want to be here in that office feeling the dampness eat into my bones."

"It has never been your home," he says, looking a little sad. "You were made on a sunlit island." He smiles. "And you want to do things your own way." I huff out a sharp breath, and he raises his bushy eyebrows. "Did you think I didn't know that? You're the image of me as a young man."

"You don't seem angry."

"How can I be? I was exactly the same. It would be like being cross with myself." He leans back in his chair. "You shall go and get Wren, and then you can go home, Mateo."

"Home?"

"The island. It has always been where you come alive. I should have known the truth when I saw you light up for Wren in the way you do when you are going home."

"But what about the business?"

"Ah, I think it is time for me to come back."

"But you've not been well."

"I've been wallowing, child. But it's coming to an end now. I feel life stirring in my bones again, and your grandmother would be horrified to see me sitting for so long. You know how she hated it. I shall go back and try to teach your father some sense." He grimaces. "I do not hold out much hope." He looks at me. "What will you do?"

I exhale slowly, freedom unfolding before me like a bright ribbon, where all I could see before was duty and boredom. "I think I might buy a hotel in Can Picafort."

He roars with laughter. "Ah, the apple doesn't fall far from the tree." He pats my hand. "Go," he says. "Go and build your own little empire. I know it will be successful. But be warned, Mateo, I shall visit you a lot. I have grown used to Wren's chatter, so be sure to have a nice room available for me and Antonio, who will, of course, accompany me."

"It shall be so," I say, unable to hide my smile.

He sobers. "But when I die, you must be prepared to take over, Mateo. This is only a holiday from the business. Your father will never inherit it. I tell you this in secrecy. I intend to settle an arm of the business on him that will suit him more. Less responsibility."

"He won't like that."

"He will do as he is told. And your father may be weak, but he is not an idiot. Half of his problems stem from the fact that he knows he is not equal to the task. He will accept the change willingly. I know him." He sits back. "So eventually, this will be yours, but by then, I think you and Wren will be ready for all the challenges, including the family. I'm giving you time, Mateo. Time to be yourself and time for you and Wren to grow strong together."

"Thank you."

A silence falls that I break by clapping my hands together. "I'm going to London first," I say, getting up.

"Why London?"

"To get Wren." I bend down and hug him. "*Ti voglio bene, nonno.*"

He pats my cheek. "You are a good boy but not so bright."

"Pardon?"

He points at the window. "Did you fail to notice the fog?"

I look at the window with a start. I've been so focused on Wren that I haven't paid attention to the weather. No wonder Luca was going so slowly on the water.

"You mean—?"

He nods. "It has grounded all aircraft."

I start to smile, excitement and purpose rising in my chest. "Wren's still here," I say. "I have to go." After hugging him again, I race out of the room, nearly colliding with my stepmother.

"Mateo, slow down," she scolds.

"I can't," I shout over my shoulder. "I'm leaving."

"What do you mean?"

I stop and turn to her. "I'm going. We're leaving this fucking place and not coming back."

"Language in front of a lady."

"I'd abide by that if I could see one." She gasps, and I grin at her. "I'm off to get Wren. You remember Wren, don't you? He's the young man you've been appallingly rude and cruel to."

"Oh, pfft. This is infatuation. He's extremely inappropriate."

"Ah, but that's where you're wrong. He's clever and funny, and just being with him makes me happier than I've ever been. You made a bit of a mistake if you don't mind me saying, Elena."

She looks suddenly cautious. "Why?"

"Because that young man is going to hold the purse strings when I take over. I'm going to put him in charge of family financing."

She goes as pale as a sheet, and I laugh and race out of the house to find my future and hopefully persuade him to take me back.

CHAPTER NINETEEN

Wren

I'm slumped in a chair and staring into space when the announcement comes over the tannoy.

"The fog has lifted now, and we will be returning to regular service. Please check the departures board for details of your flight and boarding gate."

Everyone immediately stands up and gathers their belongings as quickly as if the planes are on the tarmac and revving their engines.

I move slower, shouldering my rucksack and following the crowd as they head towards the board.

Margery turns to me. "London?" she asks. I nod. "We're at boarding gate ten, then."

"Lovely," I say with zero enthusiasm.

She chuckles. "We'll be home soon," she says happily. "Come on, Wren. You can come with us."

I follow her but not without throwing a glance back at the door to the departures lounge. Am I doing the right thing? It's a question I've been asking myself for the last few hours.

I could go back now, destroy the note, and Teo would never know. I could have another few weeks with him. More time to kiss him and smell his lemon scent and laugh together. More time to watch his face light up when he sees me—a sight that I cherish. I slump. But the end will still come, and I'll have to leave. Then at some point, I might meet him again, and he'll be as distant towards me as he was to that man in Majorca.

Mind made up, I turn and follow Margery and her husband, letting her chatter soothe the turmoil in my head as we join the long queue at the boarding gate.

Margery is just saying something about tea when there's a disturbance behind me, and I feel someone come up next to me.

I turn and gasp out loud, making her shut up instantly. "*Teo.*"

He's out of breath as if he's been running. His hair is a mess, shirt creased, and sweat standing out on his forehead. But his golden eyes are filled with purpose.

"Here you are." He's watching me steadily, and his words have such reverence—as if he's turned around and found the most precious thing in his world.

I blink back hot tears. "What are you doing here?" I mutter, aware of our two-person audience. Well, Margery is interested. Len looks as if he's contemplating finding a table to hide under away from the emotion charging the air.

"I came back," Teo says. "I left something important behind."

"Oh god, you'll be late for the board meeting," I say fretfully. "What did you leave behind?"

"You," he says, watching me, his eyes full of some emotion that makes my heart pound.

"*Me?*" I gasp.

He nods. "I realised something," he says rather chattily.

I flush as the couple behind us leans in to listen. They're so close they're breathing into my neck. Any closer, and they'd be marrying me. This is probably enlivening the dreary wait for the other passengers. I suppose we rate higher on the boredom factor than soggy mist out of a window.

"What?" I ask him out of the corner of my mouth.

"I realised that there was something far more important to me than a board meeting and a business, and I had left him behind in our bedroom. And he was sad and lonely, and I had to do something about that immediately."

His voice is very loud, and two girls ahead of us in the queue give loud, happy sighs as they crane around Len and Margery to observe us.

Teo suddenly becomes aware that we have a rapt audience. He runs his finger along his shirt collar. "Do you think we could perhaps go somewhere private to finish our discussion?" he mutters.

"Do you know anywhere?"

"I have a room," he says casually, waving a cavalier hand.

I roll my eyes. "Of course, you do," I mutter. "You probably own the bloody airport."

"Pardon?" he says, a glint in his eye telling me he heard me very well.

"That would be lovely," I say loudly. "Excuse me," I say to the rather large group who've all given up any pretence of not listening. Teo takes my bag for me, standing back as everyone grumbles unhappily.

Margery winks at me. "Lovely-looking man," she murmurs. "Is he the one you're running away from?" I nod, and she smiles. "Well, Wren, I think I'd let that one catch me if I were you." The queue starts to move, and she pats my hand. "Have a good life, Wren Roberts. I'll think of you."

"Goodbye," I say, returning her smile, and then I turn and fall into step beside Teo. He guides me through the bustling departure lounge, his hand a warm weight at the small of my back.

"I've missed my flight now," I inform him. "And that was the last of my money."

"I shall buy you a ticket if you listen to me and still want to go," he says calmly.

He directs me into a small room filled with a table and two chairs. Then his calm immediately disappears as he runs a hand through his hair and paces back and forth.

"Mateo?" I prompt.

He spins around. "I'm Teo to you," he says fiercely. "*Always*. I do not ever want you to call me anything else."

"Okay," I say slowly.

He gazes at me, his chest rising and falling rapidly. "I'm sorry," he jerks out.

I blink in surprise. "Why?"

"My family drove you away."

I shake my head immediately. "It wasn't your family, Teo. I didn't go because of them. They're just background noise." I pause. "Shitty background noise, though," I say plainly.

His eyes are wild. "But they were awful," he says loudly, pacing to the door and back, as if the room is too small to contain him. "My grandfather told me about them." He leans against the door and stares at me, his funny golden eyes intent. "The question is, why didn't you?"

I shrug. "I couldn't. They're your family. I haven't got one of my own, and I didn't want to cost you yours."

"You can certainly do that," he says dismissively. "If Elena and Francesca fell in a swamp, I'd pray that the crocodiles had health insurance." I can't help the twitch of my mouth, and he offers me a half smile. "So why go?" he says softly.

Silence falls. "Because you don't love me," I finally say wearily. "I can cope with your family. I just don't see the point in staying with you when there's no future for us."

"But I *do* love you." His declaration is loud and impassioned.

I gape at him, feeling as if I've been hit over the head with something heavy. "Pardon?" I say faintly.

"I love you very much."

"I don't understand," I gasp. "Why didn't you say it when I told you the first time?"

"I couldn't."

"Why?"

"Because I didn't *want* to be in love with you. I hadn't even admitted it to myself until today, let alone to you."

"Because I'm inappropriate?"

"No," he says passionately, striding over and taking my face in his strong hands. "You're *perfect*. It's as if you're made for me. You're funny and clever and so kind you shame me. You see things in such a different way from me, and it's a much more joyous way than I've ever known. You've taught me to relax, to ease up, and enjoy life. I realised I was in love with you on the balcony that day."

"The dance?" I say wonderingly.

He pulls me close, and his words come hot against my temple, his heart pounding under my fingers. "But I didn't want it. This love is uncontrollable. It fills me up until all I see is you, and I'm possessive and jealous. Look at what happened at the club."

I pull back and look up at him. "Teo, you were drunk. Cut yourself a little slack."

"I should not have been. I don't drink like that, but I was full of emotion and jealousy at the way Leandro looked at you. And then the fighting and the words." He shudders. "That is not how I wish to be. I am a man who can control his emotions."

"Granted, I agree with you on that. But Leandro manipulated you, and sometimes, Teo, it's good to give in to your emotion. You're like a hot Spanish powder keg. Punching Leandro was admittedly epic, and I wish I'd filmed it, but maybe next time you get jealous, you could just tell me."

"I doubted you, and I shouldn't have."

"I'm no expert in love. As far as I know, you're the only person who's ever loved me." I pause. "Wow! You love me," I say softly and smile widely at him. "You'll learn to trust me when you trust feeling love."

"You do not see yourself clearly. If you give me a chance, I will show you how loveable you are. When you believe in yourself, others will see it as clear as day." He looks steadily at me. "You're like my lighthouse, Wren. You show me the way, and your light is so clear and warm."

I bite my lip. "I barely know the way myself. You're likely to end up wrecked if you follow me too closely."

"Then how about if we journey together, one foot in front of the other, side by side?"

"With plenty of chances to admire the scenery," I say breathlessly. "And to stop and get a dog."

He gives me a wry look. "You may have whatever you like, Wren."

"And that's good because the only thing I really want is you. I love you, Teo."

His face opens in an enormous smile, and he takes me tightly in his arms, kissing me fiercely. When he pulls back, he strokes my hair away from my face.

"Shall we go home, Wren? I feel like my cuckoo should make his own nest for a change."

"Back to the palazzo?" I look at him worriedly. "They won't accept me."

"No, they probably never will."

"So, what can we do?"

"We're not going back there. We're going to Majorca."

"*What?*" Excitement runs through me. "Really?"

He smiles. "You love my island too, yes?"

I nod, and then my excitement fades. "But your work is here along with your family."

"My family is a good incentive to emigrate to the North Pole."

I laugh but go silent when he says, "I've been set free anyway."

"How?"

"My grandfather is taking back control, and he's set me free. He says I will be happier forging my own way for a bit."

I shake my head admiringly. "Your grandfather is a cunning genius."

"We will have to go back at some point," he warns me. "I will have to run the business, eventually."

"Will we be together?"

"Of course."

"Then I'll be fine. I can take on anything if I have you."

He hugs me tight, twirling me around, his face looking young and happy. "Come, then. I'm in mind to buy a rundown hotel in Can Picafort and put you in charge of it while I relax on the beach."

"You're joking."

He chuckles. "I shall wear the same pair of board shorts every day, drink sangria all night, and grow my hair down to my toes. And when people question me, I shall say, 'But my Wren loves me.'"

"He does." I grab his hand. "But how about if we do it together?"

He swallows hard. "You have the best ideas, Wren. My cuckoo."

"And finally someone who recognises the fact," I say triumphantly.

I take the hand he holds out to me, and we walk out towards our future, hand in hand and step by step.

EPILOGUE

Two Years Later

Wren

I wave goodbye to the departing happy couple and close the door with a sigh of relief.

"I give them two years at the most," Alfie says from behind me.

I lean against the hotel's glass door. "That's a trifle cynical."

He grins. "The groom spent the entire evening eyeing up the chief bridesmaid, completely unaware of the fact that the bride was doing the same."

I consider that and shrug. "I actually don't care, as long as they don't do it in my hotel."

My hotel. Part of me is still stunned by those words.

Teo was as true to his word as he ever is. When we returned to the island, he bought the hotel where we'd breakfasted on that long ago morning. The surprise was that he gave it to me, insisting that he was tired of the hotel business and wanted to grow fat and tanned sitting in the bar with the local old men. He gave me a crash course in what to do and then calmly stepped back.

I argued with him, saying I wasn't remotely qualified to run a hotel, but he insisted I could do it. And, as with many things in my life, his confidence in me encouraged me to do stuff I would never have had the courage to try before.

He believes I will do well and somehow... I do.

Of course, he never grew fat. He's far too energetic to sit still for long. I left him alone for a while. He was happy to offer advice if I asked, but he never showed any signs of wanting to take over. Instead, he let me forge my own way and at the end of each day, I would wander to the nearby bar and find him part of a laughing crowd of locals, all of whom had known him since he was a baby.

Eventually, though, I could detect the restlessness in him, so I threw a few hotel brochures into his lap and watched him set off in making his own hotel empire. It has been immensely successful, but I never doubted him. Teo has a knack for this business. It's in his blood and bone. What has surprised me is how I have it too. I might not have been born to it, but I love it just as much as him.

"I know you're thinking of Mateo," my companion says in a sing-song voice, heading into the function room where our weary waiters are starting to pack away.

"How?" I ask, following him.

He laughs. "You're breathing, and there's a 'y' in the name of the day."

My cheeks heat. "I can't help it."

He waves a careless hand. "I'd be moony-eyed if I had that man at home. Is it my imagination, or is he getting hotter? I know he treated his forty-second birthday like he would expire at any moment, but the reverse is true. He's like a hot Spanish Benjamin Button with his happy ever after."

"I don't think you've ever seen that film. It isn't quite as sunny as you think," I say, smiling at the waiters. "Leave everything," I instruct them. "There isn't a function tomorrow. Do it in the morning after a good night's sleep." I look at Alfie. "You, too."

"Does Mateo like your bossiness?" he says, leaning against the bar.

"He sort of sees it as a by-product of my personality."

"Well, your by-product is right. I'm knackered."

He stretches, and I look at the man who is now my manager. The warm and funny waiter we met here now has full rein in the hotel and it suits him. We work well together, and he's quickly become my best friend.

"Don't forget that Enzo is flying back tomorrow," I say, opening my diary and rifling through the pages. "He's staying for six months while he does the installation in our Cala d'Or hotel. I've given him the same room he had last time. He likes looking at the sea."

To my astonishment, he grimaces. "I know he's coming back. You've told me a billion times. So why doesn't he stay with you and Mateo?"

"He likes his privacy." I stare at him. "Why are you making that face? You got on very well with Enzo last time I saw you together." He flushes, and my attention sharpens. "Alfie?"

He waves his hand. "Of course, I like him," he says. It's a careless voice, but there's an undercurrent to it, but before I can question him, he checks his watch. "Isn't Mateo due back now?"

I check my own watch and whoop. "He is." I open my office door and smile at the little creature waiting patiently for me in her basket. "Are you ready, Gertie?"

The little dog immediately bounces over to me, her tail wagging. She was a birthday present from Teo who found her wandering by the side of the road. He'd had to spend a long time coaxing her into the car, as she seemed to prefer walking over riding in his Mercedes. I'd been reading a book about the female explorer Gertrude Bell at the time, and when he gave the dog to me, I'd promptly named her Gertrude. She quickly became Gertie, and she travels everywhere with me, sitting in the front seat of the Jeep, looking out for adventure like her namesake.

I look at Alfie as he follows me and Gertie to the hotel's entrance. "I still want to know about Enzo."

"Out," he says briskly, pushing me out of the door. "You can interrogate me another time."

"It would only be a few little *questions*," I shout as he shuts the hotel door in my face, but I get no reply, and I hasten to the Jeep with Gertie at my heels. Teo is home.

I steer the Jeep down the familiar coastal road to home feeling excitement fizz in my body. I can't wait to see him, as he's been in Venice this week for a family board meeting. It's not very often we're separated, because I usually go with him on these trips. But this time I needed to stay in Majorca to help with the wedding the hotel is hosting—it's being covered by a big magazine.

I've missed him so much. I've raced home each night for his video calls and news about his family's complete ridiculousness.

His family have grown used to me now. Teo says it isn't familiarity but wariness. Whatever it is, I'll take it. So, we live in a state of polite neutrality, always with the knowledge that when Grandfather dies, the business and their livelihoods will be in my and Teo's hands.

I marvel that the boy I was will someday be in charge of the Rossi fortune, but my confidence comes from proving myself again and again. Teo was the one who taught me to trust my instincts, and my successes have cemented that belief.

As I drive, the moonlight and stars shimmer on the restless sea, the sea wind blowing through the Jeep's window, and soon I'm drawing into my parking space outside our home.

We built the villa on the very spot where Teo took my virginity, and I love the place passionately. It's our very own slice of heaven in the form of honey-coloured stone and big open rooms with wooden floors and exposed bricks and beams. In the summer, it's cool and fresh, but in the winter, when the sea winds blow, it's warm and snug.

The furniture is big and comfortable, made to sink into and scattered with bright cushions. Artwork lines the walls in the few spaces where there aren't bookshelves. The books that Teo bought me stand in pride of place along with many others that we've gathered over the years. Teo is just as much of a reader as I am now, and he has more time for it, so books fill the shelves, some from trips away but more from Teo's insistence that I need the top one hundred fiction and non-fiction titles. He buys them every six months, and unpacking the boxes is just as exciting as the first time.

My lips twitch as I climb out of the Jeep and see Teo's suitcase sitting on the steps leading up to the big blue wooden door. I know he'll have come home and gone straight around the back to look at the sea. It's his favourite part of the place. He'll then have forgotten his case. You can take the boy away from the palace, but he still expects the servants.

I look up at my home. In a minute, I will race inside and into Teo's arms, but just for a moment, I marvel at the fact that I have a home. It's a place that I never grow tired of, one I will always love no matter where Teo and I end up in the world. We hope his grandfather will be with us for many years, but change will come. It's inevitable. And when it does, I will walk by Teo's side to wherever life takes us, and I will do it happily because I know that my home's not made of bricks and mortar. I hold this knowledge deep inside my heart where he has the most important spot.

My kind and clever man is my home. Not bad for a little cuckoo.

Mateo

It's early evening when the taxi drops me off at home. After paying the driver and smiling my thanks, I gather my case and step out onto the forecourt of the villa. The heat of the day is dissipating a little, and there's a welcome breeze coming from the sea, gifting me with the scent of wildflowers and brine.

I look up at the villa that is now our home. It's similar to the blueprints I had drawn up all those years ago, but just like he's added so many unexpected things to my life, Wren has done the same with the house.

I can still feel his breath on the side of my neck as he hung over my shoulder in the architect's office, staring down at the blueprints and offering careful suggestions. The architect had worn a bemused look as I'd agreed to every single thing Wren had suggested. When Wren had left, the architect had queried me, but I'd simply explained that I had many homes, but this was Wren's first, and he was to be given whatever he asked for.

However, then, as always, Wren had intervened. His only demand is that his voice is heard. He pushes me to be his partner and not his keeper. He'd declared we couldn't do anything to the house unless we both loved it. And despite the architect's concerns, the house has turned out perfectly.

It was a little taste of what my grandfather calls the Wren Ripple. He has an unerring instinct for life and love and eventually wins over even those who might doubt him.

I smile up at the stone of the villa. It glows a soft honey colour in the sun and looks warm and welcoming.

Leaving my case on the ground, I make my way around to the back, where I wander past the swimming pool, its azure depths ruffled as the wind plays games with the water and tugs at the wind chimes. We use the pool a lot, but we love our first swim of the morning to be in the sea, always naked and before breakfast.

I raise my face into the breeze. It's cooling slightly, a sign that the summer is nearly over.

My steps take me to the bottom of the garden, a path I could take blindfolded. I stand and look down at our cove where the *Luna Azul* bobs quietly in her new mooring. We try to take her out at the weekends. Wren has proved to be a capable sailor, and he adores the boat as much as I do. I love those days when it is just him and me. We come back with windswept hair and sunburnt noses and his kisses always taste of the sea.

The cove's official name is Diamante Point because of the light on the white rocks, but Wren persists in calling it Penetration Point. Warmth rolls through me at the thought of that first time with him. We've made love *many* times since then, and Wren is older now and much more mature and confident about what he wants, but some small caveman part of me wants to beat my chest in happiness that I am his first and only.

I'd wondered whether he'd want to explore sexually once the first flush of excitement had worn off us, but when I'd asked him about it with a feeling of hidden dread, he'd turned a confused face to me, declaring that he had enough with one exasperating man so why would he take on another? I'd accepted that with a light heart, and I've never asked again.

I let the peace of our cove steal over me, quietening the thoughts in my head and easing any residual tension from my travels. Then, withdrawing my key, I walk back to the house and let myself in.

Mick Jagger greets me with a noisy demand for food, sounding as though he hasn't been fed for a hundred years, I wander into the kitchen as he attempts to inflict bodily harm on me by twining around my ankles. The scrawny kitten that we rescued is now a sleek cat with soft fur and bright eyes. My mother had presented him to us as a housewarming present when we came back to the island. I'd been about to refuse, but one look at Wren's eager eyes had me capitulating as always.

It's good that he doesn't push for things, because he could have the shirt off my back whenever he asks. Mick seems to love it here. He doesn't stray too far and has even taken to Gertie. I quite often find them curled up together.

I know Wren is still at work, so I have a leisurely shower in our bathroom with its floor-to-ceiling views of the sea. Wren had insisted on a huge bath in here in front of that window, and many are the nights that we've lain together in the water, letting the sea breeze blow over us, talking and laughing over our days.

I climb out of the shower and wander naked into our bedroom. The bi-folding doors are open, and I let the warm breeze dry me as I extract clothes from my dressing room—a pair of shorts and the T-shirt that Wren bought me so many years ago. The print on it is a little faded now, but it makes my heart warm every time I see it.

As I come back into the bedroom, I catch sight of Wren's bedside table. There's a stack of books there that my grandfather sent to him, and the familiar figure of the little glass cuckoo. Wren had put it there when we moved in, insisting that it be the first thing he wanted to see in the morning other than me. The little bird glistens in the sunshine, its eyes bright and somehow knowing. I smile and touch its tiny beak.

Hearing the sound of a car engine, I move to the window over-looking the front of the house and watch as Wren manoeuvres my old Jeep around the steep bend. It's just as battered as it was. In fact, it bears a few more dents since Wren started driving it, but when he passed his test, he'd refused all my offers of a brand-new car. I'd ignored him and bought him a very expensive car, but the first time he drove it, he was so nervous that he didn't engage the brake, and it ended up at the bottom of the pool, at which point he'd asked for my Jeep. I'd grumbled, but it still thrills me when I see him in it as he zips all over the island. As if, when we are not together, a part of me is still with him.

I fasten my watch onto my wrist as I hear the front door fly open.

"Teo?" he shouts, and my heart gives its usual little skip and jump.

I'd worried at one point that I had heart problems so often did it jump, but my grandfather had just laughed, telling me I had heart trouble all right, but it was called Wren, and there was no cure.

"Up here," I shout.

His footsteps thunder up the stairs, and he appears in the doorway. He's filled out a little now, his lanky thinness vanishing under a layer of muscle that comes from our runs across our beach and the fact that he's rarely still. His hair is lightened from the sun, but his face is the same with those warm eyes, beaky nose, and full lips. However, his eyes now bear a contented expression as if all is right with his world. I hope so because my own world has rather narrowed now to Wren Roberts.

"Did you forget to hire the butler who is going to bring up your case?" he enquires, his eyes sparkling.

I laugh and open my arms, and he runs into them, lifting his mouth for my kiss. I oblige him, hunger stirring quickly because of the time we've been apart. When he pulls back, his eyes are heavy, his mouth full, and I can feel his cock against me.

"I'm so happy you're home," he says.

I bend and lick his pouty lower lip. "Show me," I murmur.

His methods of exhibition last a while, and when he's finished, we're a sweaty, muddled heap amongst the tumbled sheets. We lie, letting our breaths slow, his leg thrown over mine and his head on my chest, his fingers twining gently in the hair there. Finally, he looks up, propping his chin on my chest, and I tangle my fingers in his hair, feeling the silky strands slip through them. He tilts his head into my touch, his eyes smiling.

"Missed you so much," he says fervently.

I bring him up for a kiss. "I missed you too," I say when our mouths separate.

He resumes his earlier position. "How was the board meeting?"

"It's a very appropriate word. I was bored."

"You were not." He bites his lip. "How's your father and his new bride?"

I roll my eyes. "She is rather histrionic, which is entirely in keeping with his tastes."

"Like calls to like, then. I bet it's bloody noisy in that house."

"You have no idea. Yesterday, she cut all his suits into tiny pieces, poured mustard over them, and then threw them out of a window onto a passing boat full of nuns."

He starts to laugh. "I so wish I'd been there."

I grin. His relationship with my family is so different now. He no longer acts as an interloper—like the cuckoo that he considered himself to be. Instead, he strides at my side with his head held high, and my family have learnt to respect him, to respect that canny judgement of his and his unerring eye for detail. However, I keep a keen eye on everyone. If they upset him, they will have me to deal with.

"Grandfather was peeved that you were not with me. I believe he prefers you to me."

His eyes light up. "Is he okay?"

"Hale and hearty and as bossy as ever. He says he will be visiting us for a month or so until my father's honeymoon phase peters out. Either that or the marriage."

"Yes." He grins. "I have a couple of books to discuss with him. I'll get his room ready."

My grandfather has taken to spending a few weeks with us in the autumn, claiming that the heat helps his old bones. He descends on us with forty tons of luggage and the ever-faithful Antonio and stays for a few weeks, conducting business on the phone and forcing executives to come to him. He and Wren are closer than ever and constantly have their heads together. I think Wren sees him as a father/grandfather hybrid and flourishes under his words of advice and grumbly love. And in return, my grandfather thrives on helping him. It is pleasant to watch.

"How is the hotel?" I ask. "How did the wedding go?"

"Brilliantly. They were thrilled, and the photographer from *Brides* took some stunners. The article should be in next month's edition."

"Did they take any of you?"

He shrugs. "He took a few."

"I bet he did."

Wren is beautiful. I don't know whether it's his looks or his confidence or the fact that he knows he's loved now, but my Wren is a stunning man. I can get jealous of men who look sideways at him, but I never lose sight of the fact that I am the one who takes him home at night. And sometimes they are late nights. The hotel business is a demanding mistress, especially with the Can Picafort property. He made the changes we talked about on the morning we first visited the hotel, and that, together with his unerring eye for detail and his genuine warmth and interest in people, have made it into a huge success, and we are booked solid all year round.

The hotel business suits my Wren. For him, it's almost as if it isn't work. He spends his days talking to people, overseeing the staff who love him, and conferring with his manager. He'd kept the spiky waiter on from that day and made him a manager, which was another genius idea, as Alfie took to it like a duck to water. They make an unbeatable combination.

For a while, I lazed about, enjoying the release from the hotel business. But eventually, I grew bored, and Wren forced me into action, declaring that whether I liked it or not, the hotel business was in my blood and not to be given up so easily. He'd unleashed a stack of brochures into my lap of properties for sale. I'd declared arrogantly that I was fine, but when he was at work, I'd found myself driving around the island looking at the hotels. As I gazed at them and ran through my mind what needed to be done, I'd found my long-dormant interest awakening and a sense of that old excitement that the hotel trade had initially stirred in me.

We now have seven hotels, but they're vastly different from my family's properties. They are small boutique hotels where guests are treated as individuals. And somehow, and much to my grandfather's satisfaction, my own little empire is thriving.

I have to go back to Venice every month, and my old responsibilities are waiting for me, but I will have Wren at my side when I step back into that world. My partner and my lover, always ready with his warm smile and quick wit. And even though there will be challenges ahead, we will face them side by side and always together.

I look down at him, smiling at the sight of him asleep at my side in the sheets, his tanned olive skin a warm colour against the white cotton. I stroke his hair back tenderly, watching him breathe slowly and evenly.

Then I lie back, watching the inky black mass of the sea move in the night and hearing the wind whistle through the pine trees. I run my hand idly up and down his back, his skin as soft as silk and the vulnerable knobs of his spine firm beneath my fingers.

Wren always said he was a cuckoo, but I don't agree with the characterization, because my boy has the sweetest soul. He'd never have pushed anyone out of the nest. Instead, he'd have invited more and more birds in until the nest was too small. I know this because our house always has visitors, and the phone constantly rings with the people Wren collects with his sweet nature and those bright, observant eyes.

I press kisses into the waves of his hair and then place a final, whimsical kiss on the end of his beaky nose. I'm profoundly lucky to have found Wren, and I'm very grateful to the old man who convinced me to listen to this particular cuckoo's call. I found the deepest love and a home for myself in the warm boy lying next to me.

NEWSLETTER

Thank you for reading. I hope you enjoyed Wren's and Teo's story.

If you'd like to be the first to know about my book releases and have access to extra content including exclusive short stories and interviews with characters, you can sign up for my newsletter here

Newsletter subscribers will also have access to the exclusive short stories, '3 Dates' and 'Playground Games'

Are you interested in Wren's handsome library manager? You'll find Charlie's story here.

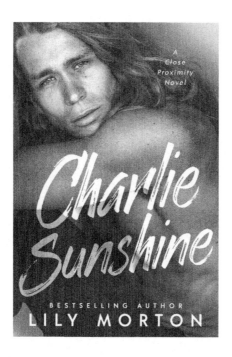

Sometimes love is a lot closer to home than you think.

Charlie Burroughs can't keep a man. All he wants is a good relationship like the ones he sees his friends having, but none of the men he picks ever work out. Despite him trying to be the perfect boyfriend, the men are either threatened by his looks or his epilepsy or a combination of the two. It's lucky that he has his best friend Misha to turn to. The two of them are closer than peas in a pod and fiercely loyal to each other. He can't imagine his life without Misha in it.

Misha Lebedinsky is the complete opposite of his best friend. Being the support system for his mum and twin sisters leaves Misha with neither the time nor the inclination for a relationship. Quick and frequent hook-ups are his favourite means of communication and any other pesky emotional needs he has are met by Charlie, who he's devoted to. He lives a life of happy compartmentalization with no intention of ever changing.

All of this changes when the two best friends move in together. Being in close proximity means that they suddenly start to see each other in a very different light. But Charlie struggles when his drive to be the perfect partner clashes with the fact that he's in love with a man who knows every little thing about him. And even if he can get past that, can a relationship ever work with a man who'd need a dictionary to tell him what love means?

From bestselling author Lily Morton comes a love story about a sunny librarian who has relationship written all over him and a cynical banker who doesn't even have it in his blurb.

Do you want to know more about the couple who Wren found so interesting in the Venetian restaurant? You'll find their story here.

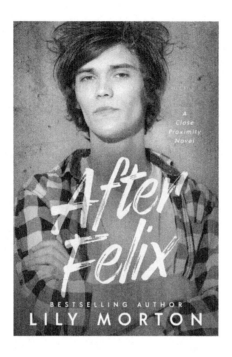

Sometimes the best love stories come in two parts.

When Felix met handsome journalist Max Travers, it was lust at first sight. It was just his luck that he then had to develop a terrible case of feelings and got his heart broken. However, two and a half years later, he's over all of that. His job is going well, he has good friends, and he doesn't lack for male company. Which, of course, is when Max has to come bursting back into his life.

Felix Jackson will always be the one who got away to Max. He's spent their time apart regretting his actions and hoping for a second chance. When an accident lands him in Felix's less than tender care, Max is determined to grab this opportunity. The only problem is that Felix is equally determined that he doesn't.

From bestselling author, Lily Morton comes a story of missed opportunities, second chances, and two very stubborn men.

This is the third book in the Close Proximity series, but it can be read as a standalone.

THANK YOU

My husband. For always being my best friend.

A big thank you to Leslie and everyone at LesCourt for everything you do. Special thanks to Mary Vitrano for all your help with the Italian phrases in the book. Any mistakes are entirely my own.

The members of my Facebook readers' group, Lily's Snark Squad. You make my group such a friendly and lovely place.

To all the bloggers who spend their valuable time reading, reviewing, and promoting the books. Also, the readers who liven up my day with their messages and photos and book recommendations. I love being a part of this community, so thank you.

Lastly, thanks to you for taking a chance on this book. I hope you enjoyed reading it as much as I enjoyed writing it. I never knew until I wrote my first book how important reviews are. So, if you have time, please consider leaving a review on Amazon or Goodreads or any other review sites. I can promise you that I value all of them.

CONTACT LILY

Website: www.lilymortonauthor.com
This has lots of information and fun features, including some extra short stories.

If you fancy hearing the latest news and interacting with other readers, do head over and join my Facebook group. It's a fun group and I share all the latest news about my books there as well as some exclusive short stories.
www.facebook.com/groups/SnarkSquad/

I'd love to hear from you, so if you want to say hello or have any questions, please contact me and I'll get back to you:
Email: lilymorton1@outlook.com

ALSO BY LILY MORTON

Mixed Messages Series

Rule Breaker

Deal Maker

Risk Taker

The Finding Home Series

Oz

Milo

Gideon

The Close Proximity Series

Best Man

Charlie Sunshine

After Felix

Black & Blue Series

The Mysterious and Amazing Blue Billings

The Quiet House

Other Books

The Summer of Us

Short Stack

Merry Measure

Beautifully Unexpected

The Cuckoo's Call

On a Midnight Clear

Short Stories and Novellas

Best Love

Spring Strings

The Stopping Place

Newsletter Exclusive Short Stories

3 Dates

Playground Games

Printed in Great Britain
by Amazon

83443793R00169